THE COLLECTED
SHORT STORIES
OF LOUIS L'AMOUR

Bantam Books by Louis L'Amour

NOVELS
Bendigo Shafter
Borden Chantry
Brionne
The Broken Gun
The Burning Hills
The Californios
Callaghen
Catlow
Chancy
The Cherokee Trail
Comstock Lode
Conagher
Crossfire Trail
Dark Canyon
Down the Long Hills
The Empty Land
Fair Blows the Wind
Fallon
The Ferguson Rifle
The First Fast Draw
Flint
Guns of the Timberlands
Hanging Woman Creek
The Haunted Mesa
Heller with a Gun
The High Graders
High Lonesome
Hondo
How the West Was Won
The Iron Marshal
The Key-Lock Man
Kid Rodelo
Kilkenny
Killoe
Kilrone
Kiowa Trail
Last of the Breed
Last Stand at Papago Wells
The Lonesome Gods
The Man Called Noon
The Man from Skibbereen
The Man from the Broken Hills
Matagorda
Milo Talon
The Mountain Valley War
North to the Rails
Over on the Dry Side

Passin' Through
The Proving Trail
The Quick and the Dead
Radigan
Reilly's Luck
The Rider of Lost Creek
Rivers West
The Shadow Riders
Shalako
Showdown at Yellow Butte
Silver Canyon
Sitka
Son of a Wanted Man
Taggart
The Tall Stranger
To Tame a Land
Tucker
Under the Sweetwater Rim
Utah Blaine
The Walking Drum
Westward the Tide
Where the Long Grass Blows

SHORT STORY COLLECTIONS
Beyond the Great Snow Mountains
Bowdrie
Bowdrie's Law
Buckskin Run
The Collected Short Stories of Louis L'Amour (vols. 1–7)
Dutchman's Flat
End of the Drive
From the Listening Hills
The Hills of Homicide
Law of the Desert Born
Long Ride Home
Lonigan
May There Be a Road
Monument Rock
Night over the Solomons
Off the Mangrove Coast
The Outlaws of Mesquite
The Rider of the Ruby Hills
Riding for the Brand

The Strong Shall Live
The Trail to Crazy Man
Valley of the Sun
War Party
West from Singapore
West of Dodge
With These Hands
Yondering

SACKETT TITLES
Sackett's Land
To the Far Blue Mountains
The Warrior's Path
Jubal Sackett
Ride the River
The Daybreakers
Sackett
Lando
Mojave Crossing
Mustang Man
The Lonely Men
Galloway
Treasure Mountain
Lonely on the Mountain
Ride the Dark Trail
The Sackett Brand
The Sky-Liners

THE HOPALONG CASSIDY NOVELS
The Riders of High Rock
The Rustlers of West Fork
The Trail to Seven Pines
Trouble Shooter

NONFICTION
Education of a Wandering Man
Frontier
The Sackett Companion: A Personal Guide to the Sackett Novels
A Trail of Memories: The Quotations of Louis L'Amour, compiled by Angelique L'Amour

POETRY
Smoke from This Altar

THE
COLLECTED
SHORT STORIES
OF
LOUIS L'AMOUR

CRIME STORIES
Volume Six, Part 1

Louis L'Amour

BANTAM BOOKS
NEW YORK

The Collected Short Stories of Louis L'Amour, Volume 6, Part 1, is a work of fiction. Names, characters, places, and incidents either are the product of the author's imagination or are used fictitiously. Any resemblance to actual persons, living or dead, events or locales is entirely coincidental.

2016 Bantam Books Mass Market Edition

Published in the United States by Bantam Books, an imprint of Random House, a division of Penguin Random House LLC, New York.

BANTAM BOOKS and the HOUSE colophon are registered trademarks of Penguin Random House LLC.

Originally published as part of *The Collected Short Stories of Louis L'Amour, Volume 6,* in the United States by Bantam Books, an imprint of Random House, a division of Penguin Random House LLC, in 2008.

ISBN 978-0-804-17977-5
ebook ISBN 978-0-553-90579-3

Cover design: Scott Biel

Photograph of Louis L'Amour by John Hamilton—Globe Photos, Inc.

Printed in the United States of America

randomhousebooks.com

9 8 7 6 5 4 3 2 1

Bantam Books mass market edition: May 2016

CONTENTS

THE COLLECTED
SHORT STORIES
OF LOUIS L'AMOUR

UNGUARDED MOMENT

ARTHUR FORDYCE HAD never done a criminal thing in his life, nor had the idea of doing anything unlawful ever seriously occurred to him.

The wallet that lay beside his chair was not only full; it was literally stuffed. It lay on the floor near his feet where it had fallen.

His action was as purely automatic as an action can be. He let his *Racing Form* slip from his lap and cover the billfold. Then he sat very still, his heart pounding. The fat man who had dropped the wallet was talking to a friend on the far side of the box. As far as Fordyce could see, his own action had gone unobserved.

It had been a foolish thing to do. Fordyce did not need the money. He had been paid a week's salary only a short time before and had won forty dollars on the last race.

With his heart pounding heavily, his mouth dry, he made every effort to be casual as he picked up his Form and the wallet beneath. Trying to appear as natural as possible, he opened the billfold under cover of the Form, extracted the money, and shifted the bills to his pocket.

The horses were rounding into the home stretch, and when the crowd sprang to its feet, he got up, too. As he straightened, he shied the wallet, with an underhand flip, under the feet of the crowd off to his left.

His heart was still pounding. Blindly he stared out at the track. He was a thief . . . he had stolen money . . . he had appropriated it . . . how much?

Panic touched him suddenly. Suppose he had been seen? If someone had seen him, the person might wait to see if he returned the wallet. If he did not, the person might come down and accuse him. What if, even now, there was an officer waiting for him? Perhaps he should leave, get away from there as quickly as possible.

Cool sanity pervaded him. No, that would never do. He must remain where he was, go through the motions of watching the races. If he were accused, he could say he had won the money. He *had* won money—forty dollars. The man at the window might remember his face but not the amount he had given him.

Fordyce was in the box that belonged to his boss, Ed Charlton, and no friend of Charlton's would ever be thought a thief. He sat still, watching the races, relaxing as much as he could. Surprisingly, the fat man who had dropped the wallet did not miss it. He did not even put a hand to his pocket.

After the sixth race, several people got up to leave, and Fordyce followed suit. It was not until he was unlocking his car that he realized there was a man at his elbow.

He was a tall, dark-eyed handsome young man, too smoothly dressed, too—slick. And there was something sharply feral about his eyes. He was smiling unpleasantly.

"Nice work!" he said. "Very nice! Now, how about a split?"

Arthur Fordyce kept his head. Inside, he seemed to feel all his bodily organs contract as if with chill. "I am afraid I don't understand you. What was it you wanted?"

The brightly feral eyes hardened just a little, although the smile remained. "A split, that's what I want. I saw you get that billfold. Now let's bust it open and see what we've got."

"Billfold?" Fordyce stared at him coldly, although he was quivering inside with fear. He *had* been seen! What if he should be arrested? What if Alice heard? Or Ed Charlton? Why, that fat man might be a friend of Ed's!

"Don't give me that," the tall young man was saying. "I saw the whole thing. Now, I'm getting a split or I'll holler bull. I'll go to the cops. You aren't out of the grounds yet, and even if you were, I can find out who used Ed Charlton's box today."

Fordyce stood stock-still. This could not be happening to him. It—it was preposterous! What ever had possessed him? Yet, what explanation could he give now? He had thrown away the wallet itself, a sure indication that he intended to keep the money.

"Come on, Bud"—the smile was sneering now—"you might as well hand it over. There was plenty there. I had my eye on Linton all afternoon. He always carries plenty of dough."

Linton—George Linton. How many times had Ed Charlton spoken of him. They were golfing companions. They hunted and fished together. They had been friends at college. Even if the money were returned, Fordyce was sure he would lose his job, his friends—Alice. He would be finished, completely finished.

"I never intended to do it," he protested. "It—it was an accident."

"Yeah"—the eyes were contemptuous—"I could see that. I couldn't have done it more accidentally myself. Now, hand it over."

There was fourteen hundred dollars in fifties and twenties. With fumbling fingers, Fordyce divided it. The young man took his bills and folded them with the hands of a lover. He grinned suddenly.

"Nice work! With my brains and your in we'd make a team!" He pocketed the bills, anxious to be gone. "Be seeing you!"

Arthur Fordyce did not reply. Cold and shaken, he stared after the fellow.

———

DAYS FLED SWIFTLY past. Fordyce avoided the track, worked harder than ever. Once he took Alice to the theater and twice to dinner. Then at a party the Charltons gave, he came face to face with George Linton.

The fat man was jovial. "How are you, Fordyce? Ed tells me you're his right hand at the office. Good to know you."

"Thanks." He spoke without volition. "Didn't I see you at the track a couple of weeks ago? I was in Charlton's box."

"Oh, yes! I remember you now. I thought your face seemed familiar." He shook his head wryly. "I won't forget *that* day. My pocket was picked for nearly two thousand dollars."

Seeing that Alice was waiting, Fordyce excused himself and joined her. Together they walked to the terrace and stood there in the moonlight. How lovely she was! And, to think he had risked all this, risked it on the impulse of a moment, and for what? She was looking up at him, and he spoke suddenly, filled with the sudden panic born of the thought of losing her.

"Alice!" He gripped her arms, "Alice! Will you marry me?"

"Why, Arthur!" she protested, laughing in her astonishment. "How rough you are! Do you always grab a girl so desperately when you ask her to marry you?"

He released her arms, embarrassed. "I—I guess I was violent," he said, "but I just—well, I couldn't stand to lose you, Alice."

Her eyes were wide and wonderfully soft. "You aren't going to, Arthur," she said quietly. "I'm going to stay with you."

"Then—you mean—"

"Yes, Arthur."

———

DRIVING HOME THAT night his heart was bounding. She would marry him! How lovely she was! How beautiful her eyes had been as she looked up at him!

He drove into the garage, snapped off the lights and got his keys. It was not until he came out to close the doors that he saw the glow of a suddenly inhaled cigarette in the shadow cast by the shrubbery almost beside him.

"Hello, Fordyce. How's tricks?" It was the man from the track. "My name's Chafey, Bill Chafey."

"What are you doing here? What do you want?"

"That's a beautiful babe you've got. I've seen her picture on the society pages."

"I'm sorry. I don't intend to discuss my fiancée with you. It's very late and I must be getting to bed. Good night."

"Abrupt, aren't you?" Chafey adopted a George Raft manner. "Not going to invite an old friend inside for a drink? An old friend from out of town—one who wants to meet your friends?"

Arthur Fordyce saw it clearly, then, saw it as clearly as he would ever see anything. He knew what this slick young man was thinking—that he would use his hold over Fordyce for introductions and for better chances to steal. Probably he had other ideas, too. Girls—and their money.

"Look, Chafey," he said harshly, "whatever was between us is finished. Now beat it! And don't come back!"

Chafey had seen a lot of movies. He knew what came next. He snapped his cigarette into the grass and took a quick step forward.

"Why, you cheap thief! You think you can brush me off like that? Listen, I've got you where I want you, and before I'm through, I'll have everything you've got!" Chafey's voice was rising with some inner emotion of triumph or hatred. "You think you're so much! Figure you can brush me off, do you?"

He stepped close. "What if I got to that fancy babe of yours and told her what I know? What if I go to Linton and tell him? You're a thief, Fordyce! A damned thief! You and that fancy babe of yours! Why—"

Fordyce hit him. The action was automatic and it was unexpected. In the movies it was always the tough guy who handed out the beatings. His fist flew up and caught Chafey on the jaw. Chafey's feet flew up, and he went down, the back of his neck hitting the bumper with a sickening crack. Then his body slipped slowly to the ground.

Arthur Fordyce stood very still, staring down at the crumpled form. His breath was coming in great gasps, and his fist was still clenched hard. Some instinct told him the man was dead.

"Mr. Fordyce?" It was his neighbor, Joe Neal, calling. "Is something wrong?"

Fordyce dropped to one knee and touched the man's head. It lolled loosely, too loosely. He felt for the heart. Nothing. He bent over the man's face, but felt no breath, nothing.

Neal was coming out on the lawn, pulling his belt tight. "Fordyce? Is anything wrong?"

He got to his feet slowly. "Yes, Joe. I wish you'd come

down here. I've been held up and I think—I think I've killed him."

Joe Neal hurried up, flashlight in hand. He threw the light on the fallen man. "Good heavens!" he gasped. "What happened?"

"He was waiting there by the tree. He stepped out with his hand in his pocket—you know, like he had a gun. I hit him before I realized."

———

THAT WAS THE story, and he made it stick. For several days it was the talk of all his friends. Fordyce had killed a holdup man. That took nerve. And a punch, too. Didn't know he had it in him. Of course, it was the bumper that actually broke his neck. Still—had there been any doubts—and there were none—a check of Chafey's record would have removed them.

He had done time and was on parole. He had gone up for armed robbery and had been arrested a score of times for investigation. He was suspected of rolling drunks and of various acts of petty pilfering and slugging. A week passed, and a second week. Arthur Fordyce threw himself into his work, never talking about what had happened.

Others forgot it, too, except Joe Neal. Once, commenting on it to his wife, he looked puzzled and said, "You know, I'd have sworn I heard voices that night. I'd have sworn it."

"You might have. They might have argued. I imagine that a man might say a lot when excited and not remember it." That was what his wife said, and it was reasonable enough. Nevertheless, Joe Neal was faintly disturbed by it all. He avoided Fordyce. Not that they had ever been friends.

———

ARTHUR FORDYCE HAD been lucky. No getting away from that. He had been very lucky, and sometimes when he thought about it, he felt a cold chill come over him. But it was finished now.

Only it wasn't.

It was Monday night, two weeks after the inquest, the first

night he had been home since it had happened. He was sitting in his armchair listening to the radio when the telephone rang. Idly, he lifted it from the cradle.

"Mr. Fordyce?" The voice was feminine and strange. "Is this Arthur Fordyce?"

"Speaking."

There was an instant of silence. Then, "This is Bill Chafey's girl-friend, Mr. Fordyce. I thought I would call and congratulate you. You seem to be very, very lucky!"

The cold was there again in the pit of his stomach. "I—I beg your pardon? I'm afraid I don't know what you mean."

"He told me all about it, Mr. Fordyce. All about that day at the track. All about what he was going to do. Bill had big ideas, Mr. Fordyce, and he thought you were his chance. Only he thought you were scared. He got too close to you, didn't he, Mr. Fordyce?"

"I'm sure," he kept his voice composed, "that you are seriously in error. I—"

She interrupted with a soft laugh, a laugh that did not cover an underlying cruelty. "I'm not going to be as dumb as Bill was, Mr. Fordyce. I'm not going to come anywhere within your reach. But you're going to pay off. You're going to pay off like a slot machine. A thousand dollars now and five hundred a month from now on."

"I don't know what you're talking about, but you are probably insane," he said quietly. "If you are a friend of Chafey's, then you know he was a criminal. I am sorry for you, but there is nothing I can do."

"One thousand dollars by Friday, Mr. Fordyce, and five hundred a month from now on. I don't think you were scared when Bill went to you, but how about the gas chamber, Mr. Fordyce? How about that?"

"What you assume is impossible." He fought to keep his voice controlled. "It's absurd to think I have that kind of money."

She laughed again. "But you can get it, Buster! You can get it when it means the difference between life and the gas chamber."

Her voice grew brusque. "Small bills, understand? Nothing bigger than a twenty. Send it to Gertrude Ellis, Box X78, at the central office. Send me that thousand dollars by Friday and send the five hundred on the fifth of every month. If you miss by as much as ten days, the whole story goes to your girlfriend, to your boss, and to the police." The phone clicked, the line buzzed emptily. Slowly, Fordyce replaced the phone.

So there it was. Now he had not only disgrace and prison before him, but the gas chamber.

A single mistake—an instant when his reason was in abeyance—and here he was—trapped.

He could call her bluff. He could refuse. The woman was obviously unprincipled and she had sounded vindictive. She would certainly follow through as she had threatened.

FOR HOURS, HE paced the floor, racking his brain for some way out, some avenue of escape. He could go to Charlton, confess everything, and ask for help. Charlton would give it to him, for he was that kind of man, but when it was over, he would drop Fordyce quickly and quietly.

Alice—his future—everything depended on finding some other way. Some alternative.

If something should happen to this woman— And it might. People were killed every day. There were accidents. He shied away from the idea that lay behind this, but slowly it forced its way into his consciousness. He was considering murder.

No. Never that. He would not—he could not. He had killed Chafey, but that had been different. It had not been murder, although if all the facts were known, it might be considered so. It had been an accident. All he had done was strike out. If he killed now, deliberately and with intent, it would be different.

He ran his fingers through his hair and stared blindly at the floor. Accidentally, he caught a glimpse of his face in a mirror. He looked haggard, beaten. But he was not beaten. There was a way out. There had to be.

Morning found him on the job, working swiftly and silently. He handled the few clients who called, talked with them and straightened out their problems. He was aware that

Charlton was watching him. Finally, at noon, the boss came over.

"Fordyce," he said, "this thing has worried you. You're doing a fine job this morning, so it looks as though you're getting it whipped, but nevertheless, I think a few days' rest would put you right up to snuff. You just go home now, and don't come in until Monday. Go out of town, see a lot of Alice, anything. But relax."

"Thanks." A flood of relief went over Fordyce as he got up, and genuine gratitude must have showed in his eyes, for Charlton smiled. "I do need a rest."

"Sure!" Ed put a hand on his shoulder. "You call Alice. Take her for a drive. Wonderful girl, that. You're lucky. Good connections, too," he added, almost as an afterthought.

The sun was bright in the street, and he stood there thinking. He would call Alice, make a date if possible. He had to do that much, for Ed would be sure to comment later. Then— then he must find this woman, this Gertrude Ellis.

He got through the afternoon without a hitch. He and Alice drove out along the ocean drive, parked by the sea, and then stopped for dinner. It was shortly after ten when he finally dropped her at her home.

He remembered what the police had said about Bill Chafey. They had known about him and they had mentioned that he had been one of several known criminals who frequented a place called Eddie's Bar. If Chafey had gone there, it was possible his girl did, too.

———

IT WAS A shadowy place with one bartender and a row of leather-covered stools and a half-dozen booths. He picked out a stool and ordered a drink. He was halfway down his second bourbon and soda before the first lead came to him.

A tall Latin-looking young man was talking to the bartender. "Gracie been around? I haven't seen her since Chafey bought it."

"You figuring on moving in there?"

"Are you crazy? That broad gives me the shivers. She's a looker, all right, but she'd cut your heart out for a buck."

"Bill handled her."

"You mean she handled him. She was the brains of that setup."

"Leave it to Bill to try to pick up a fast buck."

"Yeah, but look at him now."

There was silence, and Fordyce sipped his drink unconcernedly, waiting. After a while it started again.

"She's probably working that bar on Sixth Street."

"Maybe. She said the other day she was going to quit. That she was expecting a legacy."

A few moments later, Fordyce finished his drink and left the place. He went to Sixth Street, studied the bars as he drove along. It might be any one of them. He tried a couple but without luck.

The next morning he slept late. While he was shaving, he studied his face in the mirror. He told himself he did not look like a murderer. But then, what did murderers look like? They were just people.

He dressed carefully, thinking as he dressed. To get the money, Gertrude Ellis would have to go to the box. She would not expect him to be watching, since she would probably believe he would be at work. Even so, he would have to be careful, for she would be careful herself. She might walk by and merely glance in at first. He would have to get her to open the box. He considered that, then had an idea.

Shuffling through his own mail, he found what he wanted. It was an advertisement of the type mailed to Boxholder or Occupant. He withdrew the advertising matter to make sure his own name was not on it. Then he carefully removed the address with ink eradicator and substituted the number she had given him.

Her true name would probably be not unlike Gertrude Ellis, which was obviously assumed. The first name was Gracie, and it was a fairly safe bet the last would begin with an E. Unless, as sometimes happened, she used the name of a husband or some friend.

Considering the situation, he had another idea. Eddie's Bar and Sixth Street were not far apart. Hence, she must live somewhere in that vicinity.

HE RETURNED TO Eddie's that night, and the bartender greeted him briefly. They exchanged a few comments, and then Fordyce asked, "Many babes come in here?"

"Yeah, now and again. Most of 'em are bags. Once in a while, something good shows up."

He went away to attend to the wants of another customer, and Arthur Fordyce waited, stalling over his drink, listening. He heard nothing.

It was much later, when he had finished his third drink, and was turning to look around, that he bumped into someone. She was about to sit down, and he collided with her outstretched arm.

"Oh, I'm sorry! Pardon me."

"That's all right." She was a straight-haired brunette with rather thin lips and cool eyes. But she was pretty, damned pretty. Her clothes were not like those Alice wore, but she did have a style of her own.

She ordered a drink, and he ignored her. After a minute, she got up and went to the ladies' room. The bartender strolled over. "Speaking of babes," he said, "there's a cute one. Should be about ready, too. She's fresh out of boyfriends."

"Her? How come?"

The bartender shrugged. "Runs with some fast company sometimes. Her boyfriend tried to make a quick buck with a gun and got killed. Chafey. Maybe you read about it."

"Chafey?" Fordyce looked puzzled, although inside he was jumping. "Don't recall the name." He hesitated. "Introduce me?"

"You don't need it. Just buy her a drink." Then the bartender grinned. "But if you go home with her, take your own bottle and pour the drinks yourself. And don't pass out."

"You mean she'd roll me?"

"I didn't say that, chum. I didn't say anything. But you look like a good guy. Just take care of yourself. After all," he added, "a guy can have a good time without making a sucker of himself."

The girl returned then and sat down on her stool. He waited out her drink, and as she was finishing it, he turned.

"How about having one with me? I feel I owe it to you after bumping you like that."

She smiled quickly. "Oh, that's all right! Yes, I'll drink with you."

Her name was Gracie Turk. She had been divorced several years ago. They talked about dance bands, movies, swimming. She liked to drink, she admitted, but usually did her drinking at home.

"I'd like that," he said. "Why don't we pick up a bottle and go there?"

She hesitated, then smiled. "All right, let's go." Fordyce glanced back as he went out. The bartender grinned and made a circle of his thumb and forefinger.

Not tonight, Fordyce told himself. Whatever happens, not tonight. He will remember this. They got the bottle and went to her apartment. It was small, cheaply furnished with pretensions toward elegance. Bored, he still managed to seem interested and mixed the drinks himself. He let her see that he had money on him and, suddenly, recalled that he was expecting a business call at night.

"From back East, you know," he said by way of explanation.

He left, but with a date for the following evening. An hour later, he called back and canceled the date. His call had come, he said, and he would be out of town.

––––––

HE MADE HIS plans with utmost care. He drove out of town and deliberately wound along dusty roads for several hours, letting his car gather dust. In town, at the same time, he carefully chose a spot at which to dispose of the body.

At eight, he drove around and parked his car near the entrance to the alley behind the girl's apartment. There was a light in the window, so he went into the front entrance, hoping desperately that he would meet no one. Luck was with him, and he reached her door safely. It was around a corner in a corridor off the main hall. At the end was a door to the back stairs.

He tapped lightly and then heard the sound of heels. The door was opened, and Gracie Turk stepped back in surprise.

"Al!" That was the name he had given her. "I thought you were out of town?"

"Missed my train, and I just had a wild idea you might not have gone out."

"Come in!" She stepped back. "I was just fixing something to eat. Want a sandwich? Or a drink?"

He closed the door behind him and looked at her shoulders and the back of her head. That coldness was in the pit of his stomach again. His mouth felt dry, and the palms of his hands were wet. He kept wiping them off, as if they were already— He shook himself and accepted the drink she had fixed for him.

She smiled quickly, but her eyes seemed cold. "Well, drink up! There's more where that came from! I'll go get things ready, and then we'll eat. We'll just stay home tonight."

She had good legs, and the seams in her stockings were straight. He was cold. Maybe the drink would fix him up. He drank half of it at a gulp. It was lousy whisky, lousy— The words of the bartender at Eddie's came back to him. "Take your own bottle," he had said, "and pour your own drinks." He stared at the glass, put it down suddenly.

He sat down abruptly. She would be coming in soon. He glanced hastily around, then took the drink and reaching back under the divan, poured it, little by little, over the thick carpet. When she came back into the room, he was sitting there holding his empty glass. "Thanks," he commented. "Let me get some for *you*."

She smiled, but her eyes were still cold and calculating. She seemed to be measuring him as she took the glass from his hand. "I'll just fill this up again. Why don't you lie down?"

"All right," he said, and suddenly made up his mind. He would not wait. It would be now. She might—

If he passed out, she would open his billfold, and in his billfold was his identification! He started to get up, but the room seemed to spin. He sat down, suddenly filled with panic. He was going; he—He got his hand into his pocket, fumbled for the identification card. He got it out of the window in the billfold and shoved it down in another pocket. The money wasn't much, only—

———

HE HAD BEEN hearing voices, a girl's and a man's for some time. The girl was speaking now. "I don't care where you drop him. Just take him out of here. The fool didn't have half the money he had the other night! Not half! All this trouble for a lousy forty bucks! Why, I'd bet he had— What's the matter?"

"Hey!" The man's voice was hoarse. "Do you know who this is?"

"Who it is? What does it matter?"

Fordyce lay very still. Slowly but surely he was recovering his senses. He could hear the man move back.

"I don't want this, Gracie. Take back your sawbuck. This is *hot!* I want no part of him! None at all!"

"What's the matter?" She was coming forward. "What have you got there?"

"Don't kid me!" His voice was hoarse with anger. "I'm getting out of here! Just you try to ring me in on your dirty work!"

"Johnny, have you gone nuts? What's the matter?" Her voice was strident.

"You mean you don't know who this is? This is Fordyce, the guy who knocked off Bill."

There was dead silence while she absorbed that. Fordyce heard a crackle of paper. That letter—it had been in his pocket. It must have fallen out.

"Fordyce." She sounded stunned. "He must have found out where I was! How the—" Her voice died away.

"I'm getting out of here. I want no part of killing a guy."

"Don't be a fool!" She was angry. "I didn't know who the sap was. I met him at Eddie's. He flashed a roll, and I just figured it was an easy take."

"What gives, Gracie?" The man's voice was prying. "What's behind this?"

"Ah, I just was going to take the sap for plenty, that's all."

She stopped talking, then started again. "Bill saw him grab a wallet some guy dropped. This guy didn't return it, so Bill shook him for half of it. Then Bill figured on more, and he wouldn't stand for it."

"So you moved in?"

"Why not? He didn't know who I was or where I was. What I can't figure is how he found out. The guy must be psychic."

Arthur Fordyce kept his eyes closed and listened. While he listened, his mind was working. He was a fool. An insane fool. How could he ever have conceived the idea of murder? He knew now he could never have done it, never. It wasn't in him to kill or even to plan so cold-bloodedly. Suddenly, all he wanted was to get out, to get away without trouble. Should he lie still and wait to find out what would happen? Or should he get up and try to bluff it out?

"What are you going to do now?"

———

GRACIE TURK DID not reply. Minutes ticked by, and then the man turned toward the door. "I'm getting out of here," he said. "I don't want any part of this. I'd go for dumping the guy if he was just drunk, but I want no part of murder."

"Who's talking about murder?" Gracie's voice was shrill. "Get out if you're yellow."

Fordyce opened one eye a crack. Gracie was facing the other way, not looking directly at him. He put his hands on the floor, rolled over, and got to his feet. The man sprang back, falling over a chair, and Gracie turned quickly, her face drawn and vicious.

Fordyce felt his head spin, but he stood there, looking at them. Gracie Turk stared, swore viciously.

"Give him his ten," Fordyce told her, "out of the money you took from me."

"I will like—"

"Give it to him. He won't go for a killing, and you don't dare start anything now because he'd be a witness. For that matter, he would be a witness against me, too."

"That's right," the man said hastily. It was the same Latin-looking man he had seen in Eddie's. "Give me the sawbuck and I'll get out of here—but fast."

Gracie's eyes flared, her lips curled. "What do you think you're pulling, anyway? How'd you find me? Who told you?"

Fordyce forced himself to smile. "What's difficult about finding you? You're not very clever, Gracie." Suddenly, he saw his way clear and said with more emphasis, "Not at all clever."

The idea was so simple that it might work. He was no murderer, nor was he a thief. He had only been a fool. Now if he could assume the nerve and the indifference it would take, he could get safely out of this.

"Look," he said quietly, "like Chafey, you walked into this by accident. He misunderstood what he saw and passed it on to you, and neither of you had any idea but making a fast buck.

"Bill"— and he knew it sounded improbable "—stepped into a trap baited for another guy. You know as well as I do that Bill was never very smart. He was neither as smart nor as lucky as you. You're going to get out of this without tripping."

"What are you talking about?" Gracie was both angry and puzzled.

"The wallet I picked up"— Fordyce made his voice sound impatient "—was dropped by agreement. We were trying to convince a man who was watching that I was taking a payoff." The story was flimsy, but Gracie would accept a story of double-dealing quicker than any other. "Bill saw it, and I paid off to keep him from crabbing a big deal."

"I don't believe it!" Her voice was defiant, yet there was uncertainty in her eyes. "Was murdering Bill part of the game?"

He shrugged it off. "Look Gracie. You knew Bill. He was a big, good-looking guy who couldn't see anything but the way he was going. He thought he had me where the hair was short when he stopped me outside my garage. Once away from that track, I was clean, so he had no hold over me at all. My deal had gone through. We had words, and when he started for me, I hit him. He fell, and his neck hit the bumper. He was a victim of his own foolishness and greed."

"That's what you say."

"Why kill him? He could be annoying, but he could prove nothing, and nobody would have believed him. Nor," he added, "would they believe you."

He picked up his hat. "Give this man the ten spot for his trouble. You keep the rest and charge it up to experience. That's what I'd do."

The night air was cool on his face when he reached the street. He hesitated, breathing deep, and then walked to his car.

———

AT THE CHARLTON'S party, one week later, he was filling Alice's glass at the punch bowl when George Linton clapped him on the shoulder. "Hey, Art!" It was the first time, he thought suddenly, that anybody had called him Art. "I got my money back! Remember the money I lost at the track? Fourteen hundred dollars! It came back in the mail, no note, nothing. What do you think of that?"

"You were lucky." Fordyce grinned at him. "We're all lucky at times."

"Believe me," Linton confided, "if I'd found that fourteen hundred bucks, I'd never have returned it! I'd just have shoved it in my pocket and forgotten about it."

"That," Art Fordyce said sincerely, "is what you think!"

POLICE BAND

"CAR 134 . . . 134 . . . cancel your last call, 135 will handle. . . ."

Tom Sixte stopped turning the dial and listened. He was far over on the right side of his radio and was for the first time aware that it could pick up police calls. The book he was reading had failed to hold his interest. He put it down and lit a cigarette.

"42, station call . . . 1047 South Kashmir . . . 218, MT, Clear . . ." The signal faded in and out.

Sixte leaned back in his chair, listening with only half his attention. He had been in town to study a plan for moving an industrial plant to San Bernardino and the study was complete, his report written. At thirty-two he was successful, single, and vaguely discontented.

With only hours remaining of his stay in town, he was profoundly bored. His work had given him no time to make friends, and he had seen too many movies. Waiting got on his nerves, and he was leaving in just forty-eight hours for Bolivia.

"All units . . . stolen truck . . . commercial . . . Charles . . . Henry. . . ." The voice trailed off again and Sixte turned in his chair and poured his glass half full of Madeira, then relaxed.

The dispatcher's voice came in suddenly. "179 . . . Redondo and San Vincente, neighbor reports a man hurt, a woman screaming. . . ."

Tom Sixte sat up abruptly. That was only two blocks away! He sat still for a moment but boredom pulled him to his feet. He shrugged into his coat and, hat in hand, stepped out the door.

Upon reaching the street, he hesitated. What was he rushing for? Like a ten-year-old kid after a fire truck!

But, why not? He was doing nothing and the walk might do him good. He went to the corner. He could hear no screaming, although far off he heard the wail of a siren approaching.

He turned the corner and started for Redondo, but just before he reached it, he saw a girl cutting across a lawn, coming toward him. Her coat was open, hair flying, and she was running.

She was in the middle of the street when she saw him. She slid to a stop and in the light reflected from the corner her face seemed set and strained. Her right hand was in her pocket.

"What's the trouble?" he asked. "Do you need help?"

"No!" She spat the word. But a glance over her shoulder and her manner changed. She came up to him quickly. "Sorry, I do need help, but you frightened me. I just got away from a man."

"The police are coming. There's nothing to worry about now."

She paused, listening to the siren. "Oh, but I *can't* meet the police! I simply can't! They'd . . . my parents would hear . . ." She caught his arm impulsively. "Help me, won't you? Daddy and Mother didn't know I was out. . . ."

They were walking back toward the corner he had turned. A siren shrilled to a stop somewhere behind them. She clutched his arm. "Do you live close by? Can't we go there? Just until the police are gone? I . . . I fought him off, and he fell. He may be hurt. Take me to your place . . . oh, *please*!"

Tom Sixte shrugged. No use letting the kid get into trouble, and it would be only for a few minutes. He could not see her face well, but her voice and her figure indicated youth.

He led the way upstairs and unlocked the door. The room was small and simple. Aside from the clothes and his bags the only things in it that belonged to him were a half dozen books.

When he saw her face under the light, he felt his first touch of doubt. She must be . . . well, over thirty.

She saw the bottle. "Can I have a drink?" Without waiting for his reply, she picked up his own empty glass and poured wine into it. She tossed it off, then looked startled. "What was that?"

"It's wine. It's called Malmsey."

"It's good." She picked up the bottle and looked at it. "Imported, isn't it?" She glanced swiftly around the room, and saw the telephone. "May I make a call?"

She moved the phone and dialed. He heard the phone ringing, then a hard male voice. "Yeah?"

"Kurt? This is Phyllis. . . . Can you come and get me?" Sixte heard a male voice asking questions. "What d'you think?" Her voice became strident with impatience. "Rhubarb? I'll say! The place is lousy with cops.

"No, I'm all right . . . some guy invited me up to his place." The male voice lowered a little. "How do I know who he is?" Phyllis grew more impatient. "Look, you're in this as deep as I am! You come an' get me! . . . Sure, I'll stay here, but hurry!"

Worried now, Sixte turned on her as she hung up the phone. "I didn't bargain for this," he said, "you'll have to go. I had no idea you were running from the police."

"Sit down." There was a small automatic in her hand. "I'm not fooling. That man out there is dead."

"Dead?" Sixte was incredulous. "You killed him?"

Her laugh was not pleasant. "He was a drunken fool. It was that woman spoiled it all."

"Woman?"

"Some dame who came up while I was going over him. She started to scream so I hit her."

Tom Sixte sat down, trying to focus his thoughts. Fifteen minutes ago, he had been reading, faintly bored. Now, he was mixed up in a murder and robbery. Kurt was coming to take her away, and then . . . his good sense intervened. That would not, could not be the end. They could not afford to let him go. And if she had killed a man . . .

She poured another glass of the Madeira. Steps sounded outside the door. There was a careful knock. Keeping her eyes on Sixte, the gun out of sight, Phyllis opened the door.

The man who stepped in was cadaverous, but handsome. He could have been no more than thirty, and he wore a dark suit. The eyes that measured Sixte were cruel.

Phyllis pulled him to one side and whispered rapidly. Kurt listened, then shook out a cigarette. "Who are you?" he said then. "What are you?"

"My name is Sixte. I'm an architect."

"Get up and turn around."

Sixte felt practiced hands go through his pockets, remove his wallet, some letters.

He was told to be seated and Kurt went through his billfold. There was seventy dollars in cash, some traveler's checks—and the tickets were with his passport.

"Bolivia, huh? Whatya know about that? I got a guy wants to leave town. He'd pay plenty for this passport and these tickets."

Sixte tried to sort out his thoughts. For the first time he began to appreciate his true danger.

Kurt smiled, and it was not a nice smile. "This is sweet, Phyl, real sweet. This joker has stuff here I can sell for a grand, easy. Maybe two. Rubio has to get out of town and this is it. Rubio pays, takes the ticket—this guy is gone and nobody even looks for him."

Tom Sixte sat very still. His mind seemed icy cold. He was not going to get out of this . . . he was not going to . . . he reached over to his radio and adjusted the hands of the clock, then the volume. . . .

———

DETECTIVE LIEUTENANT MIKE Frost walked back to the lab truck. "Roll it, Joe," he said, "nothing more you can do here."

Suddenly the radio lit up. "179 . . . you up the block from the coroner's van? If so turn your radio down. We're getting complaints."

Frost picked up the microphone. "Dispatch . . . ? What's this about my radio?"

After a brief conversation Mike Frost got out of the car, spoke to Joe, and walked up the block. The sound was rolling from the hallway of a rooming house and Frost went up the steps two at a time. The door was open, and as people were emerging from the rooms and staring, Frost shoved through the door and went in. The blasting sound filled an empty room, with the light switch off.

Turning the lights on, he stepped to the radio and turned it off with a snap. Joe had come into the door behind him. "What is it, Lieutenant?"

"Oh, some crazy fool went off and left his radio turned on." He scowled. "No, it's one of those clock radios. Must have just switched on."

"Who'd want that volume?" Joe wondered. "And on a police band, too."

Mike Frost looked at Joe thoughtfully, then turned slowly and began to look around the room. It was strangely bare.

No clothes, no personal possessions. The bathroom shelves were empty, no razor, shaving cream, or powder. No toothbrush.

The simple furniture of a furnished room, towels, soap . . . a clock radio and some books. The clock radio was brand spanking new . . . so were the books.

Frost stepped back into the bathroom. The sink was still damp. Whoever had been here had left within a very few minutes. But why leave a new radio and the books? The only other thing remaining was an almost empty bottle of Madeira. The glass on the table was still wet . . . and there was lipstick on the rim. In two places . . . some woman had taken at least two drinks here.

And not twenty minutes ago, a woman had fled the scene of a killing just two blocks away.

Somebody had left this room fast . . . and why was that radio set for a time when no one would want to get up and tuned for a police band with the volume control on full power?

"Get your stuff, Joe. Give it a going-over."

Joe was incredulous. "This place? What's the idea?"

"Call it a hunch, Joe. But work fast. I think we'd better work fast."

The landlady was visiting somebody in Santa Monica.

Yes, she had a new roomer. A man. Nobody knew anything about him except that he was rarely in, and very quiet. Oh, yes! A neighbor remembered, Mrs. Brady had said he was leaving in a couple of days . . . this room would be vacant on the fifth. This was the third.

Frost walked back up to the room and stared around him. Was he wasting time, making a fool of himself? But why would a man leave a perfectly new clock radio behind him? And why leave the books?

There were six of them, all new. They represented a value of more than thirty dollars and given the condition of the spines three of them had not even been opened. Two were on South America. On Bolivia. One was a book on conversational Spanish.

Frost picked up the telephone and rang the airlines. In a matter of minutes he had his information. Three men were scheduled for La Paz, Bolivia, on the fifth . . . another check . . . at that address. Thomas Sixte. Frost put the phone back on the cradle.

He was no closer to an answer but he did have more of a puzzle and some reason behind his hunch. Why would a man, leaving within forty-eight hours, anyway, suddenly leave a comfortable room?

Where did he expect to spend the next forty-eight hours? Why did he leave his books and radio? He glanced at the dial on the radio. The man had his clock radio set to start blasting police calls within a matter of minutes after he had left his room.

Why?

Frost picked up the Madeira bottle . . . forty-eight years old. Good stuff, not too easily had . . . he checked the telephone book and began ringing. Absently, he watched Joe going over the room. His helper was in the bathroom.

The liquor store he called replied after a minute. Just closing up. "Yes, I knew Mr. Sixte. Very excellent taste, Lieutenant. Knows wines as few men do. When he first talked to me about them, I believed him to be a champagne salesman.

"That brand of Madeira? Very few stores, Lieutenant. It would be easy to . . . yes? All right."

He glanced at his watch. He had been in the vicinity so had gone to Redondo and San Vincente. That had been at 9:42 . . . twenty minutes later he heard the blasting of the radio . . . it was now 10:35.

"Only three sets of prints," Joe told him. "One of them a man's. Two are women. One of them is probably the maid or the landlady, judging by where I found 'em."

"The others?"

"Only a couple . . . some more, but smudged. Got a clear print off the wine bottle, one off the glass."

"Anything else?"

"Soap in the shower is still wet. He probably took a shower about seven or eight o'clock. Some cigarettes, all his . . . and he'd been reading that book."

Joe rubbed his jaw. "What gives, Lieutenant? What you tryin' to prove?"

Mike Frost shrugged. He was not quite sure himself. "A man is killed and a girl is slugged by a woman. We know that much. Two blocks away a man suddenly leaves his room, with no reason that figures, and minutes later his clock radio starts blasting police calls.

"A woman has been in this room within the last hour. My hunch is it was the woman who killed that guy on Redondo. I'm guessing that she got in here somehow to duck the police, and when she went away, she took him with her."

"And he turned on the radio to warn us? How does he know we're near?"

"Maybe the girl told him. Maybe he saw the murder. Maybe she followed him. It's all maybe."

"Maybe he was in cahoots with her."

"Could be . . . but why the radio?"

"Accident . . . twisted the wrong dial, maybe."

Frost nodded. "All right. Check those prints. All three sets . . . or whatever you got."

Had the girl taken the man away from here by herself? They had a call out, the area blanketed. Any girl alone would have been stopped. But if she had been with him? She might have been stopped, anyway. She was a blonde, about thirty, someone had said, slight figure . . . in a suede coat.

When Joe was gone Mike Frost sat down in the empty room and began to fiddle with the radio. After twenty minutes he had learned one thing. You just didn't turn this on to the police band. You had to hunt for it, adjust it carefully.

Heavy steps on the stairs . . . "Got something for you, Lieutenant." It was an officer from a radio car. "A girl across the street. She was parked with her boyfriend . . . high school kids . . . they saw two men and a woman come out and go to a car. Dark sedan of some kind."

"Two men?"

"Yeah . . . the car drove up while they were sittin' there. The guy who went upstairs was tall. Big in the shoulders."

It was something, but not much. There was the phone. Had the girl gotten in here she could have called her boyfriend, and he might have been waiting nearby. The murdered man had been drinking, that was obvious. Probably quite drunk . . . and probably in a bar not a dozen blocks away.

If they could find that bar they might get a description . . . beat officers were looking but it might not be fast enough . . . a man's life might be at stake.

Mike Frost stood quietly gnawing gently at his lower lip. He was a big man, wide in the shoulders, with a rather solemn, thick-boned face. His fingers dug at his reddish-brown hair and he tried to think.

This Tom Sixte . . . he was no fool. In a tight spot he had thought of the clock radio and the police calls. It had been a chance, but he had thought of it and taken it. He might think of something else but they could not depend on that.

The bank. They might try to get some money out of Sixte. Suddenly, Frost was hoping Sixte would think of that. If he did, if he could play on their greed . . .

The wine bottle . . . he had liquor stores alerted for possible purchase of the Madeira. It was a wild chance, but the girl had tried a glass of it, and to get money they might humor Sixte. "Boy," Frost said, half aloud, "I hope you're thinking, and I hope you're thinking like I am."

Forty-eight hours. They would have the flight covered long before takeoff time.

Mike Frost went back to his office and sat down at the battered, scarred old desk. He ran his fingers through his rusty hair and tried to think . . . to think. . . .

———

TOM SIXTE SAT on the divan in a quaint, old-fashioned room. The sort of furnishings that were good middle-class in 1910. It gave him a queer feeling to be sitting there like that, the room was so much like his Aunt Eunice's.

Kurt was leafing through the paper and he was smoking. Phyllis was irritable. She kept looking over at Sixte. "You're a fool, Kurt. Get rid of him."

"Take it easy." Kurt leaned back in his chair, lighting another cigarette with his left hand. With his coat off, his shoulders were not as wide and he was a little pigeon chested. "I've got a call out for Rubio. Let him do it."

Sixte's feet were tied, but his hands were free. There was no way he could move quickly, and nothing to use with his hands. He was trying to put himself in the position of the police and getting nowhere.

Suppose some neighbor had just turned off the radio? Suppose the police had become curious, would that make them look around? How smart were they?

All right. Suppose they had come, and suppose they had examined his room. Suppose they decided he had been kidnapped, all of which was a lot of supposing. But, if they had? What would they do?

Closing his eyes to shut out the room he was in, he tried to picture the situation. He knew something of police work, something of the routine. But there would be little to go on . . . the Madeira. It was the one thing that was different. That might help.

What else?

As long as they sat still, he had time. Yet as long as they sat still they could not make mistakes. He had to get them into the open, to start them moving. Sooner or later the nagging of Phyllis might irk Kurt into killing him.

But Kurt didn't want to kill, if he didn't have to . . . he wanted this Rubio to do it. Kurt didn't want to kill but Tom had no doubt that he would if pushed. Kurt might be the key, but what did he want?

He wanted money. Easy money, quick money.

Kurt hoped to sell the passport and tickets, for maybe a thousand dollars . . . a thousand dollars . . . who, if he could, would not buy his life for that sum? Or twice or three times as much? Or more?

Rubio had not called, so there was a chance. A faint, slim chance.

"Look," he said quietly, "I'm a reasonable guy. What you do is none of my business. Anyway, I'm supposed to go to South America. I don't know who either of you are, and I don't want to know, but I figure you're pretty smart."

All criminals, psychologists say, are both egotists and optimists. A good point. Flatter them—but not too much.

"Suppose you knock me off, and suppose you sell my papers to Rubio . . . will he pay a thousand bucks?"

Kurt smiled. "He does or he don't get them."

Sixte shrugged. "All right. You know him better than I do. But he knows you've got me on your hands. The only way you can make any dough is to sell those papers, otherwise you knock me off for nothing, am I right?"

"So what?"

"So he says, 'I'll give you five hundred, take it or leave it.' Then where are you?"

Kurt's smile was gone, he was studying Tom Sixte and he didn't like what he was thinking. Kurt was remembering Rubio, and he had a hunch that was just what Rubio would do—and where did that leave *him*?

"Now I want to live. I also want to go to South America. Rubio will give you a thousand bucks for my papers. All right," Sixte put his palms on his knees. "I'll boost the ante. You put me on that plane to Bolivia with my own tickets and I'll give you *five* thousand!"

"Don't listen to him, Kurt." Phyllis was uneasy. "I don't like it."

"Shut up." Kurt was thinking. Five thousand was good money. Five G's right in his mitt.

He shook his head. "You'd have them radio from the plane. What do you think I am, a dope?"

Sixte shrugged. "I know better than that. You're a sharp operator and that's what I'm banking on. Any dope can kill a man. Only a dope would take the chance at that price. Especially when he can get more."

He took his time. "See it from where I sit. I want to live. If some drunk gets killed, that's no skin off my nose. I like women, good food, I like wine. I can't have any of them if I'm dead."

Tom Sixte lit a cigarette. "I haven't got a lot of money, but I could cash a check for five thousand dollars. If I tried to get more they'd make inquiries and you might get suspicious and shoot me. I'm going to play it smart.

"So I draw five thousand. You take it and put me on the plane. I don't know who you are . . . what exactly am I going to tell them? You could be out of town, in Las Vegas or Portland before they started looking—but that's not all. I wouldn't squawk because I'd be called back as a witness. If I wasn't here there'd be nothing to connect you with the job—and brother, I can make money in Bolivia. I've got a big deal down there."

There were plenty of fallacies in his argument, but Tom Sixte would point out nothing they could not see. He drew deep on his cigarette and ran his fingers through his dark hair. He was unshaved and felt dirty. If he got out of this, it would be by thinking his way out, and he was tired. He wanted a shower and sleep.

"I got to think about it." Kurt got up. "I don't like it much."

Sixte leaned back on the divan. "Think it over. If I was in your place, I would think a lot." Kurt leaned back and lit a cigarette. His face was expressionless but Sixte was remembering the padded shoulders in Kurt's jacket. "Your girlfriend, for instance. She'd look mighty pretty in a new outfit, and you two would make a pair, all dressed to the nines."

Kurt ignored him, looking around and speaking past his cigarette. "Phyl, fix some sandwiches, will you?"

"As long as I'm paying for this," Sixte grinned at them, "why not some steaks? The condemned man ate a hearty meal. . . ." He met Kurt's cold eye and added, "Maybe you'll soon have five thousand dollars, so why not enjoy yourself?" Keeping his voice casual, he added, "And while you're at it, why not a bottle of wine? Some of that Madeira?"

DETECTIVE LIEUTENANT MIKE Frost sat behind the scarred desk. It was 10:00 A.M. and he had just checked with the morgue . . . nobody that could be Sixte had been brought in yet. But if he was dead they might never find him.

Joe stuck his head in the door. "Nothing on the prints. The man's were Sixte himself, a major in combat intelligence during the war. The woman was the landlady, who does her own cleaning up. And we drew a blank on the girl. Nothing on file."

There had been nothing on the bars, either. Nobody remembered any such couple. Frost was thinking . . . the other man had come at once, and it could not have taken him longer than ten minutes. It took time to get outside, get a car started and into the street . . . at most he would not be more than twenty blocks away. More likely within half that distance. Frost picked up the phone and started a check on bars and possible loafing places. Looking for a tall dark young man who answered a phone and left hurriedly.

Surprisingly, the break came quickly. Noonan called in. Frost remembered him as a boyish-looking officer who looked like a college halfback. A man answering the description took a call in a public booth at three minutes after ten. He paid for his drinks and went out.

Why so sure of the time? The bartender's girl was late. She usually came in at quarter to ten, so he was watching the clock and expecting a call.

"This guy didn't talk," Noonan said. "He nursed one drink for more than an hour, had just ordered the second. The bartender heard him say on the phone, 'Yes, this is Tommy Hart.'"

They ran a check on Hart . . . nothing. Noonan called back. "A guy in that bar, he says that guy Hart, if that was his name, used to hang out at a bar on Sixth Street. The Shadow Club."

It fit. A lot of hoods came and went around there. A lot of good people, too. Frost had Hart figured as small time—working through a woman—but even the small-time boys have big ideas, delusions of grandeur. And he might be afraid to turn Sixte loose.

At noon Frost went out for a sandwich. He drank two cups of coffee, taking a lot of time. He covered the ground again, step by step. The bank, the liquor stores, Hart, the airlines. The Shadow Club.

Shortly after one, he walked back to the desk. Sixte had been missing almost fifteen hours. By now he might be buried in the floor of a cellar or a vacant lot.

Tom Sixte . . . friendly, quiet, hard worker. Read a lot. Spoke French and German, studying Spanish. Expert in industrial planning . . . an unlikely man to be mixed up in anything. Mike Frost knew all about him now. Had reports on his desk from the government, from businessmen with whom he had talked . . . Sixte was top drawer. He was dark-haired, good-looking, smiled easily.

If the tickets were used, they would have their man. But Tom Sixte would be dead, a good man murdered.

Frost started thinking. Tickets to Bolivia were worth dough in the right place. So was a passport and visa . . . who wanted to get out of town? Who that they knew about? Who that was missing?

Tony Shapiro . . . from Brooklyn. A mobster. Big time. Wanted by the Feds. Something clicked in the brain of Mike Frost. Shapiro had been reported seen in Tucson . . . in Palm Springs.

Local connections? Vince Montesori, Rubio Turchi.

Frost picked up the phone. . . . Shapiro had connections in the Argentine. If he could get to South America, he might be safe.

Frost got up and put on his hat. He went down into the street, squinting his eyes against the sunlight. He walked west, then north. After a while he stopped for a shine.

The shine boy was a short, thickset man with a flat face

and there was nobody around. He had never heard of Tommy Hart or anybody like him. Montesori was working his club, same as always. Rubio? The shine boy bent further over the detective's shoes. Nothing . . .

It all added up to nothing.

Back at the desk, Frost checked the file on Rubio. He had kept his nose clean since coming out of Q. He . . . Mike Frost picked up the telephone and began checking on Rubio and San Quentin . . . his cell mate had been in for larceny. Twenty-six years old, tall, dark hair, name . . . Kurt Eberhardt. He hung up the phone.

Kurt Eberhardt . . . Tommy Hart. It could be. It was close enough, and the description was right.

He had something to go on now. Check the Shadow Club on Eberhardt . . . check with the stoolies, his contacts on the criminal side. It might be a blind alley, but it could fit. There was nothing substantial, anywhere. A bottle of Madeira . . . he dropped in at a liquor store. Three principal varieties of Madeira sold here. Sercial, a dry wine. Boal was on the sweet side. Malmsey was a dessert wine, and sweeter. It was Malmsey that Sixte fancied.

At four o'clock, he was sitting at the scarred desk, thinking about Sixte. If the guy was alive, he was sweating about now. Time was drawing the strings into a tight knot around his throat.

All over town the wheels were meshing, the department was working . . . and they had nothing. Nothing at all.

Rubio Turchi could not be found. He had been around until shortly after midnight the previous night, and he dropped out of sight . . . the time tied in . . . which might be an accident. Mike Frost swore softly and irritably at the loose ends, the flimsy angles on which he must work. Nothing really . . .

A report from the Shadow Club. They remembered Eberhardt. A free spender when he had it. Some figured he had been rolling drunks for his pocket money. Always with a girl . . . a brunette. Her name was Lola, a Spanish girl, or Mexican.

Find Lola.

More wheels started to mesh. No rumble from the bank. Nothing on the wine. Nothing on Turchi, nothing on anybody.

At ten o'clock, Mike Frost went home and crawled into bed. At 2:00 A.M., he awoke with a start. He sat up and lit a cigarette.

He called Headquarters. They had Lola. He swore, then got into his clothes. Sleepy, unshaven, and irritable, he walked into his office. Lola was there, with Noonan.

Frost lit a cigarette for her. "You're not in trouble," his tone was conversational, "you'll walk out of here in a few minutes and Noonan can drive you home.

"All we want to know is about a guy named Eberhardt, Kurt Eberhardt."

She turned on Frost and broke into a torrent of vindictive Spanish. Sorting it out, he learned she knew nothing about him, nor did she want to, he was a rat, a pig, a—she quieted down.

A few more questions elicited the information that she had not seen him in three months. He had left her . . . a blonde, a girl named Phyllis Edsall.

Lola talked and talked fast. Kurt Eberhardt thought he was a big shot, smart. That was because he had been in prison with Rubio Turchi. He had driven a car for Turchi a few times, but he bragged too much; Turchi dropped him. She had not seen him in three months.

Now they had another name, Phyllis Edsall. No record. A check on Edsalls in the telephone book brought nothing. They did not know her. Reports began to come in from contacts in the underworld. . . . Eberhardt probably had stuck up a few filling stations, but usually he had his girl get drunks out where he could roll them. Sometimes it was the badger game, sometimes plain muscle.

Nobody knew where he lived. Nobody knew where the girl lived.

Nothing more from the Shadow Club. Nothing from the bank. Nobody in the morgue that fit the description. Rubio Turchi still missing.

Mike Frost and Noonan went out for coffee together. They

stopped by the liquor store where Sixte had been buying his Madeira. The fat little proprietor looked up and smiled. "Say, you were asking about Madeira. I sold a bottle yesterday afternoon. I started to call, but the line was busy, and . . ."

Frost found his hands were shaking. Noonan looked white. "Who bought it? Who?" Frost's voice was hoarse.

"Oh," the little man waved his hand, "just some girl. A little blonde. I told her—"

"You told her what?"

The little man looked from Frost to Noonan. His face was flabby. "Why . . . why I just said that was good wine, even the police were interested, and—"

Mike Frost felt his fist knot and he restrained himself with an effort. "You damned fool!" he said hoarsely. "You simple-minded fool!"

"Here!" The little man was indignant. "You can't talk to me like—"

"That girl. Did she wear a suede coat?" Noonan asked.

The little man backed off. "Yes, yes, I think so. You can't—"

It had been there. They had had it right in their grasp and then it was gone. The little man had not called. She looked, he said, like a nice girl. She was no criminal. He could tell. She was—"Oh, shut up!" Frost was coldly furious.

One fat, gabby little man had finished it. Now they knew. They knew the police were looking for Sixte, that they were watching the sales of Madeira, they knew. . . .

"S'pose he's still alive?" Noonan was worried.

Frost shrugged. "Not now. They know they are hot. They probably won't go near a bank. That blew it up. Right in our faces."

"Yeah," Noonan agreed, "if he's alive, he's lucky."

———

TOM SIXTE LAY on the floor of the cellar of the old-fashioned house with his face bloody and his hands tied as well as his feet. Right at that moment he would not have agreed that it was better to be alive. When Phyllis came in with the wine, she was white and scared. She had babbled the story and Kurt had turned vicious.

"Smart guy, huh?" he had said, and then he hit Sixte. Sixte tried to rise, and Kurt, coldly brutal, had proceeded to knock him down and kick him in the kidneys, the belly, the head. Finally, he had bound his hands and rolled him down the cellar steps to where he lay. The door had been closed and locked.

Sixte lay very still, breathing painfully. His face was stiff with drying blood, his head throbbed with a dull, heavy ache, his body was sore, and his hands were bound with cruel tightness.

They dared not take him to the bank looking like this. They dared not put him on a plane now. Phyllis was sure she had not been followed. She had taken over an hour to come back, making sure. But there was no way out now. They would kill him. Unless he could somehow get free.

Desperation lent him strength. He began to struggle, to chafe the clothesline that bound him against the edge of the wooden step. It was a new board, and sharp-edged.

Upstairs, he heard a door slam and heavy feet went down the front steps. The floor creaked up above. Phyllis was still there . . . no use to ask her help, she was the one who killed the man on Redondo.

He began to sweat. Sweat and dust got into the cuts on his face. They smarted. His head throbbed. He worked, bitterly, desperately, his muscles aching.

———

Kurt EBERHARDT WAS frightened. He got out of the house because he was scared. Despite what Phyl said, they might have followed her. He walked swiftly north, stopped there on a corner, and watched the house. Nobody around, no cars parked. After ten minutes, he decided she had not been followed and walked on, slower.

He had to see Rubio. Rubio would know what to do. He went to his car, got in, and drove downtown. He tried to call Rubio . . . no answer. He called two or three places, no luck. At the last one, he asked, "When is he leavin'?"

"You nuts?" The man's voice was scoffing. "He ain't goin' noplace. He can't. He's tied up here, wit' big dough."

Then, maybe Rubio would not use the tickets, either. He wouldn't want the visa and passport.

His stomach empty and sick, Kurt Eberhardt started up the street. On the corner, he stopped and looked back, seeing the sign. The Shadow Club . . . it was early yet. It might not be open. He stood there, trying to think, looking for an out.

He had never killed a man. He had bragged about it, but he never had. When Phyllis told him she had, he was scared, but he dared not show it. The fear had made him beat Sixte.

That had been foolish. With that beat-up face . . . still, the guy was scared now, bound to be. They could say he had been in an accident. Sixte wouldn't talk out of turn. He could draw out the money . . . not a bad deal. He could even take it and the tickets and scram. No, they would stop him . . . unless he killed Sixte.

It was better to play it straight with the guy.

Phyl . . . she made the trouble. She got him into this. Too rattle-brained. Lola now, she never made a wrong move. Killing that guy, Lola wouldn't have done it. Lola . . . no use thinking about that. It was over.

He would get Rubio. He would wait at his place until he came.

———

MIKE FROST SAT at his desk. It was 4:00 P.M. The plane for Bolivia left at 9:45. The banks were closed now, but there were a few places around town where a check might be cashed . . . they were covered.

No more chance on the liquor stores. The men checking up on those were pulled off. They were still worrying over the bone of Kurt Eberhardt and that of Phyllis Edsall. No luck on either of them. Nobody seemed to know either of them beyond what they had learned.

At 4:17 P.M., a call came in. Rubio Turchi's green sedan had been spotted coming out of the hills at Arroyo and the Coast Road. It would be picked up by an unmarked police car.

At 4:23 P.M. another call. A dark sedan with a dark-haired young man had been parked in front of Rubio's apartment for more than an hour. The fellow seemed to have fallen asleep in the car, apparently waiting. It was the first time the man covering Rubio's apartment had been able to get to a phone. He gave them the car's number.

The license had been issued to one Phyllis Hart, but she had moved from the old address, left no forwarding address.

Mike Frost rubbed the stubble on his face and swore softly. He walked to the door of an adjoining office and stuck his head in. "Joe? You got that electric razor here? I feel like hell."

He carried the razor back, loosened his tie, and took off his coat. He plugged in the razor and started to shave. Rubio would meet Eberhardt, if that was him in the car, and seven to ten it was. Then they would what . . . go back to the place where Sixte was held . . . had been held? Or would it simply be a delivery of the tickets? If they split, they would be followed separately, if they went together, so much the better. He stopped shaving and called for another undercover car to be sent out to Rubio's place.

Mike Frost rubbed his smooth cheek and started on his upper lip.

———

TOM SIXTE FELT the first strand of the clothesline part, but nothing else came loose. He tugged, it was tight and strong. He waited, resting. It was getting late.

For some time now, there had been restless movements upstairs. Suddenly, the footsteps turned and started toward the cellar steps. Instantly, Sixte rolled over and over, then sat up, his face toward the steps.

Phyllis came down until she could see him, then stopped and stared. Her face was strained and white, her eyes seemed very bright.

She stared at him, and said nothing, so he took a chance. "Did he run out on you?"

Her lip curled and she came down onto the floor. For a

minute, he thought she would hit him. Then she said, "He won't run out on me. He wouldn't dare."

Sixte shook his head a little. "Man, have I got a headache! My head got hit on the steps." She made no reply, chewing on her lip. "Look," he said, "can't we make a deal? You an' me?"

Her eyes were cold, but beyond it, he could see she was scared. "What kind of deal?"

"Get me on that plane and I'll give *you* the five thousand."

It got to her, all right. He could see it hit home. "You're in this deeper than he is. Why should he collect? Seems to me he's been gone a long time."

"The banks are closed now."

"You'd know somebody. My identification is good. We could tell them I got in a scrap with your boyfriend, and want to get out of town, that I have my tickets, but need cash."

She was thinking it over. No question about that. She had it in mind. "I know a guy who might have it."

"Then it's a deal?"

"I'll give him ten minutes more," she said. "It's almost five."

She went back up the stairs, and Sixte returned to his sawing at the ropes that bound him.

———

AT 5:10 P.M., his cheeks smooth, his hair freshly combed, Mike Frost got a call. Rubio and Eberhardt had made contact. They had gone into the house and there was a man with them. He was a short, powerfully built man in a gray suit.

An unmarked police car slid into place alongside the curb under some low-hung branches. Nobody got out. A man sauntered up the street and struck a match, lighting a cigarette. It was a cloudy afternoon and there was a faint smell of rain in the air.

Mike Frost was sweating. He was guessing and guessing wild. The man in the gray suit could be Tony Shapiro. He hesitated, then picked up the telephone and dialed the FBI.

When he hung up, his phone rang. Rubio, Eberhardt, and

the other man had come out. They all got into Rubio's car and started away. They were being checked and followed.

————

At 5:22 P.M., the cellar door suddenly opened and Phyllis came down the steps sideways. She went over to Sixte and she had a gun in her hand. "You try anything, and I'll kill you," she said, and he believed her.

He had his hands loose and he brought them around in front of him. "See?" he said. "I'm playing fair. I could have let you come closer and jumped you." He began to untie the ropes on his ankles.

When he got up, he staggered. Barely able to walk, he got up the stairs. Then he brushed himself off, splashed water on his face, and combed his hair. As they reached the door, a taxi rolled up.

"Don't try anything."

The cabdriver looked around, his eyes hesitating on Sixte's bruised face.

"The Shadow Club," Phyllis said, and sat back in the seat. Her features were drawn and fine, her eyes wide open. She sat on Sixte's right and had her right hand in her pocket. "We'll get out by the alley."

They went up a set of stairs and stopped before a blank door. Phyllis knocked and after a minute a man answered. At her name, he opened the door, then wider. They walked in. When the man saw Sixte's face, his eyes changed a little. They seemed to mask, to film. The man turned, went through another door, and walked to his desk.

He was a stocky man in a striped shirt. His neck was thick. "Whatya want, Phyl?" He dropped into his chair.

"Look," she said quickly, "this guy is a friend. He's got dough in the bank and he's got to get out of town. He wants to cash a check for five G's."

"That's a lot of cash." The man looked from one to the other. "What's it worth?"

"A hundred dollars."

The man chuckled. "You tell that to Vince Montesori? It's worth more."

Sixte produced his identification, and indicated the balance in his checking account. "The check's good," he said quietly, "and I'll boost the ante to five hundred extra if you cash it right away."

Montesori got to his feet. "I gotta check. There's a guy works for the bank. If he says you're okay, I'll cash it, okay?" He indicated a door. "You wait in there."

It was a small private sitting room, comfortably fixed up. There was a bar with glasses and several bottles of wine, one of bourbon. Tom Sixte stepped to the bar. "I could use a drink. How about you?"

Phyllis was watching him carefully. "All right."

He picked up the bourbon and then through the thin wall over the bar, he heard a faint voice, audible only by straining his ears.

"Yeah," it was Montesori, "they just came in. Tell Rubio. I'll stall 'em."

Sixte finished pouring the drinks, added ice and soda. He walked back and held the drink out to Phyllis. She stood back, very carefully. "Put it down on the table," she said, "I'll pick it up."

This was not going to work. Whatever happened, he had to get out of here . . . fast.

———

At 5:47, a call came in from a radio car. They had tailed Rubio and the other two men to a frame house, old place off Mission Road. They had all gone in, then had come rushing out and piled into the car.

After they had gone, followed by other cars, a check of the house revealed some cut clothesline in the cellar, an unopened bottle of Madeira, and clothes for a girl and a man. There was some blood on the cellar floor, and a few spots on the living room carpet.

Mike Frost got up and put on his coat. It looked like a double-cross. The babe had taken Sixte and lit out, for where?

The source of information at the Shadow Club would not

talk . . . closed up like a clam. In itself, that meant something.

Frost motioned to Noonan and they walked out to the car. "The Shadow Club," he told Noonan. He sat back in the seat, closing his eyes. After a while all this waiting could get to a guy. It was time to squeeze someone and squeeze them hard. Patience got you only so far.

THE GIRL WAS too cautious, Sixte could see that. He was on edge now. It had been a long time since he had played rough. Not since the Army days. But the events of the past hours had sharpened him up. He was bruised and stiff, but he was mad; he was both mad and desperate.

"It's a double-cross," he said, looking at Phyllis. "That guy out there, that Vince Montesori. He called Rubio."

Her eyes were level and cold. He could see how this girl could kill, and quickly. He explained what he had heard. "It's your neck, too," he said, "you were making a deal on your own, but our deal stands if we get out of here."

"We'll get out. Open the door."

It was locked. No answer came from the other side. Phyllis was frightened now. Sixte turned swiftly and picked up a stool that stood beside the little bar. He had heard voices through the wall, low voices, so—he swung the stool.

The crash of smashing wood filled the room and Sixte looked quickly through the hole in the cheap dividing wall. The room beyond was empty. He smashed again with the stool, then went through the hole, and opened the door. Phyllis came out, looking at him quickly—he had not tried to trap her.

The door to the alley was locked tight. The door to the club was locked.

The alley door was metal and tightly fitted, solid as the wall itself. The door to the club was not so tight, and breaking it down might attract help from the club itself. From the patrons . . . he heard footsteps coming along the hall.

"Behind the door," he told her, "get them under the gun when they come in."

Her eyes were small and tight. There was an inner streak of viciousness in this girl. He was accepted as her ally at least momentarily. She looked at him and said, "Don't worry about Kurt. He's yellow."

A key sounded in the lock and Sixte dropped his right hand to the back of a chair. It was a heavy oak chair and he tilted it, ever so slightly.

Montesori stepped inside, behind him were Kurt and two other men. Startled, Montesori looked at him, then beyond him at the smashed panels of the wall. His face went white around the mouth.

"You busted my wall!"

Kurt stepped in, looking at Sixte like he had never seen him before. Rubio followed. "Where's she? Where's the girl?"

"Get over by the wall, Vince. You, too, Kurt. All of you." Phyllis stepped out with the gun.

Only the man in the gray suit remained in the door. Sixte gambled. He had the chair balanced and he shoved down hard on the corner of the back. The chair legs slid, shooting out from under his hand on the slick floor. The man tried to jump, but the heavy chair smashed him across the knees and he fell over it, into the room.

Tom Sixte went over him in a long dive and hit the floor sliding. Somebody yelled behind him and there was a shot, then another. Fists started pounding on the alley door, and Sixte scrambled to his feet only to be tackled from behind. Turning, with a chance to fight back for the first time, Sixte hooked a short, wicked left that caught Rubio as he scrambled to get up.

The blow smashed his nose and showered him with blood. He staggered, his eyes wide, his mouth flapping like a frightened chicken, and then Sixte was on him. Rubio tried to fight back, but Sixte was swinging with both hands. Rubio scuttled backwards into the chair and the gray-suited man who sat very still on the floor, clutching his shin, his face utterly calm.

Vince Montesori jumped through the door, scrambling over the chair, and tried to break past Sixte, but Tom Sixte was in the middle of the hall and he caught the running man coming in with a right that jolted him clear to the spine when it landed. Vince went back and down, and Sixte turned to run but suddenly the room was filled with officers in uniform.

Tom Sixte crouched over, his breath coming in gasps. Looking through the open hall door he could see Kurt lying on the floor inside. His throat had been torn by a bullet and there was a bigger hole behind his ear where it had come out.

Phyllis was handing her gun to an officer, and a big man in plainclothes walked up to Sixte. The man had rusty hair and a freckled face. He looked very tired. "You Sixte?"

"Yeah?"

Frost smiled wryly. "I'm Mike Frost. Glad to see you. . . . Heck, I'm glad to see you alive."

TIME OF TERROR

WHEN I LOOKED up from the menu, I was staring into the eyes of a man who had been dead for three years.

Only he was not dead now. He was alive, sitting on the other side of the horseshoe coffee counter, just half a room away, and he was staring at me.

Three years ago I had identified a charred body found in a wrecked car as this man. The car had been his. The remains of the suit he wore were a suit I recognized. The charred driver's license in his wallet was that of Richard Marmer. The size, the weight, the facial contours, the structure of the burned body, all were those of the man I knew. I was called upon to identify the body because I had been his insurance agent, and I had also known him socially.

On the basis of my identification, the company had paid the supposed widow one million two hundred twenty thousand dollars. Yet the man across the room was Richard Marmer, and he was not dead.

Who else could know of my mistake? His wife? Was *she* still alive? Was I the only person alive who could testify that the man across the room was a murderer? For he must be responsible for the man whose body was found. The logic of that was inevitable.

He was getting up from his place, picking up his check. He was coming around the counter. He sat down beside me. My flesh crawled.

"Hello, Dryden. Recognized me, didn't you?"

My mouth was dry and I could not find words. What could one say at such a time? I must be careful . . . careful.

He went on. "It's been a long time, but I had to come back. Now that you've seen me I guess I'll have to tell you."

"Tell me what?"

"That you're in it, too. Right up to your neck."

"I don't know what you're talking about."

"Have some more coffee, we have a lot to talk about. I took care of all this years ago . . . just in case." He ordered coffee for both of us and when the waitress had gone, he said quietly, "After the insurance was paid to my wife, one hundred thousand dollars was deposited to an account under your name at a bank in Reno."

"That's ridiculous."

"It's true. You took your vacation at June Lake that year, and you fished a little at Tahoe." Marmer was pleased with his shrewdness . . . and he had been shrewd. "I knew you went there to fish, and I knew when your vacation was so I timed it all very carefully. The bank officials in Reno will be prepared to swear you deposited that money. I forged your signature very carefully. After all"—he smiled—"I practiced it for almost a year."

They would believe I had been bribed, that I had been in on it.

He could have done it, there was no doubt of that. He had imitated me over the phone more than once; he had fooled friends of mine. It had seemed merely a peculiar quirk of humor until now!

"It wouldn't stand up," I objected, but without hope, "not to a careful investigation."

"Possibly. Only it must first be questioned, and so far there is no reason to believe that it will ever be doubted."

There *was* a reason; I was determined to get in touch with the police, as soon as I could get out of here, and take my chances.

"You see," he continued, "you would be implicated at once. And of course, you would be implicated in the murder, too."

The skin on my neck was cold. My fingers felt stiff. When I tried to swallow my throat was dry.

"If murder is ever suspected, they will suspect you, too. I even"—he smiled—"left a letter in which I said that you were involved . . . and that letter will get to the district attorney. I have been very thorough, Dryden! Very thorough!"

"Where's your wife?" I asked him.

He chuckled and it had a greasy, throaty, awful sound. "She made trouble." He turned a bit and something metallic bumped against the counter. I looked down. The butt of a flat automatic protruded from the edge of his coat. When I looked back up, he smiled.

"It's all true, Dryden. Come out to the car, I'll prove it to you."

My thoughts fluttered wildly at the bars of the cage he was building around me. And yet, I doubted that it was really a cage at all. He had killed an innocent man, now it seemed he had killed his wife, what was there to keep him from killing me, too? He had nothing to lose, nothing at all. What he had told me of the involved plot to implicate me was probably a lie. Somehow I couldn't imagine a man who would kill someone in order to cash in on his life insurance, and then kill his wife, giving up one hundred thousand dollars on the off chance that it would keep me quiet. Marmer just wanted to get me out to the car. He wanted to get me out to the car so he could kill me.

What was left for me? What was the way out? There had been an officer in the army who told us there was always a way out, that there was always an answer . . . one had only to think.

Fear.

That was my salvation, my weapon, the one thing with which I could fight! Suddenly, I knew. My only weapon lay before me, the weapon of my mind. I must think slowly, carefully, clearly. And I must be an actor.

Here beside me was a man who had killed, a man with a gun who certainly wanted to kill me. My only weapon was my own mind and the fear that lay ingrained deep in the convolutions of his brain. Though he was behaving calmly he must be a frightened, worried man. I would frighten him more. What was the old saying about the guilty fleeing when no man pursued? I must talk to him . . . I must lie, cheat, anything to keep myself alive.

His fear was my weapon, so I must spin around this man a web of illusion and fear, a web so strong that he would have no escape . . .

"All of you fellows are the same"—I picked up my coffee, smiling a little—"you plan so carefully and then overlook the obvious. I always liked you, Marmer," that was a lie, for I never had, "and I'm glad to see you now."

"Glad?" He stared at me.

"What I mean," I made my voice dry and a little tired, "should be obvious. I'll admit I was startled when I saw you here, but I was not worried because this could be an opportunity for both of us. You can save your life and I can regain my reputation with the company."

"What the hell are you talking about?" He stared at me. He was skeptical, but he was not sure. That was my weapon . . . he could not be sure.

For what mind is free of doubt? In what mind lies no fear? How great then must be the fear of a man who has murdered twice over? The world is his enemy, all eyes are watching him. All ears are listening, all whispers are about him.

When could he be sure that somebody else, some clerk, some filling station attendant, somebody who had known him . . . when could he be sure he was not seen?

A criminal always believes things will turn out right for him and he believes he is smarter, shrewder . . . or at least he believes that on the surface . . . beneath lies a morass of doubt, a deep sink of insecurity and fear.

"Marmer," I spoke carefully and in a not unfriendly tone, "you've been living in a fool's paradise. Not one instant since you committed your crime have you been free. Your wife got your insurance money so you believed your crime had been successful."

Behind the counter was a box of tea bags, it was partly behind a plastic tray of spoons but I could see CONSTANT COM . . . written on the box.

"You forgot," I continued, "about Constant."

"What?"

"Bob Constant was an FBI man, one of their crack operators. He quit the government and accepted a better paying job as head of the investigation setup in our insurance company.

"He'd been in the business a long time and such men develop a feeling for *wrongness,* for something out of place. So he had a hunch about your supposed death."

Oh, I had his attention now! He was staring at me, his eyes dilated. And then as I talked I actually remembered something that had bothered me. I seemed to see again a bunch of keys lying on a policeman's desk . . . his keys. Something about those keys had worried me, but at the time I could find nothing wrong. How blind I had been! Now, at last, I could see them again and I knew what had been wrong!

"He checked all your things, and when he came to your keys, he checked each one. Your house key was not among them."

He drew a quick, shocked breath. Then he said, "So what?" But he did not look at me, and his fingers fidgeted at his napkin.

"Why should a man's house key not be in his pocket? He was puzzled about that. It was not logical, he said. I objected that your wife could let you in, but he would not accept that. You should still have a key.

"Suppose, he asked me, that the dead man is not the insured man? Suppose the dead man was murdered and substituted, and then at the last minute the murderer remembered the key . . . perhaps his wife was away from home . . . then he would take that key from the ring, never suspecting it would be noticed.

"So he began to investigate, the money had been paid, but that was not the end. Your wife had left town, several months, at least. But probably you didn't trust her with all that money. She had said she was going to live with her sister . . . only she didn't. He knew that within a few hours. Then where had she gone?

"You see, Marmer? Bob Constant (I was beginning to admire my invention) was suspicious, so he started the wheels moving. All over the United States a description went out, a description of you and of your wife. New people in a community were quietly looked over, your relatives were checked. Your sister-in-law had been getting letters from your wife, and then they stopped. Your sister-in-law was worried.

"More wheels started turning," I said quietly, "they are looking for you now in a thousand cities. For over a year, we have known you were alive. For over two years evidence has been accumulating. They don't tell me much about it. I'm only a small cog in a big wheel."

"You're lying!" His voice was louder, there was an underlying strain there.

"We dug up the body," I continued quietly, ". . . doctors keep records of fractures, you know, and we wanted to check this body for a broken bone that had healed.

"Did you ever watch a big police system work? It doesn't look like much, and no particular individual seems to do very much, yet when all their efforts mesh on one case the results are prodigious. And you . . . you are on the wrong end of it.

"No information is safe. Baggage men, hotel people, telephone operators, all are anxious to help the police if only to be known as cooperative in case they want to fix a parking ticket."

I was talking for my life, talking because I knew this man was willing to kill me, and that he could do it now and there would be small chance that I could protect myself in any way. Suppose I grabbed him suddenly, and throttled him? Suppose I killed him? I couldn't do that. I couldn't do it because I didn't know if I could and because of the fear that he hadn't been lying, that he had, in fact, set me up.

Never had life been so beautiful as then! All the books I wanted to read, the food I wanted to taste, the hours I wanted to spend at many things, all of them seemed vastly greater and more beautiful than ever before.

Fear . . . it was my only weapon . . . if I was lucky he might let me go or, more realistically, if I got away he might choose to go into hiding rather than pursue me. I also realized I might have another weapon . . . hope.

"They can't miss, Marmer, you're not safe and you never have been. Did you ever see a man die in a gas chamber? I have. You hear that it is very quick and very easy. You can believe that if you like. And what is quick? The word is relative.

"Did you ever think how that could be, Marmer? To live, even for an instant, without hope? But in those months on death row, waiting, there is no hope."

"Shut up."

He said it flatly, yet there was a ring of underlying terror in it, too. Who was to say what responsive chords I might have touched? "Have it your own way," I said, then I moved to close the deal. "You can beat the rap if you're smart."

"What?" He stared at me, his interest captured in spite of himself. "What do you mean?"

"Look." I was dry, patient. "Do you think that I want to see you dead? Come on, man, we've been friends! The insurance company could be your ally in this. Suppose you went to them now . . . Suppose you went up there and confessed, and then offered to return what money you have left? You needn't even return it all." I was only thinking of winning my safety now. I was in there, trying. "But some is better than none. They would help you make a deal . . . extenuating circumstances. Who knows what a good lawyer could do? We've only been collecting evidence on you, that you weren't dead. We've nothing on the dead man in the car; we've nothing on your wife. They would be glad to get some of their money back and would cut a deal to help you out. You could beat the death penalty."

He sat very still and said nothing. He was crumpling the paper napkin in his fingers. I dared not speak. The wrong move or the wrong word . . . at least, he was worried, he was thinking.

"No!" He spoke so sharply that people looked up. He noticed it and lowered his voice. "Come on! We're getting out of here! Make one wrong move or say one word and I'll let you have it!"

He said no more about showing me the deposit from Reno.

Had I thrown away my chance at life by pushing him too hard? Had I forced him to kill me? We got up.

Maybe I could have done something. Perhaps I could have reached for him, but there were a dozen innocent people in that café within gun range. I wanted no one else injured or killed even though I wanted to save myself.

We paid our checks and stepped out into the cool night air . . . a little mist was drifting in over the building. It would be damp and foggy along the coast roads.

We walked to his car, and he was a bare step behind me. "Get behind the wheel," he said, "and drive carefully. Don't get us stopped. If you do, I'll kill you."

When we were moving, I spoke to him quietly. "What are you going to do, Rich? I always liked you. Even when you pulled this job, I still couldn't feel you were all wrong. Somewhere along the line you didn't get a decent break, something went wrong somewhere.

"That's why I've tried to help you tonight, because I was thinking of you."

"And not because you were afraid to die?" he sneered.

"Give me a chance to help you . . . I'd rather die than go through what you have ahead, always ducking, dodging, worrying, knowing they were always there, closing in around you, stifling you.

"And now, of course, there will be this. Those people in the café saw us leave together. They'll have a good description of you."

"They never saw me before!"

"I know . . . but they have seen me many times. I've always eaten in there by myself, so naturally the first time I sat with somebody else they would be curious and would notice you."

Traffic was growing less. He was guiding me by motions, and he was taking me out toward Palos Verdes and the cliffs along the sea. The fog rolled in, blanketing the road in spots. It was gray and thick.

"The gas isn't like this fog, Marmer," I said, "you don't see it."

"Shut up!" He slugged me backhanded with the gun. It wasn't hard, he didn't want to upset my driving.

"It isn't too late . . . yet. You can always go with me to the company."

"You stupid fool, I'm not going to turn myself in."

"You should, because it's only a matter of days now, or hours."

The gun barrel jarred against my ribs and peeled hide. "Shut up!" His voice lifted. "Shut up or I'll kill you now!"

Bitterly, I stared at the thickening fog. All my talking had been useless. I was through. I might fight now, but with that gun in my ribs I'd small chance.

Suddenly I saw a filling station. Two cars were parked there and people were laughing and talking. I was not going to die! I was . . . I casually put the car in neutral, aimed for an empty phone booth beside the road, and jerking up on the door handle, lunged from the car. The gun went off, its bullet burning my ribs, the muzzle blast tearing at my clothes. I went over and over on the pavement, the surface of the road tearing my shoulder, my knees, my hands. There was a crash of metal, the sound of breaking glass, and then silence. I rolled over, turning toward the wreck. The people at the gas station stared, frozen.

Then the car door popped open and after a moment a figure moved, trying to get out of the car, trying to escape. The hand clutching the gun banged on the roof as Marmer tried to lever himself up. The dark form took one step and cried out, his left leg collapsed under him, and he fell to the ground. He rolled on his side, the gun moved in the darkness. There was a shot.

My hands were shaking and my lips trembled. I picked myself up off the road and staggered toward the car.

Richard Marmer's head was back and there was blood on the gravel. He must have put the gun in his mouth and pulled the trigger a moment after he discovered that his leg was broken . . . a moment after he had finally realized he was trapped.

SLOWLY, MY LEGS shaking, I turned and started down the road toward the filling station.

I was alive . . . alive . . .

The fog drifted like a cool, caressing hand across my cheek. Somebody dropped a tire iron and people were moving toward me.

THE GRAVEL PIT

MURDER HAD BEEN no part of his plan, yet a more speculative man would have realized that a crime is like a lie, and one inevitably begets another, for the commission of a first crime is like a girl's acceptance of a first lover—the second always comes easier.

To steal the payroll had seemed absurdly simple, and Cruzon willingly accepted the risk involved. Had he even dreamed that his crime would lead to violence, he would never have taken the first step, for he'd never struck a man in anger in his life, and only one woman.

But once he accepted the idea of murder, it was natural that he should think of the gravel pit. In no other place was a body so likely to lie undiscovered. The pit had been abandoned long ago, used as a playground by neighborhood children until the families moved from the vicinity and left it to the oil wells. Brush had now grown up around the pit, screening it, hiding it.

Now that the moment of murder approached, Cruzon waited by the window of his unlighted room, staring into the rain-wet street, his mouth dry, and a queer, formless sort of dread running through him.

He had been pleased with the detached way in which he planned the theft. The moment of greatest danger would be that instant in which he substituted the envelope he was carrying for the one containing the payroll. Once the substitution was made, the rest was simple, and the very casualness of it made the chance of detection slight. Hence, he had directed every thought to that one action. The thought that he might be seen and not exposed never occurred to him.

Yet that was exactly what had happened, and because of it, he was about to commit a murder.

Eddie Cruzon had been eating lunch at Barnaby's for over a year. On the day he overheard the conversation, nothing was further from his thoughts than crime.

"We've used the method for years," a man beside him was saying. "The payroll will be in a manila envelope on George's desk. George will have the receipt for you to sign and the guard will be waiting."

"What about the route?"

"Your driver knows that. He was picked out and given the route not more than ten minutes ago. All you have to do is sit in the backseat and hold the fifteen thousand dollars in your lap."

Fifteen thousand was a lot of money. Cruzon considered the precautions, and the flaw was immediately apparent: the time when the payroll lay on George's desk in the busy office. For Eddie knew the office, having recognized the men talking. He worked for a parcel delivery service and had frequently visited the office on business. With that amount of money, a man could do . . . plenty. Yet, the idea of stealing it did not come until later.

Once his decision was made, the actual crime was as simple as he'd believed it would be. He merely walked into the office carrying a duplicate envelope, and seizing a moment when George was not at his desk, he put down his envelope and picked up the other. Walking out, his heart pounding, he mingled with people at the elevator, and then, in the foyer of the building, stamped and addressed the envelope to himself and dropped it in a large mailbox near the door.

It was Saturday morning and there was no delivery until Monday, so he went back to his work, pretending to be unconcerned as always. Yet when he finished his day and was once more in his room, he could scarcely restrain his exuberance.

Fifteen thousand, and all *his*! Standing before the mirror, he brushed his sleek blond hair and stared triumphantly at the vistas of wealth that opened before him. He would go about his work quietly for another month, and then make an excuse, and quit. After that, Rio, Havana, Buenos Aires! He was seeing himself immaculately clad on the terrace of a hotel in Rio when the phone rang.

"Cruzon?" The voice was low, unfamiliar. "That was pretty slick! Nobody saw it but me, and I'm not talking ... as long as I can do business with you."

Shock held him speechless. His lips were numb and his stomach had gone hollow. He managed the words, "I don't know what you're talking about. Who is this?"

"You'll know soon enough. The only reason you're not in jail is because I've kept my mouth shut."

Eddie Cruzon had stared past the curtain at the drizzle of falling rain, his mind blank, his whole consciousness clambering at the walls of fear. "No reason why we should have trouble," the voice continued. "In ten minutes, I'll be sitting in the back booth of the coffee shop on your corner. All I want is my cut."

Cruzon's lips fumbled for words.

Into the silence the voice said, "They will pay five hundred for information. Think that over."

The man hung up suddenly, and Cruzon stared at the phone as if hypnotized. Then, slowly, he replaced the handset on its cradle.

For a long time he remained perfectly still, his mind a blank. One fact stood isolated in his mind. He must share the fifteen thousand dollars.

Yet almost at once his mind refused that solution. He had planned it, he had taken the risk, he would share it with no one.

The answer to that was stark and clear. The unknown, whoever he was, would inform on him if he didn't pay up.

He could share his loot, go to prison, or ...

That was when he first thought of murder.

What right had the stranger to force his way into the affair? Theft was a rough game. If anything happened to him, it was just his bad luck.

Then he thought of the gravel pit. Only a few weeks ago he had visited the place, driving out the old road, now badly washed out and obviously unused. Curiosity impelled him to stop his car and walk up the grass-grown path along the fence.

The pit lay in the rough triangle formed by a wide field of pumping wells, the unused road, and the fence surrounding a golf course, but far from any of the fairways. It was screened by low trees and a tangle of thick brush. There was no evidence that anyone had been near it in a long time.

His car could be pulled into the brush, and it should take him no more than ten minutes to walk up to the pit and come back alone. There was small chance of being seen. It might be months before the body was found.

Even when the plan was detailed in his mind, something within him refused to accept it. He, Eddie Cruzon, was going to kill a man!

Later, looking across at the wide face of the man in the restaurant, he pretended to accept his entry into the affair with ease. "Why not?" he said. "I don't mind a split." He leaned over the table, anxious to convince the man of his sincerity. "Maybe we can work out something else. This job was a cinch."

"It was slick, all right!" The little man with the round face was frankly admiring. "Slick as anything I ever saw! It took me a minute or two to realize what had happened, and I saw it!"

Eddie had leaned forward. "The money's cached. We'll have to hire a car. . . ." He had decided not to use his own.

"I've got a car. Want to go now?" The little man was eager, his eyes bright and avid.

"Not now. I've got a date, and this girl might start asking questions. Neither of us should do anything out of the normal. We just act like we always have."

"That's right. I can see that," the fellow agreed, blinking. He was stupid, Cruzon thought, absolutely stupid! "When do we go after it?"

"Tomorrow night. You drive by and pick me up. We'll go out where I hid the money, split it two ways, have a good dinner to celebrate, and go our ways. Meanwhile, you be thinking. You're in a position to know about payrolls and can tip me to something else, later. With this parcel service job, I can go anywhere and never be noticed."

Nothing but talk, of course. Cruzon hated the milky blue eyes and the pasty face. He wanted only to be rid of him.

When he saw the car roll up before his apartment house, he felt in his waistband for the short iron bar he had picked off a junk pile. Then, pulling his hat brim lower, he walked out the door.

Weber opened the door for him, and Cruzon got in, striving for a nonchalance he did not feel. He gave directions and then sank back in the seat. His mouth was dry and he kept touching his lips with his tongue.

Out of the corners of his eyes, he studied the man beside him. Weber was shorter than he, and stocky. Once at the pit, he must kill and kill quickly, for the man would be suspicious.

They had seen no other car for miles when he motioned Weber to pull off the road. Weber stared about suspiciously, uneasily. It was dark here, and gloomy, a place of slanting rain, wet pavement, and dripping brush. "You hid it clear out here? What for?"

"You think I want it on me? What if they came to search my place? And where could I hide it where I'd not be seen?" He opened the door and got out into the rain. "Right up this path," he invited, "it isn't far."

Weber was out of the car, but he looked up the path and shook his head. "Not me. I'll stay with the car."

Cruzon hesitated. He had not considered this, being sure the man would want to be with him. Weber stared at him, then up the path. Cruzon could almost see suspicion forming in the man's mind.

"Will you wait, then?" he asked irritably. "I don't want to be left out here."

"Don't worry!" Weber's voice was grim. "And don't try any tricks. I've got a gun."

"Who wants to try anything?" Cruzon demanded impatiently. Actually, he was in a panic. What could he do now?

Weber himself made it easy. "Go ahead," he said shortly,

"and hurry. I'll wait in the car." He turned to get back into the car, and Cruzon hit him.

He struck hard with his fist, staggering Weber. The stocky man was fumbling for the gun with one hand when Cruzon jerked out the iron bar. He struck viciously. Once . . . twice . . . a third time.

And then there was only the softly falling rain, the dark body at his feet, and the night.

He was panting hoarsely. He must work fast now . . . fast. Careful to avoid any blood, he lifted the man in a fireman's carry and started up the path.

Once, when almost halfway, he slipped on the wet grass and grabbed wildly at a bush, hanging on grimly until he got his feet under him. When at last he reached the brink of the pit, he heaved Weber's body over and stood there, gasping for breath, listening to the slide of gravel.

Done!

It was all his now! Rain glistened on the stones, and the pit gaped beneath him, wide and dark. He turned from it, almost running. Luckily, there was nobody in sight. He climbed in and released the brake, starting the car by coasting. An hour later he deserted the car on a dark and lonely street, then straightened his clothes and hurried to the corner.

Walking four fast blocks, he boarded a bus and sank into a seat near the rear door. When he'd gone a dozen blocks, he got off and walked another block before catching a cab.

He was getting into the cab when the driver noticed his hand. "What's the matter? Cut yourself?"

In a panic, he looked down and saw that his hand was bloody. Weber's blood? It couldn't be. He'd worn gloves. He must have scratched his hand afterward, on the bushes.

"It's nothing," he said carelessly, "just a scratch."

The driver looked at him oddly. "Where to, mister?"

"Down Wilshire, then left."

Cruzon got out his handkerchief and wiped his hand. His trousers were wet and he felt dirty. It was a while before he got home. He stripped off his clothes and almost fell into bed.

Cruzon awakened with a start. It was broad daylight and

time to dress for work. His mind was startlingly clear, yet he was appalled at what he'd done. He had mur— He flinched at the word. He had killed a man.

He must be careful now. Any move might betray him. Reviewing his actions of the previous night, he tried to think of where he might have erred.

He had thrown the iron bar away. He had worn gloves in the car, and it had been left on a street in a bad neighborhood. He had taken precautions returning home. Above all, nobody knew he was acquainted with Weber.

There was nothing to worry about. He wanted to drive by the pit and see if any marks had been left, but knew it might be fatal. He must never go near the place again.

There was nothing to connect him with the payroll. When Weber turned up missing, there was a chance they would believe he had made the switch himself, then skipped out.

After dressing for work, he took time to carefully brush the suit he'd worn the previous night. He hurried out, drove to work, stopping only once, to buy a paper. There was nothing about the missing payroll. That puzzled and worried him, until he remembered it was Monday. That must have been in the Sunday paper, which he'd missed.

At his usual hour, he dropped around to Barnaby's. He took three papers with him, but waited until he had his coffee before opening them. A careful search netted him exactly nothing. There was no comment on the payroll robbery. Then, the two men whom he'd overheard came in and sat down near him. Another man came in a moment later, and Cruzon gasped audibly, turning cold and stiff.

The newcomer was short, stocky, and had a pale face. Cruzon almost gasped with relief when he saw the man was all of ten years older than Weber. The man carried a newspaper, and sat down one stool away from him.

Cruzon took off his uniform cap and smoothed his blond hair with a shaky hand. No use getting jumpy whenever he saw a man even built like Weber; there were lots of them.

He had finished his lunch and was on his second cup of coffee, and trying so hard to hear what his neighbors were saying that he'd been prodded twice on the arm before he realized the stocky man on his other side was speaking to him. "How about the sugar?" he asked. Then the fellow grinned knowingly. "You must have had a bad night. I had to speak three times before you heard me."

Impatiently, Cruzon grabbed the sugar and shoved it at the man. The fellow took it, his eyes questioning and curious.

Cruzon got his attention back to the other men just in time to hear one say, ". . . good joke, I'd say. I wonder who got it?"

"Could have been anybody. You've got to hand it to the boss. He's smart. He puts so many twists in that payroll delivery, nobody could ever figure it out! I'll bet he lays awake nights working out angles!"

"Did Weber come in late? I haven't seen him."

"Not yet. Say, wouldn't it be funny if he took it? He's just dopey enough to try something like that!"

They paid their checks and walked out. Cruzon stared blindly at his coffee. Something was wrong! What did they mean by saying it was a good joke? He remembered all they had previously said, about not giving out the name of the driver or the route until the last minute, but had there been other precautions? Had . . . could he have been duped?

His spoon rattled on his cup and the man beside him grinned. "You'd better take on a lot of that, friend. You're in no shape to be driving."

"Mind your own business, will you?" His irritation, fear, and doubt broke out, his tone made ugly by it.

The fat man's eyes hardened. "It is my business, chum." The man got to his feet and flipped open a leather case, displaying a detective's badge. The name, Cruzon noted, was Gallagher. "We've enough trouble without you morning-after drivers."

"Oh . . . I'm sorry, officer." Get hold of yourself, get a grip, his subconscious was saying. "I'll be careful. Thanks for the warning."

Hastily, he paid his check and left. When he got into the truck, he saw the fat man standing by the building, watching him.

Watching *him*? But why should he? How could they be suspicious of him?

For the remainder of the day he drove so carefully he was almost an hour late in finishing deliveries. He checked in his truck, then hurried to his car and got in. Even more carefully, he drove home.

He saw it as soon as he entered the hallway. Restraining an impulse to seize the envelope and run, he picked it up and walked to his room. The key rattled in the lock, and he was trembling when he put the envelope down on the table and ripped open the flap. He thrust in his hand, fumbling feverishly for the first packet. He jerked it out.

Newspapers . . . just newspapers cut in the size and shape of bills!

Desperately, his heart pounding, he dumped the envelope out on the table and pawed over the packets. More newspapers.

That was what they meant, then, and the joke was on him. On him? Or on Weber?

Only Weber was out of it; Weber was beyond shame or punishment. Weber was dead, and he had been killed for a packet of trimmed paper.

But they did not know, they could not know. Weber could not talk, and that crime, at least, was covered. Covered completely.

Cruzon dropped into a chair, fighting for sanity and reason. He must get rid of the envelope and the paper. That was the first thing. It might be months before they found Weber's body, and he could be far away by then.

Frightened as he was, he gathered up the papers and, returning them to the envelope, slipped out to the incinerator and dumped them in.

Back in his room, he left the light off, then hastily stripped off his clothes and got into bed. He lay sleepless for a long, long time, staring out into the shadowed dark.

He was dressing the following morning when he first noticed his hands. They were red.

Red? *Blood on his hands!* The blood of . . . ! He came to his feet, gasping as if ducked in cold water. But no! That was impossible! There had been no blood on his hands but his own, that scratch.

The scratch? He opened his hand and stared at it fever-ishly; he pawed at it. There was no scratch.

The blood had been Weber's.

And this? But this was not the red of blood, it was brighter, a flatter red.

Leaving the house, he pulled on his gloves. A good deal of it had washed away, and there were parts of his hands it hadn't touched. Most of it was on the palms and fingers.

All morning he worked hard, moving swiftly, crisply, effi-ciently. Anything to keep his mind off Weber, off the news-papers, off the strange red tinge that stained his hands. Then, at last, it was lunchtime, and he escaped his work and went to Barnaby's almost with relief. Even removing his gloves did not disturb him, and nobody seemed aware of the red in between his fingers. A thought crept into his mind. *Was it visible only to him?*

Cruzon was over his coffee when the two men came in again. Eddie sipped his coffee and listened feverishly to the men beside him.

This time they discussed a movie they had seen, and he fought back his anxiety to leave, and waited, listening.

The red on his hands, he thought suddenly, might have come from a package he handled. Something must have bro-ken inside, and in his preoccupied state, he had not noticed.

Then Gallagher walked in and dropped onto a stool beside him. He smiled at Cruzon. "Not so bad this morning," he said. "You must have slept well?"

"Sure," he agreed, trying to be affable. "Why not?"

"You're lucky. In my business, a man misses plenty of sleep. Like yesterday evening. We found a body."

"A body?" There was no way they could connect him with it, even if it was Weber.

"Yeah. Man found a gun alongside the road." Gallagher pulled a cheap, nickel-plated revolver from his pocket. "Not much account, these guns, but they could kill a man. Lots of 'em have. The fellow who found this gun, he brought it to us. We made a routine check, an' what d'you think? Belongs to a fellow named John Weber. He bought it a couple of days ago."

"John Weber?" So his name had been John? He had not known. "Has it been in the papers?"

"No, not yet. Well, anyway, that made us curious. A man buys a gun, then loses it right away, so we called this Weber, an' you know what? He'd disappeared! That's right! Landlady said his room hadn't been slept in, and he hadn't been to work. So we drove out to where this gun was lost and we scouted around.

"There was an old, washed-out dirt track up a hill away from the surfaced road. Nobody seemed to have been up there in a long time, but right up there on the track, we found the body."

"Where?" Even as the incredulous word escaped him, he realized his mistake. He took a slow, deep breath before speaking again. "But you said nobody had been there? How could he—"

"That's what we wondered. His head was battered, but he managed to crawl that far before he died. The killer had slugged him and dropped him over the rim of the pit."

Cruzon was frightened. Inside, he was deathly cold, and when he moved his tongue, it felt stiff and clumsy. He wanted to get away; he wanted to be anywhere but here, listening to that casual, easy voice and feeling those mild, friendly blue eyes. He glanced hastily at his watch. "Gosh! I've got to go! I'll be late with my deliveries!"

The detective dismissed his worry with a wave of the hand. "No need to rush. I feel like talking, so I'll fix it with your boss. I'll tell him you were helping me."

Eddie had a feeling he was being smothered, stifled. Something . . . everything was wrong.

The gun, for instance. He had never given it a thought, having been anxious to get away without being seen. And Weber not dead, but crawling halfway to the road!

"I won't take much longer," Gallagher said, "it wasn't much of a case."

"But I should think it would be hard to solve a case like that. How could you find out who killed him? Or how he got there?"

"That isn't hard. Folks figure the cops are dumb, but nobody is smart all the time. I ball things up, occasionally, and sometimes other cops do, but we've got something that beats them all. We've got an organization, a system.

"Now take this Weber. It didn't take us long to get the dope on him. He'd only been in town a year, no outdoor fellow, he just bowled a little and went to movies. So what do we figure from that? That it must have been the killer who knew about the gravel pit. It was an abandoned pit, unused in years. Not likely Weber would know about it.

"Meanwhile, we find there's an attempted payroll robbery where this Weber works. We figure Weber either did it or knew who did and was killed because of it. That adds up. So while some of the boys checked on him, others checked on the gravel pit."

Gallagher flipped open a notebook. "It hadn't been used in eight years. The company found a better source for gravel, but one of the guys in the department knew about kids who used to play there. So we started a check on truck drivers who hauled from there, oil field workers who knew about it, and the kids.

"The guy who's in the department, he gave us a list. His name is Ernie Russell."

Skinny Russell!

"He remembered them all. One was killed on Okinawa. One's an intern in New York. A girl works down the street in a coffee shop, and you drive a parcel delivery truck. Funny, isn't it? How things work out? All of you scattered, an' now this brings it all back."

"You . . . you mean that was the same pit where we used to play?"

"Sure, Eddie. An' you know? You're the only one who might have known Weber. You delivered to that office, sometimes."

"I deliver to a lot of offices." They had nothing on him. They were surmising, that was all. "I know few people in any of them."

"That's right, but suppose one of them called you?" The placid blue eyes were friendly. "Suppose one of them thought he saw you pick up the payroll envelope? Suppose he wanted a piece of it?"

The detective sipped coffee. "So it begins to add up. Suppose you were called by Weber? Weber was planning something because he bought that gun Saturday afternoon. He wanted to be on the safe side. And you knew about the gravel pit."

"So what? That isn't even a good circumstantial case. You can't prove I ever saw Weber."

"You've got something there. That's going to be tough unless you admit it."

He got to his feet. "I've got to go now. I've done nothing. I don't want to talk to you."

"Look, kid." Gallagher was patient. "You can tell me about it now or later. You muffed it, you know, from beginning to end. We know you met him somewhere, an' we can find it. Maybe it will take us a week, maybe two weeks or a month, but we'll find it. We've got you on the payroll job, an' we'll get you on the killing, too, kid."

"What do you mean, you've got me on the payroll job? I had nothing to do with it!"

Gallagher remained patient. "You've been trying to keep your hands out of sight. One of my boys was watching the house when you came out this morning. He was watching your hands, and he saw the red on them before you got your gloves on. He called me about it this morning. We checked your incinerator . . . closely packed papers have to be stirred around or they won't burn. Only the edges a little, and they'll brown over.

"That red on your hands? That guy in the payroll office, he's a funny one. He handles three payrolls a week for eight years, an' never lost one. He's always got an angle. The day you stole that envelope, he took the real payroll over in a taxi, all alone. But the papers you handled, they had red dye on them . . . hard to wash off."

Eddie Cruzon sat down on the stool again and stared blindly down at his coffee. He blinked his eyes, trying to think. Where was he now? What could he do?

"Another thing. Weber, he lives out in Westwood, an' he

called you from home. It was a toll call, see? We got a record of it."

The fool! The miserable fool!

Gallagher got to his feet. "What do you say, kid? You haven't a chance. Want to tell us about it? My wife, she's havin' some friends over, an' I want to get home early."

Cruzon stared at his coffee and his jaw trembled. He was cold, so awfully cold, all the way through. And he was finished . . . finished because he'd thought . . .

"I'll talk." His voice was no more than a whisper. "I'll talk."

THE HAND OF KUAN-YIN

T HERE WAS NO sound but that of the sea whispering on the sand and the far-off cry of a lonely gull. The slim black trunks of the sentinel palms leaned in a broken rank above the beach's white sand, now gray in the vague light. It was the hour before dawn.

Tom Gavagan knelt as Lieutenant Art Roberts turned the body over. It was Teo.

"It doesn't make sense," Roberts said impatiently. "Who would want to kill *him*?"

Gavagan looked down at the old man and the loneliness of death was upon him, and a sadness for this old man, one of the last of his kind. Teo was a Hawaiian of old blood, the blood of the men who had come out of the far distances of the Pacific to colonize these remote islands before the dawn of history.

Now he was dead, and the bullet in his back indicated the manner of his going. Seventy-five years of sailing the great broken seas in all manner of small craft had come to this, a bullet in the back on the damp sand in this bleak hour before daybreak. And the only clue was the figure beside him, that of a god alien to Hawaii.

"It's all we have," Roberts said, "unless the bullet gives us something."

The figure was not over fifteen inches in height, and carved from that ancient ivory that comes down to China from the islands off Siberia. The image was that of Kuan-yin, the Chinese goddess of mercy, protector of shipwrecked sailors, and bringer of children to childless women. It lay upon the sand near Teo's outstretched fingers, its deep beige ivory only a shade lighter than the Hawaiian's skin.

Wind stirred the dry fronds of the palms, whispering in

broken sentences. Somewhere down the coast a heavier sea broke among the rocks.

"What would he want with a Kuan-yin?" Roberts was puzzled. "And where did he get it?"

Gavagan got to his feet and brushed the sand from his hands. He was a tall man with a keen, thoughtful face.

"You answer that question," Gavagan said, "and you'll be very close to the man who killed him."

Roberts indicated the Kuan-yin. "What about that? Anything special?"

"The light isn't good," Gavagan said, "but my guess is you'll find nothing like it outside a museum." He studied the figure in the better light from Roberts's flash. "My guess is that it was made during the T'ang dynasty. See how the robe falls? And the pose of the body? It is a superb piece."

Roberts looked up at him. "I figured it was something special, and that's why I called you. You would know if anybody would."

"Anytime . . ." He was thinking that Teo had called and left a message with his service just two days ago. Odd, not because they had spoken only rarely in recent years, but because Teo had never liked using the telephone. He was a man at home with the sea and the winds and not comfortable or trusting around modern conveniences. Gavagan had intended to stop by and see the old man the night before but had gone to a luau up in Nanakuli instead.

Gavagan indicated the statue. "After you've checked that for prints, I'd like another look at it. You may have stumbled into something very big here."

"Like what?" Roberts pushed him. "Teo was just an old fisherman. We both knew him. Tell me what you're thinking."

"I don't know, but it's a rare piece, whatever it's doing here . . . no doubt it's why he was killed."

A car from the police lab had drawn up on the highway skirting the beach, and Tom Gavagan walked back to his convertible. In the eastern sky the clouds were blushing with a faint rose, and Gavagan sat still in his car, watching the color change, thinking.

To most things there was a semblance of order, but here

everything was out of context. What would an old fisherman like Teo be doing in the middle of the night on a lonely beach far from his home? And with a museum-quality ivory statue, of all things?

Roberts had said little, for he was not a talkative man when working on a case, but Gavagan had noticed there was scarcely any blood upon the sand. The bullet wound must have occurred somewhere else, and Teo had evidently staggered out upon the beach and died.

If so, why had he gone to that beach? And why would anyone shoot an old fisherman who was without enemies?

The only answer to that must be that Teo had something somebody wanted.

The Kuan-yin?

It was a valuable piece, a very valuable piece, but not many people would be in a position to know that. Kuan-yin figures, inexpensive ones, could be picked up in almost any curio store, and only an expert or someone with a rare appreciation for art would know this was something special.

It was a starting point, at least, for no one in the islands owned such a piece or Tom Gavagan would have known of it. Most of the islanders knew of his interest in art, and from time to time he had been asked to view almost every collection in Hawaii, sometimes to evaluate a piece for the owner, sometimes merely to share the pleasure in something beautiful.

Tom Gavagan was a curious man. He also was more than casually interested. His first voyage on deep water had been in old Teo's ancient schooner, the *Manoa,* and much of his own knowledge of the sea had been acquired from Teo aboard that vessel. Gavagan had grown up with Teo's three sons, one lost at Pearl Harbor, a second at Iwo Jima. Kamaki was the only one left, the last of his family now, for Kamaki had no children.

———

THE SUN WAS a blast of flame on the horizon when Gavagan reached the deck of the *Manoa.* For a minute or two he stood very still, looking around.

There was no sound but the lazy lap of water against the hull, yet he felt uncomfortable, and somehow wary. Teo had lived on his boat, and for years had moored it at this abandoned pier down the shore from the village. Gavagan stood listening to a car go by on the highway a quarter of a mile away, and then he walked forward, his footsteps echoing on the deck. Suddenly, he paused. On the deck at his feet lay some splinters of wood.

He had seen such wood before. It was aged and had a faint greenish tinge. Squatting on his heels, he felt of the fragments. They still seemed faintly damp. These might be slivers from the pilings of the old pier, although there was no reason for their presence here.

Or they might be wood brought up from the bottom of the sea. They looked as wood does when it has been immersed in salt water for a long time.

He dropped the fragments and walked to the companionway. Hesitating there, he looked down into the darkness below, and then once more he looked around.

There was no one in sight. At the village a half mile away, there seemed to be some movement, and across the deep water a fishing boat was putt-putting out to sea. The mooring lines creaked lonesomely, and Gavagan put a foot down the ladder, then descended sideways because of the narrowness.

The small cabin was empty, but nothing seemed unusual unless it was a pulled-out drawer. He started to go on into the cabin, then stopped.

There were indications here that the *Manoa* had recently been out to sea. There were coiled ropes against the wall, not a place that Teo would store such things but, perhaps, a place he might put them while reorganizing his gear. Sacks of food lay in the galley, opened; rice, salt, both partly used. In the forward locker Teo's ancient copper helmet and diving dress lay crumpled, still wet where the rubberized fabric had folded. Kamaki was not around and there seemed no indication of why Teo had placed the call.

Somewhere within the schooner or against the outside hull, there was a faint bump. His scalp prickled. . . .

Turning swiftly to climb the ladder, he glimpsed something on the deck to the left of and slightly behind the ladder. He picked it up, startled and unbelieving. It was a bronze wine vessel in the form of an owl or a parrot, and covered with the patina of time. He had seen one like it in the Victoria and Albert Museum; behind it there was another one. It was . . . the hatch darkened and when he looked up, Al Ribera was standing up there, looking down.

"Hello, Gavagan. Looking for something?"

There had never been anything but active dislike between them. Al Ribera had been a private detective in San Francisco and Honolulu until he lost his license first in one place, then the other. He was an unsavory character, and it was rumored that he was a dangerous man. Tom Gavagan did not doubt it for a minute.

"I was looking for Kamaki."

"Kamaki?"

"Old Teo's son. I came to tell him about his father."

Al Ribera's face was only mildly curious. "Something wrong?"

"He's dead . . . murdered."

"Tough." Ribera glanced around. "Son? I didn't know he had a son. Friend of mine over from the coast wanted to charter a schooner for some deep-sea fishing."

"Teo doesn't charter . . . didn't charter, I mean."

Ribera shrugged. "My friend wanted a Hawaiian. You know how these mainlanders are."

Gavagan thought swiftly. Not for a minute did he believe Ribera's story. There were too many dressed-up charter boats around Honolulu, boats that would appeal to a tourist much more than this battered schooner of Teo's.

Gavagan went up the ladder, and Ribera reluctantly stepped aside, glancing down the ladder as he did so. It was obvious to Gavagan that Ribera very much wanted to get below and look around.

"Where were you last night?" Gavagan asked.

Ribera's features chilled, and he measured Gavagan with cold, hard little eyes. "Are you kiddin'? What's it to you?"

"Teo was a friend of mine and Art Roberts grew up with Teo's boys, like I did."

"What's that got to do with me? If it makes any difference," he added, "I was with a doll last night."

Taking a cigarette from a pack, Ribera put it between his lips, then struck a match. He was stalling, not wanting to leave.

Gavagan leaned back against the deckhouse. "Hope Kamaki gets back soon. I've got to be back at the Royal Hawaiian to meet a guy in a couple of hours."

"I think I'll go below and have a look around." Al Ribera threw his cigarette over the side.

"No."

"What?" Ribera turned on him, angrily. "Who's telling who around here?"

"I'm telling you." Gavagan studied the man coolly. "The police want nothing disturbed . . . especially"—he glanced over—"the bronze owl."

Al Ribera stiffened sharply, then slowly let his muscles relax, but Gavagan knew he had touched a nerve. "Who's interested in owls? I don't get it."

"A lot of people are going to be interested," Gavagan explained, "especially when a man who has fished all his life suddenly turns up with a bronze owl of the Chou dynasty which any museum would cheerfully pay thousands of dollars for."

Al Ribera spread his legs slightly and lit another cigarette. He showed no inclination to leave, and Gavagan began to grasp the idea that somehow Ribera intended to get below before he left the schooner, even if it meant trouble. There was something here he wished to cover up, to obtain, or to find out.

"That owl," Gavagan said, "is a particularly fine specimen of Chinese bronze. I'd like to own it myself."

"You're welcome to it, whatever it is. I'll not say anything."

"Somewhere," Gavagan suggested, "Teo came upon several valuable pieces of art. There's nothing like any of this in the islands, and pieces like this can't very well be stolen. Or if they were stolen the thief would get nowhere near the real value from them . . . they're known pieces."

Ribera's hard eyes fastened on Gavagan. "I expect," he said slowly, "from what you say there aren't many people in the islands who would know these pieces for what they are. Am I right?"

"Maybe two . . . there might be a half dozen, but I doubt it.

"You're wasting time." Gavagan stood up. "The *Manoa* isn't for charter."

Ribera turned angrily and started for the gangway, but at the rail he paused. "Suppose I decided to go below anyway?"

"I'd stop you." Gavagan was smiling. "What else?"

Ribera turned back. "All right," he said, more mildly, "another time, another place."

The big man walked to his car, and when he started off, the wheels dug into the gravel, scattering it behind him like a volley.

————

HE GOT BACK to the gallery around five. It was a dim, tunnel-like shop that displayed African and Oceanic art by appointment only. A long canoe with outriggers hung from the ceiling; primitive drums, carved life-sized human forms, and cases of stone idols lined the walls. He snapped on the light over his desk and called his service.

He had waited several hours for Kamaki to show up, but there was no sign of him. The bronze owl he had given a quick once-over and it was as fine a piece as the Kuan-yin. He hesitated to call Roberts about this new find and the fact that Ribera had been by until he had spoken with Kamaki . . . something was up and he had no intention of getting his old friend in trouble. Finally, he'd walked down to the village and asked a couple of people to tell Kamaki to call if they saw him. He also asked them to keep an eye on the boat, suggesting that they might call the police if they saw anyone lurking about.

There were two messages: Art Roberts wanting to know if he'd had any further thoughts and a woman named Laurie Haven. She'd been by the shop, got the phone number off the door, and would be waiting until six at a place down the street called Ryan's.

————

THE GIRL AT the table was no one he had ever known, and not one he would have forgotten. She was beautiful, and she dressed with a quiet smartness that spoke of both breeding and wealth. He walked to her table and seated himself. "I'm Tom Gavagan," he said.

Her eyes, in this light at least, were dark blue, and her hair was brown. "I am Laurie Haven. I wanted to know if you had any information regarding the Madox collection."

"Those were some fabulous pieces." He was surprised and immediately cautious. Madox had once had a superb collection of Chinese art. *Once,* however, was the operative word. Both the man and his artifacts had disappeared. "A man who would take such a collection to sea was a fool," Gavagan said.

"Not at all." Laurie's eyes measured him coolly. "My uncle was an eccentric man, but he was also a good sailor."

"My apologies," Gavagan said. "That was insensitive."

"He's been missing four years. And there are probably many that share your opinion . . . all of which is beside the point." She opened her purse and took from it a ring, a dragon ring made of heavy gold and jade. "Have you ever seen that before?"

Tom Gavagan fought to keep the excitement from his voice. "Then this was not in the collection when it was lost? It is the Han ring, of course."

"It *was* lost."

Somehow this was beginning to make sense. The Kuan-yin, the bronze owl, and now this. "So how—?"

"I bought the ring, Mr. Gavagan, two days ago in Pearl. I bought it for sixty dollars from a man who believed he was cheating me."

Gavagan turned the heavy ring in his fingers. If this ring had been in the collection when lost, yet had turned up for sale in Pearl Harbor, it meant that either all of the artifacts had not been lost, or all of them had been stolen.

From the moment he had seen the bronze owl, he had begun to grasp at the edges of an explanation. He had been sure he had heard of that owl, yet there could have been more than one . . . there could have been many. Still . . .

"Why did you come to me?"

"Because I believe you can help me. You know the people who understand such things, Mr. Gavagan, and I do not believe my uncle's collection was stolen before he was lost at sea."

"Come along," he told her, "we're going to see a man about an owl."

———

ALL WAS DARK and still when the car drew up alongside the old pier where the *Manoa* was moored. There was no light on the schooner, looming black and silent upon the dark water. "I hope he's aboard," Gavagan said, "or in the village. Anyway, there's something here I want you to see. You should stay in the car, though, there've been some rough characters about."

At the plank, he hesitated. There was a faint stirring aboard the schooner. Swiftly, Gavagan went up the gangway. As his feet touched the deck, a man loomed suddenly before him.

"Kamaki?" It was too tall to be Kamaki. Gavagan heard a shoe scrape as the man shifted his feet to strike.

Gavagan lunged forward, stepping inside the punch and butting the man with his shoulder. The man staggered and started to fall, but Gavagan caught him with a roundhouse right that barely connected.

The hatch opened suddenly and Al Ribera stood framed in the light holding a pistol. "All right, Gavagan. Hold it now."

Tom Gavagan stood very still. The man he had knocked down was getting up, trying to shake the grogginess out of his head. Realization suddenly dawned on the man and he cocked himself for a swing.

"Stop it!" Ribera said harshly. "Don't be a damned fool. He can help, if he wants to live. The guy's an expert in this stuff."

Gavagan measured the distance to Ribera, but before he could move, the man he had hit was behind him and he had no chance. Ribera stepped aside, and Gavagan was shoved toward the ladder.

There had been no sound from Laurie Haven, and suddenly he realized they thought the car to be empty.

Kamaki was lying on the deck with his hands tied behind him. As Gavagan reached the bottom of the ladder, the Hawaiian succeeded in sitting erect.

Al Ribera came down the steps. There was another man, a Chinese with a scarred face whom Gavagan recalled having seen about town.

Three of them, then . . . and Ribera had a gun.

Kamaki had blood on his face from a split in his scalp and there was a welt on his cheekbone. The stocky Chinese had a blackjack in his fist. Gavagan was bound, hands behind his back, ankles tight together.

"What's the matter, Al?" Gavagan asked. "Did your perfect crime go haywire?"

Ribera was not disturbed. "*Crime?* It's a salvage job. The skipper just wouldn't cooperate with his new partners. You ever been down in a helmet and dress?"

"The word is out, Ribera, those pieces are known. They know where they came from and, soon enough, they'll know who you are."

"There's nothing to connect us with this! And for your information, when we get the rest of this stuff up we're not coming back. We took on enough provisions tonight to get to San Francisco."

"What about the ring?"

Ribera's head turned slowly. "What ring?"

"The jade and gold ring from the collection. Somebody peddled it."

Ribera stared hard at Gavagan, trying to decide whether this was a trick, yet as he stared, Gavagan could almost see his mind working. There was enough larceny in Ribera that he would be quick to suspect it of another.

Ribera turned to look at the big man Gavagan had fought with on the deck. The man's eyes shifted quickly, but he tried to appear unconcerned.

"Nielson, did you—?"

"Aw, he's lyin'!" Nielson declared. "There ain't no ring I know of."

Ribera's eyes were ugly. "Yes, there was. By the lord Harry, one of you is lyin', and I'll skin the . . ." He stopped and motioned his men out of the cabin. "Come on, let's take this on deck."

They locked the door to the cabin, and Gavagan could hear footsteps on the ladder. "What's going on here, Kamaki?"

"Sounds like you know more than I do. . . . Pops found this wreck, we brought some stuff up. He called you and was asking around about the sunken boat when Ribera showed up. He knew all about what we'd found and wanted to cut himself in. When we said no, they took over. They were going to force us to go back out. They let me go with the Chinese guy to get supplies. I guess that's when Pops escaped." He was quiet for a moment then. "Almost escaped," he said.

"He had the Kuan-yin with him when he died," Gavagan said.

Kamaki shook his head, tears showed in his eyes. "He wanted to give it to my wife . . . to help us have kids. Can you believe that? He has a chance to get away but he takes the time to steal a hunk of ivory because he thinks it might help her. He got shot and he still carried it down the beach with him. . . ." There was no sound for a moment but Kamaki quietly crying.

Then the Hawaiian took a long slow breath. "They are getting ready to cast off," he said.

"What!"

"The tide is turning, they're going to take the *Manoa* out."

Tom Gavagan heard feet moving on the deck, lines being let out, the slap of filling canvas. "Can these guys sail?" he asked.

"Yeah. The Swede and the Chinaman . . . the Chinaman can dive, too."

Soon enough they could feel the roll of the deep ocean, and Gavagan inched his way over to where Kamaki was tied.

"Let's figure a way to get loose. I don't fancy being tied up and I don't fancy going down in a helmet and dress with these guys running my lines."

"They took all the knives when they tied me up . . . even the one on the weight belt of the diving dress," Kamaki said.

"What about that?" Gavagan jerked his head at a long nail driven into the crosspiece just above the door. It was at least six inches long but had been driven into the wood only about an inch. "If we could get it out I think I could use it to get the knots untied."

"Yeah?" Kamaki suddenly grinned. "Watch me."

He wormed his way over to the bulkhead and maneuvered himself so that he was on his back with his legs extending up the wall. He arched his back until his weight was on his shoulders and his heels scooted almost a foot higher, closer to the nail. But the boat was rolling constantly now, and no sooner had he tried to hook the ropes binding his legs over the nail than the deck heeled over and he fell, his heels hitting the deck with a thud.

"Help me." Kamaki squirmed back into position. Gavagan soon got the idea. He got to his feet and, leaning against the bulkhead, blocked Kamaki's legs from sliding to the right. A locker blocked them from going too far left. Kamaki hunched, his powerful torso straining. Hunched again . . . he slipped one of the ropes binding his feet over the nail. Then he tightened his stomach muscles and fearlessly hung all of his two hundred and twenty pounds from the nail.

There was a moment where nothing happened. Then the *Manoa* listed, Kamaki's weight shifted, and with a groan the nail pulled free from the wood. Kamaki crashed to the deck.

"You okay?" Gavagan whispered.

"I'll pay for that later. I think they heard us." Kamaki tried to get back to where he had been as footsteps crossed the decking above them.

"Get down!" Kamaki demanded. But Tom Gavagan shook his head.

Al Ribera opened the hatch and came partway down the companionway, gun drawn. He saw Gavagan standing unsteadily at the bottom of the steps.

"You tryin' something?"

"Cut us loose!" Gavagan demanded.

Ribera laughed. "No chance." He leaned out and gave Gavagan a shove. Gavagan tottered on bound feet and fell to the deck. "That'll teach you to stay sitting down," Ribera smirked, and closed the hatch behind him. He never saw, or didn't pay attention to, the six-inch nail lying at Gavagan's feet.

Kamaki grunted. "You are one cool customer, Tom."

———

IT TOOK TEN minutes of finger-numbing work for Gavagan to loosen the knots on Kamaki's wrists. Less than a minute later they were free. Free but still locked in the cabin. Kamaki went to the small table protruding from one side of the locker. He pulled up on it and removed the single leg underneath. The table hinged up and fastened against the locker. They now had a weapon.

Some sort of diversion was in order, but before they could discuss what to do there came more sounds of feet on the deck over their heads and then the sound, far off but approaching rapidly, of powerful engines. There was the crackle and squawk of a bullhorn announcing words that sent relief flooding through Tom Gavagan.

"This is the United States Coast Guard! Drop your sails and heave to!"

There was no change in the motion of the *Manoa*. Suddenly the hatch was thrown open. Before Kamaki could set himself there were footsteps on the stairs and Ribera appeared, gun in hand.

"Got loose, did you? Well, tough. Get out on deck, we need hostages."

Suddenly Kamaki swung the table leg. It hit Ribera's forearm and the gun went off into the deck. Gavagan rushed him, getting inside and hitting him with a right to the jaw. The man staggered back and Gavagan wrenched the gun away. The Swede stepped into the hatch, and Gavagan pointed the gun at him and forced him back onto the deck.

They were at sea and the *Manoa* had fallen away from the wind; she was pitching erratically in the troughs of the waves. Off to the port side a powerful searchlight cut through the night. Silhouetted behind it a Coast Guard cutter stood ready, the barrel of a machine gun picking up the edge of the beam.

Kamaki dragged Ribera, none too gently, up onto the deck, and Gavagan collected the Chinese. They waited as a boat from the cutter pulled up alongside. The third man off the boat after a Coast Guard lieutenant and an ensign was Art Roberts. The fourth person out of the boat was Laurie Haven.

"Well, Tom," said Roberts, "imagine meeting you here."

"Where are we?" Gavagan located a faint glow in the sky that must be the beginnings of dawn. "And how did you get here?"

"The middle of the ocean, it seems. It looked like you were heading for Molokini Island." Roberts had a faint smile on his face.

Laurie spoke up. "I took your car and went for the police as soon as the boat left the dock."

"With a little help from Lieutenant Cargill we caught you on radar," Roberts told him.

"Here." Tom Gavagan handed the policeman Ribera's pistol. "I think the chances are pretty good that ballistics will prove this is the gun that shot Teo."

He took the pistol, produced an evidence bag, and dropped it in. "You will all have to come in to headquarters, there are a lot of questions that need answering. A Coast Guard crew will bring this boat back to port."

―――

THE SKY WAS just going from gray to blue and the lights of the island were appearing in the distance when Tom Gavagan found Laurie Haven on the deck of the cutter.

"I haven't really thanked you for saving us," he said.

"I haven't thanked you for finding where my uncle's ring came from. It's a relief just to know what ultimately happened to him. We all wondered for so long."

"With luck, Kamaki can recover much more from the wreck."

"I should pay you something. . . . I never dreamed I'd get such fast results."

"No need. But if you want to sell any of the Madox collection, I'd be honored to handle it for you." He glanced at her appraisingly. "There is a favor you could do for me . . . when the police are finished with it I would like it if you gave that Kuan-yin to Kamaki as a partial payment for recovering your uncle's collection."

Laurie looked puzzled. "I could do that, but why?"

"His father wanted him to have it, and I think his wife would appreciate it, too . . . enough said?"

Laurie smiled and leaned into the wind as the cutter rounded the breakwater and turned into the harbor.

SAND TRAP

BEFORE HE BECAME fully conscious he heard the woman's voice and some sixth sense of warning held him motionless. Her voice was sharp, impatient. "Just start the fire and let's get out of here!"

"Why leave that money on him? It will just burn up."

"Don't be such an idiot!" her voice shrilled. "The police test ashes and they could tell whether there was money or not . . . don't look at me like that! It has to look like a robbery."

"I don't like this, Paula."

"Oh, don't be a fool! Now start the fire and come on!"

"All right."

Monte Jackson held himself perfectly still. Despite the pounding in his skull he knew what was happening now. They believed him dead or unconscious and, for some reason, planned to burn the house and him with it.

From some distance away he heard footsteps and then a door closed. All was quiet except for the ticking of a clock. Returning consciousness brought with it pain, a heavy, swollen pain in the back of his head. He opened his eyes and saw linoleum, turquoise and black squares, an edge of enameled metal and beyond it, lying against the wall in what he now realized was the dark corner behind a washing machine, a man's dress sock, lightly covered with dust. His head hurt, it hurt badly and he wasn't sure he could move.

His fingers twitched . . . okay, movement was possible. He didn't get up, but he thought about it . . . were they gone? Who were *they*? A woman. He could almost remember her, something . . .

He smelled smoke. Smoke! And not wood smoke either,

burning plastic, amongst other things. He was definitely going to have to get up.

He lurched to his knees, sending a flurry of twenty- and one-hundred-dollar bills to the floor; his head swam and black spots passed before his eyes. He was in the utility room of a house somewhere, flames crackled, there was money everywhere. He grabbed the side of the washing machine and stood up, a haze of smoke hung in the doorway before him, he stumbled forward into a kitchen. Behind him there was a good two thousand dollars in currency scattered on the floor . . . but other things had his attention.

The pain and the increase in light blurred his vision. A roll of paper towels, conveniently placed near a burner on the gas range, was spreading fire to items left on the counter, brown paper bags from the market, a wooden box built to hold milk bottles, and from there to the gaily colored drapes over the sink . . . one whole side of the room was in flames. On the floor lay a man in his shirtsleeves and wearing an apron, a caked reddish-brown stain on his side. Beside him lay two items. A small pistol and a heavy, cast-iron pan.

Monte Jackson suddenly had a vision of that pan coming down on the side of his head. It was only then that he noticed the food that was splattered all over his right shoulder and sleeve. He touched his scalp and nearly lost his balance. It was split, split to the bone.

He turned, and as the lightbulb over the sink burst from the heat of the fire, staggered to a door that looked like it opened onto a side yard; he yanked at the knob. It turned but the door wouldn't open, it just rattled in the jamb. A lock? The heat was like the broiling desert sun and growing even more intense. The lock needed a key . . . and the key was not in it.

As the paint began to blister on the wall next to him, Monte Jackson dropped to all-fours and crawled into the burning kitchen, desperately headed for the door that he assumed led to the dining room. He slipped in the sauce that covered the floor near the body, his hand hit the pistol and it went skittering into a corner. He pushed through the swinging door and he was suddenly in the comparative calm of a butler's pantry.

Shadows thrown by the flames fled ahead of Jackson as he

scrambled to his feet and ran down the hallway. Past the dining room, the living room, then the front door was before him. He slid to a stop; a faint whistling sound came from under the door . . . air rushing into the house, feeding the fire that was spreading in the kitchen and licking its way down the ceiling of the hallway. He could feel its heat at his back. Jackson turned the knob and pulled the door open. It came easily, like one of those automatic doors in a supermarket, the pressure of the outside air pushing it inward. The fire roared to greater life behind him, flames pouring up the stairwell and into the second floor.

Jackson stumbled across a wide front porch and down a short set of concrete steps, the free warm air of the summer night enfolding him. He swayed on his feet. What was going on? He remembered a building with arches along the sidewalk, sitting in a bar, a girl . . .

Riverside. He was in Riverside. He had been in the bar at the Mission Inn!

Fire lit the second-floor windows of the house. He had to call the fire department . . . but, what of the man on the floor? The man was dead. The man was dead and he probably owned the house that was burning. Monte Jackson wanted to be far away. Far away in a place where none of this could have happened.

Headlights swung into the front yard and Jackson turned. But the car was not coming in from the road, it had been parked behind the house, near the detached garage.

"It's him! You idiot, get him!" He heard the woman's harsh voice again, and suddenly the car accelerated. Jackson backed up, turned, then ran. The dark sedan sprayed gravel as a heavy foot was applied to the gas. He dodged, jumped a hedge and went to his knees, but was up with a lunge and into the shrubbery, slamming blindly into a woven wire fence, hitting it hard enough to throw him back; he ploughed on. The car ground to a stop, caught in the hedge, and he heard the doors pop open. There was a shot. He felt the hot breath of the bullet pass his cheek. He crouched and ran, sighted a gate . . . how he got through it and into the orchard beyond he never knew.

Twice he stumbled and fell headlong, but forced himself to keep running until he was completely out of breath.

As his head cleared he caught the sound of tires as a car drove by on gravel. Following the sound, he emerged from the brush on the lip of a ravine dividing the wood from a county road.

It was not a main road but, by the look of it, plenty of cars were passing. If he could get a lift, get out of here, well, maybe he could figure out what happened.

He thought of his appearance and lifting a fumbling hand, felt gingerly of the wound along his scalp. There was dried blood in his hair and on his cheek and ear.

The sound of water led him to an irrigation ditch where he dropped to his knees and bathed the blood away, then dried himself with his shirt and handkerchief. Carefully, he combed hair over the wound to try to conceal it. Behind him, the orchard was silhouetted against the glowing cloud of smoke that rose from the fire.

———

So WHAT HAD happened? Well, there was the lounge at the Mission Inn. A girl, pretty enough . . . pretty enough for a man who had spent the last three months in the desert. He had caught her eye momentarily, but what would a girl like that want with him?

Unfortunately, it was all coming back to him.

The girl, woman (he had other names for her now) . . . had been well dressed but was obviously nervous. A man, a big young man, was hanging around the bar, watching her. The two never spoke but Monte Jackson hadn't been in the desert so long that he was blind; the man didn't want to be noticed, but he was watching the woman whose name, Jackson now knew, was Paula.

He had finished his drink and left the bar, there was no time in his life right now for women; few women would tolerate the way he was living. There was also no time in his life for whatever kind of drama was brewing between her and the man at the bar. He had no time for it, but when the dark sedan had pulled up beside him as he walked down the street, he had found himself involved, regardless.

———

AFTER CLEANING UP, he decided against trying to get a ride. Although he was hurt, a minor concussion, at least, a torn scalp, bruises and scrapes from his escape, and a nasty cough from the smoke he had inhaled, he had to think, and he was still sure that his appearance, especially so close to a fire, would draw unwanted attention.

His memories were sorting themselves out and he thought he knew where he was. A little farm, a nice gentlemanly farm, on the outskirts of Riverside. He turned right and started walking along the road. Occasionally cars sped past. At first he ducked into the ditch when he saw them coming, fearing a bullet from Paula or her friend. But soon after he started out he had heard fire engines in the distance, probably on a parallel road, and figured that Paula might be busier trying to explain to the cops and the fire crew what had happened than she was trying to find him. So he walked along the shoulder of the road, squinting against the dust of passing cars, until he came to an intersection. The new road was paved, and on the other side, under a streetlamp, was an empty bus stop.

———

THE BUS GOT him within a block of the El Mirage Motel where, earlier in the day, he had taken a room on the second floor. He no longer had his key but the desk clerk remembered him and gave him another. The room was as he had left it just hours before. He went to the bathroom and washed his face and scalp again. Though very painful, he cleaned the wound, and that started it bleeding again. He tore strips from a towel and bound it up as best he could; the kind of pressure it needed was impossible, for the bruising was worse than the cut. He slipped out of his torn and filthy clothes and noticed that the pockets were almost empty . . . it was not only his room key that was gone, his wallet was missing too! He sat down next to the telephone. He should call the police.

That was simple. That was the right thing to do. And what

would he tell them? Well, the truth; a woman had picked him up in her car as he left the lounge at the Mission Inn. She had said that a man was following her and that she would like him to see her home. Her husband, a local doctor, would then drive him wherever he wanted to go.

It had made sense at the time.

Once at the farm, she had asked if he wanted a drink. When he said yes, she'd suggested that he get a coaster out of the cabinet behind him. He had turned, and when he had turned back, the big man from the bar was standing there and had hit him on the head with the cast-iron pan. He'd fallen to his knees and the man had hit him again. The last thing that he remembered was the woman, Paula, fitting his hand around a small automatic pistol . . . curling his fingers around it, then carrying it away in a handkerchief.

He was a patsy. The two had set him up but it hadn't worked. He definitely should call the police.

Except that thought worried him. With his wallet gone he had no ID. No one knew him here; the year or so since leaving the service he had spent prospecting in the desert. His terminal leave pay and what he had saved financed the venture, for his expenses had been small. He'd never had an address or a job anywhere except for the Army and he'd only gone there because a judge had given him a choice, the military . . . or jail.

He had a record, that could be a problem. Breaking and entering with a gang of other kids from Tempe. His uncle, an old jackass prospector, had taken a strap to him many a time but it hadn't helped. The Army had and after eight years in a ranger company he had emerged a different man.

None of which was going to help him now. He had escaped but the woman was going to have a lot of explaining to do and he was suddenly certain of what she was going to say. The very story she had tried to set up in the first place would be her best bet now. Someone had tried to rob the dead man in the house (was it her husband?), the house had caught fire just as she was returning home. He didn't know exactly how she'd spin it but he had no doubt that she would identify him as the killer . . . and she probably had his wallet.

He felt short of breath and his throat was tight. Everything he had learned in the Army told him to call the police. But his childhood, the poor kid raised in an ovenlike trailer who had been chased by the cops down dusty alleys and through weed-grown scrap yards, said something else. The world he lived in now was not the world of the military. He could not count on officials being the hard but fair officers he had once known. He could not count on those around him to take responsibility for their actions or to take pride in their honesty.

In the end he split the difference. Quickly dressing in clean clothes, he packed his bag and, using a stash of money left in his shaving kit, paid the bill. He gingerly pulled his hat on over the makeshift bandage and set out for the bus station.

After buying his ticket he turned to a phone booth and, pulling the door shut, dropped a dime in the slot. After speaking with an operator and holding for a minute or so a voice responded. "Robbery-Homicide, Lieutenant Ragan speaking."

Jackson took a deep breath. "Lieutenant Ragan, don't think this is a crank call. I'm going to outline a case for you. Listen. . . ."

Without mentioning his name he outlined his story from the moment he'd been accosted by the woman on the street. He told how he was lured into her home, that he'd been knocked out, and the plans to fire the house. He ended suddenly. "Ragan, I need help. This man, whoever he was, was killed, shot, and these people are looking for a cover story . . . something that doesn't implicate them. I'm not a killer, but you can see the spot I'm in, can't you?"

"I guess so," the policeman said. "What do you want from me?"

"Look into it from my angle, don't just believe everything you're told."

"We never just believe what we're told." Ragan's voice was dry, nearly expressionless. "Look, it's not my case. All I can tell you to do is to give yourself up. Just come in and let us do our job."

Monte Jackson hung the receiver gently on the hook.

He had done what he could. Once on his claim, it might be

months, even years before they found him. But he knew too much to believe he could escape forever.

Yet he must have breathing space. He was in a trap, but if he had time he might think his way out or perhaps, the investigation would turn up something that led away from him. He had made an attempt to offer an element of doubt. The police might accept the woman's story, yet if they had cause to look further, what might they find?

They were calling his bus, and in a minute he was moving with the line, then boarding the bus north to Inyokern.

————

WHEN THE BUS stopped at Adelanto he glanced out the window and saw someone who gave him an idea. "Hey, Jack!" he called. "How far you going?"

"Bishop," he said, walking toward Monte. "Why?"

"Look," Monte explained. "I've got to call L.A. and I've got to leave the bus here. No use to waste my ticket, so you might as well take it and ride to Inyokern, then buy one on from there."

The fellow hesitated briefly. "Sure thing. What do you want for it?"

"Don't worry about it," Jackson said, turning away quickly. Now the bus driver would never realize he had lost a passenger, and if the ticket was traced it would have been used to Inyokern.

He was a tall young man with broad shoulders and he had always walked a lot. Fortunately, the morning was cool. If he remembered correctly it was seven miles to Oro Grande on Highway 66. He started out, walking fast along the intersecting road. Yet he was in luck, for when he had gone scarcely a mile a pickup slowed and the door opened. He got in.

"Goin' far?" He was a dark-haired man in boots and Levi's.

"Oro Grande, to catch a bus for Barstow."

"Lucky," the fellow grinned, "I'm drivin' to Barstow. On to Dagget, in fact, if you care to ride that far."

At Dagget, Jackson walked over the connecting road to Yermo and waited four hours for the bus for Baker. Arriving in Baker he walked through town to the little house owned by

Slim Garner, who worked the neighboring claim over in Marble Canyon. He found Slim watering his rough patch of lawn.

"Hey, Monte! Didn't think to see you here."

"Are you headed back to Death Valley? I could use a ride."

"Sure, no problem." He turned off the hose, looking around at the yard, which was mostly dirt. "I'm not here enough to grow weeds, I should give up and save the water. Put your haversack in the truck, I'll load up and we'll go."

———

SLIM'S POWERWAGON GROUND northward and a hot wind blustered in through the open windows. Jackson dozed in the passenger seat, trying to get some rest, although the shaking of the truck made his head throb. The radio played old songs through a speaker that was stuck to the top of the dash by the magnet in its base, the two wires connecting it running down into the defroster vent.

When the news came on, however, Monte Jackson found himself coming fully awake.

"In Riverside, a prominent doctor was killed last night. Martin Burgess was shot to death in an apparent robbery attempt and his house caught fire and burned either as a complication of the struggle or in an attempt to cover up the crime. The doctor's wife, Paula Burgess, was returning home and saw a man flee from the burning house. The assailant is still at large."

The news continued. There was a war going on in Indochina and a scandal brewing in the L.A. City Hall, the weather was expected to be hot and get hotter.

"We'll be workin' nights this week," Slim groused.

"What?" Jackson made believe he'd just woken up.

"Gonna be hot!"

"Yeah? So what else is new?"

———

LEAVING GARNER IN Marble Canyon, Monte Jackson hiked west in the long summer twilight. His claim was near

Harris Hill and coming from Slim's place was the back way in. That was good given everything that was going on right now, he thought. He wanted to have a chance to look over the site and confirm that no one was there ahead of him. If he was going to have a sit-down with the authorities, he wanted to walk into a police station under his own power like an innocent man, not be arrested, like a fugitive.

But as the light faded from the sky he could see that his cabin was undisturbed. And for about forty-eight hours, his life returned to normal.

———

THAT NIGHT HE slept long and deep, a needed escape from all that had happened. The next day he carefully cleaned the wound again, this time properly, with peroxide, and then bandaged it. He noticed, while looking in the mirror, that the pupil of his left eye was noticeably larger than the right . . . he'd been right, the man who'd hit him had given him a concussion. He puttered around the house that day doing small chores and cleaning up. He also repacked his haversack with some food and a canteen, and then cleaned his rifle, an old Savage Model 99 that had belonged to his uncle.

On the second day Monte Jackson walked up to the diggings. He wore his sunglasses until he was inside the tunnel, and that seemed to help his head a bit.

At the end of his drift he picked up a drill steel and, inserting it into the hole, started to work, yet after only a few blows with the single jack his head began aching with a heavy, dull throb, and he knew that the scalp wound had taken more out of him than he had believed.

Leaving his tools in the drift, he picked up his canteen and shirt and started back to the cabin, yet he had taken no more than a dozen steps before he heard a car. It was, he knew, still some distance off, rumbling and growling along the rough road that came in from the west. Having listened to other cars on that road he knew approximately where it would be, and he knew that before it could reach his cabin it must go south at least two miles, then back north. It was the merest trail, and the last of it uphill.

HE WAS NO more than a minute climbing the sixty feet to the crest. Lying on his stomach, he inched the last few feet and scanned the trail. It was a Willys utility wagon, the kind that was available for rent in Bishop for day trips into the Sierras, and in it were two people.

Jackson squirmed swiftly back, then arose and started at a trot for the drift. Once inside the tunnel he caught up a few handfuls of dust and dropped them from above so that they would filter down over his tools and the spot where he had worked to give an appearance that would lead them to believe he had not recently used them. Hurrying to his cabin he gathered his things, padlocked the door, and then paused to listen. There was no sound.

That meant they had left the vehicle at the spring and were coming on foot. Keeping to rocks and gravel, he went down into the arroyo and crossed it, cutting over to enter a deep gash in the hill. Then coming out of the small canyon he climbed to the crest overlooking his cabin.

After about twenty minutes he saw them coming. It was Paula and the big blond man. The man walked slightly in advance, and had an automatic pistol tucked into the waistband of his pants. Monte settled down to watch and, despite the pain in his head, was amused to find himself enjoying it. That they had come to kill him he had no reason to doubt, yet as he watched their cautious approach he found himself with a new idea.

He was the one man who actually knew Paula Burgess guilty of murder, yet by coming here they had delivered themselves into his hands. This was his native habitat. He knew the desert and they did not. Their jeep was the tenuous link to the world they knew, and if anything happened to that vehicle they were trapped.

Their incompetence was obvious from their movements. Once the man stepped on a stone that rolled under his foot, causing him to fall heavily. He caught himself on his hands, but had Monte been in the cabin he would have heard it. They looked at the lock, then peered in the windows. Certainly, no one was in the shack with a padlock on the door. After a few minutes of conversation the man started toward the drift. Paula Burgess remained alone before the cabin.

Monte Jackson stared at her with rising anger. She had chosen him for killing exactly as she might have chosen a certain fly for swatting. Now they were here, hunting him down like an animal.

He had his rifle and he could kill them both easily. For a man who had made Expert with a half-dozen weapons, two hundred yards was nothing, yet shooting was unnecessary. Of their own volition they had come into the desert but, he vowed, they would leave only when he willed it.

Sliding back from the ridge he got up and walked fast, then trotted a short distance. The sun was high and it was hot now, but he must get there first, and must have a little time.

———

THE JEEP WAGON stood near the spring. Squirming under it, he opened his clasp knife and, using a carefully chosen rock as a hammer, he punched a hole in the side of the gas tank. The fuel spurted out and, working the knife blade back and forth, he enlarged the hole. Given the angle of the vehicle and positioning of his hole he figured that no more than two gallons would soon remain in the tank and if this was like the trucks that he had used in the Army, the last half gallon might well be useless. He worried that they might see or smell the drained fuel but it was over one hundred degrees and there was no humidity, so the gas would evaporate quickly. He scattered several handfuls of sand over the widening stain to help out. Then he flattened out behind some creosote brush about twenty yards from the jeep, and waited.

———

THEY CAME DOWN the path, the woman complaining. "He's got to be around somewhere, Ash! He has to hide, and where is there a better place?"

"Well he's not here now! It was a fool idea. Let's just sit tight and wait for that insurance!" Ash shook his head. "Let him stay here and rot . . . they'd never believe him, anyway! If anybody knew we were up here it would look suspicious."

"Oh, shut up! I started this and I want to finish it!" Paula got into the jeep. Her blouse was damp on the shoulder blades and armpits and the two-mile walk had done neither of them any good. She was in heels, and he wore tight city shoes. They were good and hot now, and dry.

"I'm going to get a drink," Ash said, "it's a long ride back."

"Come on! We can stop by that last place for a Coke! I thought you wanted to get out of here?"

Ash got in and the jeep started willingly enough. When they had gone Monte Jackson got up. He took his time for there was lots of it, he knew about how far they would be able to get. He made up a few sandwiches, put them in the haversack with a blanket and his leather jacket, then stuffed cookies into his pockets and with his rifle and canteen, walked east, away from the road.

From time to time he stopped and mopped sweat from his brow, and then walked on toward Marble Canyon. They would make anywhere from five to ten miles with the gas they had, traveling in low as they would. It was only six miles to Dodd's Spring but he doubted if they would get so far.

―――――

SLIM GARNER WAS washing dishes when Jackson showed up. "Too late for coffee," he said.

"Not hungry, Slim." He grounded his rifle. Garner glanced curiously at the pack and rifle but said nothing. "Tell you what you might do, though. About the day after tomorrow you might drive over to Stovepipe Wells and call the sheriff. Ask him to meet me at Dodd's Spring and to bring Ragan from the Riverside Police Department. Robbery-Homicide. You tell him it's the Burgess case."

Garner stared. "Homicide? That's murder!"

"You're darn tootin', it is! Call him, will you?"

"You ain't fixin' to kill nobody?" Slim protested.

"No, the fact is I'm takin' a gamble to prove I haven't killed somebody already." Knowing he must not walk again until the cool of the evening, he sat down and quietly spun his yarn out while Slim listened. Garner nodded from time to time.

"So they come up here after you?" Slim asked. He chuckled, his old eyes twinkling. "Sure, I'd like to see their faces when they find they are out of gas clean over there on the edge of the Valley!"

"Do you suppose they could find Dodd's Spring?"

"Doubt it. Ain't so easy lest you know it's there." He grinned. "Let 'em sweat for a while. Do 'em good: Make 'em feel talkative."

DUSK WAS SETTLING over the desert when Monte Jackson again saw the utility wagon. Evidently gas had not been their only trouble, for a punctured tire was now lying in the backseat. The jeep was stopped on open ground and the man and woman stood beside it, arguing. Their gestures were plain enough, but when he crawled nearer, he could hear them.

"Why not start tonight? We've got to have gas and you could be there by morning."

"Are you crazy? It's twenty miles, and maybe thirty!"

"Well, what if it is?" she asked irritably.

"In this country, wearing these shoes, I'd be lucky to make it in two days! And without water? What do you think I am?"

"What a guy!" she exclaimed contemptuously. "You let me plan it all, do everything, and then you come off without enough gas to get us back!"

"Look, honey," he protested patiently, "we had enough gas. There should be seven or eight gallons left!" He dropped to his knees and peered under the rear of the vehicle. "There's a hole," he said.

"A hole?"

"He put a hole in our tank . . . or someone did."

"What do you think he intends to do?"

"Do?" Ash shrugged. "I don't know, maybe call the cops. I'm more worried about us!"

"What do you mean?"

"We're in the middle of the desert. Nobody comes out

here. We could die, okay." He sucked in a deep breath. "You're worried about the guy being a witness. You're worried about the cops. I'm worried about the fact that we're in the desert and, unless it was a rock that put a hole in our tank, this guy Jackson is the only person who knows we're here."

"So what do we do?"

"We'd better wait. Cars have been over this trail, and one might come along. If none does, then I can start walking by daylight. At night I couldn't keep to the trail."

There is no calm like the calm of a desert at dusk, there is no emptiness so vast, no silence so utterly still. Far, serrated ridges changed from purple to black, and the buttes and pinnacles pointed fingers of shadow into the wasteland. Stars were coming out, and the air grew faintly chill. Monte Jackson pulled on his coat and crawled closer . . . it was time to have a little fun.

"I'll build a fire," Ash said.

"Don't pick up a snake," Monte said.

The woman gave a little shriek, but though their eyes lifted, they were looking some distance off to his left where a rock cliff had caught the sound and turned it back to them. Ash put a hand on his gun but kept it under his shirt. When there was no other sound they moved together and stood there, looking up toward the ridge where he lay, a long low ridge of sand and rock.

"Who's there?" the man called out.

Jackson settled back against a warm rock, and waited. A tall saguaro, one of those weird exclamation points of the desert, stood off to his left, and beyond it the desert stretched away, a place of strange, far beauty, and haunting distance. A coyote broke the silence suddenly, yapping at the moon, the sound chattering plaintively against echoing cliffs until the long valley resounded with it, and then it ceased suddenly, leaving a crystalline silence.

He heard a stick cracking then and saw a flashlight moving along the ground, then more breaking sticks.

Monte turned his face toward the cliff and asked, "What about water?"

Ash peered around him in the gathering dark. "Hey you! We're in trouble, we need help!"

"Trouble?" Monte said. "No. You're not in as much trouble as you're gonna be!"

There was a brief, whispered conversation. Then . . .

"Now see here," the man blustered, "you come down! Come down and we'll talk about this."

Monte Jackson did not reply. The fire would help with the cold but it would not help their thirst. By noon tomorrow they would be suffering. They asked for it, and a little fear is a wholesome thing.

———

LEAVING HIS POSITION, Monte hiked up the wash to the spring. He ate a sandwich, had a long drink, chewed a salt tablet and settled down for the night. Awakening with the first dawning light he made coffee, ate another sandwich, and then returned before full sunup to his vantage point. The two were huddled in the jeep. But now the day was warming up, from a nighttime low in the mid-fifties, today it would be over one hundred degrees.

"It'll be over a hundred today," he called loudly. "Without water, you might last from one to three days. If you are very lucky you could make twenty miles."

Ash got out of the jeep. "Wait a minute!" he called. "I want to talk to you!" His voice tried to be pleasant, but starting toward the rocks he slipped his hand behind his back, reaching for the gun. Knowing how difficult it is to see a man who does not move, Monte lay still on the dusty ground.

Ash got close to the rocks, then looked around. "Where are you?" he asked. "Do you have gas?" Ash scrambled over rocks and peered around. "Let's talk this over. We need gas to get out of here."

Monte said nothing, Ash was closer than he liked.

After a moment Ash gave up and walked back to the jeep. It was still cool, but clambering over rocks had him sweating profusely. He got out of his coat and mopped his face.

"Better save that energy," Monte called out.

"Go to the devil!" Ash yelled. He scanned the rocks but had not yet figured out where Jackson was.

"We can go back to the spring where we left the jeep," Paula suggested in a low voice.

"You won't like the water. What do you think I did with the gasoline?" Monte lied. They both spun around.

"Damn you! Who are you, and what's this all about?" Ash squinted at the area where Monte lay, he was looking right at him but couldn't make him out in the clutter of rocks and brush. They *must* know he knew who they were; what he was doing was fun but it was also serious business and rapidly growing tiresome.

Monte Jackson decided to stop fooling around and get down to business—he stood up.

"Write out a confession and we'll talk about water. I've got a canteen, and I know where you can get gas and fix your tank."

"So it is you? Well, you don't understand. You don't understand what you saw. We can explain. Just come down . . . come down here."

"I think I understand pretty well, Ash." The man jerked a bit when Monte used his name. "I think Mrs. Burgess there killed her husband for his life insurance and then the two of you went out looking for someone to take the blame . . . preferably a dead someone."

"You're crazy!" Ash shouted.

"Am I? I think murder is a crazy thing, myself. I also think a man's crazy to let a woman suck him into a mess like this."

He let that soak in for a moment. "You're an accessory, Ash, but, of course, they might believe you were in on it."

"I've an alibi!" Ash shouted, but his voice lacked confidence. "Come down and talk. There's money in this. We've got money right here. We can do business."

"Toss your pistol up here and I'll come."

Ash swore. Neither of them had believed he knew of the pistol. "Like hell!" Ash yelled.

"All right by me, but don't get any ideas. I've got a rifle."

Waiting would just make it hotter, and after a while this

seemed to dawn on them, yet the sun was blazing hot before they finally started. It was what he had hoped: to delay them until the sun was high.

"It's twenty miles to Keeler. Or you can strike south for the Death Valley highway, but you might get lost, too."

"Shut up!" Ash roared. "If I could get my hands on you, I'd . . . !"

"Get the beating of your life," Jackson said cheerfully. "Why, you're soft as butter, while I've drilled thousands of holes in hard rock by hand! You two think it over. A confession for water; you don't think it's a good deal now . . . but you will." He backed into cover then turned and walked off, climbing the ridge until he was a safe distance away and out of sight.

They seemed to be talking it over then; after about half an hour, they again started walking south, down the road. The man glanced around occasionally, worried, no doubt, that they both might get a bullet in the back. Well, let him worry.

Monte followed and did not try to hide his progress. Ash caught sight of him, paralleling their track about one hundred yards west, and pointed him out to Paula. They didn't like it, but there was little they could do.

———

THE SUN WAS hot and Monte had long since folded his jacket into the haversack. Neither of them had a hat and he did, and unlike Ash, Monte kept his shirtsleeves rolled down. He picked up a piece of float and examined it. They were walking steadily, but Paula lagged a little, and he had an idea that Paula wanted to bargain on her own. Obviously, she wanted to talk.

Ash slowed. "Come on, honey! If we're going to get anywhere we've got to keep moving!"

"You go ahead. I'll be right behind. I can't walk fast in these shoes."

Ash walked on, Paula glanced around and Monte let his head show over the ridge. She stopped at once. "I want to talk to you," she invited. "Come on down!"

Selecting his spot, he sat down, making her come to him.

When she was twenty yards away, he stopped her. "Close enough!" he said. "What do you want?"

Paula obviously wanted to come closer. She was accustomed to getting what she wanted from men, although after a night in a jeep she was considerably less attractive than he remembered her. "Why don't you forget this and come in with me?" she invited. "You've got a rifle, and we don't need him. There's a lot of money."

"What about that rap in L.A.?"

"We could say it was Ash. Come on, my husband was insured for seventy thousand dollars, and the house besides! Think what we could do with that!"

"Just think!" he said sarcastically. "Seventy thousand dollars, and us on the run for the rest of our lives. Funny, it doesn't sound like enough to me."

She stared at him, trying to figure him out. At that moment Ash showed over the last rise. When he saw them together he shouted and started to run toward them.

Jackson leaned his elbows on his knees and calculated the distance. The fool! Didn't he know he shouldn't run that hard in this heat? He watched him come. The effective range of a pistol is not great, but the actual range is greater than supposed. He would take no chances. He lifted the rifle. Ash slowed, then stopped, panting hoarsely. "No you don't!" he shouted. "You don't cross me up!"

Paula stared at him. "Quick!" she said eagerly. "Shoot him!"

"I'm sorry. I'm just not much interested in money. And, it's really not that much money."

"It's enough!" she protested. ". . . and you could have me." She stepped forward, as if offering herself to him.

He grinned at her. "You should see yourself!" Her makeup was streaked and her hair mussed and dulled by dust. She'd been attractive back in the bar in Riverside, but here . . .

"I'd rather just take the money," he said.

She screamed, her face contorted, hurling epithets at him. Ash had come closer and now he brought up the pistol, so Monte stood, and with four sprinting steps was in the brush and rocks beyond the arroyo.

From his concealment he could hear their angry voices, and then Ash showed on the crest, the muzzle of his pistol a questing eye. His face was haggard and strained, his shirt soaked with sweat. He wouldn't sweat much longer.

Monte took a pull at the canteen and rested in the shade of a clump of brush. Walking was okay but the running did not do his head any good. When he looked again they had started on and made almost half a mile. Paula Burgess looked beaten.

After a while he moved to follow, staying in the shade from the nearby ridge. When he again saw them they had stopped and were seated near some saltbush. They had reached the fork of the old desert trail.

From this point it branched south and then west to Keeler and north across the vast waste of the Saline Valley, waterless and empty. Paula had her shoes off and so did Ash. Obviously, they'd had enough although they'd come just five miles from the jeep. From where he crouched in the shadow of a rock he could see their faces were beginning to blister, and their lips looked puffed and cracked.

"How about it?" he called. "Want to write out a confession, and sign it? I've got water, you know."

Neither made a reply, nor did they speak to each other.

He'd heard that it was typical of criminals that they are optimistic and always see themselves as successful. This seemed to have left these two with few resources when faced with failure.

"It's only three. Even once the sun goes down the heat will hang on because it takes time for the rocks to cool off. By six it should be better. If you're alive then."

"Give us a break!" Ash pleaded.

"You're not far from water. A couple of hundred feet straight down."

"Listen!" Ash got up. "I'd nothing to do with this! She roped me in on it, and I had no idea she was going to kill anybody!"

His voice was hoarse and it hurt him to speak. "That's tough," Monte agreed, "toss your gun over here and we'll discuss it."

"Nothing doing!"

"Forget it then. I won't even talk until I have that pistol."

Heat waves danced in the distance and a dust devil picked a swirl of dust from the valley floor and skipped weirdly across the desert until it died far away in the heat-curtained distance. Ash had moved nearer, and now Paula was hobbling toward him.

"Throw me the gun! Otherwise I'm going back to my claim!"

Ash hesitated, standing there with one hand in his pocket, his face drawn and haggard.

"You fool!" Paula screamed at him. "Give me that!" She grabbed the hand emerging from the pocket and before he could move to prevent her she pointed it at Monte.

He flattened out and the gun barked viciously. Sand stung his face and in a panic he rolled over into the low place behind him and, grabbing his rifle, broke into a run, dodging into the brush even as she topped the rise where he had been lying.

Ash shouted at her, but Paula was beyond reason, firing wildly. Monte hit shelter behind a boulder, then heard Paula scream once more, the gun sounded again and he looked back. They were standing on the rise, struggling furiously, with Paula clawing at his face. But then Ash was backing away, and he had the gun.

"Four shots," Monte warned himself. "There's more to come."

"Come on back! You can have the gun if you'll give us water!"

Monte was beyond easy pistol range. He got to his feet and lifted the rifle. "Fire another shot, and I leave you for the buzzards!"

He walked toward them, watching Ash. "Give me the gun and I'll tell you where there's water."

Ash hesitated no longer, but tossed the gun toward Monte. Jackson picked it up by the trigger guard, carefully wrapped it in his handkerchief and dropped it into the haversack.

Their faces were fiery red and there were ugly streaks on the man's cheek where it had been raked by Paula's fingernails. She stared at Monte, her eyes sullen with hatred. She was no longer pretty, for the desert sun and the bitterness of her hatred had etched lines into her face.

"There's water in the radiator of your jeep," he told them.

"Huh?" Hope flared, then died in the man's eyes. "Aw, hell, man, give us a break!"

"Like she gave her husband? Like you planned to give me? Many a man's been damned glad to get water out of a radiator and stay alive. It's only five miles from here."

He watched them, studying their faces. "Or, you can write out complete confessions, one for each of you, and then I'll see that you both drink."

Their faces were sullen. "You know," he added, "you're not really in a bad way yet. Soon it'll start getting complicated. You're losing salt, without it your bodies won't be able to process water even if I give you some . . . you could die of dehydration in a swimming pool." He took a salt pill out of his pocket and popped it into his mouth. "Soon water really won't be the problem."

They looked at each other in something approaching horror. He could see that they could just barely imagine what another two days would be like.

"That's not human!" Paula protested. "You can't do a thing like that to a woman!"

"Look who's talking! You started this!" He shook his head. "I don't care what happens to you. When a woman starts killing she is entitled to no special treatment."

He sat down on a rock, but it was much too hot and he got up immediately. Neither of them was sweating now. Their skins looked parched and dry. "Ash could probably get off with a few years. You'll have as much of a lawyer as you can buy, and who knows what a good lawyer can do. Out here it's a different thing . . . there's going to be no appeal when the sun comes up tomorrow."

Without warning, Ash leaped at him, swinging, and instantly, Paula darted forward, her eyes maniacal.

Monte sprang back and, swinging the rifle, clipped Ash alongside the head with the barrel. He turned, and sank the butt into Paula's stomach. They both went down, though Monte had pulled the blows. Ash wasn't even bleeding.

"Don't be foolish," he said. "Exertion will only make the end come quicker. You've both stopped sweating, that's usually a bad sign."

Ash cursed, glaring up at him from the ground.

Monte Jackson walked away and when thirty yards off, lifted the canteen and took a long pull, then sloshed the water audibly. They stared at him, their hatred displaced only by thirst. Knowing the desert, he knew neither of these people were as badly off as they believed, but by noon tomorrow . . .

"You think it over." He took a pad and pencil from his pocket, the pencil strapped to the pad with a rubber band. "When you're ready, start writing." He laid it on the ground.

Then he turned and walked into the desert toward a small corner of shade. His life, his freedom, everything depended on success, and if he failed now it would leave him in an even worse position with the law.

————

THE HOUR DRAGGED slowly by, then another half hour. They were no longer at the fork when he walked back, but their tracks were plain. They were returning to the utility wagon.

He turned off toward Dodd's Spring, drank, then refilled the canteen. They had taken the pad and pencil with them. He walked slowly after them; when he caught up, they were still a mile from the jeep, and both were seated. Ash, behind a clump of brush, was writing on the pad, squinting his eyes against the sun's glare on the paper.

————

THE SHERIFF CAME at noon on the following day, driving up to Dodd's Spring in an open jeep with Ragan on the seat beside him, and Slim Garner in the rear to show the way. Behind them was a weapons carrier with three more deputies. Monte Jackson walked down from the rocks to meet them.

"How are you, Jackson?" He had talked several times with

the sheriff in Baker and elsewhere. "Ragan tells me you've had some trouble."

"Did Slim tell you what I told him?"

"He sure did. You know where they are?"

"Up the road a few miles. Let's go." He got into the jeep beside Garner. While they rode he handed the two confessions to Ragan. "That about covers it. Right now there's a chance they will both talk. Ash figures he will get off because he didn't actually kill anybody."

"We got a few facts," Ragan admitted. "Somebody planned to burn the house, all right. We found the oil-soaked rags and some spilled kerosene on the counter in the kitchen. Lucky for all of us the place didn't burn completely. Then we found out about Ash Clark, he's the guy down there, right? He promised his landlady payment in a few days, said he was coming into money. It's definitely a case with a few loose ends."

Monte took the pistol from the haversack, and Ragan accepted it as the trucks rolled to a stop. Paula Burgess was haggard and the blazing desert sun had burned her fiercely. Ragan cuffed them and put them in with the deputies. Then they all turned and headed for town. Monte Jackson relaxed, looking back as the long desert road spun out behind the jeep. Long shadows stretched across the landscape, and dust devils danced like ghosts on the wide, sandy flats. A mirage glowed in the distance, looking for all the world like a cool and placid lake.

The desert, he thought, can be a friendly place . . . if only one showed it the proper respect.

UNDER THE HANGING WALL

I

THE BUS BUMPED and jolted over the broken, heat-ribbed pavement, and I fought my way out of a sodden sleep and stared at the road ahead. My face felt sticky and my head ached from the gas fumes and heat. Twisting and turning in my sleep had wound my clothes around me, so I straightened up and tried to pull them back into place again.

We were climbing a steep, winding road that looked as if it had been graded exclusively for mountain goats. I ran my fingers through my hair and tried pulling my pants around to where they would be comfortable. In the process, my coat fell open and revealed the butt of my gun in its shoulder holster.

The fat man stared across the aisle at me. "Better not let 'em catch you with that rod," he advised, "or you'll wind up in jail."

"Thanks," I said.

"Insurance is my line," he said, "Harbater's the name. Ernie Harbater. Do a lot of business up this way."

It was hot. The air in the bus was like the air over a furnace, and when I looked off across the desert that fell away to my left, the horizon was lost to dancing heat waves.

There were five people on the bus. Harbater, who wore a gray gabardine suit, the trousers stretched tight over fat thighs, his once white shirt bulging ominously over his belt, was the only one who sat near me. He looked as uncomfortable as I felt, and lying beside him on the seat was a crumpled and dog-eared copy of a detective magazine with a corner torn off the cover.

Three seats ahead a girl with stringy and streaked blond

hair, and lipstick that didn't conform to the shape of her mouth, sweltered in her own little world. Across the aisle from her was another girl, who wore a gray tailored suit. The coat lay over the back of the seat beside her.

The fifth passenger was another man, with the rough physique and pale skin of a mining man. He squinted placidly out the window as the bus groaned unhappily and crept over the brow of the mountain. For a moment there was a breeze that was almost cool, and then we started down from the wide world in which we had existed, and into the oven of a tight little canyon.

We rounded a curve finally, and Winrock lay ahead of us, a mining town. Most of the buildings were strewn along the hillsides, empty and in ruins, the one graded street lying along the very bottom of the canyon. The business buildings were all frame or sheet metal but two. One was the brick bank, a squat and ugly thing on a corner, the other an ancient adobe that had once been a saloon. One of the reasons that I had gotten this job was because I'd worked in places like this, but that didn't mean I was wild about coming back.

Harbater had dozed off, so I shucked my gun from its holster and thrust it beneath my belt, under my shirt. Then I stowed the holster in my half-empty bag and slid gratefully out of my coat. My shirt was sweat-soaked.

The bus ground to a halt and dust sifted over it. Groggily, I crawled to my feet. Coat over one arm, and my bag in the other hand, I started for the door. The girl with the stringy hair was gathering up some odds and ends, and she looked up at me with that red blotch that passed for a mouth. Her lips, normally not unattractive, were lipsticked into what passed for a cupid's bow, and it looked terrible.

The other girl had awakened suddenly, and when I glanced down at her, I looked into a pair of wide, intelligent gray eyes. She sat up, pushing back a strand of hair. I swung down into the street, bag in hand.

Several loafers sat on a bench against the wall of the Winrock Hotel. I glanced at the sign, then walked up on the porch and shoved the door open with my shoulder.

A scrawny man in a green eyeshade got up from behind the desk and leaned on it. "Got a room?" I asked.

"Got fifty of 'em," the clerk said. He dug out a key and tossed it on the desktop. "End of the hall, second floor," he said. "Bath's next door."

I picked up my bag.

"That'll be ten dollars," he said.

I put the bag down again and fished for some bills. I pulled off two fives and handed them over, then went up the worn steps and down the creaky hall. If anybody ever dropped a match, the place would go up in one whopping blast of flame. It was old, and dry as tinder.

"You got yourself a lulu this time!" I said disgustedly. "What a guy will do for money!"

Tossing the bag on the old iron bed, I threw the coat over the back of a chair and peeled off my shirt. It was so wet it stuck to my back. Then I took off my shoes and socks and had started on my pants when I recalled the bath was next door. Still disgusted, I picked up a towel and, barefoot, stuck my head into the hall. There was nobody in sight, so I came out and went into the bathroom.

When I'd bathed and dressed, I put my gun back in my waistband and, taking my coat over my arm, walked downstairs.

The wide, almost empty room that did duty for a lobby had a bar along one side, two worn leather chairs and an old-fashioned settee down the middle, and four brass cuspidors.

Two men loafed at the bar. One of them was a big-shouldered, brown-faced man with a powerful chest. He was handsome in a heavy, somewhat brutal fashion and had the look of a man it would be bad to tangle with. The other was a shorter man, evidently one of the oldest inhabitants. I put a foot on the rail and ordered a bourbon and soda.

The brown-faced man looked at me. He had hard eyes, that guy. I turned to the bartender, who was an overstuffed party in a dirty shirt. He had a red fringe around a bald head, and red hair on his arms and the backs of his hands.

"Where do I find the law around here?"

He opened his heavy-lidded eyes, then jerked his head toward the brown-faced man. "He's it," he said.

"You the deputy sheriff?" I asked. "Are you Soderman?"

He looked at me and nodded.

I walked down the bar and flipped my badge at him. "Bruce Blake, I'm a private detective," I said. "I'm here to look over the Marshall case."

"It's closed." His hard eyes studied me like I was something dirty he'd found in his drink.

"His brother wanted it looked into. Just routine."

He hesitated, tipping his glass and studying his drink carefully. Then he shrugged. "All right. It's your time."

I shrugged my own shoulders and grinned. "Actually, it's Lew Marshall's time. I'm just going through the motions."

"You want to talk to Campbell? He's in jail, waitin' trial."

"Uh-huh. Might just as well."

———

ON THE WAY to the jail, Soderman told me about the case. "This Campbell owned the Dunhill mine. It had been rich once, then the vein petered out and they shut down. Campbell, he wouldn't believe the hole was finished. He'd helped locate the original claims, he an' Dunhill together. Ten years he worked around, tryin' to find what happened to that vein. Then he found a pocket and got enough ore out of it to hire an engineer. He hired Tom Marshall.

"Marshall came in here and worked for two months, and then quit, turning in a report that it was useless, the mine was played out. Campbell gave up then, and he took a regular job, mostly to pay his daughter's tuition at some school she was goin' to out in Los Angeles.

"Finally, he got an offer for the mine. It wasn't much, but it was something, and he sold. Sold it out for a few thousand dollars."

Soderman looked up, grinning wryly. His teeth were big, white and strong looking. "When the new outfit moved in, Marshall was the superintendent. They opened the mine up an' he had the vein uncovered in less than a week!"

"That's bad. He finds the vein, lies to Campbell, then gets backing. That was dirty."

"You said it!" Soderman's voice was hard with malice. I couldn't blame him. Probably most of the townspeople sympathized with Campbell.

"Anyway," he continued, "the day shift came out of the hole, and Marshall went down to look it over. They didn't have a night shift, but were plannin' one. Nobody ever saw Marshall again alive."

"How does Campbell tie in?"

"Weber, he was watchman at the mine, saw Campbell go into the mine. He ran to stop him, but Campbell was already inside. So Weber let him go."

"When did they find Marshall?"

"Day shift man found him when he came on the next morning."

"Nobody looked for him that night? What about his wife?"

Soderman shook his head. "Marshall usually worked at night, slept during the day. He'd been working night shifts a long time, and got used to it. Habit he had."

"Work at home?"

"He had an office at the mine."

I shifted my coat to the other arm and pulled the wet sleeve free of the flesh. Then I mopped my brow. The jail was at the far end of town. It was hotter than blazes, and as we plodded along in the dust, little whorls lifted toward our nostrils. Dust settled on my pantlegs, and my shoes were gray with it.

This looked like they said, pretty open and shut. Why was Lew Marshall suspicious? He had told me nothing, just sent me along with a stiff retainer to look into the killing.

The jail was a low concrete building with three cells. It was no more than a holding tank for prisoners who would be sent on to the county building up north.

"You got him in there?"

The big man laughed. "The old fool cussed the prosecutor at the preliminary hearing. He wouldn't post a bond, so the judge sent him back here."

The air was like an oven inside. There was an office that stood with the door open, and we walked in. As we stepped into view of the three barred doors, I saw the gray-eyed girl from the bus standing in front of one of them. She started back as she saw us.

"Who are you?" Soderman wasn't the polite sort.

"I'm Marian Campbell. I've come to see my father."

"Oh?" He looked at her, then he smiled. I had to admit the guy was as good-looking as he was tough. I left him looking at her and stepped to the cell door.

Campbell was standing there. He was a short, broad man with heavy shoulders and a shock of white hair.

"I'm Bruce Blake, a private detective," I said. "They sent me down here to look into Marshall's death. You the guy who killed him?"

"I haven't killed anybody an' I told 'em so!" He looked right straight at me and his gray eyes reminded me of the girl's. "Tom Marshall was a double-crossing rat, an' maybe he needed a whippin', but not killin'. I'd not waste my time killin' him."

"What did you go to the mine for?" I mopped my brow. Soderman and the girl were both listening.

"To get some of that ore for evidence. I was going to start a suit against him."

"You see him?"

He hesitated. "No," he said finally. "I never saw hide nor hair of him. The snake!"

If I was going to ask intelligent questions I was going to need more information. I ran my fingers through my hair. "Whew!" I said. "It's hot here. Let's go."

Soderman turned away and I followed him out into the white heat of the street. It was a climb back, and that didn't make me any happier. Certainly, Campbell had motive and opportunity. The guy looked straight at you, but a lot of crooks do that, too. And he was the type of western man who wouldn't take much pushing around. However, that type of western man rarely dodged issues on his killings.

"What do you think?" Soderman wanted to know. He stopped, sticking a cigarette between his lips. He cupped a match and lighted it.

"What can a guy think? Crotchety. Seems like he might have the temper to do it."

"Sure. Ain't even another suspect."

"Let's talk to the wife."

"Why talk to her?" Soderman said roughly. "She's been bothered enough."

"Yeah, but I can't go back and turn in a report when I haven't even talked to his wife."

Grudgingly, he admitted that. When he started up to the house, it was easy to see why he'd hesitated. It was a climb, and a steep one.

"What the devil did they live up here for?" I asked. "It would be a day's work to climb this hill, let alone anything else!"

"This ain't their home. She's just livin' here a few days. The Marshall house is even further up, but it's easier to get at." He pointed to a small white house with two trees standing on the open hillside in full view of the town. "That's it."

II

DONNA MARSHALL WAS sitting in the living room when we rapped on the door. She looked up quickly when she heard Soderman's voice and started up from the divan.

"Private detective to see you," Soderman said sharply. "I tried to head him off."

She was something to look at, this Donna Marshall was. She made a man wonder why Tom Marshall worked nights. On second thought, if they had been married long, you could imagine why he might work nights.

She was a blonde, a tall, beautifully made woman who might have been a few pounds overweight, but not so that any man would complain. She was a lot of woman, and none of it was concealed.

"Come in, won't you?" she said.

We filed into the room and I sat on the lip of an overstuffed chair and fanned myself with my hat. "It's too hot," I said.

She smiled, and she had a pretty smile. Her eyes were a shade hard, I thought, but living in this country would make anything hard.

"What is it you wish to know?"

"I just thought I'd see you and ask a few questions. It looks like Soderman here has the right man in jail, so this is mostly routine. Anyway, it's too hot for a murder investigation."

She waited, a cigarette in her fingers. There was a bottle of beer on the stand beside the divan. I could have used one myself.

"Been married long?"

She nodded. "Six years."

"Happy?"

"Yes." Her answer was careless, and she didn't seem very positive or much interested. Her eyes strayed past me toward Soderman.

"Like living in these hick mining towns?"

For the first time she seemed to look at me, and she smiled. "I don't see how anybody could," she said. "There's simply nothing to do. I didn't care for it, but Tom had his work to consider."

Somehow I couldn't picture her fitting into such a town as Winrock. She was the sort of woman who likes nightclubs, likes dining and dancing. I didn't blame her for not liking Winrock, however, I didn't care for it myself.

"How much did Marshall have invested in this mine?"

"Not much," she said. "It was mostly a job."

Was that what she thought? I stared at the floor, faintly curious. Lew and Tom Marshall owned this mine, and from all the evidence it had turned into a whale of a rich hole. Well, maybe Tom Marshall was the cagey sort. Maybe he didn't tell his wife everything.

"Are you going to stay here?"

"Here?" She spoke so sharply that I glanced up. Her voice and her expression told me what she thought of the town a lot better than what she had to say. "I wouldn't stay here even a minute longer than I have to!"

She rubbed out her cigarette in the ashtray. Soderman got up. "Any more questions?" he asked. "We'd better move on."

"I guess that's right." We all got up, and Soderman turned toward the door. He sure was one big man. When he moved you could see the weight of muscle in his shoulders.

Donna Marshall started after him, and it gave me a chance to pick up a familiar-looking magazine that lay on the table near the ashtray. It wasn't exactly the thing to do, but I slid it into my coat pocket as casually as possible. They were going to the door together, so the move went unnoticed.

When we got outside in the sun, I mopped my brow again. "Good-lookin' woman," I said. "If I had a woman like that, I'd stay home nights."

He looked around at me, a question in his eyes. They weren't nice eyes when they looked at you like that, and I found myself being glad I wasn't a crook who had to come up against him. This Soderman could be a rough customer.

"Where to now?" he asked.

"Let's go up to their house," I said, "up where they lived."

"You got a craze for walkin'," he said with disgust. "Can't we let it ride until later? When it cools off a little?"

"You go on down if you want," I said. "I'll just look around a little more. I want to finish up and get out of here. I haven't lost anything in this town."

————

He LED THE way along the path that led to the Marshall house, and we swung back the gate and entered.

Once inside, I stopped and looked back. From the door you could see all the way down the winding path to the town and the Dunhill mine beyond. You could see everything that happened in town from this viewpoint, and likewise, anyone on the street in town could see anyone who came and went from this house.

There was little enough to see once we were inside. There were three rooms in the house, and a wide porch. The kitchen and living room offered nothing. There were dirty dishes on the table and in the sink, and one thing was plain enough: Donna Marshall was no housekeeper.

I wandered into the bedroom, not sure what I was looking for. More than anything, I was looking and hoping for a break, because I didn't even know why I was up here. Lew Marshall had given me little to nothing with which to work, merely telling me he wanted his brother's murderer punished and wanted to be very sure they got the right person.

Soderman had seated himself on the edge of the porch outside. He was plainly disgusted with me, and he wasn't alone. I was disgusted with myself, so when I'd taken a quick look around, I turned to go. Then I saw something under the head of the bed. I knelt quickly and picked up several fragments of dried red mud.

After studying them a few minutes, I put them into an envelope and slid them into my pocket. Then I took the head of the bed and, with a lift, swung it clear of the wall. The dust under the bed was thick, but it had been disturbed recently, for something had been lying under that bed, something long and heavy, something that could have been a man, or the body of a man. I also noticed the clock on the nightstand, though at the time I didn't realize why.

"What've you found?" Soderman appeared in the door behind me, the last person I wanted near right then. He must have moved swiftly and silently when he heard me moving the bed. He was staring at me now, and his lips were drawn over his white teeth. I shrugged and motioned vaguely at the room.

"Nothing," I said. "Just looking around."

"Haven't you had enough yet?" he demanded impatiently. "I'm gettin' fed up!"

"Then suppose you go on down to town?" I suggested. "I can find my way around now."

His eyes could be ugly. "No," he said, and I didn't like the way he said it. "If you turn up anything, I want to be the first to know."

As we went out I palmed a map of the mine that I had noticed on the sideboard. It was creased where it had been folded to fit in someone's, probably Tom Marshall's, pocket. We started back down the steep path. I asked, "Rained around here lately?"

He hesitated before answering my question, and I could

see he was weighing the question in his mind, trying to see what it might imply.

"Yes, it rained a few days ago," he said finally. "In fact, it rained the day before the killing."

The day before? I glanced off across the canyon. Whatever had been under that bed, it could scarcely have been Marshall's body, although it looked like something of the sort had been lying there. No man, not even so powerful a man as Soderman, could have carried a body from here, across town, and to the mine shaft.

Not even if he dared take a chance in leaving the house with an incriminating load when he had to cross the town from here. Certainly, crossing the town was not much of a task, but at any time, even in the dead of night, he might meet someone on that path or in the street itself. And if he, or anyone else, had done such a thing, he would have had to pass several houses.

There was no way a car could approach the house. It was on a steep canyon side, and there was no road or even a trail beyond the path on which we had come.

One thing remained for me to do. To have a look at the mine itself, to examine the scene of the crime. There was, in the back of my mind, a growing suspicion, but as yet it was no more than the vaguest shadow bolstered by a few stray bits of evidence, none of which would stand for a minute in court under the examination of a good lawyer. And none of them actually pointed to the guilty party or parties.

There was the magazine, a bit of red mud that might have come from a shoe, and some disturbed dust under a bed. There was also a very attractive young woman of a type who might have caused trouble in more selective circles than were to be found among the lusty males of Winrock . . . and she was tied in with a mining engineer who did not sleep at home.

———

WE WALKED BACK to the jail. It sat close against the mountainside, and there had been some excavation there to fit the building into the niche chosen for it. There was a pump set off to one side of the entrance that leaked into the earth to one side of the path. Bright yellow bees hovered around the evaporating pool in a landing pattern like water bombers on their way to a forest fire. Soderman led the way inside. The jail office was scarcely more than the size of one of the cells.

"What did he have on him when he was found?" I asked.

Impatiently, Soderman opened his desk and dumped an envelope on the desktop. I loosened the string and emptied the contents. It was little enough. A box of matches, a tobacco pouch, some keys, a pocket knife, a couple of ore samples, and a gun.

The gun was a .38 Police Positive, an ugly and competent-looking gat, if you asked me. It was brand spanking new. There were no marks in the bluing from the cylinder having been rotated, no dirt between the rear of the barrel and the top frame, and no lead in the rifling. It was fully loaded and had never been fired.

That gun was something to set a man thinking, and it needed no more than a glance to tell me how new the gun was. Why had Tom Marshall suddenly bought a gun, apparently just a few days before he was murdered?

"Wonder what he had that for?" I mused.

Soderman shrugged. "Snakes, maybe. Lots of us carry guns around here."

"He hasn't had it long."

"Listen." Soderman leaned his big heavy hands on the desk and glared at me. "What are you gettin' at? You've been nosin' around all day, diggin' into a closed case. We've got the guilty party right in this jail, an' we've got enough evidence for a conviction."

It was time to start something. If I was going to crack this one, I was going to have to get things rolling. If I could get the right people worried, perhaps I could jolt something loose. Anything I told him would get around. I hoped it would get to the right people.

"Then you can guess again," I told him. "I've a hunch Campbell didn't do it, and a better hunch who did!"

He leaned farther over the desk and his face swelled. "You tryin' to make a fool of me? You tryin' to come in here an' show me up? Well, I'm tellin' you now! *Get out!* Get out of town on the next bus!"

"Sorry," I said, "I'm not leaving. I'm here on a legitimate job, and I'll stay until it's wound up. You can cooperate or not as you please, but I tell you this: I'm going to hang this on the guilty parties, you can bet your last dollar on that!"

Turning on my heel, I left him like that, and walked back to the hotel. He didn't know how much of a case I had, and to be honest, I didn't have a thing. The mine remained to be looked at, and I was hoping there would be something there that would tell me what I wanted to know. Above all, something concrete in the way of evidence.

Yet why had Tom Marshall bought a gun before he was killed?

Why was the alarm clock in the Marshall home set for five A.M., when Tom Marshall remained at the mine all night?

And who, or what, had been under the bed on that last rainy day?

These things and a cheap magazine were what I had for working points, and none of them indicated a warrant for an arrest. And I had nothing to offer a jury.

Had he been afraid of Campbell, would he not have bought the gun before his return? Tom Marshall had been a rugged specimen, much more than a physical match for Campbell, and he did not seem to be a man who resorted to guns.

Hence, it stood to reason that he bought the gun for a man he could not handle with his fists. Flimsy reasoning, perhaps, but there it was.

Tom Marshall had spent his nights at the mine, and Donna Marshall wasn't one to rise at five in the morning. So who had set the alarm I'd noticed beside the bed? It was set for five, and Soderman and I had been in the house from a quarter to five in the afternoon until at least quarter after. No alarm had gone off.

Daylight came shortly after five. Supposing someone wanted to be away from the house while it was still dark . . . An interesting speculation.

That afternoon I sent a wire, in code, to my home office.

Soderman would find out that I had sent it, and that coded message was going to worry him.

My feet ached from walking. I went up the stairs to my room and lay down across the bed. There had to be an angle, somewhere. I sat up and took off my shoes, but when I had the left one in my hand, I froze with it there and stared at the rim of the sole and the space in front of the heel.

Both were marked with still-damp red mud!

It hit me like an ax. That red mud came from the wet place around the pump near the jail! Anybody getting water from that pump would get mud on their shoes. On a rainy day, it would be much worse.

Soderman.

Certainly it might not have been Soderman who killed Marshall. And yet it could have been.

III

I T WAS FULL dark when I opened my eyes. Groggily, soaked with perspiration, I climbed off the bed and passed a shaky hand over my face. My head ached and I felt tired.

Fighting a desire to lie down again, I stripped off my clothes and had another bath. I dressed in fresh clothing and slid my gun back into my waistband. Then I walked along the hall and down the stairs.

The usual gang was in the lobby. Four or five men loafed at the bar, and one of them was Soderman. He glanced up when I came down the steps, and he didn't look friendly. He looked as if he hated my innards. Several of the townspeople looked at me, but I didn't stop. Across the street was a small cafe, catering mostly to tourists. I walked over. I felt better, felt like eating.

A tall teenager waited on me, a girl who had not yet grown into her lanky body or her large, interested eyes.

When she put the glass of water on my table, she said, "There was a woman in here looking for you. Very pretty, too."

"Yeah?" I was surprised. "Not Mrs. Marshall?"

The waitress made a face. "No, much nicer!"

I said, "I take it that you don't care for Donna Marshall?"

"She's none of my business. I don't imagine she'll be here long, now that she has his money."

"This your home?"

"Me and my mother, she owns this place."

"Father?"

"Dead. He was killed in the mine."

"Cave-in?"

"Yes. It happened about ten years ago. They had to open a new drift into the mine, and sink a new shaft. The old one was down in the canyon, east of the new entrance."

The coffee was good. So was the steak.

"They never use that old entrance?" I asked her.

"Oh, no! It's very dangerous! No one has been in that way in years. It was tried, but there's a hanging wall of stone that is all cracked and it might collapse. Nothing has ever been done about it as they never go that way, but Jerry Wilson was in partway, and he said he never saw a worse-looking place. A shout or a sharp sound might bring the whole thing down. Anyway, the new part of the mine is west of there and so it doesn't matter."

That was interesting. Mines weren't new to me, especially hard rock mines. I'd run a stoper and a liner, those were drilling rigs, in more than one hole, and had done my share of timbering and mucking. I knew, too, that in a town of this size, in mining country, nearly everybody worked in the mines at one time or another.

A woman was looking for me. That would probably be the Campbell girl, but whatever she wanted would have to wait. I had plans. This was going to be my busy night, and with luck I could wind this case up tighter than a drum.

With luck.

It was going to take the devil's own luck to help me, for I was going to stick my neck out, way out.

Weber, the watchman at the mine, was the backbone of the case against Campbell. Weber had seen Tom Marshall go into the mine. He had seen Campbell go in, and nobody else had gone in at all. Campbell had motive and opportunity, and if others had motives, and none had been brought up, they hadn't had opportunity.

When I thought of what lay ahead, I had a notion to chuck it. A good night's sleep, the morning bus, and back to Los Angeles in a matter of hours. Lew Marshall hadn't told me how long I should stay on the job, only that I look into it. Well, I had looked into it. I had interviewed Donna Marshall, talked with the deputy sheriff and the accused, and I'd examined the situation. Out of that I could make a tight, accurate report that would earn me my money and look all right to anyone.

What it wouldn't do would be plenty. It would leave the murderer in the clear, for in my own mind I was morally certain that Campbell was not guilty. I've always thought there is no such thing as a perfect crime; there are just imperfect investigators. Contrary to what many believe, P.I.'s rarely get to solve crimes, but if I had a shot at it here, I didn't want myself listed with the imperfect.

Marshall went into the mine. Campbell went in. Campbell came out, and Marshall was found dead. That would make sense to any jury.

For me, it wasn't enough. I was always a contrary sort of a cuss, and when I looked at that sultry babe who had done duty as Marshall's wife, I began to wonder. She was sexy, she was lazy, she was untidy, but she had a body that would have stirred excitement in the veins of a crutch-using octogenarian.

Moreover, if I had ever looked into the eyes of a woman who was completely and entirely selfish, it was Donna Marshall.

Add to that one young, rugged, and handsome deputy sheriff and you've got trouble. They could have Campbell. For me, I'd hang my case on the skirts of Donna Marshall. She was the kind who bred murder and violence. And unless I had made a serious mistake, she had Soderman in the palm of her hand.

Or did she? Men like Soderman are not easy to handle. They live on a hair trigger and they backfire easily.

Sitting over my coffee, thinking of that, I heard the screen door slam and glanced up to see Marian Campbell coming toward me. She must have been hot and tired, but she looked as neat and lovely as she had when I first saw her getting on the bus in L.A.

She came right over to my table and sat down, and then the door opened again and the fat man I'd met on the bus came in. He glanced at me, then at Marian, and then he walked to another table and sat down. He ordered beer.

"What have you found out?" Marian's gray eyes were wide and beautiful.

"Not much, yet." It pays to be cautious. After all, why give her hope when there was no evidence?

"I know he didn't do it! You've got to believe me. Is there any way I can help?"

"Not yet," I said. Harbater was guzzling his beer. He looked at me, his sharp eyes probing.

The poor fool wonders if I'm still carrying that gun, I thought. Busybody if I ever saw one.

Marian Campbell sat there across the table from me, the picture of unhappiness. Me, I'm a sucker for an unhappy girl, and I looked up and stuck my neck out all the way.

"I don't want to raise any hopes," I said, "but I know in my own mind your father is innocent. And if I can, I'll prove it."

Her head came up sharply, and the look in her eyes was an excuse for anything. "Oh, if you could save him, I'd do anything for you!"

Why are women so free with promises like that?

The fat man was looking at me, then at the girl. I wondered what he was thinking, and if he had overheard. Suddenly, I was willing to bet a nickel he had.

The door slammed open and Soderman came in. He looked around, then saw me talking to Marian. He came across the room and sat down at the table, jerking a chair out with a quick movement and sitting down hard. He rested those big forearms on the table and stared at me, his eyes ugly.

"Didn't I tell you to leave town?" He spoke harshly, and it stirred something in me.

I've never hunted trouble, but in a lifetime of knocking around in rough places, I've had more than my share. Big guys always aroused something in me. They made the hair along the back of my neck stiffen like a strange bulldog would.

"You've been watching too many movies," I answered. "I told you I was staying, and I meant that. Until this case is busted wide open, I am staying."

Now I followed it up by saying too much, and I knew it, but I was mad. Mad clear through. "You've arrested an innocent man, and maybe you know he's innocent, but I'm going to free him, and brother, when I do, I'm going to hang a noose around the neck of the guilty parties!"

The veins in his forehead swelled and I thought he was coming right across the table at me. He glared for a moment or two, his big hands on the tabletop, and I sat there, tipped back a little in my chair, but my feet braced for quick movement.

Slowly, his face changed and it turned white around the eyes. He eased back into his chair, relaxing all his muscles. He was worried as well as mad. I knew then that I had him. If he had known nothing beyond what he was supposed to know, if he had been sure Campbell was guilty and not had some doubts of his own, he'd have slugged me.

"You're asking for trouble," he said, looking out from under his eyebrows at me, "and you're biting off more than you can chew."

"That's possible," I agreed, "but so has somebody else, and what they bit off is going to give them acute indigestion."

I shoved my hands down in my pockets. "Soderman," I said, "you've been a miner. You know enough about mines to get around in one. Well, I've worked in a few myself. And," I added, "I know something of the history of this one. Enough to know that Weber's evidence isn't worth a tinker's damn!"

His eyes flickered a little. "If you're thinking about the old shaft, you're wrong. It can't be used."

"Tried it?" I suggested.

He could see where that led, and he let something come

into his eyes that told me he was going to like taking a poke at me.

"No," he said. "But it was abandoned because it was too dangerous. A man would be a fool to crawl into that hole. The hanging wall of that big stope needs only a jar and the whole blamed mountain would come down. It gives me the creeps even to look in there."

Knowing what unmaintained tunnels were like, I could agree with him. It made me sweat to think of it, and yet I knew then that I was going to sweat some more, because I *was* going to try it. If I could get from the old workings into the new, to the place where Marshall was killed, then I could establish a reasonable doubt as to Campbell's guilt.

Soderman shoved back from the table and got up. When he did, I happened to glance at Harbater sitting over his beer. His eyes were on Soderman, and in them was contempt . . . contempt and something more. The something more was hate.

Why should a stranger hate Soderman?

After a few more words I got up and left Marian, paid the check and went out.

It was cool and dark in the street, and I turned toward the hotel, taking my time. Across the way, and on the side of the ravine, the gallows frame over the shaft of the Dunhill loomed against the sky. It was too early for that. I went back to the hotel, up to my room.

Although I turned on the light, I didn't stay there. Stepping out into the hall, I took a quick gander each way, then moved down to the door of a room about twenty feet from my own. The lock was simple for my pick, and I went in, easing the door shut. The bag was locked, but a few moments with another pick and it opened. In the bag I found a pair of coveralls and a flashlight. Also, there was a small carbide miner's lamp, and a couple of letters that I glanced at, and some business cards.

"So?" I muttered. "It's like that, is it, my fat friend?"

There was no more time so I snapped the bag shut and slipped into the empty hall, locked the door, and returned to my own room. Ernie Harbater would have some things to explain, and it offered a new angle. I stretched out on the bed.

───

WHEN MY EYES opened, I was wide awake. A quick glance at my watch told me it was after midnight. Easing out of bed, I dressed, checked over my gun, and then picked up a carbide lamp, a more modern model than the one my neighbor down the hall had with him. For luck, I dropped a pencil flashlight in my pocket, then another clip for the rod.

The hall was like a tomb. I listened a moment, then slipped out and closed the door. At the end of the hall, I opened the back door and slipped out to the stairway. Cool air blew across my face. The door shut after me.

Only one light showed. It was the watchman's shack at the Dunhill. I turned and started away toward the ravine and the old workings that the girl in the cafe had told me about. The trail was overgrown with coarse grass, and at one point a small slide had blocked it. I crawled over and went along the trail to the collar of the old inclined shaft. There was a vague light, reflected off the nearby rocks from the shack above. It was just enough to see where I was walking and the shape of things nearby.

The abandoned hoist house was there, and beyond it I could see the shaft slanting steeply down. Rusted tracks were under my feet, and once I stubbed a toe on the end of a tie.

When I got there, to the collar of the shaft, I stopped. It had seemed cool, but I was sweating now.

IV

HERE, WHERE I stood, there was a level place where waste rock from the mine had been dumped and smoothed off. Across the narrow canyon the opposite side loomed up black against the night, and above it there was a scattering of bright desert stars. It was still, so still a person might almost have heard the movement of a bat's wing.

Breeze touched my face gently, drying the perspiration on my cheeks.

To my left the mine opened, black as death. Nobody needed to tell me this might be my last look at the stars. Old mines were something I knew all too well. I knew the thick, loose dirt of the floor, gray and ancient, untouched by any breeze, undisturbed by any walking foot. I knew the pale dust that gathers on the side walls of the drifts and lies in a mantle over the chutes and the rusted ore cars.

I knew how the ancient timbers crack and groan with the weight of a mountain on their shoulders, and I knew how the strain on those timbers grew, how the hanging walls of the drifts and stopes began to buckle. Water would seep through, finding cracks and private ways, weakening the vast weight above. The guts of the mountain lay there suspended, a gigantic trap for the unwary.

I walked into the mine entrance. When I had felt my way along for thirty feet, and the opening was gray light in back and above me, I put my hand over the reflector of the carbide lamp and struck sharply to light it, brushing the tiny wheel against the flint. Flame spurted from the burner; a long, knifelike jet of flame standing out at least six inches and hissing comfortably. I turned it down to a mere two inches and, drawing a deep breath, started down the steep incline that led into the old workings of the mine.

When I had gone fifty yards or so, the floor became level and I passed the first ladder leading upward into a stope and, beside it, two chutes. Under one of them stood an ancient, rusted ore car.

A little farther on there were more chutes, and I continued walking. So far the timbering was in fair shape. From my few careful inquiries and a study of the map I'd obtained, I thought I could tell where the troublesome area began, but when I had gone beyond the last of the chutes, I realized I need not have worried about that. I stopped and flashed my light farther ahead; then I knew what hell was like.

When a vein of ore is discovered off of a mine tunnel, the miners follow it, hollowing out the richest rock to form what they call a stope. These man-made caverns are often too large to be supported by timbers and are the most dangerous areas in a mine . . . especially an older, unmaintained mine.

The tunnel before me fell away into blackness and vanished. It was not hard to see what had happened. Evidently, there had been a stope below the level on which I stood, and the unreinforced ceiling, or hanging wall, had caved in. Dead ahead of me the floor of the drift broke sharply off, and it was a good ten feet to the heaped-up, broken rock below. I raised my eyes and looked across at least a hundred feet of open space, lighted weirdly by the flame, turned up to its highest now.

The roof of the drift above me had been hollowed out, turning this section of tunnel into another stope, probably trying to follow the vein of ore from below. Flashing my light upward, I could vaguely see the hanging wall of the section ahead, and for the first time I could appreciate the term. The roof of upper stope was, literally, hanging.

Great cracks showed, and the rock on either side of the cracks sagged ominously. Water dripped through and the whole roof of the huge chamber bulged downward, waiting, it seemed, for no more than a gesture or a sudden sound to give way with all the crushing power of the mountain above it.

How long it had hung that way, I did not know. And I had to lower myself down to the rubble below and make my way across it to the tunnel beyond. I could not see that drift, nor did I know exactly where it was. I only knew it was there, and if I was to prove my theory, I had to cross this open stretch alive.

For a moment I stood, listening. There is no soundlessness such as the silence far under the earth. There is no dark such as that absolute blackness where there is complete absence of light. Yet here, it was not quite soundless, for there was something, vague, yet ominously present. A drip of water so quiet as not to be identified? A distant trickling of sand? Whatever it was, at times the mountain seemed to sigh, the earth to move, ever so slightly, like a restless sleeper.

Putting my lamp down on the lip of the cave-in at my feet,

I lowered myself as far as I could, got my lamp in one hand, then let go. It was a short drop and I landed safely. Carefully, trying to forget the threatening bulges above my head, I began working my way over the heaped-up boulders and debris, mingled with a few timbers from smashed chutes, toward the opposite wall.

When I was almost halfway across, something made me turn and look back. On the lip of the old drift where a few minutes ago I had stood, there was a light!

Fear came up in my throat like a strangling hand. Backing away, I watched the light like a bird watches a snake. I am not a coward, nor yet a brave man. A fight I always liked, but one thing I knew—I wanted no fighting here.

Then I saw the gun.

The man, or woman, who held the light had a gun. I could see the shine of the barrel in the glow from the flame. I was not afraid of being shot, for a bullet would mean nothing here. If that pistol was fired in this stope, neither of us would ever live to tell the story. It would mean complete and sudden extinction.

Moving back again, I saw the gun lift, and I spoke, trying to keep my voice low, for any sudden sound might be all that was needed.

"If you want to live, don't fire that gun. If you do, we'll both die. Look at the hanging wall."

The light held still.

"Look at the roof," I said. "The top of the stope."

The light lifted and pointed up, showing those ugly cracks and the great bulge of rocks.

"If you fire that gun, the whole roof will cave in. It will take that drift with it." I was still backing up with occasional swift glances around as the light allowed some vague outline of what lay behind me.

My mind was working swiftly as I backed away. I knew something now, something that had been disturbing me all day. It was a new idea and, while a puzzling one, it revealed much and made many things clear.

Whoever it was showed hesitation now. I could almost feel the mind working, could sense what he or she must be thinking. Trying to judge what was true and what not. The person over there wanted, desperately, to kill me, yet there was an element of danger.

Suddenly, the light went out. Then I heard a grating, a slide, and a sodden sound. Whoever it was had dropped to the floor of the stope!

Instantly, I put my own light out.

We were in complete darkness now. Gently, I shifted a foot. Backing as carefully as I could, I got to the wall. I wanted the killer, and I was sure in my own mind that the killer faced me in the stope, yet I wanted no trouble there. The slightest vibration might bring that hanging wall down, and I wanted no part of that.

My foot hit the wall behind me. If the drift was there, it would be above me, probably out of reach. The muck over which I had been crawling had been slanting down, carrying me even lower than the original ten feet.

I heard a rock fall, and knew the killer was coming up on me in the dark. He was closing in.

What did he expect to do? The chances were, he also had a knife. Sweat poured down my face and ran down my skin under my shirt. Dust came up in my nostrils. The air seemed very hot, and very close. I backed up. Then, suddenly, a cool movement of air touched my cheek.

Keeping it in my face, I edged toward it. I put my hand out and found emptiness. Feeling around, I found the arch of the top of a tunnel. The hole was no more than two feet wide, and chances were the drift was not over seven or eight feet high. Wedging myself in the hole, I dropped.

My feet hit first and there was a tiny splash of water. I got my balance and started rapidly along the drift. Once, I bumped hard into the wall at a turn, and once around it I got my light going, but turned it down to a very feeble glow. Then I ran swiftly along the drift, my lungs gasping for air.

Tom Marshall's body had been discovered at the bottom of a winze well back in the mine. Calculating my own descent through the stope, I believed myself to be on the level where the body had been found. He had been knocked on the head and dropped down the winze.

Hurrying on through the old workings of the mine, I came suddenly to some recent timbering. I had just crawled over a pile of waste that almost filled a crosscut running from the dead-end drift of the old workings into the new. In a matter of minutes I had found the winze.

Here it was. Dark stains on the rock were obvious enough. Once, I thought I heard a sound, and flashed the light down the drift that ran out the other side of the air shaft. There was nothing. Kneeling, I began to study the rocks. It was just a chance I could find something, some clue.

The tiny splash of water between the ties of the track jerked me out of a brown study. My lamp hung on the wall, and I came up fast. I was too slow.

A gigantic fist smashed out of somewhere, and I was knocked rolling. Lights exploded in my brain and I rolled over, getting to my knees. Soderman was calmly hooking his lamp to the wall. He turned then and started toward me, and I made it to my feet, weaving. He swung, low and hard, and I caught the punch on my forearm and swung my right. It caught him on the side of the face but he kept coming. Toe-to-toe we started to slug it out, weaving, smashing, swinging, forward and back, splashing in the water, our bodies looming black and awful in the glare of the two flickering lights.

There was blood in my mouth and my breath was coming hard. He closed with me, trying for a headlock, but I struck him behind the knee and it buckled, sending him down. I jerked my head free and kicked him in the ribs. He lunged to his feet and I hit him again, then he dived for me and I gave him my knee in the face.

Bloody and battered, he lunged in, taking my left and getting both hands on me. His fingers clamped hard on my throat and blackness swam up and engulfed me. Agonizing pains swept over me, and I swung my legs up high and got one of them across the top of his head, jerking him back. Then I crossed the other one over his face and, with all the power that was in them, crushed him back toward the floor. He was on his knees astride me, and I thought I'd break his back, but he was old at this game, too, and suddenly he hurled himself back, giving way to my pressure, and got his legs free.

Both of us came up, bloody and staggering. I swung one from my heels into his wind. He grunted like a stuck hog, and I let him have the other one. At that, it took three of them to bring him down, and I stood there in the flickering light, gasping to get my breath back.

Then the tunnel swam around me, the floor seemed to heave, and our lights went out. A moment later there came a dull boom.

V

SODERMAN, ON THE floor at my feet, came out of it with a grunt.

"What . . . was that?" The words were muffled through his swollen lips.

Feeling along the wall for my lamp, I let him have it. "I think they've blown the entrance to this drift."

Holding the lamp in my left hand, I struck at the reflector with my palm. On the third strike I got a light. The flame leaped out, strong and bright.

Soderman was sitting up. His face looked terrible but his eyes were clear. "Blown up?" The idea got to him. "Bottled us in, huh!" That made me think, and I watched him closely.

He didn't throw a fit or start rushing around or exclaiming, and I liked that. He got up. Then he stared at me, frankly puzzled.

He said, "Who would do it? Why?"

"Soderman," I said, "you're a good fighter, but you've got nothing for brains. You and me, we're the only two people alive who know who killed Tom Marshall, and I'm the only one knows why!"

He stared at me, blinking. Then he got his light and set it going. He shook his head. "That ain't reasonable. It can't be!"

"It is," I said, "and it isn't going to do us much good. If I'm not mistaken, we're bottled up here. Anybody know you were coming here?"

"She did. Nobody else."

"Nobody knew I was coming, either. That means nobody is going to start wondering for a while where either of us are."

"She wouldn't do that! Why, she—" He was taking it hard.

"Buddy, Donna Marshall may have preferred you to her husband, enough to play around a little, anyway, but there was something she preferred to either of you."

"What was that?" He scowled at me, not liking it.

"Money."

"But how would she figure money?"

"This mine is worth dough. Also, Tom Marshall had a hundred thousand in insurance."

He studied that one over for a while, staring at his light. Then he started to move. "Let's have a look."

Soderman led the way and we slogged along through the mud and water toward where the main elevator station should be. Coming up from the old workings as I did, I had not been through here before, there was more to that hole than it looked like, and both of us were tired. Suddenly, after ten minutes or so of walking, our lights flashed on a slide of rock closing off the drift. He looked around a little, and his face got grim.

"Oh, they did it right!" he said. "They did it very right! This is a hundred yards inside the main drift. The chances are it caved all the way to the elevator station. We couldn't dig through that in a month!"

We didn't waste any time talking about it. We turned around and started back. "You must have come in through the big stope," he said over his shoulder. "How was it?"

"Nasty," I said, "and I'd bet a pretty penny there's no stope there now. That roof was the shakiest-looking thing I've seen."

"Roof?" he said. "I thought you were a miner. You mean, hanging wall."

"Yes," I said, "that's what I mean." The reason I said it was because I was checking up on him, just to be sure, and things were clicking into place in my skull. "If I get out of this," I added, "I'm gonna see somebody swing!"

We only needed one look. The big stope through which I'd come a short time before was gone. Debris bulged into the drift from it, and part of the drift down which I'd come had caved in. We were shut off, entombed.

He stood there, staring at me, and he looked sick. I'd bet a plugged dime I looked sicker.

"Listen," I said, "you've worked in this hole. I haven't. Isn't there anyplace we could get out? An air shaft? An old prospect hole? Anything?"

"No." He shook his head. "Looks like we've bought it, bud."

———

I SAT DOWN on a boulder and got out my map.

"Let's look this over," I said. "If there's an angle, it's here."

Over my shoulder, he started to study it with me. Here, on paper, was a blueprint of the mine. And a cross section of all the workings, old and new.

We didn't have to study that blueprint long to know we were bottled up tighter than a Scotchman at a wake. There had been only two openings to this section of the mine, and they were plugged. On the other side of the elevator station there was a series of vent shafts, but they could just as well have been in China.

"We're sunk!" Soderman said. "She's fixed us plenty."

That blueprint lay there on my knee. "Hey!" I said. "Didn't I see a powder locker back down this drift?"

"Uh-huh, so what? Do we blow ourselves up?"

"Look at this two-twenty drift," I suggested. "It cuts mighty close to the edge of the hill. Supposing we set up a liner and see what we can do?"

He looked at me, then he bent over and turned a valve on the air pipe. It blasted a sharp, clear stream of air. "The compressor's still running." He looked at me and then chuckled. "What have we got to lose?"

The two-hundred-twenty-foot drift was higher than ours but it didn't connect to any of the shafts leading out of the mine. All the ore from that level was dropped down chutes to this level to be trammed out. We got a drill and carried it up into the two twenty and set it up facing the wall of the drift. Then we rustled some drill steel. None of it was very sharp, but there was still some part of an edge on it.

Neither of us was saying a thing. We both knew what the joker was. There were no figures on that blueprint to show how much distance there was between the wall of the drift and the outside. It might be eight feet, it might be ten, or twenty or fifty. The one figure we needed wasn't on that blueprint.

We didn't think about that because we didn't want to. Regardless of our fight, we went into this like a team. After all, we were miners, even though it had been a time since either of us had run a machine.

We connected the air hoses and started to work. The rattle and pound of the drill roared in the closed-in drift. He bored in with one length of steel, but when he'd drilled in as far as the steel would go, he didn't change to a longer bit, he shifted to another hole instead of completing this one. If need be, we could always load what we had and blast on chance.

Hour after hour passed. At times, despite the fact that we were afraid they would shut the main compressor down, we let the air blast freely into the drift, cooling us and making sure we had breathing air. Then we would connect the hose again and go back to work.

Nobody ever put in eight holes any faster than we did. Taking turns, we ran them in as deep as we could, having an ugly time fighting that dull steel. While he was working, I combed the mine for more of it, and while I was working, he brought up some powder and primers from the store on the level below.

We finally tore our machine down and lugged it out of there. Then we loaded the holes and split the fuses. Then we got as far away as we could, and waited with our mouths open for the blast. Maybe that wasn't necessary. Waiting with our mouths open, I mean, but neither of us knew what effect the blast would have when both openings of the mine were sealed.

We heard the *thump thump thump* of the blasts, and got up and started in after counting the shots. The air was still blue with powder smoke, but we moved over the muck to the face. A nice little crosscut was blasted, but there was solid rock at the end of it.

Without any talk, we mucked out a space and set up the liner again. This time he used several bits in the same hole, and I watched him. Suddenly, the drill leaped ahead. He just turned and looked at me, and neither of us needed to say a word. It had gone through!

We ran another hole and then, getting impatient, we loaded them and came out of the drift again. When the shots went, we started on the run, and before we had gone fifty feet we could feel the cool night air on our faces!

The hole wasn't big, but we got out. Soderman looked at me.

"We did it, pal! We did it!" he said. Then he added, "Mister, that's the last time I *ever* go underground until they bury me! I mean it!"

Me? I was already walking. I am not a guy who gets sore very often, but I was sore now, and I had my own ideas about what to do. My rod was still in my waistband, and that was where I wanted it.

———

THERE WERE SWARMS of people around the shaft collar when we came down the hill. Somebody saw us, and a yell went up. "Who set off that powder? Were you in there?"

Neither of us said anything; we saw Donna Marshall standing there in slacks and a sweater, and her face looked yellow as yeast. Behind her was a short, fat man with thick thighs and a round, pasty face. When I first saw him, I'd thought his eyes were cruel, and even now they looked it, frightened as he was.

Ten feet away from them, I stopped, and the crowd sort of fell back. I turned to Soderman. "Do it," I said.

"Donna Marshall!" he called out. "I'm arresting you for the murder of your husband, Tom Marshall!"

Harbater was edgy, and while I'd looked at her, I had an

eye on him, too. When Soderman spoke her name and everyone's eyes shifted, Harbater's hand jabbed down in his pocket and he shot so fast it made me blink. The bullet went into the ground between my feet, and because he'd never pulled the gun clear of his pocket, he was having trouble raising it farther. He tried to jerk it out of his coat. I aimed and shot, my bullet breaking his kneecap and knocking him down. Then I stepped in, kicked his hand away, and pulled the gun from his pocket. He lay on the ground groaning.

We locked them up and called for the doctor. Mrs. Marshall cursed the deputy like a truck driver, then demanded a lawyer and went to sit in the corner of her cell. When we came out, Soderman was scowling at me. "Now fill me in. Who is this guy?" he wanted to know.

"He's the insurance salesman who sold Tom Marshall his policy. I met him coming up here. He had been reading a magazine on the bus, all crumpled and one corner torn off the cover. Later, I saw that magazine at Donna Marshall's, where he had evidently forgotten it. We probably only missed him by a few minutes.

"At first, I couldn't figure the guy. But I saw some papers in his room and everything began to click into place. The only thing that messed me up was you."

"Me?" Soderman looked around, his neck getting red.

"Well," I said, "she's a good-looking babe, and you wouldn't be the first guy who got into trouble over one. I think Tom Marshall bought that gun for you. He was wise to you, but didn't want to tackle you barehanded. I guess we'll never know. That alarm clock set for five was partly the tipoff. I knew *he* didn't need it." I chuckled. "It must have been tough that last time, under that bed. How long did you have to stay there?"

He scowled at me. "How did you know *that*?" Then he grinned sheepishly. "The alarm didn't go off that morning, and when I looked out of the window, he was coming up the hill. There I was in full sight of the whole town if I tried to leave, so I crawled under the bed, and that guy stayed there all day long!"

I laughed, and he scowled at me again. "It ain't funny!" he

said. "And to think that babe made a sucker out of me! I thought you were tryin' to frame her to save the estate for Lew Marshall."

He rubbed his ear. "Who do you think actually did the killing?"

"I'm betting on the insurance man. Came in through that old working and killed Marshall, then got out. He followed me in there tonight, but I got away. Then he went back and blasted the tunnel entrance. But that'll be tough to prove."

"Oh, no. His pants will prove it. In that old working there's a streak of limestone, blue lime, and the ore evidently occurred as replacements of the limestone. In the new workings the ore mostly occurs with quartz monazite. There's no limestone at all in the new workings. If he crawled over those rocks in the big stope, some of that lime will be in his clothes."

"Now that's good!" I chuckled. "I've got more on Harbater. I frisked his room in the hotel and found some coveralls he used and a miner's lamp. He probably used the coveralls the first time he came into the mine. We could test those too. You know, it would have been easy," I added, "if you hadn't come into it from so many angles!"

"Coverin' up for a dame," he said. "Well, that cures me! They ain't any good for a man!"

"Some of them are, all right," I maintained, thinking of one in particular. "Some of them are very much all right."

I got up and started for the door. It was going to be nice to see Marian at breakfast and tell her that her father was cleared. It was one part of this job I was going to like. I was still planning the way I'd tell her when I fell asleep.

TOO TOUGH TO KILL

THE BIG TRUCK coughed and roared up the last few feet of the steep grade and straightened out for the run to Mercury. Pat Collins stared sleepily down the ribbon of asphalt that stretched into the darkness beyond the reach of the lights. Momentarily, he glanced down at Ruth. She was sleeping with her head on his shoulder. Even Deek Peters, the deputy sheriff detailed to guard him, had been lulled to sleep by the droning of the heavy motor and the warmth of the cab.

Pat shook himself, and succeeded in opening his eyes wider. He had been going day and night for weeks it seemed. The three-hundred-mile run to Millvale and back was to be his last trip. Two weeks off for his honeymoon, and then back at a better job. Right now he and Ruth would have been on the train headed west if it hadn't been for the killing.

Why couldn't Augie Petrone have been given the works somewhere else than right in front of his truck as he left Mercury! Because of that they had detained him several hours for questioning in Millvale, and now, knowing him to be the only witness, they had detailed Peters to guard him. He wished Tony Calva and Cokey Raiss would do their killing elsewhere next time. It had been them all right. He remembered them both from the old days and had seen them both clearly as they pumped shot after shot into Petrone's body as his car lay jammed against a fire hydrant. There had been another man, too, a big gunman. He hadn't recognized him, but he would remember his face.

Suddenly a long black car shot by the truck and wheeled to a stop. Almost in the same instant, three men piled out into the road. Two of them had tommy guns. For an instant Pat hesitated upon the verge of wheeling the truck into them, full speed. Then he remembered Ruth there beside him, Ruth the girl he had just married but a few hours before. With a curse he slammed on the brakes as Deek Peters suddenly came to life.

"All right," Calva snarled, motioning with the .45 he carried. "Out of that cab! One wrong move an' I'll blast the guts out of you!"

Peters let out an oath, and whipped up his shotgun. The .45 barked viciously, and then again, and the deputy sheriff slumped from the seat to the pavement. Shakily, Pat helped Ruth down and they stood to one side. Her eyes were wide and dark, and she avoided looking at the tumbled body of the deputy.

"Well, would you look who's here!" Raiss grinned, stepping forward. "The smart boy who talks so much has brought his girlfriend along for us!"

"All right, you two!" Calva snapped. "Crawl in that car and don't let's have a single yap out of you!"

Pat's face was white and tense. He squeezed Ruth's hand, but his mouth felt dry, and he kept wetting his lips with his tongue. He knew Tony Calva and Cokey Raiss only too well. Both were killers. It was generally believed that Raiss had been the man behind the gun in most of the gang killings around Mercury in the past three years. Tony Calva was bodyguard for Dago John Fagan. There were two other men in the car, one sat at the wheel, and the other had stopped in the door, a tommy gun lying carelessly in the hollow of his arm.

Ruth got in, and the man with the tommy gun gave her a cool, thin-lipped smile that set the blood pounding in Pat's ears. The gun muzzle between his shoulders made him realize that there was still a chance. They hadn't killed him yet, and perhaps they wouldn't. As long as he was alive there was a chance of helping Ruth.

"You guys got me," he said suddenly. "Let my wife go, why don't you? She'll promise not to talk!"

"Fat chance!" Raiss sneered. "Why didn't you keep your trap shut? If you hadn't spouted off to those coppers in Millvale you might have picked up a couple of C's some night."

He paused, and turned to stare at Ruth. "No, we'll keep the twist. She's a good-lookin' dame, and we boys may have to hide out somewhere. It gets kinda lonesome, you know."

Pat's muscles tightened, but he held himself still, watching for a chance. The car swung off down the paving in the direction from which he had come, and then wheeled suddenly into a rutted side road. Sitting in the darkness of the car with a gun behind his ear, Pat tried to think, tried to remember.

———

THE ROAD THEY were on was one he hadn't traveled in years, but he did know that it led to the river. The river!

Suddenly, the car stopped. While the thin, white-faced gunman held a pistol to his head, he was forced from the car. Raiss was waiting for him, and Calva sat in the car watching Ruth like a cat watching a mouse.

They were on the bridge. Pat remembered the current was strong along here, and the river deep. There were four of them, and they all had guns. He might get one, but that wouldn't help. They might turn Ruth loose, they might just be talking that way to torture him.

"Don't shoot, Cokey," Calva said suddenly. "Just knock him in the head and let the river do it. There's a farm up here on the hill."

Suddenly, Ruth tried to leap from the car, but Calva caught her by the arm and jerked her back. Pat's face set grimly, but in that instant Raiss moved forward and brought the gun barrel down across his head in a vicious, sideswiping blow.

An arrow of pain shot through him, and he stumbled, and almost went down. He lurched toward Raiss, and the gunman hit him again, and again. Then suddenly he felt himself falling, and something else hit him. He toppled off the bridge, and the dark water closed over his head.

———

HOURS LATER, IT seemed, he opened his eyes. At first he was conscious of nothing but the throbbing pain in his head, the surging waves of pain that went all over him. Then slowly, he began to realize he was cold.

He struggled, and something tore sharply at his arm. Then he realized where he was and what had happened. He was caught in a barbed-wire fence that extended across the river about three hundred yards below the bridge from which his body had been tumbled.

Cautiously, he unfastened his clothes from the wire, and clinging to the fence, worked his way to shore. He walked up the bank, and then tumbled and lay flat upon his face in the grass. For a long time he lay still, then he sat up slowly.

He had no idea of how much time had passed. It was still dark. They had, it seemed, tumbled him off the bridge for dead, not knowing about the fence. It was only a miracle that he hadn't gone down to stay before the barbs caught his clothing and held him above water.

Gingerly, he ran his fingers along his scalp. It tingled with the pain of his touch, and he realized it was badly cut. He groped his way to his feet, and started toward the road. He remembered the farm they had said was up above. Almost blind with pain, he staggered along the road, his head throbbing.

Ahead of him the fence opened, and he could see the black bulk of the farmhouse looming up through the night. Amid the fierce barking of a big shepherd dog, he lurched up to the door and pounded upon it.

It opened suddenly. Pat Collins looked up and found himself staring into the wide, sleepy eyes of an elderly farmer.

"Wha—what's goin' on here?" the farmer began. "What you mean—!"

"Listen," Pat broke in suddenly. "I'm Pat Collins. You call the sheriff at Mercury an' tell him Raiss an' Calva waylaid my truck an' knocked me in the head. Tell him they got my wife. Tell him I think they went to The Cedars."

The farmer, wide awake now, caught him by the arm as he lurched against the doorpost, "Come in here, Collins. You're bad hurt!"

Almost before he realized it the farmer's wife had put some coffee before him and he was drinking it in great gulps. It made him feel better.

"You got a car?" he demanded, as the farmer struggled to raise central. "I want to borrow a car."

The farmer's wife went into the next room and he hurriedly pulled on the dry clothes she had brought him.

"Please, I need help. You know me, I'm Pat Collins, and I drive for the Mercury Freighting Company, Dave Lyons will back me. If there's any damage to the car I'll pay."

The farmer turned from the telephone. "Mary, get this young man my pistol and those extra shells, an' get the car key out of my pants pocket." He paused, and rang the phone desperately. Then he looked back at Collins. "I know you, son, I seen you down about the markets many a time. We read in the paper today about you witnessin' that killin'. I reckon they published that story too soon!"

———

As THE FARMER'S car roared to life, Pat could hear the man shouting into the phone, and knew he had reached Mercury and the sheriff. Coming up the hill from the river the memory of Dago John's old roadhouse at The Cedars had flashed across Pat's mind. A chance remark from one of the gunmen came to him now as he swung the coupe out on the road, and whirled off at top speed.

It had only been a short time since they had slugged him and dropped him in the river. They would be expecting no pursuit, no danger.

Two miles, three, four, five. Then he swung the car into a dark side road, and stopped. The lights had been turned off minutes before. Carefully, he checked the load in the old six-shooter, and with a dozen shells shaking loose in his pocket, he started down the road.

His head throbbed painfully, but he felt surprisingly able. It wasn't for nothing that he had played football, boxed, and wrestled all his life.

He reached the edge of the fence around the acres where the old roadhouse stood. The place had been deserted since prohibition days. Dago John had made this his headquarters at one time. Carefully, he crawled over the fence.

Pat Collins was crouched against the wall before he saw

the car parked in the garage behind the building. The door had been left open, as though they hadn't contemplated staying. Through a thin edge of light at the bottom of a window he could see what went on inside.

Three men, Tony Calva, Cokey Raiss, and the white-faced gunman, were sitting at the table. Ruth was putting food on the table.

Pat drew back from the window, and suddenly, his ear caught the tiniest sound as a foot scraped on gravel. He whirled just in time to see the dark shadow of a man loom up before him. He lashed out with a vicious right hand that slammed into the man's body, and he felt it give. Then Pat stepped in, crashing both hands to the chin in a pretty one-two that stretched the surprised gangster flat.

Quickly, Pat dropped astride him and slugged him on the chin as hard as he could lay them in. Afraid the sound had attracted attention, he crawled to his feet, scooping the gun-man's automatic as he got up. He opened the door.

"Come on in, Red," the gunman said, without looking up, but Pat fired as he spoke, and the white-faced gangster froze in his chair.

With an oath, Calva dropped to the floor, shooting as he fell. A bullet ripped through Pat's shirt, and another snapped against the wall behind his head and whined away across the room. Pat started across the room. Suddenly he was mad, mad clear through. Both guns were spouting fire, and he could see Raiss was on his feet, shooting back.

Something struck Pat a vicious blow in the right shoulder, and his gun hand dropped to his side. But the left gun was still there, and Raiss sagged across the table, spilling the soup. Coolly, Pat fired again, and the body twitched. He turned drunkenly to see Calva lifting a tommy gun. Then Ruth suddenly stepped through the door and hurled a can of tomatoes that struck Calva on the head.

Pat felt his knees give way, and he was on the floor, but Calva was lifting the tommy gun again. Pat fired, and the gangster sagged forward.

Collins lurched to his feet swaying dizzily. Far down the

road he could hear the whine of police sirens, and he turned to stare at Ruth.

What he saw instead was the short blocky gunman who had been in the car, the one that had shot down Petrone, and the gunman was looking at him with a twisted smile and had him covered.

———

THEY FIRED AT the same instant, and even as he felt something pound his chest, he knew his own shot had missed. He lurched, but kept his feet, weaving. The heavyset man's face bobbed queerly, and he fired at it again. Then, coolly, Pat shoved a couple more shells into his pistol, hanging the gun in his limp right hand. He took the gun in his good left hand again, and then he saw that the other man was gone.

He stared, astonished at the disappearance, and then his eyes wavered down and he saw the man lying on the floor.

Suddenly the door burst open, and the police came pouring into the room.

———

WHEN HE REGAINED consciousness he was lying on a hospital bed, and Ruth was sitting beside him.

"All right?" she whispered. He nodded and took her hand. Pat grinned sleepily.

ANYTHING FOR A PAL

TONY KINSELLA LOOKED at his platinum wristwatch. Ten more minutes. Just ten minutes to go. It was all set. In ten minutes a young man would be standing on that corner under the streetlight. Doreen would come up, speak to him, and then step into the drugstore. Once Doreen had put the finger on him, confirming that he was, in fact, the man they sought, the car would slide up, and he, Tony Kinsella, Boss Cardoza's ace torpedo, would send a stream of copper-jacketed bullets into the kid's body. It would be all over then, and Tony Kinsella would have saved his pal from the chair.

He looked up to the driver's seat where "Gloves" McFadden slouched carelessly, waiting. He noted the thick neck, and heavy, prizefighter's shoulders. In the other front seat "Dopey" Wentz stared off into the night. Kinsella didn't like that. A guy on weed was undependable. Kinsella shrugged; he didn't like it but the whole mess would soon be over.

This kid, Robbins, his name was, he'd seen Corney Watson pull the Baronski job. Tomorrow he was to identify Corney in court. Corney Watson had sprung Kinsella out of a western pen one time, so they were pals. And Kinsella, whatever his failings, had one boast: he'd do anything for a pal. Tony was proud of that. He was a right guy.

But that was only one of the two things he was proud of. The other the boys didn't know about, except in a vague way. It was his brother, George. Their name wasn't Kinsella, and George had no idea that such a name even existed. Their real name was Bretherton, but when Tony had been arrested the first time, he gave his name as Kinsella, and so it had been for a dozen years now.

Tony was proud of George. George was ten years the

youngest, and had no idea that his idolized big brother was a gangster, a killer. Tony rarely saw him, but he'd paid his way through college, and into a classy set of people. Tony smiled into the darkness. George Bretherton: now wasn't that a classy name? Maybe, when he'd put a few grand more in his sock, he'd chuck the rackets and take George off to Europe. Then he'd be Anthony Bretherton, wealthy and respected.

Kinsella leaned back against the cushions. This was one job he was pulling for nothing. Just for a pal. Corney had bumped "Baron" Baronski, and this kid had seen it. How he happened to be there, nobody knew or cared. Tomorrow he was going to testify, and that meant the chair for Corney unless Tony came through tonight, but Tony, who never failed when the chips were down, *would* come through.

They had located Robbins at a downtown hotel, a classy joint. Cardoza sent Doreen over there, and she got acquainted. Doreen was a swell kid, wore her clothes like a million, and she was wise. She had put the finger on more than one guy. This Robbins fellow, he wasn't one of Baronski's guns, so how had he been there at the time? Tony shrugged. Just one of those unfortunate things.

Why didn't George write, he wondered? He was working in a law office out west somewhere. Maybe he'd be the mouthpiece for some big corporation and make plenty of dough. That was the racket! No gang guns or coppers in that line, a safe bet.

Tony wondered what Corney was doing. Probably lying on his back in his cell hoping Kinsella would come through. Well, Tony smiled with satisfaction; he'd never botched a job yet.

SUDDENLY DOPEY HISSED: "Okay, Tony, there's the guy."

"You think! When you see Doreen comin', let me know. I'm not interested 'til then."

He suddenly found himself wishing it was over. He always felt like this at the last minute. Jumpy. Prizefighters felt that way before the bell. Nerves. But when the gun started to jump he was all right. He caressed the finned blue steel of the barrel lovingly.

"Get set, Tony, here she comes!" The powerful motor came to life, purring quietly.

Kinsella sat up and rolled down the window. The cool evening air breathed softly across his face. He looked up at the stars, and then glanced both ways, up and down the street. It was all clear.

A tall, broad-shouldered fellow stood on the corner. Tony could see Doreen coming. She was walking fast. Probably she was nervous too. That big guy. That would be him. Tony licked his lips and lifted the ugly black muzzle of the submachine gun. Its cold nose peered over the edge of the window. He saw a man walk out of the drugstore, light a cigar, and stroll off up the street. Tony almost laughed as he thought how funny it would be if he were to start shooting then, how startled that man would be!

There! Doreen was talking to the man on the corner. Had one hand on his sleeve . . . smiling at him.

God, dames were coldblooded! In a couple of minutes that guy would be kicking in his own gore, and she was putting him on the spot and smiling at him!

Suddenly she turned away and started for the drugstore on some excuse or other. As she passed through the door she was almost running. The car was moving swiftly now, gliding toward the curb, the man looked up, and the gun spouted fire. The man threw up his arms oddly, jerked sharply, and fell headlong. McFadden wheeled the car and they drove back, the machine gun spouting fire again. The body, like a sack of old clothes, jerked as the bullets struck.

———

THE NEXT MORNING Tony lay on his back staring at the ceiling. He wondered where Doreen was. Probably the papers were full of the Robbins killing. Slowly he crawled out of bed, drew on his robe, and retrieved the morning paper from his apartment door. His eyes sought the headliners, blaring across the top in bold type:

GANG GUNS SLAY FEDERAL OPERATIVE.
MACHINE GUNS GET WATSON WITNESS.

Tony's eyes narrowed. A federal man, eh? That wasn't so good. Who would have thought Robbins was a federal man? Still, they were never where you expected them to be. Probably he'd been working a case on Baronski when Corney bumped him off. That would be it.

His eyes skimmed the brief account of the killing. It was as usual. They had no adequate description of either Doreen or the car. Then his eyes glimpsed a word in the last paragraph that gripped his attention. His face tense, he finished the story.

Slowly, he looked up. His eyes were blank. Walking across to the table he picked up his heavy automatic, flipped down the safety, and still staring blankly before him, put the muzzle in his mouth and pulled the trigger.

His body toppled across the table, the blood slowly staining the crumpled paper and almost obliterating the account of the Robbins killing. The final words of the account were barely visible as the spreading stain wiped it out:

"A fact unknown until the killing was that Jack Robbins, witness for the prosecution in the Baronski killing, was in reality George Bretherton, a Federal operative recently arrived from the Pacific Coast and working on his first case. He is survived by a brother whose present whereabouts are unknown."

FIGHTER'S FIASCO

GOOD HEAVYWEIGHTS ARE scarcer than feather pillows in an Eskimo's igloo, so the first time I took a gander at this "Bambo" Bamoulian, I got all hot under the collar and wondered if I was seeing things. Only he wasn't Bambo then, he was just plain Januz Bamoulian, a big kid from the Balkans, with no more brains than a dead man's heel. But could he sock! I'm getting ahead of myself. . . .

———

I AM WALKING down the docks wondering am I going to eat, and if so, not only when but where and with what, when I see an ape with shoulders as wide as the rear end of a truck jump down off the gangway of a ship and start hiking toward another guy who is hustling up to meet him. It looks like fireworks, so I stand by to see the action, and if the action is going to be anything like the string of cuss words the guy is using, it should be good.

This guy is big enough to gather the Empire State Building under one arm and the Chrysler Tower under the other, and looks tough enough to buck rivets with his chin, so I am feeling plenty sorry for the other guy until he gets closer and I can get a flash at him. And that look, brother, was my first gander at the immortal Bambo Bamoulian.

He is about four inches shorter than the other guy, thicker in the chest, but with a slim waist and a walk like a cat stepping on eggs. He is a dark, swarthy fellow, and his clothes are nothing but rags, but I ain't been in the fight racket all these years without knowing a scrapper when I see one.

Me, I ain't any kind of a prophet, but a guy don't need to be clairvoyant to guess this second lug has what it takes. And what is more, he don't waste time at it. He sidles up close to the big guy, ducks a wide right swing, and then smacks him with a fist the size of a baby ham, knocking him cold as a Labrador morning!

Old Man Destiny doesn't have to more than smack me in the ear with a ball bat before I take a hint, so I step up to this guy.

"Say," I butt in. "Mightn't you happen to be a fighter?"

"How would you like to take a walk off the pier," he snarls, glaring at me like I'd swiped his socks or something. "You double-decked something-or-other, I am a fighter! What does that look like?" And he waves a paw at the study in still life draped over the dock.

"I mean for money, in the ring. You know, for dough, kale, dinero, gelt, sugar, geetus, the—"

"I get it!" he yelps brightly. "You mean for money!"

What would you do with a guy like that?

"That's the idea," I says, trying to be calm. "In the ring, and with the mitts."

"It's okay by me. I'll fight anybody for anything! For money, marbles, or chalk, but preferably money. Marbles and chalk are kind of tough on the molars."

"Then drop that bale hook and come with me. I am the best fight manager in the world, one of the two smartest guys in the universe, an' just generally a swell mug!"

"That's okay. I like you, too!" he says.

Ignoring what sounds faintly like a crack, I say, "They are wanting a fighter over at the Lyceum Club. And we'll fight whoever they got, we don't care who he is."

"We? Do both of us fight one guy? Mister, I don't need no help."

"No, you fight. I'm the brains, see? The manager, the guy that handles the business end. Get it?"

"Oh, so you're the brains? That's swell, it gives you some-thin' t' do, an' we'll manage somehow."

I looks at him again, but he is walking along swinging those big hooks of his. I catch up, "Don't call me mister. My name is McGuire, 'Silk' McGuire. It's Silk because I'm a smooth guy, see?"

"So is an eel smooth," he says.

A few minutes later, I lead my gorilla into Big Bill Haney's office and park him on a chair in the outer room with his cap in his mitts. Then I breeze inside.

"Hello, Bill!" I says cheerfully. "Here I am again! You got that heavyweight for the four-rounder tonight?"

"What d' you care?" he says, sarcastic. "You ain't had a fighter in a year that could punch his way out of a paper bag!"

"Wrong," I says coldly. "Climb out of that swivel chair and cast your lamps over this—" And I dramatically swing the door open and give him a gander at my fighter, who has parked his number tens on the new mahogany table.

"Hell," he says, giving Bambo the once-over. "That ain't no fighter. That chump is fresh off the boat."

"No wisecracks. That guy is the greatest puncher since Berlenbach and faster than even Loughran. He's tougher than a life stretch on Alcatraz, and he ain't never lost a battle!"

"Never had one, either, huh?"

Big Bill looks Januz over with a speculative glint in his eyes, and I know what he sees. Whatever else he may have, he does have color, and that's what they pay off on. My bohunk looks like a carbon copy of the Neanderthal man, whoever he was, only a little tougher and dumber.

"Okay," Haney says grudgingly. "I'll give him the main go tonight with 'Dead-Shot' Emedasco. Take it or leave it."

"With who?" I yelps. "Why, that guy has knocked over everyone from here to China!"

"You asked for a fight, didn't you?" he sneers. "Well, you got one. That clown of yours would've dragged down about twenty bucks for getting bounced on his ear by some preliminary punk; with the Dead-Shot he'll get not less than five centuries. Why are you kicking?"

"But this guy's a prospect. He can go places. I don't want him knocked off in the start, do I? Chees, give a guy a chance, won't you?"

"Forget it. That's the only spot open. I filled that four-rounder yesterday, and then Hadry did a run-out on the main event, so I can shove your boy in there. If he lives through it, I'll give him another shot. What do you call him?"

"Hey, buddy?" I barks at him. "What d' you call yourself?"

"Me? I come without calling," he grins. "But my name is Bamoulian. Januz Bamoulian. J-a-n-u-z—"

"Skip it!" I says hastily. "We'll call you Bambo Bamoulian!"

———

I TOUCH HANEY for a fin, so we can eat, and we barge down to Coffee Dan's to hang on the feed bag. While Dan is trying to compose a set of ham and eggs, I go into a huddle with myself trying to figure out the answers. This big tramp Dead-Shot Emedasco is poison. Or that's the way he sounds in the papers. I have never seen him, but a guy hears plenty. I usually get all the dope on those guys, but this is one I missed somehow. He has been touring the sticks knocking over a lot of guys named Jones, and on paper looks like the coming heavyweight champ.

The way Bambo charges them ham and eggs, I decide we better fight early and often, and that I'd rather buy his clothes than feed him. But while I am on my third cup of coffee, me not being a big eater myself as I'm nearly out of money again, I look up and who should be steering a course for our table but "Swivel-Neck" Hogan.

Now, I like Swivel-Neck Hogan like I enjoy the galloping cholera, and he has been faintly irritated with me ever since a poker game we were in. He had dealt me a pair of deuces from the bottom of the deck, and I played four aces, which relieved him of fifty bucks, so I know that whenever he approaches me there is something in the air besides a bad smell.

"Hey, you!" he growls. "The skipper wants ya."

"Say, Bambo," I says, "do you smell a skunk or is that just Swivel-Neck Hogan?"

"Awright, awright," he snarls, looking nasty with practically no effort. "Can dat funny stuff! The chief wants ya!"

As I said, I like Swivel-Neck like the seven-year itch, but I have heard he is now strong-arming for "Diamond-Back" Dilbecker, a big-shot racketeer, and that he has taken to going around with a gat in every pocket, or something.

"Act your age," I says, pleasant-like. "You may be the apple of your mother's eye, but you're just a spoiled potato to me." Then I turns to Bambo and slips him my key. "Take this and beat it up to the room when you get through eating, an' stick around till I get back. I got to see what this chump wants. It won't take long."

Bambo gets up and hitches his belt up over his dinner. He gives Swivel-Neck a glare that would have raised a blister on a steel deck. "You want I should bounce this cookie, Silk?" he says, eagerly. "Five to one I can put him out for an hour."

"It'd be cheap at twice the price," I chirps. "But let it ride."

WHEN WE GET to Dilbecker's swanky-looking apartment, there are half a dozen gun guys loafing in the living room. Any one of them would have kidnapped and murdered his own nephew for a dime, and they all look me over with a sort of professional stare as though measuring up space in a cornerstone or a foundation. This was pretty fast company for yours truly, and nobody knows this better than me.

Dilbecker looks up when I come in. He is a short, fat guy, and he is puffy about the gills. I feel more at home when I see him, for Diamond-Back Dilbecker and me is not strangers. In fact, away back when, we grew up within a couple of blocks of each other, and we called him Sloppy, something he'd like to forget now that he's tops in his racket.

"McGuire," he says, offhand. "Have a cigar." He shoves a box toward me, and when I pocket a handful I can see the pain in his eyes. I smile blandly and shove the stogies down in my pockets, figuring that if I am to go up in smoke it might just as well be good smoke.

"I hear you got a fighter," he begins. "A boy named Bamoulian?"

"Yeah, I got him on for tonight. Going in there for ten stanzas with Emedasco." Now, I wonder as I size him up, what is this leading up to? "And," I continue, "he'll knock the Dead-Shot so cold, he'll keep for years!"

"Yeah?" Dilbecker frowns impressively. "Maybe so, maybe no. But that's what I want t' see you about. I got me a piece of Emedasco's contract, and tonight I think he should win. I'd like to see him win by a kayo in about the third round."

Dilbecker slips out a drawer and tosses a stack of bills on the desk. "Of course, I'm willing to talk business. I'll give you a grand. What do you say?"

I bit off the end of one of his cigars, taking my time and keeping cool. Actually, I got a sinking feeling in my stomach and a dozen cold chills playing tag up and down my spine.

Dilbecker's at a loss for patience. "Take it, it's a better offer than you'll get five minutes from now," he growls. "Things could happen to you, bad things . . . if you know what I mean."

He's right, of course. He's got a room full of bad things on the other side of the door. I hate to give in to this kid I used to know on the old block but what the hell . . . lookin' at him I realize it may be my life on the line. Nevertheless, a man's got to have his pride.

"Don't come on hard with me, Dilbecker. You may be a tough guy now because you got a crowd o' gun guys in the next room but I remember when the kids from St. Paul's used to chase you home from school!"

"Yeah? Well you forget about it!" he says. "Set this fight and don't make me mad or both you and the Slavic Slugger'll wake up to find yourselves dead!"

Now, I'm not bringing it up but I helped him escape from the parochial school boys a time or few and I took my lumps for it, too. I'm not bringing it up but it's got my blood pressure going anyway.

"Awright, you said your piece," I says, as nasty as I can make it. "And now I'm sayin' mine. I'm sending my boy out there to win and you can keep your money and your gunsels and your damned cigars!" I tossed the load from my pocket on his desk. "I got connections, too. You want to bring muscle? I'll bring muscle, I'll bring guns and sluggers, whatever it takes."

He laughs at me, but it's not a nice laugh. "Muscle? You? You're a comedian. You should have an act. You bum, you been broke for months. You know better than to put the angle on me. Now get out of here, an' your boy dives t'night, or you'll get what Dimmer got!"

Only a week ago they dragged "Dimmer" Chambers out of the river, and him all wound up in a lot of barbed wire and his feet half burned off. Everybody knows it is Dilbecker's job, but they can't prove nothing. I am very sensitive about the feet, and not anxious to get tossed off no bridges, but Bamoulian will fight, and maybe—a very big maybe—he can win!

Also, I don't like being pushed around. So, am I brave? I don't know. I get out of there quick. I got the rest of my life to live.

———

So WE GO down to the Lyceum and I don't tell the big ape anything about it. He's happy to see me and raring to go; I don't want to distract him any. I'm bustin' a sweat because I've got no connections, no muscle, no gun guys and Sloppy Dilbecker has. I do, however, call in some favors. There's an old car, which is sitting right outside the dressing-room door, and a pawnshop .38, which is in my pocket. And running shoes, which is on my feet.

Now it's nearly time and I am getting rather chilled about those feet by then, although it looks like they'll be warm enough before the evening is over. Several times I look out the dressing-room door, and every time I stick my head out there, there is a great, big, ugly guy who looks at me with eyes like gimlets, and I gulp and pull my head in. I don't want Bambo worried going into the ring, although he sure don't look worried now, so I says nothing. He is cheerful, and grinning at me, and pulling Cotton's kinky hair, and laughing at everybody. I never saw a guy look so frisky before a battle. But he ain't seen Dead-Shot Emedasco yet, either!

Once, I got clear down to the edge of the ring, looking the crowd over. Then I get a chill. Right behind the corner where we will be is Sloppy Dilbecker and three of his gun guys. But what opens my eyes and puts the chill in my tootsies again is the fact that the seats all around them are empty. The rest of the house is a sellout. But those empty seats . . . It looks like he's saving space for a whole crew of tough guys.

It is only a few minutes later when we get the call, and as we start down the aisle to the ring, I am shaking in my brand-new shoes. Also, I am wondering why I had to be unlucky enough to get a fighter stuck in there with one of Dilbecker's gorillas. And then, all of a sudden I hear something behind me that makes my hair crawl. It is the steady, slow, shuffling of feet right behind me.

When I look back, I almost drop the water bottle, for right behind me is that big dark guy who has been doing duty right outside our door, and behind him is a crowd of the toughest looking cookies you ever saw. They are big, hard-looking guys with swarthy faces, square jaws, and heavy black eyebrows.

While Bambo takes his stool, I see them filing into the empty seats behind Sloppy, and believe me they are the toughest crowd that ever walked. I ain't seen none of them before. And except for one or two, they ain't such flashy dressers as most of Dilbecker's usual gun guys, but they are bigger, tougher, and meaner looking and when Cotton touches me on the arm, I let a yip out of me and come damn near pulling a faint right there. Who wouldn't, with about fifty of those gun guys watching you?

WHEN I LOOK around, Emedasco is already in the ring. He is a big mug weighing about two hundred and fifty pounds and standing not over six feet seven inches!

We walk out for instructions, and as the bunch of us come together in the center of the ring, Bambo hauls off and takes a swing at Dead-Shot's chin that missed by the flicker of an eyelash. Before we can stop them, Emedasco slammed a jarring right to Bambo's head, and Bambo came back with a stiff left to the midsection! Finally we got them separated, and I tell Bambo to hold it until the fight starts, and when the bell rings we are still arguing.

Emedasco charged out of his corner like a mad bull and takes a swing at Bamoulian that would have torn his head off had it landed, but Bambo ducked and sank a wicked left into the big boy's stomach. Then, as Emedasco followed with a clubbing right to the head, he clinched, and they wrestled around the ring until the referee broke them. They sparred for a second or two, and then Bambo cut loose with a terrific right swing that missed, but hit the referee on the side of the head and knocked him completely out of the ring and into the press benches.

Then those two big lugs stood flat-footed in the center of the ring and slugged like a couple of maniacs with a delirious crowd on its feet screaming bloody murder. Emedasco was a good sixty pounds heavier, but he was in a spot that night, for if ever a man wanted to fight, it was my Bambo Bamoulian.

I was so excited by the fight that I forgot all about Dilbecker, or what might happen if Bamoulian won, which looked like it could happen now.

When the next bell sounded, Bambo was off his stool and across the ring with a left he started clear from his own corner, and it knocked Emedasco into the ropes. But that big boy was nobody's palooka, and when he came back, it was with a volley of hooks, swings, and uppercuts that battered Bambo back across the ring, where he was slammed to the floor with a powerful right to the beezer.

The dumbfounded crowd, who had come to see Emedasco knock over another setup, were on their chairs yelling like mad, seeing a regular knock-down-and-drag-out brawl like everybody hopes to see and rarely finds. Bambo was right in his element. He knocked Dead-Shot Emedasco staggering with a hard left to the head, slammed a right to the body, and then dropped his hands and laughed at him. But Emedasco caught himself up and with one jump was back with a punch that would have shook Gilbraltar to its base. The next thing I know, Bambo is stretched on his shoulder blades in my corner, as flat as a busted balloon.

I lean over the ropes and yell for him to get up, and you could have knocked me cold with an ax when he turns around and says, grinning, "I don't have to get up till he counts nine, do I?"

At nine he's up, and as Emedasco rushes into him, I yell, "Hit him in the wind! Downstairs! In the stomach!"

Holding the raging Emedasco off with one hand while the big guy punches at him like a crazy man, my prize beauty leans over and says, "What did you say, huh?"

"Hit him in the stomach, you sap!" I bellowed. "Hit him in the stomach!"

"Oooh, I get it!" he says. "You mean hit him in the stomach!" And drawing back his big right fist, he fired it like a torpedo into Emedasco's heaving midsection.

With a grunt like a barn had fell on him, Emedasco spun halfway around and started to drop. But before he could hit the canvas, Bambo stepped in and slammed both hands to the chin, and Emedasco went flying like a bum out of the Waldorf, and stayed down and stayed out.

We hustled back to the dressing room with the crowd cheering so loud you could have heard them in Sarawak, wherever that is, and believe me, I am in a sweat to get out of there.

As we rush by, I hear a wild yell from the big ugly guy who has had his eye on me all evening, and when I glance back that whole crowd is coming for me like a lot of madmen, so I dive into the dressing room and slam the door.

"Hey, what's the idea?" Bambo demands. "Somebody might want to come in!"

"That's just what I'm afraid of!" I cry. "The hallway is full of guys that want to come in!"

"But my brother's out there!" Bambo insists, and jerks the door open, and before you could spell Dnepropetrovak, the room is full of those big, tough-looking guys.

I make a break for the door, but my toe hooked in the corner of Bambo's bathrobe, which has fallen across a chair, and I do a nosedive to the floor. The gun goes sliding. Then something smacks me on the dome, and I go out like a light.

When I came to, Bambo is standing over me, and the guy with the black eyes is holding my head.

"Awright, you got me! I give up!" I said. "You got me, now make the most of it."

"Say, you gone nuts?" Bambo squints at me. "What's eatin' you, anyway? Snap out of it, I want you t' meet my brother!"

"Your who?" I yelps. "You don't mean to tell me this guy is your brother?"

"Sure, he came to see me fight. All these guys, they my people. We come from the Balkans together, so they come to see me fight. They work on the docks with me."

———

I AM STILL laughing when we drop in at the Green Fan for some midnight lunch, and it isn't until we are all set down that I remember it is one of Sloppy Dilbecker's places. Just when I find I am not laughing anymore from thinking of that, who should come up but Swivel-Neck Hogan. Only he is different now, and he walks plenty careful, and edges up to my table like he is scared to death.

"Mr. McGuire?" he says.

"Well, what is it?" I bark at him. I don't know why he should be scared, but bluff is always best. And if he is scared, he must be scared of something, and if a gun guy like Swivel-Neck is calling me mister, he must be scared of me, so I act real tough.

"Sloppy—I mean Diamond-Back—said to tell youse he was just ribbing this afternoon. He ain't wantin' no trouble, and how would youse like to cut in on the laundry an' protection racket with him? He says youse got a nice bunch of gun guys, but there is room enough for all of youse."

For a minute I stare at him like he's nuts, and then it dawns on me. I look around at those big, hard-boiled dock workers, guys who look like they could have started the Great War, because, when it comes right down to it . . . they did. I look back at Swivel-Neck.

"Nothing doing, you bum. Go an' tell Sloppy I ain't wanting none of his rackets. I got bigger an' better things to do.

But tell him to lay off me, see? And that goes for you, too! One wrong crack an' I'll have the Montenegran Mafia down on you, get me?"

He starts away, but suddenly I get an inspiration. Nothing like pushing your luck when the game is going your way.

"Hey!" I yells. "You tell Sloppy Dilbecker that my boys say they want the treats on the house t'night, an' tell him to break out the best champagne and cigars he's got, or else! Understand!"

I lean back in my chair and slip my thumbs into the armholes of my vest. I wink at Bambo Bamoulian, and grin.

"All it takes is brains, my boy, brains."

"Yeah? How did you find that out?" he asks.

SIDESHOW CHAMPION

WHEN MARK LANNING looked at me and asked if I would take the Ludlow fight, I knew what he was thinking, and just what he had in mind. He also knew that there was only one answer I could give.

"Sure, I'll take it," I said. "I'll fight Van Ludlow any place, for money, marbles, or chalk."

But it was going to be for money. Lanning knew that, for that's what the game is about. Also, it had to be money because I was right behind the eight ball for lack of it.

Telling the truth: if I hadn't needed the cash as bad as I did, I would never have taken the fight. Not me, Danny McClure.

I'd been ducking Ludlow for two years. Not because I didn't want a shot at the title, but because of Lanning and some of the crowd behind him.

Mark Lanning had moved in on the fight game in Zenith by way of the slot machine racket. He was a short, fat man who wore a gold-plated coin on his watch chain. That coin fascinated me. It was so much like the guy himself, all front and polish, and underneath about as cheap as they come.

However, Mark Lanning was *the* promoter in Zenith. And Duck Miller, who was manager for Van Ludlow, was merely an errand boy for Mark. About the only thing Lanning didn't control in the fight game by that time was me. I was the uncrowned middleweight champ and everybody said I was the best boy in the division. Without taking any bows, I can say yes to that one.

The champ, Gordie Carrasco, was strictly from cheese. He won the title on a foul, skipped a couple of tough ones, and beat three boys on decisions. Not that he couldn't go. Nobody ever gets within shouting distance of any kind of title unless he's good. But Gordie wasn't as good as Ludlow by a long ways. He wasn't as good as Tommy Spalla, either. And he wasn't as good as me.

Ludlow was a different kinda deal. I give the guy that. He had everything and maybe a little more. Now no real boxer ever believes anybody is really better than he is. Naturally, I considered myself to be the better fighter. But he was good, just plenty good, and anybody who beat him would have to go the distance and give it all he had. Van Ludlow was fast. He was smart, and he could punch. Added to it, he was one of the dirtiest fighters in the business.

That wasn't so bad. A lot of good fighters have been rough. It isn't always malicious. It's just they want to win. It's just the high degree of competitive instinct, and because among top grade fighting men the fight's the thing, and a rule here or there doesn't matter so much. Jack Dempsey never failed to use every advantage in the book, so did Harry Greb, and for my money they were two of the best who ever lived.

If it had just been Ludlow, I'd have fought him long ago. It was Lanning I was ducking. Odd as it may seem, I'm an honest guy. Now I've carried a losing fighter or two when it really didn't matter much, but I never gypped a bettor, and my fights weren't for sale. Nor did I ever buy any myself. I won them in the ring and liked it that way.

The crowd around Lanning was getting a stranglehold on the fight game. I didn't like to see that bunch of crooks, gunmen, and chiselers edging in everywhere. I had ducked the fights with Ludlow because I knew that when I went in there with him, I was the last chance honest fighting had in Zenith or anywhere nearby. I was going to be fighting every dirty trick Lanning and his crowd could figure out. The referee and the judges would be against me. The timekeeper would be for Ludlow. If there was any way Lanning could get me into the ring without a chance, he'd try it.

Yet, I was taking the fight.

The reason was simple enough. My ranch, the only thing in the world I cared about, was mortgaged to the hilt. I'd blown my savings on that ranch, then put a mortgage on it to stock it and build a house and some barns. If it hadn't been for Korea, it would have been paid off. But I was in the army, and Mark Lanning located that note and bought it.

The mortgage was due, and I didn't have even part of a payment. Without that ranch, I was through. My days in the ring weren't numbered, but from where I stood I could see the numbers. I'd been fighting fourteen years, and Lanning had the game sewed up around there, so nobody fought unless they would do business. I cared more about that ranch than I did the title, so I could take a pass on Gordie Carrasco. But Van Ludlow couldn't. Lanning had him aimed at Gordie but he wouldn't look so good wearing the belt if the man all the sportswriters called "the uncrowned champ" wasn't taken down, too. Lanning now had it all lined up. I had to fight or give up on my future.

And then, there was Marge Hamlin.

Marge was my girl. We met right after I mustered out, when I first returned to Zenith. She was singing at the Rococo, and a honey if there ever was one. We started going together, became engaged, and were going to marry in the summer.

I *had* to take the fight. That was more the truth of it.

I went over to Lanning's. Duck Miller was there. We talked.

"Then," Lanning said, smiling his greasy smile, "there's the matter of an appearance forfeit."

"What d'you mean?" I asked. "Ever know of me running out on a fight?"

He moved one pudgy hand over to the ashtray and knocked off the gray ashes from his expensive cigar. "It ain't that, Danny," he said smoothly, "it's just business. Van's already got his up to five thousand dollars."

"Five thousand?" I couldn't believe what I heard. "Where would I get five thousand dollars? If I had five thousand you would never get me within a city block of any of your fights."

"That's what it has to be," he replied, and his eyes got small and ugly. He liked putting the squeeze on. "You can put up your car an' your stock from the ranch."

For a minute I stared at him. He knew what that meant as well as I did. It would mean that come snakes or high water,

I would have to be in that ring to fight Ludlow. If I wasn't, I'd be flat broke, not a thing in the world but the clothes on my back.

Not that I'd duck a fight. But there are such things as cut eyes and sickness.

"Okay," I said, "I'll put 'em up. But I'm warnin' you. Better rig this one good. Because I'm going to get you!"

I wasn't the bragging kind, and I saw Duck Miller looked a little worried. Duck was smart enough, just weak. He liked the easy dough, and the easy money in Zenith all came through Mark Lanning. Lanning was shrewd and confident. He had been winning a long time. Duck Miller had never won, so Miller could worry.

The thing was, Miller knew me. There had been a time when Duck and I had been broke together. We ran into some trouble out West when a tough mob tried to arrange one of my fights to make a cleanup. I refused to go along, and they said it was take the money or else.

Me, I'm a funny guy. I don't like getting pushed around, and I don't like threats. In that one, everybody had figured the fight would go the distance. This guy was plenty tough. Everybody figured me for the nod, but nobody figured he would stop me or I'd stop him. The wise boys had it figured for me to go in the tank in the sixth round.

I came to that fight all rodded up. They figure a fighter does it with his hands or no way. But these hombres forgot I'm a western man myself, and didn't figure on me packing some iron.

Coming out of the Arizona Strip, the way I do, I grew up with a gun. So I came down to that fight, and when this Rock Spenter walked out of his corner I feinted a left and Rock threw a right. My right fist caught him coming in, and my left hook caught him falling. And at the ten count, he hadn't even wiggled a toe.

I went down the aisle to the dressing room on the run, and when the door busted open, I was sitting on the rubbing table with a six-shooter in my mitt. Those three would-be hard guys turned greener than a new field of alfalfa, and then I tied two of them up, put the gun down, and went to work on the boss.

When I got through with him, I turned the others loose one at a time. Two of them were hospital cases. By that time the sheriff was busting down the door.

That old man had been betting on me, and when I explained, he saw the light very quickly. The sure-thing boys got stuck for packing concealed weapons, and one of them turned out to be wanted for armed robbery and wound up with ten years.

I'm not really bragging. I'm not proud of some of the circles I've traveled in or some of the things I've done. But I just wanted you to know what Duck Miller knew. And Duck may have been a loser, but he never lost anything but money. So far, he was still a stand-up guy.

When I had closed the door I heard Duck speak. "You shouldn't have done it, Mark," he said. "He won't take a pushing around."

"Him?" Contempt was thick in Lanning's voice. "He'll take it, and he'll like it!"

Would I? I walked out of there and I was sore. But that day, for the first time in months, I was in the gym.

The trouble was, I'd been in the service, spent my time staring through a barbed-wire fence in a part of Korea that was like Nevada with the heat turned off, and during that time I'd done no boxing. Actually, it was over three years since I'd had a legitimate scrap.

Van Ludlow had a busted eardrum or something and he had been fighting all the time. It takes fights to sharpen a man up, and they knew that. Don't think they didn't. They wanted me in the tank or out of the picture, but bad. Not that Van cared. Ludlow, like I said, was a fighter. He didn't care where his opponent came from or what he looked like.

———

MARGE WAS WAITING for me, sitting in her car in front of the Primrose Cafe. We locked the car and went inside and when we were sitting in the booth, she smiled at me.

Marge was a blonde, and a pretty one. She was shaped to

please and had a pair of eyes you could lose yourself in. Except for one small thing, she was perfect. There was just a tiny bit of hardness around her mouth. It vanished when she smiled, and that was often.

"How was it?" she asked me.

"Rough," I said. "I'm fighting Van in ninety days. Also," I added, "he made me post an appearance forfeit. I had to put it up, and it meant mortgaging my car and my stock on the ranch."

"He's got you, hasn't he?" Marge asked.

I smiled then. It's always easy to fight when you're backed in a corner and there's only one way out.

"No," I said, "he hasn't got me. The trouble with these smart guys, they get too sure of themselves. Duck Miller is a smarter guy than Lanning."

"Duck?" Marge was amazed. "Why, he's just a stooge!"

"Yeah, I know. But I'll lay you five to one he's got a little dough in the bank, and well, he'll never wind up in stir. Lanning will."

"Why do you say that?" Marge asked quickly. "Have you got something on him?"

"Uh-uh. But I've seen his kind before."

———

LIKE I SAY, I went to the gym that day. The next, too. I did about eight rounds of light work each of those two days. When I wanted to box, on the third day, there wasn't anybody to work with. There were a dozen guys of the right size around, but they were through working, didn't want to box that day, or weren't feeling good. It was a runaround.

If I'd had money, I could have imported some sparring partners and worked at the ranch, but I didn't. However, there were a couple of big boys out there who had fooled with the mitts some, and I began to work with them. Several times Duck Miller dropped by, and I knew he was keeping an eye on me for Lanning. This work wasn't doing me any good. I knew it, and he knew it.

Marge drove out on the tenth day in a new canary-colored coupe. One of those sleek convertible jobs. She had never looked more lovely. She watched me work, and when I went over to lean on the door, she looked at me.

"This won't get it, Danny," she said. "These hicks aren't good enough for you."

"I know," I said honestly, "but I got a plan."

"What is it?" she asked curiously.

"Maybe a secret," I told her.

"From me?" she pouted. "I like to know everything about you, Danny."

She did all right. Maybe it was that hardness around her mouth. Or put it down that I'm a cautious guy. I brushed it off, and although she came back to the subject twice, I slipped every question like they were left-hand leads. And that night, I had Joe, my hand from the ranch, drive me down to Cartersville, and there I caught a freight.

––––––

THE GREATER AMERICAN Shows were playing county fairs through the Rocky Mountain and prairie states. I caught up with them three days after leaving the ranch. Old Man Farley was standing in front of the cook tent when I walked up. He took one look and let out a yelp.

"No names, Pop," I warned. "I'm Bill Banner, a ham an' egg pug, looking for work. I want a job in your athletic show, taking on all comers."

"Are you crazy?" he demanded, low voiced. "Danny McClure, you're the greatest middleweight since Ketchell, an' you want to work with a carnival sideshow?"

Briefly, I explained the pitch. "Well," he said, "you won't find much competition, but like you say, you'll be fightin' every night, tryin' all the time. Buck's on the show, too. He'd like to work with you."

Almost fifteen years before, a husky kid, just off a cow ranch in the Strip, I'd joined the Greater American in Las Vegas. Buck Farley, the old man's kid, soon became my best pal.

An ex-prizefighter on the show taught us to box, and in a few weeks they started me taking on all comers. I stayed with the show two years and nine months, and in that time must have been in the ring with eight or nine hundred men.

Two, three, sometimes four a night wanted to try to pick up twenty-five bucks by staying four rounds. When I got better, the show raised it to a hundred. Once in a while we let them stay, but that was rare, and only when the crowd was hot and we could pack them in for the rest of the week by doing it.

When I moved on, I went pro and had gone to the top. After three years, I was ranking with the first ten. A couple of years later I was called the uncrowned champ.

"Hi, Bill!" Buck Farley had been tipped off before he saw me. "How's it going?"

Buck was big. I could get down to one sixty, but Buck would be lucky to make one ninety, and he was rawboned and tough. Buck Farley had always been a hand with the gloves, so I knew I had one good, tough sparring partner.

That night was my first sideshow fight in a long time. Old Man Farley was out front for the ballyhoo and he made it good. Then, I don't have any tin ears. My nose has been broken, but was fixed up and it doesn't show too much. A fighter would always pick me for a scrapper, but the average guy rarely does, so there wasn't any trouble getting someone to come up.

The first guy was a copper miner. A regular hard-rock boy who was about my age and weighed about two hundred and twenty. The guy's name was Mantry.

When we got in the ring, the place was full.

"Maybe you better let me take it," Buck suggested, "you might bust a hand on this guy."

"This is what I came for," I said. "I've got to take them as they come."

THEY SOUNDED THE bell and this gorilla came out with a rush. He was rawboned and rugged as the shoulder of a mountain. He swung a wicked left, and I slid inside and clipped him with two good ones in the wind. I might as well have slugged the side of a battleship.

He bulled on in, letting them go with both hands. I caught

one on the ear that shook me to my heels and the crowd roared. Mantry piled on in, dug a left into my body and slammed another right to the head. I couldn't seem to get working and circled away from him. Then I stabbed a left to his mouth three times and he stopped in his tracks and looked surprised.

He dropped into a half crouch, this guy had boxed some, and he bored in, bulling me into the ropes. He clipped me there and my knees sagged and then I came up, mad as a hornet with a busted nest. I stabbed a left to his mouth that made those others seem like brushing him with a feather duster and hooked a right to his ear that jarred him for three generations. I walked in, slamming them with both hands, and the crowd began to whoop it up.

His knees wilted and he started to sag. This was too good to end, so I grabbed him and shoved him into the ropes, holding him up and fighting with an appearance of hard punching until the bell rang.

Mantry looked surprised, but walked to his corner, only a little shaky. He knew I'd held him up, and he was wondering why. He figured me for a good guy who was taking him along for the ride.

When we came out he took it easy, whether from caution or because I'd gone easy on him, I couldn't tell. I stabbed a left to his mouth that left him undecided about that, then stepped in close. I wanted a workout, and had to get this guy back in line.

"What's a matter, chump?" I whispered. "You yella?"

He went hog wild and threw one from his heels that missed my chin by the flicker of an eyelash. Then he clipped me with a roundhouse right and I went back into the ropes and rebounded with both hands going. He was big and half smart and he bored in, slugging like crazy.

Mister, you should have heard the tent! You could hear their yells for a half mile, and people began crowding around the outside to see what was going on. Naturally, that didn't hurt the old man's feelings.

Me, I like a fight, and so did this Mantry. We walked out there and slugged it toe-to-toe. What I had on him in experience and savvy, he had in weight, strength, and height. Of course, I'd never let old Mary Ann down the groove yet.

The crowd was screaming like a bunch of madmen. I whipped a right uppercut to Mantry's chin and he slumped, and then I drove a couple of stiff ones into his wind. The bell rang again and I trotted back to my corner.

The third was a regular brannigan. I dropped about half my science into the discard because this was the most fun I'd had in months. We walked out there and went into it and it would have taken a smarter guy than any in that crowd to have seen that I was slipping and riding most of Mantry's hardest punches. He teed off my chin with a good one that sent up a shower of sparks, and when the round ended, I caught him with two in the wind.

Coming up for the fourth, I figured here is where I let him have it. After all, Farley was paying one hundred bucks if this guy went the distance. I sharpened up in this one. I didn't want to cut the guy. He was a right sort, and I liked him. So I walked out and busted him a couple in the wind that brought a worried expression to his face. Then I went under his left and whammed a right to the heart that made him back up a couple of steps. He shot two fast lefts to the head and one to the chin, then tried a right.

I stepped around, feinted with a left, and he stepped in and I let Mary Ann down the groove. Now you can box or you can slug but there's none out there that can do both at once. A fighter's style is usually one or the other. Boxing will win you points and it'll keep you from getting hit too much, but slugging puts them on the canvas. The only problem is you have to stop boxing for an instant and plant your feet to do it. It's in that instant that you can get hit badly, if your opponent is on the ball. Mantry took the feint, however, and that was the end of him.

It clipped him right on the button and he stood there for a split second and then dropped like he'd been shot through the heart.

I walked back to my corner and Buck looked at me. "Man," his eyes were wide, "what did you hit him with?"

When the count was over, I went over and picked the guy up.

"Lucky punch!" one of the townies was saying. "The big guy had it made until he clipped him!"

When Mantry came around, I slapped him on the shoulder. "Nice fight, guy! Let's go back an' dress.

"Pop," I said when we were dressing, "slip the guy ten bucks a round. He made a fight."

Pop Farley knew a good thing when he saw it. "Sure enough." He paid the big guy forty dollars, who looked from me to Pop like we were Santa Claus on Christmas Eve. "Why don't you come back an' try it again?" Pop suggested.

"I might," Mantry said, "I might at that!"

———

THAT WAS THE beginning. In the following sixty days, I boxed from four to twelve rounds a night, fighting miners, lumberjacks, cowpunchers, former Golden Glove boys, Army fighters, anything that came along. Mantry came back twice, and I cooled him twice more, each one a brawl.

Those sixty days had put me in wonderful condition. I was taking care of myself, not catching many, and tackling the varied styles was sharpening me up. Above all, every contest was a real fight, not practice. Even an easy fight keeps a man on his toes, and a fighter of strength can often be awkwardly dangerous if he knows a little. And every one of these men was trying.

Buck knew all about my troubles. He was working with me every day, and we had uncovered a good fast welter on the show who had quit fighting because of a bad hand. The light, fast work was good for me.

"It won't go this easy," Buck told me. "I heard about Mark Lanning. He's dangerous. If he intends to clear the way to the title, he'll not rest until he knows where you are, and just what you're doin'."

———

LATER, I HEARD about it. I didn't know then. Buck Farley had voiced my own thoughts, and in a different way, they were the thoughts of Mark Lanning and Duck Miller.

"Well," Lanning had said, "if he's taken a powder he's

through. Might be the best way at that, but I hate to think of him gettin' away without a beatin', and I hate to think of blowin' the money we'd win on the fight."

"He ain't run out," Duck said positively. "I know that guy. He's smart. He's got something up his sleeve. What happened to him?"

"We traced him to Cartersville," Gasparo said. Gasparo was Lanning's pet muscle man. "He bought a ticket there for Butte. Then he vanished into thin air."

It was Marge Hamlin who tipped them off. I found that out later, too. I hadn't written her, but she was no dumb Dora, not that babe. She was in a dentist's office, waiting to get a tooth filled, when she saw the paper. It was a daily from a jerkwater town in Wyoming.

CARNIVAL FIGHTER TO MEET PAT DALY

Bill Banner, middleweight sharpie who has been a sensation in the Greater American Shows these past two months, has signed to meet Pat Daly, a local light-heavyweight, in the ten-round main event on Friday's card.

Banner, a welcome relief from the typical carnie stumblebum, has been creating a lot of talk throughout the Far West with his series of thrilling knockouts over local fighters. Pop Farley, manager and owner of Greater American, admits the opposition has been inexperienced, but points to seventy-six knockouts as some evidence. One of these was over Tom Bronson, former AAU champ, another over Ace Donaldson, heavyweight champion of Montana.

She grabbed up that paper and legged it down to Mark Lanning. "Get a load of this," she tells him. He studies it and shrugs. "You don't get it?" she inquired, lifting an eyebrow. "Ask Duck. He knows that Danny used to fight with a carnival."

"Yeah," Duck looked up, "got his start that way. Greater American Shows, it was."

Lanning's eyes lit up triumphantly. "You get a bonus for that, Chick," he tells Marge. Then he turned his head. "Gasparo, take three men. Get Tony Innes. I'll contact him by phone. Then get a plane west. I want Tony Innes to fight in this Daly's place."

"Innes?" Miller sat bolt upright. "Man! He's the second best light-heavy in the business!"

Lanning leered. "Sure! An' he belongs to me. He'll go out there, substitute for Daly. He'll give McClure a pasting. One thing, I want him to cut Danny McClure's eye! Win or lose, I want McClure's eye cut! Then when he goes in there with Ludlow, we'll see what happens!"

Outside in the street, Duck Miller lit a cigarette and looked at Marge Hamlin.

"So he's got you on the payroll, too," he said. "What a sweet four-flusher you turned out to be!"

Marge's face flushed and her lips thinned. "What about *you*?" she sneered.

Duck shrugged. "I'm not takin' any bows, kid," he said grimly, "but at least he knows which side I'm on. He's a square guy. You like blood? Be there at the ringside when he gets that eye opened. You'll see it. I hope it gets on you so bad it'll never wash off!"

"He chose this game," Marge said angrily. "If he doesn't know how it's played, that's his problem."

"And you chose him." Duck snapped his match into the street. "I guess the blood's there and won't wash off already."

ALL THAT I heard later. The Greater American was playing over in Laramie, but Pop and Buck Farley were with me, ready to go in there with Pat Daly. All three of us were in the dressing room, waiting for the call, when the door busted open.

Pat Daly was standing there in his street clothes. He had blood all over and he could hardly stand.

"Who in blazes are you?" he snarled. "Y' yella bum! Scared of me an' have your sluggers beat me up so's you can put in a setup!"

Buck took him by the arm and jerked him inside. "Give," he said, "what happened?"

"What happened?" Daly was swaying and punch-drunk, but anger blazed in his eyes. "Your sluggers jumped me. Ran my car off the road, then before I was on my feet, they started slugging me with blackjacks. When I was out cold they rolled me into the ditch and poured whiskey on me!"

"What about this substitute business?" Pop demanded.

Suddenly, I knew what happened. Mark Lanning had got me located. From here on in, it would be every man for himself.

"You knew all about it!" Daly swore. "When I got in, Sam tells me he heard I was drunk and hurt in an accident, and that they have a substitute. You tell me how you knew that!"

The door opens then, and Sam Slake is standing there. He looks at Daly, then he looks at me. His face is hard.

"Daly can't fight," he says, "which is your fault. Your handpicked substitute is out there, so you can go in with him. But I'm tellin' you, don't bring your crooked game around here again. I'm callin' the D.A., so if you want to play games you can play them with him."

I got to my feet then, and I was sore. "Listen!" I snapped. "I'll tell you what this is all about! Get the newspaper boys in!"

It was time for the main go, and the crowd was buzzing. They had had a look at Pat Daly, some of them, and the arena was filled with crazy stories. The newspaper boys, three of them, came down into my dressing room.

"All right," I said, "this is the story. My name isn't Bill Banner. It's Danny McClure."

"What?" one of these reporters yelped. "The uncrowned middleweight champ? But you're signed to meet Van Ludlow!"

"Right!"

Briefly, quickly as I could, I told them about how I was pushed into the fight with Ludlow, all about the methods Lanning used. How I couldn't get sparring partners, and how I came west and joined the show I'd been with as a kid. And how Lanning had sent his sluggers to the show. That I didn't know who the substitute was, but before the fight was over, they'd know it was no frame. Some of it was guess-work, but they were good guesses.

"Maybe I'll know him. I'll bet money," I told them, "he's good. I'll bet plenty of dough he was sent out here to see that I go into the ring with Ludlow hurt. I got to go, or the commission in Zenith belongs to Lanning and I lose my ranch."

"Wow! What a story! The best middleweight in the game fights his way into shape with a carnival!" The reporters scrambled to beat me to the ring.

By that time the arena was wild. So I grabbed my robe and got out of the dressing room with Buck Farley and Pop alongside of me. I could see both of them were packing heaters.

When I crawled through the ropes, I looked across the ring and saw Tony Innes.

"Who is he?" Buck asked.

I told him and his face went white. Tony Innes was tough. A wicked puncher who had fought his way to the top of the game with a string of knockouts.

The announcer walked into the center of the ring and took the microphone, but I pushed him aside. Gasparo, in Innes's corner, started up. Before he could get over the edge of the ring, Buck Farley tugged him back. The crowd was wild with excitement, but when I spoke, they quieted down.

"Listen, folks! I can't explain now! It will all be in the papers tomorrow, but some guys that want me out of the fight racket had Pat Daly slugged and brought out a tough boy to stick in here with me. So you're goin' to get your money's worth tonight!

"In that corner, weight one hundred and seventy-five pounds, is Tony Innes, second-ranking light-heavyweight in the world! And my name isn't Bill Banner! It's Danny McClure, and tonight you're going to see the top-ranking light-heavyweight contender take a beating he'll never forget."

The crowd just blew the roof off the auditorium, and Tony Innes came on his feet and waved a wildly angry glove at the mike. "Get it out of here!" he snarled. "Let's fight!"

Somebody rang the bell, and Buck Farley just barely got

out of the way as Innes crossed the ring. He stabbed a left that jerked my head back like it was on a hinge, and he could have ended the fight there, but he was crazy mad and threw his right too soon. It missed and I went in close. Never in all my life was I so sore as then.

I ripped a right to his muscle-corded middle and then smashed a left hook to the head that would have loosened the rivets on the biggest battleship ever built, but it never even staggered this guy. He clipped me on the chin with an elbow that made my head ring like an alarm clock. If *that* was the kind of fight it was going to be, I was ready! We slugged it across the ring and then he stepped out of the corner and caught me with a right that made my knees buckle.

I moved into Tony, lancing his cut mouth with a straight left. He sneered at me and bored in, rattling my teeth with a wicked uppercut and clipping me with a short left chop that made my knees bend. I slammed both hands to the body and jerked my shoulder up under his chin. When the bell for the first sounded, we were swapping it out in the middle of the ring.

The minute skipped by and I was off my stool and halfway across the ring before he moved. The guy had weight and height on me and a beautiful left. It caught me in the mouth and I tasted blood and then a right smashed me on the chin and my brain went smoky and I was on the canvas and this guy was standing over me, never intending to let me get up. But I got up, and brought one from the floor with me that caught him on the temple and rolled him into the ropes.

I was on top of him but still a little foggy, and he went inside of my right and clinched, stamping at my arches. I shoved him away with my left, clipped him with a right, and then we started to slug again.

You had to give it to Innes. He was a fighter. There wasn't a man there that night who wouldn't agree. He was dirty. He had sold out. He was a crook by seventeen counts, but the guy could dish it out, and, brother, he could take it.

And those people in that tank town? They were seeing the battle of the century, and don't think they didn't know it! The leading world contenders for two titles with no holds barred.

Yeah, they let it go on that way. The sheriff was there, a red-hot sport and fight fan.

"Let the voters get me!" I heard him say between rounds. "I'm a fightin' man, an' by the Lord Harry I wouldn't miss this no matter what happens. Nobody interrupts this fight but the fighters. Understand!"

If a guy was to judge by that crowd, the sheriff could hold that office for the rest of his life. Me, I was too busy to think about that then. Van Ludlow, Marge Hamlin, Duck Miller, and Lanning were a thousand miles away. In there with me was a great fighting man, and a killer.

Maybe I'd never fight Ludlow, but I was going to get Innes.

————

DON'T ASK ME what happened to the rounds. Don't ask me how we fought. Don't ask me how many times I was down, or how many he was down. We were two jungle beasts fighting on the edge of a cliff, only besides brawn, we had all the deadly skill, trained punching power, and toughness of seasoned fighters. A thousand generations had collected the skill in fighting we used that night.

He cut my eye . . . he cut both my eyes. But his were, too, and his mouth was dribbling with blood and he was wheezing through a broken nose. The crowd had gone crazy, then hoarse, and now it sat staring in a kind of shocked horror at what two men could do in a ring.

Referee? He got out of the way and stood beside the sheriff. We broke, but rarely clean. We hit on the breaks, we used thumbs, elbows, and heads, we swapped blows until neither of us could throw another punch. The fight had been scheduled for ten rounds. I think it was the fourteenth when I began to get him.

I caught him coming in and sank my right into his solar plexus. He was tired, I could feel it. He staggered and his mouth fell open and I walked in throwing punches to head and body. He staggered, went down, rolled over.

Stand over him? Not on your life! I stepped back and let the guy take his own time getting up! It wasn't because I was fighting fair. I wanted him to see I didn't need that kind of stuff. I could do it without that.

He got up and came in and got me with a right to the wind, and I took it going away and then I slipped on some blood and I hit the canvas and rolled over. Innes backed off like I had done, and waved at me with a bloody glove to get up and come on!

The crowd broke into a cheer then, the first he'd had, and I could see he liked it.

I got up and we walked in and I touched his gloves. That got them. Until then it had been a dirty, ugly fight. But when I got up, I held out both gloves and with only a split second of hesitation, he touched my gloves with his, a boxer's handshake!

The crowd broke into another cheer. From then on there wasn't a low blow or a heeled glove. We fought it clean. Two big, confident fighting men who understood each other.

But it couldn't last. No human could do what we were doing and last. He came for me and I rolled my head and let the glove go by and then smashed a right for his body. He took it, and then I set myself. He was weaving and I took aim at his body and let go.

The ropes caught him and he rolled along them. He knew he was going to get it then, but he was asking no favors, and he wasn't going to make it easy for me.

Again I feinted, and when he tried to laugh, a thin trickle of blood started from a split lip. He wouldn't bite on that.

"Quit it!" I heard him growl. "Come an' get me!"

I went. Then I uncorked the payoff. I let Mary Ann go down the groove!

The sound was like the butt end of an axe hitting a frozen log, and Tony Innes stood like a dummy in a doze, and then he went over on his feet, so cold an iceberg would have felt like a heat wave. And then I started backing up and fell into the ropes and stood there, weaving a little, my hands working, so full of battle I couldn't realize it was over.

———

THE NEWS REPORT of the fight hit the sport pages like an atomic bomb. Overnight everybody in the country was talking about it and promoters from all over the country were offering prices on a return battle. Above all, it had started a fire I didn't think Mark Lanning could put out. But he could still pull plenty behind the smoke.

Most people will stand for a lot, but once a sore spot gets in front of their eyes, they want to get rid of it. The rotten setup at Zenith, which permeated the fight game, was an example. The trouble was, it was a long time to election and Lanning still had the situation sewed up in Zenith, and most of the officials.

More than ever, he'd be out to get me. The season was near closing for Greater American so Pop turned the show over to his assistant and came east with me. Buck came, too, and he brought that .45 Colt along with him.

Maybe I had spoiled Lanning's game. Time would tell about that, but on the eve of the Ludlow fight, I had two poorly healed eyes, and the ring setup back home was no better than it had been. Despite all the smoke, I was still behind the eight ball.

The publicity would crab the chance of Lanning pulling any really fast stuff. But with my eyes the way they were, there was a good chance he wouldn't have to. I was going into a fight with a cold, utterly merciless competitor with two strikes against me. And with every possible outside phase of the fight in question.

You think the timekeeper can do nothing? Suppose I got a guy on the ropes, ready to cool him, or suppose I get Ludlow on the deck and the referee says nine and there are ten seconds or twenty seconds to go, and then the bell rings early and Ludlow is saved?

Or suppose I'm taking a sweet socking and they let the round go a few seconds. Many a fight has been lost or won in a matter of seconds, and many a fighter has been saved by the bell to come on to win in later rounds.

Duck Miller was lounging on the station platform when I got off of the train. He glanced at my eyes and there was no grin on his lips.

"Well, Duck," I said, "looks like your boss got me fixed up."

"Uh-huh. He's the kind of guy usually gets what he wants."

"Someday he's going to get more than he asks for," I said quietly.

Duck nodded. "Uh-huh. You got some bad eyes there."

"It was a rough fight."

Duck's eyes sparked. "I'd of give a mint," he said sincerely, "to have seen it! You and Tony Innes, and no holds barred! Yeah, that would be one for the book." He looked at me again. "You're a great fighter, kid."

"So's Ludlow." I looked at Duck. "Miller, at heart you're a right guy. Why do you stick with a louse like Lanning?"

Duck rubbed his cigarette out against his heel. "I like money. I been hungry too much. I eat now, I got my own car, I got a warm apartment, I have a drink when I want. I even got a little dough in the bank."

I looked at him. Duck was down in the mouth. His wide face and hard eyes didn't look right.

"Is it worth it, Duck?"

He looked at me. "No," he said flatly. "But I'm in."

"Seen Marge?" I asked.

That time he didn't look at me. "Uh-huh. I have. Often."

Often? That made me wonder. I looked at him again. "How's she been getting along?"

Duck looked up, shaking out a smoke. "Marge gets along, don't ever forget that. Marge gets along. Like me," he hesitated, "she's been hungry too much."

He turned on his heel and walked away. He was there to look at me, to report to Lanning how I looked so they could figure on Ludlow's fight. Well, I knew how I looked. I'd been through the mill. And what he'd said about Marge I didn't like.

She was waiting for me at the ranch, sitting in the canary-yellow convertible. She looked like a million, and her smile was wide and beautiful. Yet somehow, the change made her look different. I mean, my own change. I'd been away. I'd been through a rough deal, I was back, and seeing her now I saw her with new eyes. Yes, she was hard around the eyes and mouth.

When I kissed her something inside me said, "Kid, this is it. This babe is wrong for you."

"How's it, honey?" I said. "Everything all right?"

"Yes, Danny, but your eyes!" she exclaimed. "Your poor eyes are cut!"

"Yeah. Me an' Tony Innes had a little brawl out West. Maybe," I said, "you read about it?"

"Everybody did," she said frankly. "Do you think it was wise, Dan? Telling that stuff about Mark Lanning?"

"Sure, baby. I fight in the open, cards on the table. Guys like Lanning don't like that." I looked down at her. "Honey, he's through."

"Through? Mark Lanning?" She shook her head. "You're whistling in the dark, Dan. He's big, he's too strong. He's got this town sewed up."

"It's only one town," I said.

Right then I didn't know she was working with Lanning. I didn't know she was selling me out. Maybe, down inside, I had a hunch, but I didn't know. That was why I didn't see that I'd slipped the first seed of doubt into her thoughts.

That evening two black sedans pulled up the drive and stopped in front of the porch where I was sitting, feet up, reading the newspaper. Something about the men that got out, maybe it was their identical haircuts or the drab suits that they wore, said "government" in square, block lettering.

"Evening," the first one said. "I'm special agent Crowley, FBI." He flipped open his wallet to show me his ID. "This," he indicated a taller man from the second car, "is Bill Karp, with the State Attorney General's office. We'd like to talk to you about a story we read in the newspaper . . ."

Before they were done we'd talked for four hours, and a court reporter took it all down.

———

THREE DAYS I rested, just working about six rounds a day with the skipping rope and shadowboxing. Then I started in training again, and in earnest. We had a ring under the trees, and I liked it there. Joe Moran was with me, and Buck Farley.

It went along like that until two days before the fight. Then

Pop came in, he had a long look at me, and he pushed his wide hat back on his head and took the cigar from his lips.

"Kid," he said, "I got a tip today. Your dame's bettin' on Ludlow."

If anybody had sprung that on me, even Pop Farley, before I went west, I'd have said he was a liar. Now I just looked at him. Pop was my friend. Maybe the best one I had. I was like a son to him, and Pop wouldn't lie to me.

"Give it to me, Pop," I said. "What do you know?"

"Saw her coming from Mark Lanning's office. I got curious and I had her followed. I found out she's hocked her jewelry to bet on Ludlow. I traced the sale of that yellow car. Lanning paid for it."

Well, I got out of the ring and walked back to the house. I pulled on my pants and a sweater, I changed into some heavy shoes. Then I went for a walk.

There was work to be done. Fences needed mending, one barn would soon need a new roof, over the winter I would have to repair my tractor, which hadn't worked right in years ... I always dreamed I was doing it for someone, someone besides me, that is. Suddenly I realized that person wasn't Marge and never would be.

Marge Hamlin meant a lot to me, but hurt as it did, it wasn't as bad as it would have been before I went west. That trip had made me see things a lot clearer.

I walked in the hills, breathing a lot of fresh, cool air, and before long I began to feel better. Well, maybe Duck was right. She had been hungry too much. Somehow, I didn't find any resentment in me.

———

We WERE SITTING on the porch the day of the fight when Marge drove up. She'd been out twice before, but I was gone. She looked at my eyes when I walked down to the car. I heard Pop and Buck get up and go inside.

Marge looked beautiful as a picture, and just as warm.

"Marge," I said, "you shouldn't have bet that money." Her eyes went sharp, and she started to speak. "It's okay," I said, "we all have to live. You play it your way, it's just that you'll lose, and that'll be too bad. You're going to need the money."

"What do you mean? Who told you how I bet?"

"It doesn't matter. Copper those bets if you can, because I'm going to win."

"With those eyes?" She was hard as ice now.

"Sure, even with these eyes. Tony Innes was a good boy. I beat him. Outweighed fifteen pounds, I beat him. I'll beat Ludlow, too."

"Like fun you can!" Her voice was bitter. "You haven't a chance!"

"Take my tip, Marge. And then," I added, "cut loose from Mark. He won't do right by you. He won't be able to, even if he wanted to."

"What do you mean? What can you do to Mark?" Contempt was an inch thick in her voice.

"It isn't me. That story from out West started it. Mark's through. He's shooting everything on this fight. He still thinks he's riding high. He isn't. Neither are you."

She looked at me. "You don't seem much cut up about this," she said then.

"I'm not. You're no bargain, honey. In fact you've been a waste of my time."

That got her. She had sold me out for Mark Lanning and his money, but she didn't like to think I was taking it so easy. She had set herself up to be the prize, but now she wasn't the prize I wanted. She started the car, spun the wheel and left the ranch with the car throwing gravel as I walked back inside.

———

THAT NIGHT YOU couldn't have forced your way into the fight club with a crowbar. The Zenith Arena was jammed to the doors, and when Ludlow started for the ring, a friend told me and I slid off the table and looked at Pop.

"Well, Skipper," I said, "here goes everything."

"You'll take him," Buck said, but he wasn't sure. It's hard to fight with blood running into your eyes.

When we were in the center of the ring, Buck Farley was with me. I turned to him. "You got that heater, Buck?"

"Sure thing." He showed me the butt of his .45 under his shirt.

The referee's eyes widened. Ludlow's narrowed and he touched his thin lips with his tongue.

"Just a tip." I was talking to the referee. "Nobody stops this fight. No matter how bloody I get, or no matter how bloody Ludlow gets, this fight goes on to the end. When you count one of us out, that will be soon enough.

"Buck," I said, "if this referee tries to give this to Ludlow any way but on a knockout or decision at the end of fifteen rounds, kill him."

Of course, I didn't really mean it. Maybe I didn't. Buck was another guess. Anyway, the referee was sure to the bottom of his filthy little soul that I did mean it. He was scared, scared silly.

Then I went back to my corner and rubbed my feet in the resin. This was going to be murder. It was going to be plain, unadulterated murder.

The gong sounded.

Van Ludlow was a tough, hard-faced blond who looked like he was made from granite. He came out, snapped a fast left for my eyes, and I went under it, came in short with a right to the ribs as he faded away. He jabbed twice and missed. I walked around him, feinted, and he stepped away, watching me. The guy had a left like a cobra. He stabbed the left and I was slow to slip it. He caught me, but too high.

Ludlow stepped it up a little, missed a left and caught me with a sweet right hand coming in. He threw that right again and I let it curl around my neck and smashed both hands to the body, in close. We broke clean and then he moved in fast, clipped me with a right uppercut and then slashed a left to my mouth that hurt my bad lip. I slipped two lefts to the head and went in close, ripping both hands to the body before he tied me up. He landed a stiff right to the head as the bell rang.

Three rounds went by just like that. Sharp, fast boxing, and Ludlow winning each of them by a steadily increasing margin. My punches were mostly to the body in close. In the fourth the change came.

He caught me coming in with a stiff left to the right eye and a trickle of blood started. You could hear a low moan from the crowd. They had known it was coming.

Blood started trickling into my eye. Ludlow stabbed a left and got in close. "How d'you like it, boy?"

"Fine!" I said, and whipped a left hook into his ribs that jolted him to his socks.

He took two steps back and I hit him with one hand, then the other. Then the fight turned into a first-rate blood-and-thunder scrap.

———

Van Ludlow could go. I give him that. He came in fast, stabbed a left to my mouth, and I went under another one and smashed a right into his ribs that sounded like somebody had dropped a plank. Then I ripped up a right uppercut that missed but brought a whoop from the crowd.

Five and six were a brawl with blood all over everything. Both my eyes were cut and there was blood in my mouth. I'd known this would happen and so was prepared for it. Ludlow threw a wicked right for my head in the seventh round and I rolled inside and slammed my right to his ribs again. He backed away from that one.

"Come on, dish face!" I told him politely. "You like it, don't you?"

He swung viciously, and I went under it and let him have both of them, right in the lunch basket. He backed up, looking unhappy, and I walked into him blazing away with both fists. He took two, slipped a left, and rocked me to my number nines with a rattling right hook.

He was bloody now, partly mine and partly his own. I shot a stiff left for his eye and just as it reached his face, turned my left glove outside and ripped a gash under his eye with the laces that started a stream of blood.

"Not bleeding, are you?" I taunted. "That wasn't in the lesson for today. I'm the one supposed to bleed!"

The bell cut him off short, and he glared at me. I took a deep breath and walked back to my corner. I couldn't see myself. But I could guess. My face felt like it had been run through a meat grinder, but I felt better than I had in months. Then I got the shock of my life.

TONY INNES WAS standing in my corner.

"Hey, champ!" He looked at me, got red around the gills, and grinned. "Shucks, man! You're a fighter. Don't tell me the guy who licked me can't take Van Ludlow."

"You ever fight Ludlow?" I was still standing up. I didn't care. I felt good.

"No," he said.

"Well," I told him, "it ain't easy!"

When the bell sounded, I went out fast, feeling good. I started a left hook for his head and the next thing I knew the referee was saying "Seven!"

I rolled over, startled, wondering where the devil I'd been, and got my feet under me. I came up fast as Van moved in, but not fast enough. A wicked right hand knocked me into the ropes and he followed it up, but fast. He jabbed me twice, and blind with blood, I never saw the right.

That time it was the count of three I heard, but I stayed where I was to eight, then came up. I went down again, then again. I was down the sixth time in the round when the bell rang. Every time I'd get up, he'd floor me. I never got so tired of a man in my life.

Between rounds they had my eyes fixed up. Tony Innes was working on them now, and he should have been a second. He was as good a man on cut eyes as any you ever saw.

The ninth round opened with Ludlow streaking a left for my face, and I went under it and hit him with a barrage of blows that drove him back into the ropes. I nailed him there with a hard right and stabbed two lefts to his mouth.

He dished up a couple of wicked hooks into my middle

that made me feel like I'd lost something, and then I clipped him with a right. He jerked his elbow into my face, so I gave him the treatment with my left and he rolled away along the ropes and got free.

I stepped back and lanced his lip with a left, hooked that same left to his ear, and took a wicked left to the body that jerked my mouth open, and then he lunged close and tried to butt.

"What's the matter?" I said. "Can't you win it fair?"

He jerked away from me and made me keep my mouth shut with a jolting left. I was counterpunching now. He started a hook and I beat him with an inside right that set him back on his heels. He tried to get his feet set, and rolled under a punch. I caught him with both hands and split one of his eyes.

Ludlow came in fast. It was a bitter, brutal, bloody fight and it was getting worse. His eyes were cut as badly as mine now, and both of us were doing plenty of bleeding. I was jolting him with body punches, and it was taking some of the snap out of him. Not that he didn't have plenty left. That guy would always have plenty left.

Sweat streamed into my eyes and the salt made me blink. I tried to wipe the blood away and caught a right hook for my pains. I went into a crouch and he put a hand on my head, trying to spin me. I was expecting that and hooked a left high and wide that caught him on the temple. It took him three steps to get his feet under him, and I was all over him like a cold shower.

He went back into the ropes, ripping punches with both hands, but I went on into him. He tried to use the laces and hit me low once, but that wasn't stopping me. Not any. I was out to get this guy, and get him but good. I hung him on the ropes and then the bell sounded and I turned and trotted to my corner.

Tony Innes was there, and he leaned over. "Watch yourself, kid. Mark's got some muscle men here."

"Don't let it throw you," Buck said grimly, "so've we!"

I looked at him, and then glanced back at the crowd. Lanning was there, all right, and Gasparo was with him, but they both looked unhappy. Then I recognized some faces. Bulge Mahaney, the carnival strong man from Greater American, had a big hand resting on Lanning's shoulder. Beside him, with a heavy cane I knew to be loaded with lead, was Charley Dismo, who ran the Ferris wheel.

Behind them, around them, were a half-dozen tough carnival roughnecks. I grinned suddenly, and then, right behind my corner, I saw somebody else. It was Mantry, the big guy I fought several times. He lifted a hand and waved to me, grinning from ear to ear. Friends? Gosh, I had lots of friends.

Yet, in that minute, I looked for Marge. No, there was no love in me for her, but I felt sorry for the girl. I caught her eye, and she was looking at me. She started to look away, but I waved to her, and smiled. She looked startled, and when the bell rang I got a glimpse of her again, and there were tears in her eyes.

Van Ludlow wasn't looking at tears in anybody's eyes. He came out fast and clipped me with a right that rang all the bells in my head. I didn't have to look to see who these bells were tolling for. So I got off the canvas, accepted a steamy left hand to get close and began putting some oomph into some short arm punches into his middle.

He ripped into me but I rolled away, and he busted me again, and then I shoved him away and clipped him. His legs turned to rubber and I turned his head with a left and set Mary Ann for the payoff. He knew it was coming, but the guy was still trying; he jerked away and let one come down the main line.

That one got sidetracked about a flicker away from my chin, but the right that I let go, with all the payoff riding on it, didn't. It took him coming in and he let go everything and went down on his face so hard you'd have thought they'd dropped him from the roof!

A cloud of resin dust floated up and I walked back to my corner. I leaned on the ropes feeling happy and good, and then the referee came over and lifted my right and the crowd went even crazier than they had already. The referee let go my hand, and when I started to take a bow, I bowed all the way to the canvas, hit it, and passed out cold.

Only for a minute, though. They doused me with water and picked me up. They were still working over Van Ludlow. I walked across toward his corner, writing shallow figure S's with my feet, and put my hand on his shoulder.

Duck Miller was standing there with his cigar in his face and he looked at me through the smoke.

"Hi, champ," he said.

I stopped and looked at him. "I won some dough on this fight," I said. "I'm going to open a poolroom, gym, and bowling alley in Zenith. I need a manager. Want the job?"

He looked at me, and something came into his eyes that told me Duck Miller had all I'd ever believed he had.

"Sure," he said, "I'd never work for a better guy!"

I walked back to my corner then, and Buck Farley slipped my robe around my shoulders and I crawled through the ropes. I walked back to the dressing room. Pop was leaning on the table with a roll of bills you could carry in a wheelbarrow. "I bet some money," he said happily, "a lot of money!" He looked up. "And you," he said, "even if you never get a middleweight title fight, you are still going to be a wealthy young man!"

When I came out, Marge was sitting in the canary convertible.

"Everything all right?" I asked.

"Yes." She looked at me.

"If it isn't," I said, "let me know."

She sat there looking at me, and then she said, "I guess I made a mistake."

"No," I said, "you weren't brave enough to take a chance."

All the way back to the ranch I could hear Pop and Buck talking about how the G-men came in and picked Lanning up for some gyp deal on his income tax, an investigation stirred up by my stories from the West. But I wasn't thinking of that.

I was thinking that in the morning I'd slip on some old

brogans and a sweater to take a walk over the hills. I'd watch the grass shifting in the wind, see the brown specks of my cattle in the meadows, the blunt angles of my corrals and barns. I was thinking that after the frozen winters in Korea, the blood and sweat of the ring—choking down that smoky air . . . how I loved and hated it—I had a chance with something that was really mine. I had no one to fight anymore.

FIGHTERS SHOULD BE HUNGRY

I

A BRUTAL BLOW in the ribs jerked Tandy Moore from a sound sleep. Gasping, he rolled into a fetal position and looked up to see a brakeman standing over him with his foot drawn back for another kick. With a lunge Tandy was on his feet, his dark eyes blazing. Fists cocked, he started for the brakeman, who backed suddenly away. "Unload!" the man said harshly. "Get off! An' be quick about it!"

Tandy was a big young man with wide shoulders and a sun-darkened face, darkened still further by a stubble of black beard. He chuckled with cold humor.

"Nope," Tandy said grimly, and with relish. "If you want me off, you put me off! Come on, I'm going to like this!"

Instead of a meek and frightened tramp, the brakeman had uncovered a wolf with bared teeth. The brakeman backed away still farther.

"You get off!" he insisted. "If that bull down to the yards finds you here, he'll report it an' I'll get chewed out!"

Tandy Moore relaxed a bit. "You watch yourself, mister! You can lose teeth walkin' up an' kickin' a guy that way!" He grabbed the edge of the gondola and lifted himself to the top, then swung his feet over to the ladder. "Say, Jack? What town is this anyway? Not that it makes much difference."

"Astoria, Oregon. End of the line."

"Thanks." Tandy climbed down the ladder, gauged the speed of the train, and dropped off, hitting the cinders on the run.

As though it had been planned for him, a path slanted down off the grade and into a dense jungle of brush that lined the sides and bottom of a shallow ditch. He slowed and started down the path.

Astoria was almost home, but he wasn't going home. There was nothing there for him anymore. He trotted along near the foot of a steeply slanting hill. He could smell the sea and the gray sky was spitting a thin mist of rain.

At the bottom of the muddy path lay a mossy gray plank bridging a trickle of water, and beyond it the trail slanted up and finally entered a patch of woods surrounded by a wasteland of logged-off stumps.

Almost as soon as Moore entered the thicket, he smelled the smoke of a campfire. He stopped for a moment, brushing at his baggy, gray tweed trousers with his hand. He wore a wool shirt open at the neck, and a worn leather jacket. His razor, comb, and toothbrush lay in one pocket of the jacket. He had no other possessions. He wore no hat, and his black hair was a coarse mass of unruly curls. As presentable as a hobo could be, he started forward.

Of the four men who sat around the fire, only two commanded his attention. A short, square-shouldered, square-faced man with intelligent eyes reclined on the ground, leaning on an elbow. Nearby a big man with black hair freely sprinkled with gray stood over the fire.

There was something familiar about the big man's face, but Tandy was sure he had never seen him before. His once-powerful build was apparently now overlaid with a layer of softness, and his eyes were blue and pleasant, almost mild.

The other two were typical of the road, a gray-faced man, old and leathery, and a younger man with dirty skin, white under the grime, and a weak chin and mouth.

"How's for some coffee?" Tandy asked, his eyes shifting from one to the other.

"Ain't ready yet, chum. Don't know that we have enough, anyway." The white-faced young man looked up at him. "They booted you off that drag, huh?"

Tensing, Tandy turned his head and looked down at the fellow, his eyes turning cold. It was an old song and this was how it always started.

"I got off on my own," he said harshly. "Nobody makes me do nothin'!"

"Tough guy?" The fellow looked away. "Well, somebody'll take all that out of you."

Tandy reached down and collared him, jerking him to his tiptoes. They were of the same age, but there the resemblance ceased, for where there was bleak power in Tandy's hard young face, there was only weakness in the tramp's.

"It ain't gonna be you, is it, sucker? You crack wise again and I'll slap some sense into you!" Tandy said coolly.

"Put him down," the big man said quietly. "You've scared the wits out of him now. No use to hit him."

Tandy had no intention of hitting him unless he had to, but the remark irritated him more. He dropped the kid and turned.

"Maybe *you* want to start something?" he demanded.

The big man only smiled and shook his head. "No, kid, I don't give a damn what you do. Just don't make a fool of yourself."

"Fool, huh?" Tandy could feel them backing him up, cornering him. "You listen to me, you yellow . . ." He reached for the big man.

A fist smashed into his mouth, and then another crossed to his jaw and he hit the dirt flat on his back.

Tandy Moore lay on the ground for an instant, more amazed at the power of that blow than hurt. The big man stood by the fire, calm and unruffled. Rage overcame Tandy, he came off the ground with a lunge and threw everything he had into a wicked right hand.

It caught only empty air, but a big, hard-knuckled fist slammed into his chest and stopped his rush, then a right crossed on his jaw and lights exploded in his brain. He went down again but threw himself over and up in one continuous movement. His head buzzing, he spat blood from broken lips and began to circle warily. This big fellow could punch.

Tandy lunged suddenly and swung, but the big man side-stepped smoothly and Tandy fell past him. He cringed, half expecting a blow before he could turn, but none came. He whirled, his fists ready, and the big man stood there calmly, his hands on his hips.

"Cut it out, kid," he said quietly. "I don't want to beat your skull in. You can't fight a lick on earth!"

"Who says I can't!" Tandy lunged and swung, only this time he was thinking and as he swung with his right, he shifted suddenly and brought up a short, wicked left into the big man's liver.

The fellow's face went gray, and the square-faced man on the ground sat up suddenly.

"Watch it, Gus!" he warned.

Gus backed away hastily, and seeing his advantage, Tandy moved in, more cautious but poised and ready. But he ran into something different, for the big man was moving now, strangely graceful. A left stiffened his mouth, a right smashed him on the chin, and another left dropped him to his knees.

Tandy got to his feet and licked his cut lips. The old guy was fast.

"You can punch, darn you!" he growled. "But this scrap ain't over. I'll fight until you drop!"

"Kid," the man warned, "we're fightin' for no good reason. You're carrying a chip but it's not for us. If I put you down again, I'll not let you get up. You know I'm not yellow, and I know you've got nerve enough to tackle all of us. What do you say we cut this out?"

Tandy hesitated, backing up. The man on the ground spoke, "Come on, son, have some coffee."

Tandy dropped his hands with a shrug.

"Mister," he said with a shamefaced grin, "I shouldn't have gone off like I did. I asked for it." He eyed Gus with respect. "You can sure use your dukes, though!"

"Don't take it hard, kid." The square-faced man smiled at him. "He used to be a prizefighter."

Across the fire the white-faced kid kept his mouth shut, not looking at either of them.

Tandy Moore shrugged. "Well he got me, but that fancy stuff ain't no good in a real scrap! Why, there's plenty of men in the lumber camps and mines could beat Joe Louis's head in if they had the chance."

"Don't kid yourself," Gus said quietly. "Fightin' is like anything else. A professional fighter does his job better than a greenhorn because he knows how.

"That fancy stuff, as you call it, is nothin' but a lot of things a lot of fighters learned over a thousand years or more. That's how scientific boxing was born. You were using it when you feinted and hit me with the left."

Tandy stared at him, then shrugged. "Ahhh, I figure you can either fight or you can't!"

Gus smiled at Tandy. "How many times have you been licked, kid?"

"Me?" Tandy bristled. "Nobody never licked me!"

"That's what I figured," Gus said. "You are big enough, tough enough, and aggressive enough so you could fight every night around hobo jungles like this one and never lose. In the ring, almost any half-baked preliminary boy would cut you to ribbons.

"I was through as a fighter ten years ago. I haven't trained since but right now I could chop you into pieces and never catch a punch. I was careless, or you wouldn't have clipped me as you did."

Tandy scoffed. "Maybe, but if I had a chance at one of those prelim boys you talk about, I'd show you!"

"Gus"—the square-faced man had seated himself on a log—"maybe this is the guy? What do you think?"

Gus stared at Tandy with a new expression in his eyes. He looked him over thoughtfully, nodded slowly. "Maybe . . . Kid, did you mean what you said? Would you want to try it?"

Tandy grinned. "I sure would! If there was a shot at some dough!"

———

THE GYMNASIUM IN Astoria was no polished and airy retreat for overstuffed businessmen. It was a dim and musty basement with a heavy canvas bag, darkened around the middle by countless punches thrown by sweat-soaked gloves, a ring slightly smaller than regulation, its ropes wound with gauze, three creaking speed bags, and a broken horse. In one corner there were barbells made from different sizes of car and truck brake drums. A wan light filtered through dirty windows set high in the walls.

It was there, in a borrowed pair of blue trunks that clung precariously to his lean hips, and under them a suit of winter underwear rescued from a basement table by Gus Coe, that Tandy Moore began the process of learning to be a fighter. Their sole capital was a ten-dollar advance from a bored promoter, and five dollars Gus wheedled from a poolroom proprietor. Briggs, Gus's friend of the square face, leaned back against the wall with a watch in his hand, and Gus stood by while Tandy, bored and uncomfortable, looked at the heavy bag doubtfully.

"Now look," Gus said patiently, "you got a left hand but you don't use it right. Lift that left fist up to shoulder height an' hold it well out. When you hit, punch straight from the shoulder and step in with that left foot. Not much, just a couple of inches, maybe. But step in. Now try it."

Tandy tried it. His gloved fist smacked the bag solidly but without much force. Tandy looked unhappily at Gus.

"You mean like that? I couldn't break an egg!"

"You keep trying it. Shoot it straight out, make it snap. An' bring your fist back on the same line your punch traveled." He stepped up to the bag. "Like this—"

The left shot out and the bag jumped with the explosive force of the blow. Tandy Moore looked thoughtful.

It worked when Gus threw it, no question about that. Well, the least he could do was humor the guy. He was beginning to like Gus Coe. The big, easygoing ex-fighter was shrewd and thoughtful. And Briggs . . .

Briggs puzzled Tandy. He was quiet, so quiet you almost forgot he was around, but somehow he always gave Tandy the feeling of being dangerous. He was a man you would never start anything with. Tandy also knew that Briggs carried a gun. He had seen him with it, a small Browning automatic in a shoulder holster.

This training was nonsense. The exercise was okay, it got your muscles in shape, but as for the rest of it, Tandy shrugged mentally. You could either fight or you couldn't.

Just let him get in the ring with one of those fancy Dans. He'd show them a thing or two!

II

THAT NIGHT TANDY stayed up late talking to his two new companions. He watched them closely, trying to figure out just what it was they were up to.

"What's the angle?" Tandy finally demanded. "I mean, down there in the jungle, Briggs said something about maybe I was the guy?"

Gus dropped on the rooming-house bed opposite him. "It's like this, kid. A guy gave me an awful jobbing a while back. The guy is a big-shot manager and he's got money. The Portland and Seattle gamblers are with him, and that means a lot of muscle men, too. He got to one of my fighters, and one way and another, he broke me an' got me run out of town. Briggs knows all about it."

"But where do I come in?" Tandy asked.

"Both of us figured we might get a fighter and go back an' try him again. The best way to get to him is to whip his scrapper . . . take his money on the bets."

"Who's his fighter?" Tandy asked.

Gus grinned at him. "A Portland boy, Stan Reiser," he said. *"Reiser!"* Tandy Moore came off the chair with a jump.

"Sure." Gus nodded. "He's probably one of the three top men on the coast right now, but you don't take him on your first fight." He looked at Tandy. "I thought you wanted to fight those guys? That you figured you could run any of them out of the ring?"

"It ain't that," Moore said, quieter now. "It's just that it isn't what I expected." His face turned grim and hard. "Yeah," he agreed, "I'll go along. I'd like to fight that guy. I'd like to lick him. I'd like to beat him until he couldn't move!"

Turning abruptly, Tandy walked out of the room and they heard his feet going down the stairs. Briggs stared at the door.

"What do you make of that?" Gus asked.

Briggs shrugged. "That kid's beyond me," he said. "Sometimes he gives me cold chills."

"You, too?" Gus looked understandingly at Briggs. "Funny, a kid like that making us feel this way."

Briggs rubbed out his cigarette. "Something's eatin' him, Gus. Something deep inside. We saw it this morning an' we may have just hit on it again, though what it has to do with Reiser or your situation I ain't gonna guess."

———

THEY WALKED INTO a hotel restaurant the night of the fight. It was early, late afternoon really. The wind was whipping in off the Pacific in blasts that slammed the door closed as they came through. In these new surroundings, they looked shabby and out of place. This was blocks from the cheap rooming house where they lived, blocks from the beanery in which they had been eating.

They sat on stools at the restaurant counter, and a girl brought the menus. Tandy Moore looked up, looked into the eyes of the girl beyond the counter.

She smiled nervously and asked, "What can I get for you?"

Tandy jerked a thumb at Gus. "Ask him," he said, and stared down at his knuckles. He was confused for there had been something in the girl's eyes that touched him. It made him feel scared and he hated it.

She looked from Gus to Briggs. "Who is this guy?" she asked. "Can't he order for himself? What do you do, poke it to him with a stick?"

Tandy looked up, his eyes full of sullen anger. That closed-in feeling was back. Gus dropped a hand on his arm.

"She's ribbin' you, kid. Forget it." He glanced down at the menu and then looked up. "A steak for him, an' make it rare. And just coffee for us."

When she turned away, Tandy looked around and said, low-voiced, "Gus, that'll take all the dough we've got! You guys eat, too. I don't need that steak."

"You fight tonight, not us," Gus replied, grinning. "All we ask is that you get in there and throw them."

The waitress came back with their coffee. She had caught the word "fight."

"You're fighting tonight?" she asked Tandy.

He did not look up. "Yeah," he said.

"You'd not be bad-looking," she said, "if you'd shave." She waited for a response, then glanced over at Gus, smiling. "Is he always like this?"

"He's a good kid," Gus said.

She went off to take another order but was back in a moment and, glancing around cautiously, slid a baked potato onto his plate. "Here's one on the house. Don't say I never gave you anything."

He didn't know how to reply so he mumbled thanks and started to eat. She stood there watching him, the tag on her uniform said "Dorinda."

"Come back and tell me about it." She looked at Tandy. "If you're able," she added.

"I'll be able!" he retorted. Their eyes met, and he felt something stir down deep within him. She was young, not over nineteen, and had brown hair and blue eyes. He looked at her again. "I'll come," he said, and flushed.

When they finished dinner, they walked around the block a couple of times to start warming up, then headed for the dressing room.

———

AN HOUR AND a half later Gus Coe taped up Tandy's hands. He looked at the young man carefully.

"Listen, kid, you watch yourself in there. This guy Al Joiner can box and he can punch. I would've got you something easier for your first fight, but they wanted somebody for this Joiner. He's a big favorite in town, very popular with the Norskies."

He cleared his throat and continued.

"We're broke, see? We get fifteen bucks more out of this fight; that's all. It was just twenty-five for our end, and we got ten of it in advance. If we win, we'll get another fight. That means we'll be a few bucks ahead of the game.

"I ain't goin' to kid you; you ain't ready. But you can punch, and you might win.

"You're hungry, kid. You're hungry for things that money can buy, an' you're mad." His eyes bored into Tandy's. "Maybe you've been mad all your life. Well, tonight you can fight back. Dempsey, Ketchell, lots of hungry boys did it in there. You can, too!"

Tandy looked down at Gus's big, gnarled hands. He knew the kindly face of the man who spoke to him, knew the worn shirt collar and the frayed cuffs. Gus had laundered their clothes these last days, using a borrowed iron for pressing.

Suddenly he felt very sorry for this big man who stood over him, and he felt something stirring within him that he had never known before. It struck him suddenly that he had a friend. Two of them.

"Sure," he said. "Okay, Gus."

———

IN THE CENTER of the ring, he did not look at Joiner. He saw only a pair of slim white legs and blue boxing trunks. He trotted back to his corner, and looked down at his feet in their borrowed canvas shoes.

Then the bell rang and he turned, glaring across the ring from under his heavy brows and moving out, swift and ready.

Al Joiner was taller than he was with wide, powerful shoulders. His eyes were sharp and ready, his lips clenched over the mouthpiece. They moved toward each other, Joiner on his toes, Tandy shuffling, almost flat-footed.

Al's left was a darting snake. It landed, sharp and hard, on his brow. Tandy moved in and Al moved around him, the left darting. A dozen times the left landed, but Tandy lunged close, swinging a looping, roundhouse right.

The punch was too wide and too high, but Joiner was careless. It caught him on the side of the head like a falling sledge and his feet flew up and he hit the canvas, an expression of dazed astonishment on his face. At seven he was on his feet and moving more carefully.

He faded away from Tandy's wild, reckless punches. Faded

away, jabbing. The bell sounded with Tandy still coming in, a welt over his left eye and a blue mouse under the right.

"Watch your chance an' use that left you used on me," Gus suggested. "That'll slow this guy down. He's even faster than I thought."

The bell sounded and Tandy walked out to meet a Joiner who was now boxing beautifully, and no matter where Tandy turned, Joiner's left met him. His lips were cut and bleeding, punches thudded on his jaw. He lost the second round by an enormous margin.

The third opened the same way, but now Joiner began to force the fighting. He mixed the lefts with hard right crosses, and Tandy, his eyes blurred with blood, moved in, his hands cocked and ready. Al boxed carefully, aware of those dynamite-laden fists.

The fourth started fast. Tandy went out, saw the left move and threw his right, and the next thing he knew he was flat on his back with a roaring in his head and the referee was saying "Six!"

———

TANDY CAME OFF the canvas with a lunge of startled fury. A growl exploded from him as he swept into the other fighter, smashing past that left hand and driving him to the ropes. His right swung for Joiner's head and Al ducked, and Tandy lifted a short, wicked left to the liver and stood Joiner on his tiptoes.

Tandy stabbed a left at Joiner's face, then swung a powerful right. Joiner tried to duck and took the punch full on the ear. His knees sagged and he pitched forward on his face.

The referee made the count, then turned and lifted Tandy's hand. The fighter on the floor hadn't moved.

In the dressing room, Tandy stared bleakly at his battered face. "For this I get twenty-five bucks!" he said, grinning with swollen lips.

"Don't worry, kid!" Gus grinned back at him. "When you hit me with your left that day in the woods, I knew you had it. It showed you could think on your feet. You'll do!"

When they came out of the dressing room suddenly Gus

stopped and his hand on Tandy's arm tightened. Two men were standing there, a small man with a tight white face and a big cigar, and a big younger man.

"Hello, Gus," the man with the cigar said, contempt in his voice. "I see you've got yourself another punk!"

Tandy's left snaked out and smashed the cigar into the small man's teeth, knocking him sprawling into the wall, and then he whirled on the big man, a brawny blond whose eyes were blazing with astonishment.

"Now, you!" he snarled. His right whipped over like an arrow, but the big man stepped back swiftly and the right missed. Then, he started to step in, but Briggs stopped him.

"Back up, Stan!" he said coldly. "Back up unless you want lead for your supper! Lift that scum off the floor. It's lucky the kid didn't kill him!"

Stan Reiser stooped and lifted his manager from the floor. The black cigar was mashed into the blood of his split lips and his face was white and shocked, but his eyes blazed with murderous fury.

"I'll get you for this, Coe!" His voice was low and vicious. "You an' that S.O.—" His voice broke off sharply as Tandy Moore stepped toward him.

Moore glanced at Reiser. "Shut him up, Stan. I don't like guys who call me names!"

Reiser looked curiously at Tandy. "I know you from somewhere," he said thoughtfully, "I'll remember . . ."

Tandy's face was stiff and cold. "Go ahead!" he said quietly. "It will be a bad day for both of us when you do!"

OUTSIDE ON THE street, Gus shook his head. "What the hell is up with you?" he asked. "You shouldn't have done it, but nothin' ever did me so much good as watchin' you hit that snake. I don't believe anybody ever had nerve enough to sock him before, he's been king of the roost so long." Both Gus and Briggs looked at him quizzically.

"It's my business," Tandy growled and would say no more.

He said nothing but he was thinking. Now they had met again, and he did not know if he was afraid or not. Yet he knew that deep within him, there was still that memory and the hatred he had stifled so long, it was a feeling that demanded he face Reiser, to smash him, to break him.

"How would I do with Reiser?" he asked suddenly.

Gus looked astonished. "Kid, you sure don't know the fight game or you'd never ask a question like that. Stan is a contender for the heavyweight title."

Tandy nodded slowly. "I guess I've got plenty to learn," he said.

Gus nodded. "When you know that, kid, you've already learned the toughest part."

III

THREE WEEKS LATER, after conniving and borrowing and scraping by on little food, Tandy Moore was ready for his second fight. This one was with a rough slugger known as Benny Baker.

The day of the fight, Tandy walked toward the hotel. There would be no steak today, for they simply hadn't money enough. Yet he had been thinking of Dorinda, and wondering where she was and what she was doing.

She was coming out of the restaurant door as he walked by. Her eyes brightened quickly.

"Why, hello!" she greeted him. "I wondered what had happened to you. Why don't you ever come in and see me?"

He shoved his hands in the pockets of the shabby trousers. "Looking like this? Anyway, I can't afford to eat in there. I don't make enough money. In fact"—he grinned, his face flushing—"I haven't any money at all!"

She put a hand on his arm. "Don't let it bother you, Tandy. You'll do all right." She looked away, then back at him. "You're fighting again, aren't you?"

"Tonight. It's a preliminary." His eyes took in the softness of her cheek, the lights in her dark brown hair. "Come and see it. Would you?"

"I'm going to be there. I'll be sure to be there early to see your fight."

He looked at her suddenly. "Where are you going now? Let's take a walk."

Dorinda hesitated only an instant. "All right."

They walked along, neither of them saying much, until they stopped at a rail and looked down the sloping streets to the confusion of canneries and lumber wharves along the riverfront. Off to the northwest the sun slanted through the clouds and threw a silver light on the river, silhouetting a steam schooner inbound from the rough water out where the Columbia met the Pacific.

"You worked here long?" he asked suddenly.

"No, only about two months. I was headed to Portland but I couldn't find a job. I came from Arizona. My father has a ranch out there, but I thought I'd like to try singing. So I was going to go to school at night, and study voice in my spare time."

"That's funny, you being from Arizona," he said. "I just came from there!"

"You did?" She laughed. "One place is all sun, the other all rain."

"Well, I grew up here. In St. John's, over near Portland. My dad worked at a box-shuck factory there. You know, fruit boxes, plywood an' all."

"Is he still there"—she looked into his eyes—"in Portland?"

"No." Tandy had to look away. "Not anymore."

Dorinda suddenly glanced at her watch and gave a startled cry.

"Oh, we've got to go! I'm supposed to be back at work!"

They made their way along the street and down the hill. He left her at the door of the restaurant.

"I probably won't get a chance to see you after the fight," she said. "I've been invited to a party at the hotel."

Quick jealousy touched him. "Who's giving?" he demanded.

"The fellow who is taking me, Stan Reiser."

He stared at her, shocked and still. "Oh . . ."

He blinked, then turned swiftly and walked away, trembling inside. Everywhere he turned it was Stan Reiser. He heard her call after him, heard her take a few running steps toward him, but he did not stop or turn his head.

———

HE WAS BURNING with that old deep fury in the ring that night. Gus looked at him curiously as he stood in the corner rubbing his feet in the resin. In a ringside seat were Dorinda and Reiser, but Gus had not seen them yet. Briggs had. Briggs never missed anything.

"All right, kid," Gus said quietly, "you know more this time, and this guy ain't smart. But he can punch, so don't take any you can miss."

The bell sounded and Tandy Moore whirled like a cat. Benny Baker was fifteen pounds heavier and a blocky man, noted as a slugger. Tandy walked out fast and Benny sprang at him, throwing both hands.

Almost of its own volition, Tandy's left sprang from his shoulder. It was a jab, and a short one, but it smashed Benny Baker on the nose and stopped him in his tracks. Tandy jabbed again, then feinted, and when Baker lunged he drilled a short right to the slugger's chin.

Benny Baker hit the canvas on the seat of his pants, his eyes dazed. He floundered around and got up at six, turning to meet Tandy. Baker looked white around the mouth, and he tried to clinch, but Tandy stepped back and whipped up a powerful right uppercut and then swung a looping left to the jaw.

Baker hit the canvas on his shoulder blades. At the count of ten, he had not even wiggled a toe.

Tandy Moore turned then and avoiding Dorinda's eyes looked squarely at Reiser. It was only a look that held an instant, but Stan's face went dark and he started half to his feet, then slumped down.

"Go back to Albina Street, you weasel," Tandy said. "I'll be coming for you!" Then he slipped through the ropes and walked away.

Gus Coe watched the interchange. The big ex-fighter took his cigar from his mouth and looked at Stan thoughtfully. There was something between those two. But what?

WITH THEIR WINNINGS as a stake they took to the road. The following week, at the armory in Klamath Falls, Tandy Moore stopped Joe Burns in one round, and thereafter in successive weeks at Baker City and Eugene he took Glen Hayes in two, Rolph Williams in one, Pedro Sarmineto in five, and Chuck Goslin in three.

Soon the fans were beginning to talk him up and the sportswriters were hearing stories of Tandy Moore.

"How soon do I get a chance at Reiser?" Tandy demanded, one night in their room.

Gus looked at him thoughtfully. "You shouldn't fight Reiser for a year," he said, and then added, "You've got something against him? What is it?"

"I just want to get in there with him. I owe him something, and I want to make sure he gets it!"

"Well," Gus said, looking at his cigar, "we'll see."

A little later, Gus asked, "Have you seen that girl lately, the one who used to work in the restaurant?"

Tandy, trying not to show interest, shrugged and shook his head.

"No. Why should I see her?"

"She was a pretty girl," Gus said. "Seemed to sort of like you, too."

"She went to the fights with Reiser."

"So what? That doesn't make her his girl, does it?" Gus demanded. "Did you ask her to go? I could have snagged a couple of ducats to bring her and a friend."

Tandy didn't answer.

Gus took the cigar from his teeth, changed the subject abruptly.

"The trouble is," he said, "you got Reiser on your mind, and I don't know just how good you are. Sometimes when a man wants something awful bad, he improves pretty fast. In the short time we've been together, you've learned more than any scrapper I ever knew. But it's mighty important right now that I know how good you are."

Tandy looked up from the magazine he was thumbing. "Why now?"

"We've got an offer. Flat price of five grand, win, lose, or draw, for ten rounds with Buster Crane."

"Crane?" Tandy dropped the magazine he was holding to the tabletop. "That guy held Reiser to a draw. He had him on the floor!"

"That's the one. He's good, too. He can box and he can hit, and he's fast. The only thing is, I'm kind of suspicious."

Briggs, who had been listening, looked up thoughtfully. "You mean you think it's a frame?"

"I think Bernie Satneck, Reiser's manager, would frame his own mother," Gus answered. "I think he's gettin' scared of the kid here. Tandy wants Reiser, an' Satneck knows it. He's no fool, an' the kid has been bowling them over ever since he started, so what's more simple than to get him a scrap with Crane when the kid is green? If Crane beats him bad, he is finished off and no trouble for Satneck."

Conscious of Tandy Moore's intent gaze, he turned toward him. "What is it, kid?"

"Satneck, I want to take him down, too! Him and his brother."

"I didn't know he had a brother," Briggs said.

"He may have a dozen for all I know," Gus said.

"Go ahead," Tandy said, "take that fight. I'll be ready." He grinned suddenly. "Five thousand? That's more than we've made in all of them, so far."

He walked out and closed the door. Briggs sat still for a while, then he got up and started out himself.

"Where you goin'?" Gus asked suspiciously.

"Why," Briggs said gently, "I'm getting very curious. I thought I'd go find out if Satneck has a brother and what they have to do with our boy here."

"Yeah," Gus said softly, "I see what you mean."

THE MONTH THAT followed found Tandy Moore in Wiley Spivey's gym six days a week. They were in Portland now, across the river from downtown and back in Tandy's home territory, although he mentioned this to no one. He worked with fighters of every size and style, with sluggers and boxers, with skilled counterpunchers. He listened to Gus pick flaws in their styles, and he studied slow-motion pictures of Crane's fights with Reiser.

He knew Buster Crane was good. He was at least a hundred percent better than any fighter Tandy had yet tackled. Above all, he could hit.

Briggs wasn't around. Tandy commented on that and Gus said, "Briggs? He's away on business, but will be back before the fight."

"He's quiet, isn't he? Known him long?"

"Twelve years, about. He's a dangerous man, kid. He was bodyguard for a politician with enemies, then he was a private dick. He was with the O.S.S. during the war, and he was a partner of mine when we had that trouble with Satneck and Reiser."

IV

TANDY MOORE STOPPED on the corner and looked down the street toward the river, but he was thinking of Buster Crane. That was the only thing that was important now. He must, at all costs, beat Crane.

Walking along, he glimpsed his reflection in a window and stopped abruptly. He saw a tall, clean-shaven, well-built young man with broad shoulders and a well-groomed look. He looked far better, he decided, than the rough young man who had eaten the steak that day in the restaurant and looked up into the eyes of Dorinda Lane.

Even as his thoughts repeated the name, he shied violently from it, yet he had never forgotten her. She was always there, haunting his thoughts. Remembering her comments, he never shaved but that he thought of her.

He had not seen her since that night when she came to the fight with Stan Reiser. And she hadn't worked at the restaurant in Astoria anymore after he returned from Klamath Falls.

Restlessly, Tandy Moore paced the streets, thinking first of Dorinda and then of Stan Reiser and all that lay behind it.

It was his driving urge to meet Reiser in the ring that made him so eager to learn from Gus. But it was more than that, too, for he had in him a deep love of combat, of striving, of fighting for something. But what?

———

GUS COE WAS sitting in the hotel lobby when Tandy walked in. Gus seemed bigger than ever, well, he was fatter, and looked prosperous now. He grinned at Tandy and said something out of the corner of his mouth to Briggs, who was sitting, and the Irishman got up; his square face warm with a smile.

"How are you, Tandy?" he said quietly.

"Hey, Briggsie, welcome back." He glanced at Gus. "Say, let's go to a nightclub tonight. I want to get out and look around."

"The kid's got an idea," Briggs said. "We'll go to Nevada Johnson's place. He's putting on the fight and it'll be good for the kid to be seen there. We can break it up early enough so he can get his rest. It would do us all good to relax a little."

Gus shrugged. "Okay."

The place was fairly crowded, but they got a table down front, and they were hardly seated before the orchestra started to play, and then the spotlight swung onto a girl who was singing.

Gus looked up sharply, and Tandy's face was shocked and still, for the girl outlined by the spotlight was Dorinda Lane.

Tandy stared, and then he swallowed a sudden lump in his throat. Her voice was low and very beautiful, and he had never dreamed she could look so lovely. He sat entranced until her song ended, and then he looked over at Gus.

"Let's get out of here," he said.

"Wait—" Gus caught his wrist, for the spotlight had swung to their table and the master of ceremonies gestured toward him.

"We have a guest with us tonight, ladies and gentlemen! A guest we are very proud to welcome! Tandy Moore, that rising young heavyweight who meets Buster Crane tomorrow night!"

Tandy looked trapped but took an uneasy bow. The spotlight swung away from him, and Gus leaned over.

"Nice going, kid," he said. "You looked good. Do you still want to go?"

They started for the door, and then Tandy looked over and saw Bernie Satneck sitting at a table on the edge of the floor. Reiser was with him, and another man who was a younger tougher version of the manager! Tandy locked his eyes forward and walked toward the lobby.

At the door he was waiting for Gus and Briggs to get their hats, when he heard a rustle of silk and looked around into Dorinda's face.

"Were you going to leave without seeing me?" she asked, holding out her hand.

He hesitated, his face flushing. Why did she have to be so beautiful and so desirable? He jerked his head toward the dining room.

"Stan Reiser's in there," he said. "Isn't he your boyfriend?"

Her eyes flashed her resentment. "No, he's not! And he never was! If you weren't so infernally stubborn, Tandy Moore, I'd have . . ."

"So, how did you get this job?"

Her face went white, and the next thing, her palm cracked across his mouth. The cigarette girl turned, her eyes wide, and the headwaiter started to hurry over, but Gus Coe arrived just in time. Catching Tandy's arm, he rushed him out the door.

Tandy was seething with anger, but anger more at himself than her. After all, it was a rotten thing for him to say. Maybe that hadn't been the way of it. And if it had, well, he'd been hungry himself. He was still hungry, no longer for food now, but for other things. And then the thought came to him that he was still hungry for her, Dorinda Lane.

———

THE CROWD WAS jammed to the edge of the ring when he climbed through the ropes the next night. His face was a somber mask. He heard the dull roar of thousands of people, and ducked his head to them and hurried to his corner.

In the center of the ring during the referee's briefing, he got his first look at Buster Crane, a heavyweight with twenty more pounds than his own one-ninety, but almost an inch shorter, and with arms even longer.

When the bell rang, he shut his jaws on his mouthpiece and turned swiftly. Crane was moving toward him, his eyes watchful slits under knitted brows. Crane had a shock of white blond hair and a wide face, but the skin was tight over the bones.

Crane moved in fast, feinted, then hooked high and hard. The punch was incredibly fast and Tandy caught it on the temple, but he was going away from it. Even so, it shook him to his heels, and with a queer kind of thrill, he realized that no man he had ever met had punched like Buster Crane. He was in for a battle.

Tandy jabbed, then jabbed again. He missed a right cross and Crane was inside slamming both hands into his body. He backed up, giving ground. He landed a left to the head, drilled a right down the center that missed, then shook Buster up with a short left hook to the head.

From there on, the battle was a surging struggle of two hard-hitting young men filled with a zest for combat. The second round opened with a slashing attack from Crane that drove Tandy into the ropes, but his long weeks of schooling had done their job and he covered up, clinched, and saved himself. He played it easy on the defensive for the remainder of the round.

The third, fourth, and fifth rounds were alike, with vicious toe-to-toe scrapping every bit of the way. Coming out for the sixth, Tandy Moore could feel the lump over his eye, and he was aware that Crane's left hook was landing too often. Thus far, Crane was leading by a margin, and it was that hook that was doing it.

A moment later the same left hook dropped out of nowhere and Tandy's heels flew up and he sat down hard.

Outside the ring, the crowd was a dull roar and he rolled over on his hands and knees, unable to hear the count. He glanced toward his corner and saw Gus holding up four, then five fingers. He waited until the ninth finger came up, and then he got to his feet and backed away.

Crane moved in fast and sure. He had his man hurt and he knew it. He didn't look so good or feel so good himself, and was conscious that he wanted only one thing, to get this guy out of action before he had his head ripped off.

Crane feinted a left, then measured Moore with it, but Tandy rolled inside the punch and threw a left to the head, which missed. Crane stepped around carefully and then tried again. This time he threw his left hook, but Tandy Moore was ready. He remembered what he had been taught, and when he saw that hook start, he threw his own right inside of it.

With the right forearm partially blocking, his fist crashed down on Crane's chin with a shock that jarred Tandy to the shoulder!

Buster Crane hit the canvas on his face, rolled over, and then climbed slowly to his knees. At nine he made it, but just barely.

Tandy walked toward him looking him over carefully. Crane was a puncher and he was hurt, which made him doubly dangerous. Tandy tried a tentative left, and Crane brushed it aside and threw his own left hook from the inside. Tandy had seen him use the punch in the newsreel pictures he had studied, and the instant it started, he pulled the trigger on his own right, a short, wicked hook at close range.

Crane hit the canvas and this time he didn't get up.

When he was dressed, Tandy walked with Gus Coe to the promoter's office to get the money. Briggs strolled along, his hands in his pockets, just behind them.

When they opened the door, Tandy's skin tightened, for Stan Reiser and Bernie Satneck were sitting at a table with a tall, gray-haired man whom Tandy instantly recognized as "Nevada" Johnson, the biggest fight promoter in the Northwest.

The rest of the room was crowded with sportswriters.

"Nice fight, tonight, Moore," Johnson said. "We've been waiting for you. How would you like to fight for the title?"

"The championship?" Tandy was incredulous. "Sure, I'd like to fight for it! But don't I get to fight him first?"

He gestured at Reiser and saw the big heavyweight's eyes turn ugly.

"See?" Nevada Johnson said to Satneck. "He's not only ready, but anxious to fight your boy. You say that Reiser deserves a title bout. Six months ago, I would have said the same thing, but now the situation has changed. Moore has made a sensational rise from nothing, although knowing Coe was his manager, I'm not surprised."

"This kid isn't good enough," Satneck protested. "The fans won't go for it. They'll think he's just a flash in the pan and it won't draw!"

Johnson looked around at the sportswriters and asked, "What about that?"

"If Bernie will forgive me," Hansen of the *Telegraph* said quietly, "I think he's crazy! A Tandy Moore and Stan Reiser fight will outdraw either of them with the champ, as long as we mention that the winner goes for the title. It's a natural if there ever was one."

"Frankly," Coe said quietly, "I can understand how Satneck must feel. After all, he's brought Reiser a long way, and it seems a shame to get his fighter whipped when the title is almost in his hands."

"Whipped?" Satneck whirled on Coe. "Why, that stinking little . . ." He looked at Tandy and his voice faded out and he flushed.

"I'd *like* to fight him," Tandy said, pleasantly enough. "I'd like nothing better than to get Reiser where he could take a poke at me when my back's not turned!"

Johnson and several of the sportswriters sat forward.

Reiser's face went dead-white but his eyes were thoughtful. He turned to his manager.

"Sign it!" he snapped. "Let's get out of here!"

Satneck glanced from Stan's face to Tandy's, and then at Gus, who was grinning mysteriously.

"What was that about?" the reporters asked, but Tandy just shook his head. Without another word, he grabbed the fountain pen that Johnson offered and signed.

———

AT THE HOTEL that night, when Tandy was in bed, Briggs and Gus sat in Gus's room. Neither of them spoke for a moment.

"I dug it up," Briggs said quietly "An' don't worry, Tandy's okay. His old man was a rummy, he worked down here at the factory by the bridge. He was a better than fair street-scrapper when sober. Satneck's brother got lippy with him once, an' Tandy's old man mopped up the floor with him. Then, one night when he was tight, an' all but helpless, two of them held him while Reiser beat him up. It was an ugly mess. The kid came up on them and they slugged him."

"What about the kid?" Gus said, impatient.

"I was coming to that," Briggs said. "They knocked him out. Reiser did it, I think, with a sap. But when the kid came out of it, his old man was all bloody and badly beaten. Tandy got him home and tried to fix him up. When his old man didn't come to, Tandy called a doctor. The kid's father had a bad concussion and never was quite right after that. The slugging they gave him affected his mind and one side of his body. He could never work again."

"Did it go to court?"

"Uh-huh, but Tandy was one against a dozen witnesses, and they made the kid out a liar and he lost the case. The father died a couple of years ago. The kid's not quite ten years younger than Reiser, and couldn't have been more than a youngster when it all happened. I guess he's been on the bum ever since."

"The kid's hungry to get Stan Reiser into a ring with him," Gus said slowly.

"It's easy to see why Reiser didn't recognize him," Briggs said. "Tandy must have changed a lot since then. As far as that goes, look how much he's changed since we met him. You'd never know he was the same person. He's filled out, hardened up, and he looks good now."

"Well, I'm glad that's all there was," Gus said thoughtfully. "I was worried."

Briggs hesitated. "It isn't quite all, Gus," he said. "There is more."

"More?"

"That wasn't the first time the kid and Reiser met. They had a scrap once. Reiser was always mean, and he teased Tandy once when the kid was selling papers on a corner out here on Albina Street. The kid had spunk and swung on him, and I guess the punch hurt, because Stan darn near killed him with his fists. I think that's what started the row with his father."

Gus Coe scowled. "That's not good. Sometimes a beating like that sticks in the mind, and this one might. Well, all we can do is to go along and see. Right now, the kid's shaping up for this fight better than ever.

"You know, one of us has got to stay with him, Briggsie. Every minute!"

"That's right." Briggs sat down. "Bernie won't stand for this. We just blocked him from the championship and no matter what Reiser thinks, Bernie is scared. He's scared Tandy can win, and as he used every dirty trick in the game to bring Stan along, he certainly won't change now."

Gus nodded.

"You're right. He'll stop at nothing. The kid got under Reiser's skin tonight, too, and once in that ring, it will be little short of murder . . . for one or the other of them."

Briggs nodded. "You know, Gus, maybe we should duck Reiser."

Gus was thoughtful for a moment, and then he said, "I know. The kid may not be afraid of Reiser. But frankly, I am. I wanted to get even with Satneck and Reiser for the one they pulled on us, but that's not important anymore. Tandy is. I like him and he's goin' places."

"Yeah," Briggs agreed. "I like the kid, too."

———

TANDY MOORE, HIS cuts healed, went back to the gym under Spivy's Albina Street Pool Room with a will. In meeting Reiser, he would be facing a man who wanted to maim and kill. Reiser had everything to lose by this fight and Tandy had all to gain. Reiser was the leading contender for the title, and was acknowledged a better man than the current champion. If he lost now, he was through.

Going and coming from the gym, and in his few nights around town, Tandy watched for Dorinda. He wanted to call and apologize for the nightclub scene, but was too proud, and despite his wish, he could see no reason for thinking he might not have been right. Yet he didn't want to believe it, and deep within himself, he did *not* believe it.

As the days drew on and the fight came nearer, Tandy was conscious of a new tension. He could see that Gus Coe and Briggs were staying close to him; that Coe's face had sharpened and grown more tense, that Briggs was ever more watchful, and that they always avoided dark streets and kept him to well-lighted public thoroughfares.

To one who had been so long accustomed to the harsh and hard ways of life, it irritated Tandy even while he understood their feelings and knew they were thinking of him. He was realist enough to know that Bernie Satneck was not going to chance losing a fighter worth a million dollars without putting up a battle.

Bernie Satneck would stop at nothing. Nor would Stan Reiser, when it came to that.

Come what may between now and the day of the fight, Tandy Moore knew that all would be settled in the ring. He also knew that although Reiser was a hard puncher and a shrewd, dangerous fighter who took every advantage, he was not afraid of him. This was his chance to get some revenge both for himself and his father . . . and it was legal.

V

ONE DAY, HANSEN, the reporter, dropped around to the second-floor hotel where they were staying. Tandy was lying on the bed in a robe, relaxing after a tough workout. The smell of Chinese food from the café downstairs drifted in through the window. The sportswriter dropped into a chair and dug out his pipe; he lit it up.

"I want to know about you and Stan Reiser," he suggested suddenly. "You knew him when you were a kid, didn't you? Out in St. John's? Wasn't there bad blood between you?"

"Maybe." Tandy turned his head. "Look, Hansen, I like you. I don't want to give you a bum steer or cross you up in any way. Whatever you learn about Stan or myself is your business, only I'm not telling you anything. Whatever differences we have, we'll settle in the ring."

"I agree." Hansen nodded, sucking on his pipe. "I've looked your record over, Tandy. Actually, I needn't have. I know Gus, and there isn't a straighter guy in this racket than Gus Coe. And Briggs? Well, Briggs is not a good man to get in the way of, not even for Bernie Satneck."

His eyes lifted, testing him with the name, and Tandy kept his face immobile.

"You've got a record since taking up with Coe that's as straight as a die," the reporter said. "If there ever was anything in your past, you have lived it down. I wouldn't say as much for Stan Reiser."

"What do you mean?" Tandy demanded.

"Just this. Bernie Satneck is running a string of illegal enterprises that touches some phase of every kind of crookedness there is. I've known about that for a long time, but it wasn't until just lately that I found out who was behind him—that he's not the top man himself."

"Who is?" Tandy didn't figure it really mattered, he wasn't after anything but a settling of old accounts.

"Stan Reiser." Hansen nodded as he said it. "Sure, we know; Bernie Satneck is his manager, and the manager is supposed to be the brains. Well, in this case that isn't so. Bernie is just a tool, a front man."

Hansen drew thoughtfully on his pipe. "I've been around the fight game a long time, had thirty years' experience around fighters. Once in a while, you strike a wrong gee among them. I think less so than in most professions or trades, because fighting demands a certain temperament or discipline. Despite their associations, most fighters are pretty square guys."

"You say Reiser isn't?"

"I *know* he isn't. I want to get him completely out of the fight game, and so do some others we know. If you put him down, get him out of the running for the championship, we'll keep him down. Don't underestimate the power of the press. Are you sure you don't want to tell me your story?"

"I'll fight him in the ring, that's all," Tandy said quietly. "Whatever there is between Reiser and me can be settled inside the ropes."

"Sure. That's the way I figured it." Hansen stopped as he was leaving. "I know about your father, but I won't write that story unless you give me the go-ahead."

GUS LEFT TANDY in the room on the day of the fight and went off on an errand across town. Briggs was around somewhere, but where Tandy did not know.

He removed his shirt and shoes and lay down on the bed. He felt anything but sleepy, so he opened a magazine and began to read.

There was a knock on the door and when it opened it was Dorinda Lane.

She was the last person he expected to see and he hastily swung his feet to the floor and reached for a shirt.

"Is it all right for me to come in?"

"Sure," he said. "You . . . well, I wasn't expecting anybody."

She dropped into a chair. "Tandy, you've got to listen to me! I've found out something, something I've no business to know. I overheard a conversation last night. Bernie Satneck and Stan Reiser were talking."

"Look." He got up and walked across the room. "If you shouldn't, don't tell me. After all, if Reiser is a friend of yours."

"Oh, don't be silly!" Dorinda declared impatiently. "You're so wrong about that! I never had but one date with him. He had nothing at all to do with my coming to the city. Long before I met you, I had found an agent and was trying to get a singing job through him. Reiser didn't even recommend me to Nevada Johnson, I've just run into him there. But that's not important, Tandy." She stepped closer to him. "It's what Reiser and Satneck have planned!"

"You mean you know? You overheard?"

Dorinda frowned. "Not exactly, I did hear them talking in

the club. Stan Reiser believes he can beat you. He was furious when he found that Bernie Satneck wasn't sure, but he did listen, and Satneck has suggested that they should take no chances. What they have planned, I don't know, as I missed part of it then, but it has something to do with the gloves, something to get in your eyes."

Tandy shrugged. "Maybe it could be resin. But they always wipe off the gloves after a man goes down, so it couldn't be that. Did you hear anything more?"

"Yes, I did. They had quite an argument, but finally I heard Reiser agree that if he hadn't stopped you by the ninth round, he would do what Bernie wanted."

Tandy Moore's eyes grew sharp. He looked down at his hands.

"Thanks, Dory," he said at last. "That'll help."

She hesitated, looking at him, tenderness and worry mingled in her eyes. Yet he was warned and he would be ready. It was nice to know.

———

As HE CRAWLED into the ring, Tandy Moore stared around him in amazement at the crowd. It rolled away from the ring in great banks of humanity, filling the ball park to overflowing. The blowing clouds parted momentarily and the sun blasted down on the spotless white square of canvas as he moved across to his corner.

Gus, in a white sweater, was beside him and Briggs stood at the edge of the ring, then dropped back into his seat. An intelligent-looking man with white brows was in the corner with Gus. He was a world-famed handler of fighters, even more skillful than Gus himself.

The robe was slid from his shoulders, and as Tandy peered from under his brows at Gus, he grinned a little and smiled.

"Well, pal, here we are," he said softly.

"Yeah." Gus stared solemnly across the ring. "I wish I knew what they had up their sleeves. They've got something, you can bet on it. Neither Bernie Satneck nor Stan Reiser ever took an unnecessary chance."

Tandy stared down at his gloved hands. He had an idea of

what they had up their sleeves, but he said nothing. That was his problem alone. He hadn't mentioned it to Gus and he was no nearer a solution now than ever. They might not try anything on him, but if they did he would cope with it when the time came.

The referee gave them their instructions and he and Reiser returned to their corners, and almost instantly the bell sounded.

Tandy whirled and began his swift, shuffling movement to the center of the ring. His mouth felt dry and his stomach had a queer, empty feeling he had never known before. Under him the canvas was taut and strong, and he tried his feet on it as he moved and they were sure.

Stan Reiser opened up with a sharp left to the head. It landed solidly and Tandy moved away, watching the center of Reiser's body where he could see hands and feet both at the same time.

Reiser jabbed and Tandy slipped the punch, the glove sliding by his cheekbone, and then he went in fast, carrying the fight to the bigger man.

He slammed a right to the ribs, then a left and right to the body. Stan backed up and he followed him.

Reiser caught him with a left to the head, and Tandy landed a right. He felt the glove smack home solidly in Stan's body, and it felt good. They clinched, and he could feel the other man's weight and strength, sensing his power.

He broke and Stan came after him, his left stabbing like a living thing. A sharp left to the mouth, then another.

Both men were in excellent shape and the murderous punches slid off their toughened bodies like water off a duck's back.

Just before the bell, Reiser rushed him into the ropes and clipped him with a wicked right to the chin.

Tandy was sweating now and he was surprised to see blood on his glove when he wiped his face.

When the bell rang for the second, he went out, feinted, and then lunged. Reiser smashed a right to the head that knocked him off balance, and before he could get his feet under him, the bigger man was on him with a battering fury of blows.

Tandy staggered and retreated hastily, but to no avail. Stan was after him instantly, jabbing a left, then crossing a right. Tandy landed a right uppercut in close and Stan clipped him with two high hooks.

Sweaty and bloody now, Tandy bored in; lost to the crowd; lost to Gus, to Dorinda, and to Briggs, living now only for battle and the hot lust of combat. It lifted within him like a fierce, unholy tide. He drove Stan back and was in turn driven back, and they fought, round after round, with the tide of battle seesawing first one way and then another, bloody and desperate and bitter.

In the seventh round, they both came out fast. The crowd was in a continuous uproar now. Slugging like mad, they drove together. Stan whipped over a steaming right uppercut that caught Tandy coming in and his knees turned to rubber. He started to sink and Stan closed in, smashing a sharp left to the face and then crossing a right to the jaw that drove Tandy to his knees.

His head roaring, Tandy came up with a lunge and dove for a clinch, but Stan was too fast. He stepped back and stopped the attempt with a stiff left to the face that cut Tandy's lips, and then he rushed Tandy, smashing and battering him back with a furious flood of blows, driving him finally into the ropes with a sweeping left that made Tandy turn a complete somersault over the top rope!

His head came through them again and he crawled inside, with Reiser moving in for the kill.

Retreating, Tandy fought to push his thoughts through the fog from the heavy punches. He moved back warily, circling to avoid Reiser. The big man kept moving in, taking his time, more sure of himself now, and set for a kill.

Tandy Moore saw the cruel lips and the high cheekbones, one of them now wearing a mouse, he saw a thin edge of a cut under Stan's right eye, and his lips looked puffed. His side was reddened from the pounding Tandy had given it, and Tandy's eyes narrowed as he backed into the ropes. That eye and the ribs!

Reiser closed in carefully and stabbed a left. More confident now, Tandy let the punch start, then turned his shoulders behind a left jab that speared Stan on the mouth. It halted him and the big fighter blinked.

Instantly, Tandy's right crossed over the left jab to the mouse on the cheekbone.

It landed with a dull thud and Stan's eyes glazed. His nostrils alive with the scent of sweaty muscles and blood, Tandy jabbed, then crossed, and suddenly they were slugging.

Legs spread apart, jaws set, they stood at point-blank range and fired with both hands!

The crowd came up roaring. The pace was too furious to last and it finally became a matter of who would give ground first. Suddenly Tandy Moore thrust his foot forward in a tight, canvas-gripping movement. Tandy saw his chance and threw a terrific left hook to the chin but it missed and a right exploded on his own jaw and he went to the canvas with a crash and a vast, roaring sound in his skull.

He came up swinging and went down again from a wicked left hook to the stomach and a crashing right to the corner of his jaw.

Rolling over, he got to his knees, his head filled with that roaring sound, and vaguely he saw Stan going away from him and realized with a shock that he was on his feet and that the bell ending the round was clanging in his ears!

One more round! It must be now or never! Whatever Reiser and Bernie had planned, whatever stratagem they had conceived, would be put into execution in the ninth round, and in the next, the eighth, he must win. He heard nothing that Gus Coe said. He felt only the ministering hands, heard the low, careful tone of his voice, felt water on his face and the back of his neck, and then a warning buzzer sounded and he was on his feet ready for the bell.

VI

THE BELL RANG and Tandy went out, a fierce, driving lust for victory welled up within him until he could see nothing but Stan Reiser. This was the man who had beaten his father, the man who had whipped him, the man who was fighting now to win all he wanted, all he desired. If Tandy could win, justice was at hand.

He hurled himself at Reiser like a madman. Toughened by years of hard work, struggle, and sharpened by training, he was ready. Fists smashing and battering he charged into Reiser, and the big heavyweight met him without flinching. For Stan Reiser had to win in this round, too. He must win in this round or confess by losing that he was the lesser man. Hating Tandy with all the ugly hatred of a man who has wronged another, he still fought the thought of admitting that he must stoop to using other methods to beat this upstart who would keep him from the title.

Weaving under a left, Tandy smashed a right to the ribs, then a left, a right, a left. His body swayed as he weaved in a deadly rhythm of mighty punching, each blow timed to the movements of Stan Reiser's body.

The big man yielded ground. He fell back and tried to sidestep, but Tandy was on him, giving no chance for a respite.

Suddenly the haze in Tandy's head seemed to clear momentarily and he stared upon features that were battered and swollen. One of Stan's eyes was closed and a raw wound lay under the other. His lips were puffed and his cheekbone was an open cut, yet there was in the man's eyes a fierce, almost animal hatred and something else.

It was something Tandy had never until that moment seen in a boxer's eyes. It was fear!

Not fear of physical injury, but the deeper, more awful fear of being truly beaten. And Stan Reiser had never been bested in that way. And now it was here, before him.

It was an end. Reiser saw it and knew it. Nothing he could do could stop that driving attack. He had thrown his best punches, used every legitimate trick, but there was one last hope!

Tandy feinted suddenly and Reiser struck out wildly, and Tandy smashed a right hand flush to the point of his chin!

Stan hit the ropes rolling, lost balance, and crashed to the floor. Yet at seven he was up, lifting his hands, half blind, but then the bell rang!

THE NINTH ROUND. Here it was. Almost before he realized it, the gong sounded and Tandy was going out again. But now he was wary, squinting at Stan's gloves.

Were they loaded? But the gloves had not been slipped off. There was no time, and no chance for that under the eyes of the crowd and the sportswriters. It would be something on the gloves.

He jabbed and moved away. Stan was working to get in close and there was a caution in his eyes. His whole manner was changed. Suddenly Reiser jabbed sharply for Tandy's head, but a flick of his glove pushed the blow away and Tandy was watchful again.

The crowd seemed to sense something. In a flickering glimpse at his corner, Tandy saw Gus Coe's face was scowling. He had seen that something in Reiser's style had changed; something was wrong. But what?

Stan slipped a left and came in close. He hooked for Tandy's head and smeared a glove across his eye. The glove seemed to slide on the sweat, and Tandy lowered his head to Stan's shoulder and belted him steadily in the stomach. He chopped a left to the head and the referee broke them. His right eye was smarting wickedly.

Something on the gloves! And in that instant, he recalled a story Gus had told him; *it was mustard oil!* So far he'd gotten little of it, but if it got directly in his eyes—

He staggered under a left hook, blocked a right, but caught a wicked left to the ribs. Sliding under another left, he smashed a right to the ribs with such force that it jerked Reiser's mouth open. In a panic the bigger man dove into a clinch, and jerking a glove free ground the end of it into Tandy's eye! He gritted his teeth and clinched harder.

"You remember me; the newsboy?" Tandy hissed as they swung around in a straining dance.

The referee was yelling, *"Break!"*

Stan hooked again but Tandy got his shoulder up to take the blow. "I'm going to take you down and if I don't I'll tell my story to anyone who'll listen!" Panic and fear haunted Stan Reiser's eyes and then something in him snapped; there was no longer any thought of the future just a driving, damning desire to punish this kid who would dare to threaten him.

Tandy jerked away and Stan hooked viciously to the jaw. Staggering, he caught the left and went to the canvas. He rolled over and got up, but Stan hooked another wicked left to his groin, throwing it low and hard with everything he had on it!

Tandy's mouth jerked open in a half-stifled cry of agony and he pitched over on his face, grabbing his crotch and rolling over and over on the canvas!

Men and women shouted and screamed. A dozen men clambered to the apron of the ring; flashbulbs popped as the police surged forward to drag everyone back. Around the ring all was bedlam and the huge arena was one vast roar of sound.

Tandy rolled over and felt the sun on his face, and he knew he had to get up.

Beyond the pain, beyond the sound, beyond everything was the need to be on his feet. He crawled to his knees and while the referee stared, too hypnotized by Tandy's struggle to get up to stop the fight, Tandy grabbed the ropes and pulled himself erect.

Blinded with pain from his stinging eyes, his teeth sunk into his mouthpiece with the agony that gnawed at his vitals, Tandy brushed the referee aside and held himself with his mind, every sense, every nerve, every ounce of strength, concentrated on Stan Reiser. And Reiser rushed to meet him.

Smashing Reiser's lips with a straight left, Tandy threw a high hard one and it caught Reiser on the chin as he came in. Falling back to the ropes, fear in every line of his face, Stan struggled to defend against the tide of punches that Tandy summoned from some hidden reserve of strength.

With a lunge, Reiser tried to escape. As he turned Tandy pulled the trigger on a wicked right that clipped Stan flush on the chin and sent him off the platform and crashing into the cowering form of Bernie Satneck!

Stan Reiser lay over a chair, out cold and dead to the world. Bernie Satneck struggled to get out from beneath him.

Then, Gus and Briggs were in the ring and he tried to see

them through eyes that streamed with tears from the angry smart of the mustard oil.

"You made it, son. It's over." Gus carefully wiped off his face. "You'll fight the champ, and I think you'll beat him, too!"

Dory was in the ring, her eyes bright, her arm around his shoulders.

"It's just a game now, Gus." He sank to the mat, gasping. "I'll do whatever you say."

"Your poor face." Dorinda's eyes were full of tears, her hand cool on his cheek.

"Just don't complain about my beard." He grinned. "It could be weeks before I can shave."

Gus and Briggs got him to his feet. "Hell," he grumbled, "I hope it isn't weeks before I can walk."

Supported by his two friends, trailed by Dorinda, who had caught up his robe and towel, Tandy limped toward the dressing rooms.

"I wish my dad could have seen," he whispered. "I wish my dad could have seen me fight."

THE MONEY PUNCH

I

THE GIRL IN the trench coat and sand-colored beret was on the sidelines again. She was standing beside a white-haired man, and as Darby McGraw crawled through the ropes, she was watching him.

Darby grinned at his second and trainer, Beano Brown. "That babe's here again," he said. "She must think I'm okay."

"She prob'ly comes to see somebody else," Beano said without interest. "Lots of fighters work out here."

"No, she always looks at me. And why is that, you ask me? It's because I'm the class of this crowd, that's why."

"You sure hate yourself," Beano said. "These people seen plenty of fighters." Beano leaned on the top rope and looked at Darby with casual eyes. The boy was built. He had the shoulders, a slim waist and narrow hips, and he had good hands. A good-looking boy.

"Wait until I get in there with Mink Delano. I'll show 'em all something then. When I hit 'em with my right and they don't go down, they do some sure funny things standing up!"

"You come from an awful small town," Beano said. "I can tell that."

Darby moved in, feeling for the distance with his left. He felt good. Sammy Need, the boy he was working with, slipped inside of Darby's left and landed lightly to the ribs. Darby kept his right hand cocked. He would like to throw that right, just once, just to show this girl what he could do.

He liked Sammy, though, and didn't want to hurt him. Sammy was fast, and Darby wasn't hitting him very often, but that meant nothing. He rarely turned loose his right in workouts, and it was the right that was his money punch.

That right had won his fights out in Jerome, and those fights had gotten him recommended to Fats Lakey in L.A.

Fats was his manager. Fats had been a pool hustler who dropped into Jerome one time and met some of the guys in the local fight scene. He'd been looking for new talent, and so the locals had talked McGraw into going to the coast and looking him up. With nine knockouts under his belt, Darby was willing.

He felt good today. He liked to train and was in rare shape. He moved in, and as he worked, he wondered what that girl would say if she knew he had knocked out nine men in a row. And no less than six of these in the first round. Neither Dempsey nor Louis had that many kayos in their first nine fights.

When he had worked six rounds, he climbed down from the ring, scarcely breathing hard. He started for the table to take some body-bending exercise and deliberately passed close to the girl. He was within ten feet of her when he heard her say distinctly, "Delano will win. This one can't fight for sour apples."

Darby stopped, flat-footed, his face flushing red with sudden anger. Who did she think she was, anyway, talking him down like that! He started to turn, then noticed they were paying no attention to him, hadn't noticed him, in fact, so he wheeled angrily and went on to the table.

I'll show 'em! he told himself. He was seething inside. Why, just for that, he'd murder Delano; knock him out, like the others, in the very first round!

———

DARBY MCGRAW'S ANGER had settled to a grim, bitter determination by the night he climbed into the ring with Mink Delano. Fats Lakey was standing behind his corner, swelling with importance, a long cigar thrust in his fat, red cheek. He kept talking about "my boy McGraw" in a loud voice.

Beano Brown crawled into Darby's corner as second. He was not excited. Beano had seen too many of them come and go. He had been seconding fighters for twenty-two years, and it meant just another sawbuck to him, or whatever he could get. He was a short black man with one cauliflowered ear. Tonight he was bored and tired.

Darby glanced down at the ringside and saw the girl in the beret. She glanced at him, then looked away without interest.

"The special event was a better fight than this semifinal will be," he heard her say. "I can't see why they put this boy in that spot."

Darby stood up. He was mad clear through. I'll show her! he told himself viciously. I'll show her! He wouldn't have minded so much if she hadn't had wide gray eyes and lovely, soft brown hair. She was, he knew, almost beautiful.

They went to the center of the ring for their instructions. The crowd didn't bother him. He was impatient, anxious to get started and to feel his right fist smashing against Mink's chin. He'd show this crowd something, and quick! Why, it took them four hours to bring Al Baker back to his senses after Baker stopped that right with his chin!

The bell clanged and he wheeled and went out fast. Delano was a slim, white, muscled youngster who fought high on his toes. Darby moved in, feinted swiftly, and threw his right.

Something smashed him in the body, and then a light hook clipped him on the chin. He piled in, throwing the right again, but a fast left made him taste blood and another snapped home on his temple. Neither punch hurt, but he was confused. He steadied down and looked at Mink. The other boy was calm, unruffled.

Darby pawed with his left, but his left wasn't good for much, he knew. Then he threw his right. Again a gloved fist smashed him in the ribs. Darby bored in, landing a light left, but taking a fast one to the mouth. He threw his right and Mink beat him to it with a beautiful inside cross that jolted him to his heels. The bell sounded and he trotted back to his corner.

"Take your time, boy," Beano said. "Just take your time. No hurry."

Darby McGraw was on his feet before the bell sounded. He pulled up his trunks and pawed at the resin. This guy had lasted a whole round with him, and this after he'd sworn to get him in the first, too. The bell rang and he lunged from his corner and threw his right, high and hard.

A fist smashed into his middle, then another one. He was hit three times before he could get set after the missed punch. Darby drew back and circled Mink. Somehow he wasn't hitting Delano. He was suddenly vastly impatient. Talk about luck! This guy had it. Mink moved in and Darby's right curled around his neck. He smiled at Darby, then smashed two wicked punches to the body.

Darby was shaken. His anger still burning within him, he pawed Delano's left out of the way and slammed a right to the body, but Mink took it going away and the glove barely touched him.

Darby stepped around, set himself to throw his right, but Mink sidestepped neatly, taking himself out of line. Before Darby could change position, a left stabbed him in the mouth. Darby ducked his head and furrowed his brow. He'd have to watch this guy. He would have to be careful.

Delano moved in now, landing three fast left jabs. Darby fired his right suddenly, but it slid off a slashing left glove that smashed his lips back into his teeth and set him back on his heels. He took another step back and suddenly Delano was all over him. Before Darby could clinch, Mink hit him seven times.

Three times in the following round he tried with his right. Each time he missed. When the bell ended the round, he walked wearily back to his corner. He slumped on the stool. "Use your left," Beano told him. "This boy, he don't like no lefts. Use a left hook!"

Darby tried, but he had no confidence in that left of his. It had always been his right that won fights for him. All he had to do was land that right. One punch and he could win. Just one. He feinted with his right and threw his left. It was a poorly executed hook, more of a swing, but it caught Mink high on the head and knocked him sprawling on the canvas.

Darby was wild. He ran to a corner and waited, hands weaving. Delano scrambled to his feet at the count of nine and Darby went after him with a rush and threw a roundhouse right. Mink ducked inside of it and grabbed Darby with both hands.

Wildly, McGraw tore him loose and threw his right again.

But Mink was crafty and slid inside and clinched once more. Darby could hear someone yelling to use his left. He tried. He pushed Delano away and cocked his left, but caught a left and right in the mouth before he could throw it.

In the last round of the fight he was outboxed completely. He was tired, but he kept pushing in, kept throwing his right. He didn't need to look at the referee. He kept his eyes away from the girl in the trench coat. He did not want to hear the decision. He knew he had lost every round.

Fats Lakey was waiting in the dressing room, his fat face flushed and ugly. "You bum!" he snarled. "You poor, country bum! I thought you were a fighter! Why, this Delano is only a preliminary boy, a punk, and he made a monkey out of you! Nine knockouts, but you can't fight! Not for sour apples, you can't fight!"

That did it. All the rage and frustration and disappointment boiled over. Darby swung his right. Fats, seeing his mistake too late, took a quick step back, enough to break the force of the blow but not enough to save him. The right smashed against his fat cheek and Lakey hit the floor on the seat of his pants, blood streaming from a cut below his eye.

"I'll have you pinched for this!" he screamed. He got up and backed toward the door. "I'll get you thrown in the cooler so fast!"

"No, you won't!" It was the white-haired man who had sat with the girl in the beret. They were both there. "I heard it all, Lakey, and if he hadn't clipped you, I would have. Now beat it!"

Fats Lakey backed away, his eyes ugly. The white-haired man had twisted a handkerchief around his fist and was watching him coolly.

II

WHEN FATS WAS gone, the girl walked over to Darby. "Hurt much?"

"No," he said sullenly, keeping his eyes down. "I ain't hurt. That Delano couldn't break an egg!"

"Lucky for you he couldn't," she said coolly. "He hit you with everything but the stool."

Darby's eyes flashed angrily. He was bitter and ashamed. He wanted no girl such as this to see him beaten. He had wanted her to see him win.

"He was lucky," he muttered. "I had an off night."

"Oh?" Her voice was contemptuous. "So you're one of those?"

His head came up sharply. "One of what?" he demanded. "What do you mean?"

"One of those fighters who alibi themselves out of every beating," she said. "A fighter who is afraid to admit he was whipped. You were beaten tonight—you should be man enough to admit it."

He pulled his shoelace tighter and pressed his lips into a thin line. He glanced at her feet. She had nice feet and good legs. Suddenly, memory of the fight flooded over him. He recalled those wild rights he had thrown into empty air, the stabbing lefts he had taken in the mouth, the rights that had battered his ribs. He got to his feet.

"All right," he said. "If you want me to admit it, he punched my head off. I couldn't hit him. But next time I'll hit him. Next time I'll knock him out!"

"Not if you fight the way you did tonight," she said matter-of-factly. "Fighting the way you do, you wouldn't hit him with that right in fifty fights. Whoever told you you were a fighter?"

He glared. "I won nine fights by knockouts," he said defiantly. "Six in the first round!"

"Against country boys who knew even less about it than you did, probably. You might make a fighter," she admitted, "but you aren't one now. You can't win fights with nothing but a right hand."

"You know all about it," he sneered. "What does a girl know about fighting, anyway?"

"My father was Paddy McFadden," she replied quietly, "if you know who he was. My uncle was lightweight champion of the world. I grew up around better fighters than you've ever seen."

He picked up his coat. "So what?" He started for the door, but feeling a hand on his sleeve, he stopped. The white-haired man was holding out some money to him.

"I was afraid Lakey might forget to pay you, so I collected your part of this."

"Thanks," Darby snapped. He took the money and stuffed it into his pocket. He was out the door when he heard Beano.

"Mr. McGraw?"

"Yeah?" He was impatient, anxious to be gone. "Fats, he forgot to give me my sawbuck."

The Negro's calm face quieted Darby. "Oh?" he said. "I'm sorry. Here." He reached for the money. It wasn't very much. He took a twenty from the thin packet of bills and handed it to Beano. "Here you are, and thanks. If I'd won, I'd have given you more."

He ducked out through the door and turned into the damp street, wet from a light drizzle of rain. Suddenly, he was ashamed of himself. He shouldn't have talked to the girl that way. It was only that he had wanted so much to make a good showing, to impress her, and then he had lost. It would have been better if he had been knocked out. It would have been less humiliating than to take the boxing lesson he'd taken.

With sudden clarity he saw the fight as it must have looked to others. A husky country boy, wading in and wasting punches on the air, while a faster, smarter fighter stepped around him and stuck left hands in his face.

What would they be saying back home now? He had told them all he would be back, welterweight champion of the world. His nine victories had made him sure that all he needed was a chance at the champion and he could win. And he'd been beaten by a comparatively unknown preliminary boxer!

Hours later he stopped at a cheap hotel and got a room for the night. What was it she had said?

"You can't win fights with nothing but a right hand."

She had been right, of course, and he'd been a fool. His few victories had swollen his head until he was too cocky, too sure of himself. Suddenly, he realized how long and hard the climb would be, how much he had to learn.

FOR A LONG time he lay awake that night, recalling those stabbing lefts and the girl's scorn. Yet she'd come to his dressing room. Why? She had bothered enough to talk to him. Darby McGraw shook his head. Girls had always puzzled him. But this one seemed particularly puzzling.

In the morning he recovered his few possessions at the hotel where he and Fats had stayed. Fats was gone, leaving the bill for him to pay. He paid it and had twelve dollars left.

He found Beano Brown leaning against the wall at Higherman's Gym. "Beano," he said hesitantly, "what was wrong with my fight last night?"

The Negro looked at him, then dug a pack of smokes from his pocket and shook one into his hand. "You ain't got no left," he said, "for one thing. Never was no great fighter without he had a good left hand. You got to learn to jab."

"Will you show me how?"

Beano lit his smoke. "You ain't goin' to quit? Well, maybe I might show you, but why don't you go to Mary McFadden? She's got a trainin' farm. Inherited it from her daddy. She's got Dan Faherty out there. Ain't no better trainer than him."

"No." Darby shook his head, digging his hands into his coat pockets. "I don't want to go there. I want you to show me."

"Well," Beano said. "I guess so."

DARBY MCGRAW WAS a lean six feet. His best weight was just over one hundred forty-five, but he was growing heavier. He had a shock of black, curly hair and a hard, brown face. The month before he had turned nineteen years old.

In the three weeks that followed his talk with Beano, he trained, hour after hour, and his training was mostly to stand properly, how to shift his feet, how to move forward and how to retreat.

He eked out a precarious existence with a few labor jobs and occasional workouts for which he was paid.

He saw nothing of Mary, but occasionally heard of her. He heard enough to know that she was considered to be a shrewd judge of fighters. Also, that she had arranged the training schedules of champions, that there was little she didn't know about the boxing game, and that she was only twenty-two.

"Seems like a funny business for a girl," he told Beano.

The Negro shrugged. "Maybe. Ain't no business funny for no girl now. She stuck with what she knowed. Her daddy and her uncle, she heard them talkin' fight for years, talkin' it with ever'body big in business. She couldn't help but know it. When her daddy was killed, she kept the trainin' farm. It was a good business, and Dan Faherty's like a father to her."

Beano looked at him suddenly. "Got you a fight. Over to Justiceville. You go four rounds with Billy Greb."

———

JUSTICEVILLE WAS A tank town. There were about two thousand people in the crowd, however. Benny Seaman, crack middle, was fighting in the main go.

Darby went in at one hundred fifty. He was outweighed seven pounds. Beano leaned on the top rope and looked at him.

"You move around, see?" he instructed. "You jab him. No right hands, see?"

"All right," Darby said.

The bell sounded and he went out fast. Greb came into him swinging and Darby was tempted. He jabbed. His left impaled Greb, stopping his charge. Darby jabbed again. Then he feinted a right and jabbed again. Billy kept piling in and swinging.

Just before the bell, Greb missed a right and Darby caught him in the chin with a short left hook. Greb hit the canvas with his knees. He was still shaken when he came out for the second. Darby walked in slowly. He feinted a right and made Greb's knees wobble with another left. He jabbed twice, working cautiously. Then he feinted and hooked the left again. Greb's feet shot out from under him and he hit flat on his face. He never wiggled during the count.

"With my left!" Darby said, astonished. "I knocked him out with my left!"

"Uh-huh. You got two hands," Beano said. "But you got lots of work to do. Lots of work."

"All right," Darby said.

THE NEXT DAY he met Mary McFadden on the street. They recognized each other at the same moment and she stopped.

"Hello," he said. He felt himself blushing, and grinned sheepishly.

"Congratulations on your fight. I heard about you knocking out Bill Greb."

"It wasn't anything," he said, "just a four round preliminary."

"All fighters start at the bottom," she told him.

"I had to find that out," he admitted. "It wasn't easy."

"They want you back there, at Justiceville," Mary said. "Mike McDonald was over at the camp yesterday. He said they wanted you to fight Marshall Collins."

"Do you think I should?" He looked at her. "They tell me you know all about this boxing game."

"Oh, no!" she said quickly. "I don't at all." She looked up at him. "Tell Beano not to take Collins. Tell him to insist on Augie Gordon."

"But he's a better fighter than Collins!" Darby exclaimed.

"Yes, he is. Much better. But that isn't the question. Marshall Collins is very hard to fight. Augie Gordon is good, but he doesn't take a punch very well. He will outpoint you for a few rounds, but you'll hit him."

"All right," he said.

Mary smiled and held out her hand. "Why don't you come out and work with us? We'd like to have you."

"Can't afford it," he said. "Your camp is too expensive."

"It wouldn't be if you were fighting for us," she said. "And Beano thinks you should be out there. He told me so. He's worried. You're causing him to work, and Beano likes to take his time about things."

He grinned. "Well, maybe. Just to make it easy on Beano." He started to turn away. "Say . . ." He hesitated and felt his face getting red. "Would you go to a show with me sometime?"

"You're an attractive man, Darby . . . but right now this is business. Maybe later, if you're still around."

"I will be," he stated.

"Then we both have something to look forward to."

Darby walked off feeling light-headed, although he realized that he didn't know what that "something" was.

———

AUGIE GORDON WAS fast. His left hand was faster than Mink Delano's. He was shifty, too. Darby pulled his chin in and began to weave and bob as Beano had been teaching him. He lost the first round, but there was a red spot on Gordon's side where Darby had landed four left hands.

Darby lost the second round, too, but the red spot on Augie's ribs was bigger and redder, and Gordon was watching that left. Augie didn't like them downstairs. Darby started working on Augie's ribs in the third, and noticed that the other fighter was slower getting away. The body punches were taking it out of him.

Darby kept it up. He kept it up with drumming punches through the fourth. In the fifth he walked out and threw a left at the body, pulled it, and hooked high and hard for the chin. Augie had jerked his stomach back and his chin came down to meet Darby's left. Augie Gordon turned halfway around before he hit the canvas.

He got up at nine, but he could barely continue. Remembering how Delano had stepped inside of his wild right-hand punches when he tried to finish him, Darby was cautious. He jabbed twice, then let Gordon see a chance to clinch. Augie moved in, and Darby met him halfway with a right uppercut that nearly tore his head off.

Mary was waiting for him when he climbed out of the ring. "Your left is getting better all the time," she said.

Dan Faherty smiled at him. "Mary says you may be coming out to the farm. We've got some good boys to work with out there."

"All right," he said, "I'll come." He grinned. "You two and Beano have made a believer out of me."

He started for his dressing room feeling better than he ever had in his life. He had stopped Augie Gordon. He had stopped Billy Greb. It looked like he was on his way. But next he wanted Mink Delano. That was a black mark on his record and he wanted it wiped clear. He pushed open the door of his dressing room and stepped inside.

Fats Lakey was sitting in a chair across the room. He was smiling, but his little eyes were mean. With him were two husky, hard-faced men.

"Hello, kid," Fats said softly. "Doin' all right, I see."

III

BEANO'S FACE WAS a shade paler and he kept his eyes down. "Yeah," Darby said, "I'm doing all right. What do you want?"

"Nothin'." Fats laughed. "Nothin' at all, right now. Of course, there's a little matter of some money you owe me, but we can take that up later."

"I owe you nothing!" Darby said angrily. He didn't even start to take off his bandages. "You never did a thing for me but try to steal my end of the gate and run away without paying Beano. The less I see of you, the better. Now beat it!"

Fats smiled, but his lips were thin. "I'm not in any hurry, Darby," he said. "When I get ready to go, I'll go. And don't get tough about it. I owe you a little something for that punch in the face you gave me, and if you don't talk mighty quiet, I'll let the boys here work you over."

Darby pulled his belt tight and slid into his sweater. He looked from one to the other of Fat's hard-faced companions, and suddenly he grinned.

"Those mugs?" he said, and laughed. "I could bounce 'em both without working up a sweat, and then stack you on top of them."

One of the men straightened up and his face hardened. "Punk," he said, "I don't think I like you."

"What do I do?" Darby snapped. "Shudder with sobs or something?"

"Take it easy, kid!" Fats said harshly. "Right now I want to talk business. I happen to know you're going in there next with Mink Delano."

"So what?"

"So you'll beat him. With that left you've worked up, you'll beat him. Then they'll have something else for you. When the right time comes, we can do business, and when you're ready, you'll do it my way. If you don't, bad things will happen to you and yours. . . . Get me?"

Fats got up, his face smug. "Wise punks don't get tough with me, see? You're just a country punk in a big town. If you want to play our way, you can make some dough. If you don't act nice, we'll see that you do."

He turned to go. "And that McFadden floozy won't help you none, either."

Darby dropped one hand on the rubbing table and vaulted it, starting for Fats. The gambler's face turned white and he jumped back.

"Take him, boys!" he yelled, his voice thin with fear. "Get him, *quick*!"

The bigger of the two men lunged to stop Darby, and McGraw uncorked a right hand that clipped him on the chin and knocked him against the wall with a thud. Then he leaped for Fats. But he had taken scarcely a step before something smashed down on his skull from behind. Great lights exploded in his brain and his knees turned to rubber.

He started to fall, but blind instinct forced stiffness into his legs, and he turned. Another blow hit him. He lashed out with his left, then his right, but suddenly Fats had sprung on his back, pinioning his arms. What happened after that, he never knew.

———

HIS FACE FELT wet and he struggled to get up, but somebody was holding him. "Just relax, son. Everything will be all right." The voice was gentle, and he opened his eyes to see Dan Faherty on his knees beside him. "Lie still, kid. You've taken quite a beating," Faherty said. "Who was it?"

"Fats Lakey and two other guys. Big guys. They had blackjacks. I hit one of 'em, but then Fats jumped on me and held my arms. I'll kill him for that!"

"No you won't. Forget it," Faherty said quietly. "We'll take care of them later."

A week later he was in Mary McFadden's gym, taking light exercise. Fats had been right in one thing. McDonald the promoter wanted him against Mink Delano in a semi-final. A warrant had been sworn out against Fats, but he seemed to be nowhere around. Beano, with a knot on his skull from where he, too, had been sapped, was working with Darby.

The gym at the McFadden Training Farm was a vastly different place from the dingy interior of the gym in the city. Higherman's was old, the equipment worn, and fighters crowded the floors. This place was bright, the air was clean, and there were new bags, jump ropes, and strange exercise equipment that had come all the way from Germany.

In the week of light work before he moved on to heavier boxing, Dan Faherty worked with him every day, showing him new tricks and polishing his punching, his blocking, and his footwork.

"Balance is the main thing, Darby," the older man advised. "Keep your weight balanced so you can move in any direction, and always be in position to punch. Footwork doesn't mean a lot of dancing around. A good fighter never makes an unnecessary movement. He saves himself. There's nothing fancy about scientific boxing. It's simply a hard, cold-blooded system, moving the fastest and easiest way, punching to get the maximum force with minimum effort.

"There's no such thing as a fighter born with know-how. He has to be a born fighter in that he has to have the heart and the innate love of the game. Then there is always a long process of schooling and training. Dempsey was just a big, husky kid with a right hand until Kearns got him and taught him how to use a left hook, and DeForest helped sharpen him up. Joe Louis would still be working in an automobile plant in Detroit if Jack Blackburn hadn't spent long months of work with him."

Darby McGraw skipped rope, shadowboxed, punched the light and heavy bags, and worked in the gym with big men and small men. He learned how to slip and ride punches, learned how to feint properly, how to make openings, and how to time his punches correctly.

"That Fats," Beano told him one night, "he's a bad one. A boy I know told me Fats is tied in with Art Renke."

"Renke?" Faherty had overheard the remark. "That's bad. Renke is one of the biggest and crookedest gamblers around, and he has a hand in several rackets."

———

THE ARENA WAS full when Darby crawled through the ropes for his fight with Mink Delano. Since beating him, Mink had gone on to win five straight fights, two of them by knockouts. He had beaten Marshall Collins and Sandy Crocker, two tough middleweights who were ranked among the best in the area.

The bell sounded and Darby went out fast. He tried a wild right, and Mink stabbed with the left. But Darby had been ready for that and he rolled under the left and smashed a punch to the body. Then he worked in, jabbed a left and crossed a short right. Mink backed up and looked him over. The first round was fast, clean, and even.

The second was the same, except that Mink Delano forged ahead. He won the round with a flurry of punches in the final fifteen seconds. The third found Mink moving fast, his left going all the time. He won that round and the fourth.

Dan Faherty and Beano were in Darby's corner. Dan smiled as McGraw sat down. He leaned into the fighter.

"Take him this round," he said quietly. "Go out there and get him. You've let him pile up a lead, get confident. Now the fun's over. Go get him!"

When the bell sounded, Delano came out briskly confident. He jabbed a left, but suddenly Darby exploded into action. He went under the left and slammed a savage right to the ribs that made the other fighter back up suddenly, but McGraw never let him get set. He hooked his left hard to the body, and then threw a one-two for the head, moving in all the time.

Delano staggered and attempted to clinch, then whipped out of it and smashed a wicked right to Darby's jaw. It hurt, and Darby started to clinch, then tore loose and smashed both fists to the body. He stabbed at Delano with a left. Fighting viciously, they drove back and forth across the ring.

Mink straightened up and started a jab. Anxious, Darby sprang in, smashing two ripping hooks to the body, then lifting the left to the chin. Delano sidestepped and tried to get away, but Darby was after him. He stabbed a left, another left, then feinted and drilled his right all the way down the groove.

Mink tried to step inside of it, but took the steaming punch flush on the point of the chin. He hit the floor flat on his face.

Faherty was gathering up Darby's gear when he looked up. "Fats surrendered to the police," he said. "I don't get it. If the assault can be proved, he'll get a stiff sentence."

"There's me and Beano," Darby said. "We can prove it. Even if he has three witnesses. Nobody can deny I got beat up. I've got the doctor's report."

"Uh-huh." But Faherty was worried, and Darby could see it.

————

HE WAS EVEN more worried at workout time the next day. "You seen Beano?" he asked.

"No. Ain't he here?" Darby pulled on his light punching-bag mitts. "I saw him last night after the fights. He went down to Central Avenue, I think."

"He hasn't come back." Faherty shrugged. "He's probably got a girl down there. He'll be back.

"There's something else," he went on. "I've got you a fight, if you want it. Or rather, Mary got it. A main event with Benny Barros."

"Barros?" Darby was surprised. "He's pretty good, isn't he?"

"Uh-huh. He is good. But you've improved, Darby. You're getting to be almost as good as you thought you were in the beginning."

McGraw grinned, running his fingers through his thick hair. "Well," he said, "that big spar-boy, Tony Duretti, was hitting me with a left today, so I guess I can get better. When do I fight him?"

"Not for two months," Faherty advised. "In the meantime, we're taking a trip. You're fighting in Toledo, Detroit, Cleveland, and Chicago. Once every ten days, then train for Barros."

"Gosh." Darby grinned. "Looks like I'm on my way, doesn't it?" He sobered suddenly. "I wish Beano would get back."

———

TWO DAYS LATER when the plane took off for Toledo, Beano Brown was still among the missing. In Toledo, Darby McGraw, brown as an Indian, his shoulders even bigger than they had been, and weighing one fifty-seven, knocked out Gunner Smith in one round. In Detroit he stopped Sammy White in three and flew on to Cleveland, where he beat Sam Ratner. Ratner was on the floor four times, but lasted the fight out by clinching and running. The tour ended in Chicago with a one-round kayo over Stob Williams.

The morning after their return to the coast, Darby rolled out of bed and dug his feet into his slippers. He shrugged into his robe and walked into the bathroom. There was a hint of a blue mouse over his right eye, and a red abrasion on his cheekbone. Other than that, he had never felt better in his life.

When he had bathed and shaved, he walked outside to the drive that ended at the main house. Mary's car was parked under a big tree, where she had left it the night before. She'd been strangely quiet all the way home from the airport. It was unusual for her to be quiet after one of his fights, but he had said nothing.

The sun was warm and it felt good. He walked across the yard, dappled with shadow and sunlight, toward the car. He dropped his hand on the wheel, the wheel Mary had been handling the night before, and stood there, thinking of her. Then he noticed the paper. He picked it up, idly curious if there was anything in the sport sheet about his fight with Williams.

He stiffened sharply.

FIGHTER DIES IN AUTO ACCIDENT

Beano Brown, former lightweight prizefighter, was found
dead this morning in the wreck of a car on the Ridge Route.
Brown, apparently driving back to Los Angeles, evidently
missed a turn and crashed into a canyon. He had been dead
for several days when found.

"No," Darby whispered hoarsely. "No!"
The screen door slammed, but he did not notice, staring
blindly at the paper. He had known Beano only a short time,
but the Negro had been quiet, unconcerned, yet caring. In the
past few weeks he had come to think of the man as his best
friend. Now he was dead.

"Oh, you found it!" Mary exclaimed. She had come up
behind him with Dan Faherty. "Oh, Darby, I'm so sorry! He
was such a fine man!"

"Yeah," Darby replied dully, "he sure was. He didn't have
a car, either. He didn't have any car at all. He wouldn't go
driving out of town because he couldn't drive!"

"He couldn't?" Dan Faherty demanded. "Are you sure?"

"Of course I'm sure. You can ask Smoke Dobbins, his
friend. Smoke offered him the use of his car one day, and
Beano told him he couldn't drive."

Faherty looked worried. "Without him, it's only your un-
supported word against Fats Lakey and his two pals that you
were beat up. We'll never make it stick."

"But a killing?" Mary protested. "Surely they wouldn't
kill a man just to keep him from giving evidence in a case
like that!"

"I wouldn't think so," Dan agreed, "but after all, they
could get five years for assault, or better. And Fats wouldn't
have had any trouble getting someone to help him with the
job, since he's Renke's brother-in-law."

"He is?" Darby scowled. He hadn't known that. He did
know that Fats was vicious. He suddenly recalled things he
had heard Fats brag about, thoughts he had considered just
foolish talk at the time. Now he wasn't so sure.

"Renke manages Benny Barros," Dan said suddenly. "They'll be out to get you this time."

"It still doesn't seem right," McGraw persisted. "Not that they'd kill him. Beano was peculiar, though. He kept his mouth shut. Maybe there was something else he knew about Fats or Renke?"

IV

SMOKE DOBBINS WAS six-feet-four in his sock feet and weighed one hundred fifty pounds. He was lean and stooped, a sad-faced Negro who never looked so sad as when beating some luckless optimist who tried to play him at pool or craps. Darby McGraw, wearing a gray herringbone suit and a dark blue tie, found Smoke at the Elite Bar and Pool Room.

"You know me?" he asked.

Smoke eyed him thoughtfully, warily. "I reckon I do," he said at length. "You're Darby McGraw, the middleweight."

"That's right. Beano Brown was my trainer."

"He was?" Dobbins looked unhappier than ever. He shook out a cigarette and lit it thoughtfully.

"I liked Beano," Darby said. "He was my friend. I think he was murdered." He drew a long breath. "I think he knew something. To be more specific, I think he knew something about Renke or Fats Lakey."

"Could be." Smoke looked at his cigarette. "Ain't no good for you to be seen talkin' to me," he added. "Plenty of bad niggers around here, most of 'em workin' for Renke. They'll tell him."

"I don't care," Darby snapped. "Beano was my friend."

Smoke threw him a sidelong glance. "He was just a colored man, white boy. Just another nigger!" The man's voice took on a bitter tone.

"He was my friend," Darby persisted stubbornly. "If you know anything, tell me. If you're afraid, forget it."

"Afraid?" Smoke looked at his shoes. "I reckon that's just

what I am. That Renke, he's a mighty bad man to trifle with. But," he added, "Beano was my friend, too."

Smoke looked up and met the fighter's eyes then. "Me, I don't rightly know from nothin', but I got an idea. You ever hear of Villa Lopez?"

"You mean the bantamweight? The one who died after his fight with Bobby Bland?"

"That's right. That's the one. Well . . ." Smoke took his hat off and scratched his head without looking at Darby. "Beano, he was in Villa's corner that night. Mugsy Stern was there, too. Mugsy was one of Renke's boys. At least, he has been ever since.

"Lots of people thought it mighty funny the way Villa died. He lost on a knockout, but he wouldn't take no dive. He got weak in the third round and Bobby knocked him out. Villa went back to his corner and died."

"You think Beano knew something?" Darby demanded. He was keeping an eye on a big Negro across the street. The Negro was talking to a white man who looked much like one of those with Fats that night when he got beat up.

"You fightin' Benny Barros, ain't you? What if somethin' happen to you? What if Beano was afraid somethin' goin' to happen to you? Somethin' like happened to Villa? Maybe if he thought that, he told Renke if anything funny happened, he would tell what he knew."

"The police? Go to the police, you mean?"

"No, not to the police." Smoke smiled. "Renke, he's got money with the police, but Villa, he had six brothers. A couple of them have been with the White Fence Gang. They good with knives. Good to stay away from. Even Renke is afraid of the Lopez brothers. If they thought, even a little thought, that something was smelling in that fight, there would be trouble for Renke."

"Where are they?" Darby demanded. "Where could I find them?"

"Don't you go talkin'," Smoke said seriously. "You talk an' you sure goin' to start a full-sized war. Those Lopez brothers, they are from East L.A. and down to San Pedro. Two of them are fishermen."

Darby McGraw walked down to the car stop when he left Smoke. When he glanced around, the tall colored man was gone. Then he saw two men walking toward him through the gathering dusk. The big Negro and the white man who had been with Fats. The man's name was Griggs. Darby stood very still, his thumbs hooked in his belt. He looked from one to the other. He was going to have to be careful of his hands, the fight was only three days off. There was no sign of the streetcar.

He waited and saw the space between the two men widening. They were going to take him. They were spreading out to get him from both sides.

"What you askin' that dinge?" Griggs demanded. "What you talkin' to that Dobbins for?"

"Takin' a collection for some flowers for Beano," Darby said. "You want to put some in?"

"I don't believe it," Griggs said. "I think you need a lesson. I thought you'd learned before, but I guess you didn't."

They were getting close now, and Darby could see the gleam of a knife in the Negro's hand, held low down at his side. He stepped away from them, stepping back off the curb. It put Griggs almost in front of him, the big Negro on his extreme left. Griggs took the bait and stepped off the high curb to follow Darby.

Instantly, Darby McGraw sprang, and involuntarily, Griggs tried to step back and tripped over the curb. He hit the walk in a sitting position, and Darby swung his right foot and kicked him full on the chin. Griggs's head went back like his neck was broken and he slumped over on the ground.

Quick as a cat, Darby wheeled. "Come on!" he said. "I'll make you eat that knife!"

"Uh-uh," Smoke Dobbins grunted, materializing from behind a signboard. He held the biggest pistol Darby had ever seen. "You don't take no chances with your hands. I'll tend to this boy. I'll handle him."

The big Negro's face paled as Smoke walked toward him. "You drop that frog sticker!" Smoke said. "Drop it or I'll bore a hole clear through you!"

The knife rattled on the walk. "You get goin', Darby," Smoke said. "I'm all right. I got two more boys comin'.

We'll put these two in a freight car, and if they get out before they get to Pittsburgh, my name ain't Smoke Dobbins."

McGraw hesitated, and then as the streetcar rolled up, he swung aboard. He did not look back. It was the first time in his life he had ever kicked a man. But Griggs had once slugged him with a blackjack from behind, and they had intended to cut him up this time.

———

FAHERTY HELD A watch on him next day. "You look good," he told Darby. "Just shorten that right a little more." He threw the towel around Darby's neck. "There's a lot of Barros money showing up. Mary's worried."

"She needn't be," Darby said quietly. "I want this boy and bad!"

"He's good," Dan told him, "he's three times the man Delano was. He knocked out Ratner. He stopped Augie Gordon, too. He's probably the best middleweight on the coast."

"All right, so he's good. Maybe I'm better."

Dan grinned. "Maybe you are," he said. "Maybe you are, at that!"

———

BEANO BROWN HAD lived in a cheap rooming house near Central Avenue. Darby knew where it was, and he had a hunch. Beano had always been secretive about his personal affairs, but he had told Darby one thing. He kept a diary.

The night before the fight, Darby borrowed Dan's car for a drive. He didn't say why, but he knew where he wanted to go.

It was a shabby frame addition built on the rear of an old red brick building. He had been there once many months ago. A man named Chigger Gamble had lived there with Beano. Chigger was a fry cook in a restaurant on Pico. He was a big, very fat Negro who was always perspiring profusely. If there was a diary, Chigger would know.

Darby parked the car two blocks away near an alley and walked along the dimly lighted street toward the side door of the building. If Beano had been murdered, Darby McGraw was going to see that somebody paid the price of that murder.

In his young life, Darby had learned the virtue of loyalty. Beano had given it to him, and if he was right, and if Smoke was right, Beano had died trying to protect him. In warning Renke away from him, Beano had possibly betrayed the fact that he knew the story behind the death of Villa Lopez. If that theory was correct, and Darby could think of no reason to doubt it, and if Renke had bet a lot of money and Villa had refused to go in the tank, Renke would not hesitate to dope him. Either the dope had killed him or left him so weakened that Bland's punches had finished him off.

Mugsy might have handled the dope in the corner, and somehow Beano had guessed it. Now Beano had died, and Darby meant to get the evidence if there was any.

The street was dark and the narrow sidewalk was rough and uneven. It ran along a high board fence for a ways. Behind the fence he could see the rooming house. There was a little dry grass growing between the sidewalk and the fence. Darby glanced right and left, then grabbed the top of the fence and pulled himself over. He was guessing that if Renke and Fats had not already found Beano's place, they would be hunting it. They might even be watching it.

The back door opened under his hand and he stepped into a dank, ill-smelling hallway. Beano and Chigger had lived on the second floor. He went up the back stairs and walked along the dimly lit hall to the door of number twelve.

He tapped lightly, but there was no response. He tapped again. After waiting for a moment, he dropped his hand to the knob and opened the door. He stepped quickly inside, then switched on a fountain-pen type flashlight.

The small circle of light fell on the dead, staring eyes of Chigger Gamble!

Quickly, Darby McGraw turned and felt for the light switch. The lights snapped on.

The room was a shambles of strewn clothing. Darby touched Chigger's shoulder. The man was still warm. Darby felt for his pulse. It was still, dead. He started to turn for the door to get help when he remembered the diary.

Yet, when he glanced around the room, he despaired of finding it here. Every conceivable place seemed to have been searched. A trunk marked with Beano's name stood open, and in the bottom of it was an open cigar box. Just such a place as the diary might have been kept. Darby switched off the light and went out the door.

A shadowy figure flitted from another doorway nearby and started down the hall on swift feet. "Hold it!" Darby called. "Wait a minute!"

But the man didn't wait, charging down the stairs as fast as he could run, with Darby right after him. They wheeled at the landing and the man went out the same door Darby had come in.

The fighter lunged after him and was just in time to see the man throwing himself over the fence. Darby took the fence with a lunge and went after him. He could see a car parked in the shadows near a trestle. He lunged toward the man as he fought to get the door unlocked.

It was Griggs, and the man grabbed wildly at his hip. Darby dropped one hand to Griggs's right wrist and slugged him in the stomach with the other. He slugged him three times, short, wicked blows, then twisted the right hand away and jerked out the gun, hurling it far out over the tracks. Then he smashed Griggs's nose with a left and clipped him with a chopping right to the head.

The big man went down, and Darby bent over him.

In his pocket was a flat, thick book. On the flyleaf it said, BEANO BROWN, 1949.

Darby turned and walked swiftly back to Dan's car. He was almost there when he saw the other car parked behind it. Suddenly he wished he had kept the gun.

But when the door of the second car opened, a girl stepped out and ran toward him. It was Mary.

"Oh, Darby!" she cried. "Are you all right?"

"Sure. Sure, I'm all right," he said. "How'd you get here?"

"I followed you," she said, "but I didn't see you leave the car and didn't see which house you went into. Then I saw the man come over the fence, but I couldn't tell who was after him. I waited."

"Let's go," he said, "we'd better get out of here fast."

They stopped in an all-night restaurant. "I got it," he said.

"Beano Brown's diary. If he knew anything about the Lopez fight, it'll be in here."

The waiter stopped by their table, putting down two glasses of water. He was thin and dark. He looked at Darby, then at the book in his hand.

"What do you want, Mary?" McGraw asked.

"Coffee," she said. "Just coffee."

He opened the diary and started glancing down the pages while Mary looked over his shoulder. Suddenly, she squeezed his arm.

"Darby, that waiter's on the telephone!" she whispered excitedly. "I think he's talking about us!"

Darby looked up hastily. "Why should he? What does he know? Unless . . . unless Renke owns this joint. No, that's too much of a coincidence to figure we've hit one of Renke's places by accident."

"Not one of *his* places, Darby, but Renke's boss of the numbers racket here. All these places handle the slips. All of them have contact with Art Renke. And he pays off for favors."

"Finish your coffee," Darby said. "We'll save the diary."

They started to get up, and the thin, dark man came around the counter very fast. "Want some more coffee? Sure, have some . . . on the house."

"No," Mary said, "not now."

"Come on," the waiter said, smiling, "it's a cold night."

"The lady said no," Darby told him sharply, then turned to Mary. "Let's get out of here!"

They got into their cars and started them fast, but not fast enough. Just as Mary started to swing her car out from the curb, an old coupe with a bright metallic paint job wheeled around the corner and angled across in front of it. Two men got out and started toward her.

V

DARBY LEFT HIS car door hanging and started back, slipping on a pair of skintight gloves. Both men were small and swarthy, and both were dressed in flashy clothes. They looked at the girl and then at him. One of them had a gun.

"You gotta book, *señor*? You give it to me, yes?"

"No," Darby said.

"You better," the man replied harshly. "Hurry up quick now, or I'll shoot!"

The fighter hesitated, his jaw set stubbornly. This time there was Mary to think of. "If we give it to you, do we both go?"

"*Si*. Yes, of course. You give it up and you go."

Without a word, Darby handed over the diary. The two men turned instantly and got in their own car.

"Well," Mary said, "that's that. We had it and now we don't have it. Fats and Renke are just as much in the clear as ever."

DARBY WAS LED through the crowd toward the ring. The place was packed and smoke hung in the air around the suspended lights. Coming through the stands, Darby and his second skirted a group of men and ran face-to-face with Fats Lakey. Fats grinned evilly; sweat ran down his neck. He wagged his finger. "Next fight, country boy ... next time you fight you're gonna make me some money." He laughed and dodged back into the crowd. Darby knew what that meant. They would try to make him take a dive. His jaw tightened.

Darby tried to clear his mind. That was in the future, maybe. Tonight was what he had to worry about now.

Benny Barros was shorter than Darby McGraw by three inches. He was almost that much wider. He was certainly more than three inches thicker through the chest.

He was a puncher and built like one. Portuguese, and flat-faced, with a thick, heavy chest and powerful arms. He came into the ring wearing red silk trunks, and he didn't smile. He never smiled. When they came together in the center of the ring, he kept his eyes on the canvas, and then he walked back to his corner and they slipped off his robe, revealing the dark brown and powerful muscles of his torso. He looked then, with his flat, rattlesnake's eyes, at Darby McGraw. Just one look, and then the bell sounded.

Barros came out fast. He came out with his gloves cocked for hooking, and he moved right straight in. Darby's left was a streak that stabbed empty air over Benny's shoulder. Benny's right glove smashed into McGraw's midsection and Darby turned away, hooking a left to the head.

Both men were fast. Darby felt the sharpness of Barros's punches and knew he was in for a rough evening. He jabbed, then hooked a solid blow to the head, and Benny blinked. His face seemed to turn a shade darker and his lips flattened over his mouthpiece.

Between rounds Dan Faherty worked over Darby. "Renke's here," he said. "So is Fats."

"I know. I wish I had that diary, though," Darby said. "We'd have them both in jail before the night is over."

The bell sounded for the second round. Barros feinted and threw a high right that caught Darby on the chin. Darby took a quick step back and sat down. The crowd came to its feet with a roar and Darby shook his head, fighting his way to one knee. The suddenness of it startled him and he was badly shaken.

He got up at seven and saw Barros coming in fast, but Darby stabbed a left into Benny's mouth that started a trickle of blood. However, the punch failed to stop him. He got to Darby with both hands, blasting a right to the head and then digging a left into his midsection just above the belt band on his trunks. Darby jabbed a left and clipped Barros with a solid right to the head.

Darby stepped away and circled warily, then, as Barros moved in, he stabbed a left to the face and hooked sharply with the same left. Barros ducked under it, slamming away at his body with both hands. Barros's body was glistening with sweat and his flat, hard face was taut and brutal under the bright glare of the light. A thin trickle of blood still came from the flat-lipped mouth, and Barros slipped another left and got home a right to Darby's stomach that jerked a gasp from him.

But Darby stepped in, punching with both hands, and suddenly Benny's eyes blazed with fury and triumph. Nobody had ever slugged with Benny Barros and walked away under his own power. The two lunged together and, toe-to-toe, began to slug it out. Darby spread his feet and walked in, throwing them with both hands, his heart burning with the fury of the battle, his mind firing on the smashing power of his fists.

He dropped a right to Benny's jaw that staggered the shorter man and made him blink, then he took a wicked left to the head that brought a hot, smoky taste into his mouth, and the sweat poured down over his body. The bell clanged, and clanged again and again before they got them apart.

Benny trotted back to his corner and stood there, refusing to sit down while he drew in great gulps of air. The crowd was still roaring when the bell for the third round sounded and both men rushed out, coming together in mid-ring with a crash of blows. Darby stabbed a wicked left to the head that started the blood from Benny's eye, and Barros ducked, weaved, and bobbed, hooking with both hands. Benny moved in with a right that jolted Darby to his heels. McGraw backed away, shaken, and Benny lunged after him, punching away with both hands.

Darby crumpled under the attack and hit the canvas, but then rolled over and came up without a count, and as Barros charged in for the kill, Darby straightened and drilled a right down the groove that put the Portuguese back on his heels. Lunging after him, Darby swung a wide left that connected and dropped Barros.

Barros took a count of four, then came up and bored in, landing a left to the body and stopping a left with his chin. The bell sounded and both men ran back to their corners. The crowd was a dull roar of sound, and Darby was so alive and burning with the fierce love of combat that he could scarcely sit down. He glanced out over the crowd once and saw two thin, dark men sitting behind Renke, and one of them was leaning over, speaking to him.

Then, as the bell rang, he realized one of the men was the man who had taken the diary. He knew he was lagging, and he lunged to his feet and sidestepped out of the corner to beat Barros's rush, but Benny was after him, hooking with both hands. Darby felt blood starting again from the cut over the eye that Faherty had repaired between rounds, and he backed up, putting up a hand as though to wipe it away. Instantly, Barros leaped in, and that left hand Darby had lifted dropped suddenly in a chopping blow that laid Benny's brow open just over the right eye. Barros staggered, then, with an almost animal-like growl of fury, he lunged in close and one of his hooks stabbed Darby in the vitals like a knife.

He stabbed with a left that missed, then hit Darby with a wicked right hook, and Darby felt as if he had been slugged behind the knees with a ball bat. He went down with lights exploding in his brain like the splitting of atoms somewhere over the crowd. And then he was coming up from the canvas, feeling the bite of resin in his nostrils.

The dull roar that was like the sound of a far-off sea was the crowd, and he lunged to his feet and saw the brown, brutal shadow of Barros looming near. He struck out with a blind instinct and felt his fist hit something solid. Moving in, he hit by feel, and felt his left sink deep into Barros's tough, elastic body. He swung three times at the air before the referee grabbed him and shoved him toward a corner so that he could begin the count.

Darby got the fog out of his brain as Benny Barros struggled up at the count of nine. McGraw saw the brown man weaving before him and started down the ring toward him. The Portuguese lunged in, throwing both hands, and Darby lifted him to his tiptoes with a ripping right uppercut, then caught him with a sweeping left hook as his heels hit the canvas. Barros stumbled backward and Darby stepped in, set himself, and fired his right—the money punch—just like in the old days when he didn't know any better. Except now it was perfectly timed and he had the perfect opening. Barros went over backward, both feet straight out. He hit on his shoulder blades, rolled over on his face, and lay still.

The referee took a look, then touched him with a hand,

and walking over, lifted Darby McGraw's right hand. Darby wobbled to the ropes and stood there hanging on and looking.

There was a wild turmoil at the ringside that suddenly thinned out, and he could see men in uniforms gathered around. Then Dan was leading him to his corner and Darby shook the fog out of his brain.

"What happened?" he demanded, staring at the knot of policemen. Over the noise of the crowd he could hear a siren whine to a stop out on the street.

Then one of the policemen stepped aside, and he saw Art Renke sitting with his head fallen back and the haft of a knife thrust upward from the hollow of his collarbone. Beside him, Fats Lakey was white and trembling, and there was blood all down his face from a slash across the cheek.

Mary was up in his corner. "Come on! Let's get you out of here!" Darby gathered his robe around him and she led him, his knees weak and uncooperative, back to the dressing room.

Darby was just getting his focus back when Dan came bursting through the door. "It was the White Fence that got Renke," he said, "at least that's what the police think."

"The man in the cafe!" Mary gasped. "He must have been a friend of the Lopez brothers and called them!"

"Art Renke's dead," Dan said. "They just slashed Fats for luck. I'd heard they'd been suspicious, and when Beano was killed, it probably made them more so. Smoke may have told them something, too."

———

DARBY MCGRAW LET Dan unlace his gloves. "Who do I fight next?" he asked.

"You rest for a month now," Dan said. "Maybe more. Then we'll see."

"Okay," Darby said, smiling, "you're the boss." He looked at Mary. "Then we'll have time for a show, won't we? Or several of them?"

She squeezed his still-bandaged hand.

"We will," she promised. "I'll get the car."

He stopped her at the dressing-room door and took her chin in his right hand, tipping her head back.

"Thank you," he said seriously, "I'd thank Beano Brown, too, if I could." He kissed her quickly then, and headed for the showers.

MAKING IT THE HARD WAY

UNDER THE WHITE glare of the lights, the two fighters circled each other warily. Finn Downey's eyes were savagely intent as he stalked his prey. Twice Gammy Delgardo's stabbing left struck Downey's head, but Finn continued to move, his fists cocked.

As the lancelike left started once more, Downey ducked suddenly and sprang in, connecting with a looping overhand right. Delgardo's legs wavered, and he tried to get into a clinch.

Finn was ready for him, and a short left uppercut to the wind was enough to set Delgardo up for a second right. Delgardo hit the canvas on his knees, and Downey wheeled, trotting to his corner.

Gammy took nine and came up. His left landed lightly, three times, as Downey pushed close; then Finn was all over the game Italian, punching with both hands. Gammy staggered, and Finn threw the high right again. He caught Delgardo on the point of the chin, and the Italian hit the canvas, out cold.

Jimmy Mullaney had Finn's robe ready when he reached the corner.

"That's another one, kid," Mullaney said. "Keep this up an' you'll go places."

Downey grinned. He was a solidly built fellow, brown and strong, with dark, curly hair. When the crowd broke into a roar, he straightened to take a bow, then he saw the cheers were not for him. Three men were coming down the aisle, the one in the lead a handsome young fellow in beautifully fitting blue gabardine. His shoulders were broad, and as he waved at the crowd, his teeth flashed in a smile.

"Who's that?" Finn demanded. "Some movie actor?"

"That?" Mullaney said, startled. "Why, that's Glen Gurney, the middleweight champion of the world!"

"Him?" Downey's amazed question was a protest against such a man even being a fighter, let alone the champion of Downey's own division. "Well, for the love of Mike! And I thought he was tough!"

Gurney looked up at Finn with a quick smile. "How are you?" he said pleasantly. "Nice fight?"

Sudden antagonism surged to the surface in Finn. He stepped down from the ring and stood beside Gurney.

So this was the champ! This perfectly groomed young man with the smooth easy manner. Without a scar on his face! Why, the guy was a *dude*!

"I stopped him in the third, like I'll do you!" Downey blurted.

Mullaney grabbed his arm. "Finn, shut up!"

Boiling within Finn Downey was a stifled protest against such poised and sure fellows who got all the cream of the world while kids like himself fought their way up, shining shoes or swamping out trucks.

Gurney's smile was friendly, but in his eyes was a question.

"Maybe we will fight someday," he agreed, affably enough, "but you'll need some work first! If I were you, I'd shorten up that right hand!"

Eyes blazing, Downey thrust himself forward. "You tell *me* how to fight? I could lick you the best day you ever saw!"

He started for Gurney, but Jimmy grabbed him again. "Cut it out, kid! Let's get out of here!"

Gurney stood his ground, his hands in his pockets. "Not here, Downey. We fight in the ring. No gentleman ever starts a brawl."

The word "gentleman" cut Finn like a whip. With everything he had, he swung.

Gurney swayed and the blow curled around his neck as men grabbed the angry Downey and dragged him back. And the champ had not even taken his hands from his pockets!

Mullaney hustled Downey to the dressing room. Inside, Jimmy slammed the door and turned on him.

"What's got into you, Finn? You off your trolley? Why jump the champ, of all people? He'd tear your head off in a fight, and besides, he's a good guy to have for a friend!"

Downey closed his ears to the tirade, all the more irritated because there was justice in it. He showered, then pulled on his old gray trousers and his shirt. Getting his socks on, he worked the tip of the sock down under his toes so that no one could see the hole.

He was angry with himself, yet still resentful. Why did a guy like Gurney have to be champion? Well, anyway . . . when they fought he would put his heart into it.

The fight game must be going to the dogs, or no snob like Glen Gurney could ever hold a title.

Of course, there were ways of getting there by knocking over a string of handpicked setups. That, however, meant money and the right sort of connections. With money improving the challenger's odds, no wonder Gurney was champ.

Mullaney pulled out bills and paid him eighty dollars.

"That's less my cut and the twenty you owe me. Okay?"

"Sure, sure!" Finn stuffed the bills into his pocket.

Jimmy Mullaney hesitated. "Listen, Finn. You've got the wrong idea about Gurney. The champ's a good egg. He never gave anybody a bad break in his life."

Downey thrust his hands in his pockets.

"He's got a lot of nerve telling me how to throw a right! Why, that right hand knocked out seven guys in a row!"

Mullaney looked at Downey thoughtfully. "You've got a good right, Finn, but he was right. You throw it too far."

Downey turned and walked out. That was the way it was. When you were on top everybody took your word. His right was okay. Only two punches in three rounds tonight, and both landed.

He fingered the bills. He would have to give some to Mom, and Sis needed a new dress. He would have to skip the outfit he wanted for himself. His thoughts shifted back to the immaculate Glen Gurney and he set his jaw angrily. Just let him get some money! He'd show that dude how to dress!

It wouldn't be easy, but nothing in his life had been easy. From earliest childhood all he could remember were the dirty streets of a tenement district, fire escapes hung with wet clothing, stifling heat and damp, chilling cold.

Never once could he recall a time when he'd had socks or shoes without holes in them. His father, a bricklayer, had been crippled when Finn was seven, and after that the struggle had been even harder. His older brother now was a clerk for a trucking firm, and the younger worked in the circulation department of a newspaper. One of his sisters worked in a dime store, and the other one, young and lovely as any girl who ever lived, was in high school.

"Hey, Finn!"

Downey glanced up, and his face darkened as he saw a fellow he knew named Stoff. He had never liked the guy, although they had grown up on the same block. These days Stoff was hanging around with Bernie Ledsham, and the gambler was with him now.

"Hi," he returned, and started to pass on.

"Wait a minute, Finn!" Stoff urged. "You ever meet Bernie? We seen your fight tonight."

"How's it?" Finn said to Bernie, a thin-faced man with shrewd black eyes and a flat-lipped mouth. Finn had seen him around, but didn't like him either.

"How about a beer?" Bernie said.

"Never touch it. Not in my racket." Downey drew away. "I've got to be getting on home."

"Come on. Why, after winnin' like you did tonight, you should celebrate. Come with us."

Reluctantly, Finn followed them into a café. Norm Hunter, a man he also knew, was sitting at a table, and with him was a short, square-built fellow with a dark, impassive face. When Finn Downey looked into the flat black eyes, something like a chill went over him, for he recognized the man as Nick Lessack, who had done two stretches in Sing Sing, and was said to be gunman for "Cat" Spelvin's mob.

"You sure cooled that guy!" Norman Hunter said admiringly. "You got a punch there!"

Pleased but wary, Finn dropped into a seat across the table from Nick Lessack.

"He wasn't so tough," he said, "but he did catch me a couple of times."

"He got lucky," Bernie said. "Just lucky."

Downey knew that was not true. Those had been sharp, accurate punches. The lump over his eye was nothing, for black eyes or cut lips were the usual thing for him, but it bothered him that those punches had hit him. Somehow he must learn to make them miss.

Stoff had disappeared, and Finn was having a cup of coffee with Hunter, Bernie, and Nick Lessack.

"That blasted Gurney!" Bernie sneered. "I wish it had been him you'd clipped tonight! He thinks he's too good!"

"I'd like to get in there with him!" Finn agreed.

"Why not?" Bernie asked, shrugging. "Cat could fix it. Couldn't he, Nick?"

Lessack, staring steadily at Downey, spoke without apparently moving his lips. "Sure. Cat can fix anything."

Finn shrugged, grinning. "*Okay!* I'd like to get in there with that pantywaist."

"You got to fight some others first," Bernie protested. "We could fix it so you could fight Tony Gilman two weeks from tonight. Couldn't we, Nick? After he stops Gilman, a couple of more scraps, then the champ. Anybody got any paper on you, kid? I mean, like this Mullaney?"

"He just works with me." Downey felt shame at what that implied, for whatever he knew about fighting, Jimmy had taught him. "I got no contract with him."

"Good!" Bernie leaned closer. "Listen, come up and have a talk with Cat. Sign up with him, an' you'll be in the dough. Tonight you got maybe a hundred fish. Cat can get you three times that much, easy. He can give you the info on bets, too."

"Sure," Hunter agreed. "You tie up with us, and you'll be set."

"Let's go," Nick said suddenly. "We can drop the kid by his home."

Bernie paid the check and they went outside where there was a big black car, a smooth job. "Get in, kid," Nick said. "Maybe Cat'll give you a heap like this. He give this one to me."

WHEN THEY LEFT Finn Downey on the corner, the street was dank, dark, and still, and he kicked his heel lonesomely against the curb. He was filled with a vague nostalgia for lights, music, comfort, and warmth, all the fine things he had never known.

Spelvin had money. Bernie and Hunter always had it, too. Finn was not an innocent; he had grown up in the streets, and he knew why Bernie and Hunter had always had money. When they were kids, he had watched them steal packages, flashlights, and watches from parked cars or stores. Twice Bernie had been in jail, yet they had more and better clothes than he'd ever had, and they had cars and money.

Finn's sister, Aline, was waiting up for him.

"Oh, Finn! You were wonderful! The rest of them had to get up early, so they went to bed, but they told me to tell you how good they thought you were!"

"Thanks, honey." He felt for the thin wad of bills. "Here, kid. Here's for a new dress."

"Twenty dollars!" She was ecstatic. "Oh, Finn, thank you!"

"Forget it!" He was pleased, but at the same time he felt sad that it took so little money to make so much difference.

He would give Mom forty for rent and groceries. The other twenty would have to carry him until his next fight. If he fought Gilman, he'd get plenty out of that, and a win would mean a lot.

Yet there was a stirring of doubt. He wasn't so sure that beating the hard-faced young battler would be easy. Yet if Spelvin was handling him, he would see that Finn won. . . .

IN THE MORNING, Jimmy Mullaney was waiting for him at the gym. He grinned. "I'm going to get you lined up for another one right away if I can, boy."

"How about getting me Tony Gilman?"

"Gilman?" Jimmy glanced at him quickly. "Kid, you don't want to fight him! He's rugged!"

"Cat Spelvin can get him for me." Finn squirmed as he saw Jimmy's face turn hard and strange.

"So?" Jimmy's voice was like Finn had never heard it before. "He's a sure-thing man, kid. You tie in with him an' you'll never break loose. He's a racketeer."

"I ain't in this game for love!" Downey said recklessly. "I want some money."

"You throwin' me over, kid?" Mullaney's eyes were cold. "You tyin' in with Spelvin?"

"No." The voice that broke in was even, but friendly. "Let's hope he's not."

Finn Downey turned and faced Glen Gurney.

"You again?" he growled.

Gurney thrust out a hand and smiled. "Don't be sore at me. We're all working at this game, and I came down to the gym today on purpose to see you."

"Me? What do you want with me?"

"I thought I might work with you a little, help you out. You've got a future, and a lot of guys helped me, so I thought I'd pass it on."

Downey recognized the honesty in the champion's voice, but flushed at the implied criticism of his fighting ability. "I don't need any help from you," he said flatly. "Go roll your hoop."

"Don't be that way," Gurney protested. "Anything I say, it's coming from respect."

"He don't need your help," drawled another voice behind them.

Gurney and Downey turned swiftly—and saw Cat Spelvin, a short man with a round face and full lips. Beside him were Bernie and the inevitable Nick Lessack.

"We'll take care of Finn," Cat said. "You do like he said, champ. Roll your hoop."

Coolly, Gurney looked Cat over, then glanced at Nick. "They're cutting the rats in larger sizes these days," he said quietly.

"That don't get you no place," Spelvin said. "Finn's our boy. We'll take care of him."

Finn felt his face flush as he looked at the champion. For the first time he was seeing him without resentment and anger. In Gurney was a touch of something he hadn't seen in many men. Maybe that was why he was champion.

"Downey," Gurney said, "you have your own choice to make, of course, but it seems to me Mullaney has done pretty well by you, and I'm ready to help."

"I promised Spelvin," Downey said.

Gurney turned abruptly and walked away. Jimmy Mullaney swore softly and followed him.

Spelvin smiled at Downey. "We'll get along, kid. You made the smart play. . . . Bernie, is the Gilman fight on?"

"A week from Monday. Finn Downey and Tony Gilman."

"You'll get five hundred bucks for your end," Spelvin said. "You need some dough now?"

"He can use some," Bernie said. "Finn's always broke."

Finn turned resentful eyes on Bernie, but when he walked away there was an advance of a hundred dollars in his pockets.

Then he remembered the expression on Mullaney's face, and the hundred dollars no longer cheered him. And Glen Gurney . . . maybe he had been sincere in wanting to help. What kind of a mess was this anyway?

———

THE ARENA WAS crowded when Finn Downey climbed into the ring to meet Tony Gilman. Glancing down into the ringside seats, he saw Mullaney, and beside him was the champ. Not far away, Aline was sitting with Joe, the oldest of the Downey family.

When the bell sounded, he went out fast. He lashed out with a left, and the blond fighter slammed both hands to the body with short, wicked punches. He clinched, they broke, and Finn moved in, landing a left, then missing a long right.

Gilman walked around him, then moved in fast and low, hitting hard. Downey backed up. His left wasn't finding Gilman like it should, but give him time. One good punch with his right was all he wanted, just one!

Gilman ripped a right to the ribs, then hooked high and hard with a left. Downey backed away, then cut loose with the right. Gilman stepped inside and sneered:

"Where'd you find that punch, kid? In an alley?"

Finn rushed, swinging wildly. He missed, then clipped Gilman with a short left and the blond fighter slowed. Gilman weaved under another left, smashed a wicked right to the heart, then a left and an overhand right to the chin that staggered Downey.

Finn rushed again, and the crowd cheered as he pushed Gilman into the ropes. Smiling coldly at Finn, Gilman stabbed two fast lefts to his face. Finn tasted blood, and rushed again. Tony gave ground, then boxed away in an incredible display of defense, stopping any further punches.

The bell sounded, and Finn walked to his corner. He was disturbed, for he couldn't get started against Gilman. There was a feeling of latent power in the fighter that warned him, and a sense of futility in his own fighting, which was ineffective against Gilman.

The second round was a duplicate of the first, both men moving fast, and Tony giving ground before Downey's rushes, but making Finn miss repeatedly. Three times Finn started the right, but each time it curled helplessly around Gilman's neck.

"You sap!" Gilman sneered in a clinch. "Who told you you could fight?"

He broke, then stabbed a left to Finn's mouth and crossed a solid right that stung. Downey tried to slide under Gilman's left, but it met his face halfway, and he was stopped flat-footed for a right cross that clipped him on the chin.

The third and fourth rounds flitted by, and Downey, tired with continual punching, came up for the fifth despairing. No matter what he tried, Gilman had the answer. Gilman was unmarked, but there was a thin trickle of blood from Finn's eyes at the end of the round, and his lip was swollen.

In the ringside seats he heard a man say, "Downey's winning this," but the words gave him no pleasure, for he knew his punches were not landing solidly and he had taken a wicked pounding.

Gilman moved in fast, and Downey jabbed with a left that landed solidly on Tony's head, much to Finn's surprise. Then he rushed Gilman to the ropes. Coming off the ropes, he clipped Tony again, and the blond fighter staggered and appeared hurt. Boring in, Finn swung his right—and it landed!

Gilman rolled with the punch, then fell against Finn, his body limp. As Downey sprang back, Tony fell to the canvas.

The referee stepped in and counted, but there was no movement from Gilman. He had to be carried to his corner. As Finn lowered him to a stool, Tony said hoarsely:

"I could lick you with one hand!"

Flushing, Finn Downey walked slowly back across the ring, and when the cheering crowd gathered around him, there was no elation in his heart. He saw Gurney looking at him, and turned away.

As he followed Bernie and Norm Hunter toward the dressing room, the crowd was still cheering, but inside him something lay dead and cold. Yet he had glimpsed the faces of Joe and Aline; they were flushed and excited, enthusiastic over his victory.

Bernie grinned at him. "See, kid? It's the smart way that matters. You couldn't lick one side of Gilman by rights, but after Cat fixes 'em, they stay fixed!"

Anger welled up in Downey, but he turned his back on them, getting on his shoes. When he straightened up, they were walking out, headed for the local bar. He stared after them, and felt disgust for them and for himself.

Outside, Aline and Joe were waiting.

"Oh, Finn!" Aline cried. "It was so wonderful! And everyone was saying you weren't anywhere good enough for Tony Gilman! That will show them, won't it?"

"Yeah, yeah!" He took her arm. "Let's go eat, honey."

As he turned away with them, he came face-to-face with Glen Gurney and two girls.

Two girls, but Finn Downey could see but one. She was tall, and slender, and beautiful. His eyes held her, clinging.

Gurney hesitated, then said quietly, "Finn, I'd like you to meet my sister, Pamela. And my fiancée, Mary."

Finn acknowledged the introduction, his eyes barely flitting to Mary. He introduced Joe and Aline to them, then the girl was gone, and Aline was laughing at him.

"Why, Finn! I never saw a girl affect you like that before!"

"Aw, it wasn't her!" he blustered. "I just don't like Gurney. He's too stuck-up!"

"I thought he was nice," Aline protested, "and he's certainly handsome. The champion of the world . . . Do you think you'll be champ someday, Finn?"

"Sure." His eyes narrowed. "After I lick him."

"He's a good man, Finn," Joe said quietly. "He's the hardest man to hit with a right that I ever saw."

The remark irritated Finn, yet he was honest enough to realize he was bothered because of what Glen Gurney had said about his fighting. Yet he could not think of that for long, for he was remembering that tall, willowy girl with the lovely eyes, Pamela Gurney.

And she had to be the champ's sister. The man he would have to defeat for the title!

Moreover, he would probably tell her about tonight, for Finn knew his knockout of Tony Gilman would not fool a fighter of Gurney's skill. The champion would know only too well just what had happened.

Somehow even the money failed to assuage his bitterness and discontent. A small voice within told him Gilman and Bernie were right. He was simply not good enough. If Gilman had not taken a dive, he could never have whipped him, and might have been cut to ribbons.

Then, he remembered that he hadn't hit Gilman with his right. He had missed, time and again. If he could not hit Gilman, then he could not hit the champ, and the champ was not controlled by Cat Spelvin. Finn had a large picture of himself in the ring with Glen Gurney, and the picture was not flattering.

Spelvin had told him he would be fighting Webb Carter in two weeks, and Webb was a fairly good boy, though not so good as Gilman. The knockout of Gilman had established Finn Downey as a championship possibility. Now a few more knockouts, and Cat could claim a title bout.

———

AT DAYBREAK THE next morning, Finn Downey was on the road, taking a two-mile jaunt through the park. He knew what he wanted, and suddenly, as he dogtrotted along, he knew how to get it.

He wanted to be champion of the world. That, of course. He wanted the fame and money that went with it, but now he knew he wanted something else even more, and it was something that all of Cat Spelvin's crookedness could not gain for him—he wanted the respect of the men he fought, and of Jimmy Mullaney, who had been his friend.

He was jogging along, taking it easy, when from up ahead he saw Pamela Gurney. She was riding a tall sorrel horse, and she reined in when she saw him.

"You're out early, aren't you?" she asked.

He stopped, panting a little from the run.

"Getting in shape," he said. "I've got another fight comin' up."

"You did well against Tony Gilman," she said, looking at him thoughtfully.

He glanced up quickly, trying to see if there had been sarcasm in her voice, but if she knew that had been a fixed fight, she showed no sign of it.

"My brother says you could be a great fighter," she added, "if you'd work."

Finn flushed, then he grinned. "I guess I never knew how much there was to learn."

"You don't like Glen, do you?" she asked.

"You don't understand; I have to fight for what I get. Your brother had it handed to him. How can you know what it's like for me?"

Her eyes flashed. "What right have you to say that? My brother earned everything he ever had in this world!"

Suddenly, all the unhappiness in him welled to the surface. "Don't hand me that! Both of you have always had things easy. Nice clothes, cars, money, plenty to eat. Gurney is champ, and how he got it, I don't know, but I've got my own ideas."

Pamela turned her horse deliberately. "You're so very sure of yourself, aren't you?" she said. "So sure you're right, and that you know it all! Well, Mr. Finn Downey, after your fight with Tony Gilman the other night, you haven't any room to talk!"

His face went red. "So? He told you, didn't he? I might have known he would."

"Told me?" Pamela's voice rose. "What kind of fool do you think I am? I've been watching fights since I was able to walk, and you couldn't hit Tony Gilman with that round-house right of yours if he was tied hand and foot!"

She cantered swiftly away. Suddenly rage shook him. He started away, and abruptly his rage evaporated. Pamela was the girl he wanted, the one girl above all others. Yet what right did she have to talk? Glen Gurney certainly was no angel. But burning within him was a fiery resolution to become so good they could never say again what they were saying now. Pamela, Gilman, Bernie. How cheap they must think him!

He recalled the helplessness he had felt against Gilman, and knew that no matter what Glen Gurney thought of him, once in the ring he would get no mercy from the champ. He had begun to realize how much there was to learn and knew that he would never learn, at least while he was being handled by Spelvin.

What he should do was go to see Jimmy Mullaney. But he hated the thought of admitting he was wrong. Besides, Jimmy might not even talk to him, and there was plenty of reason why he should not. Still, if he could learn a little more by the time he fought Carter, he might make a creditable showing.

He found Mullaney in the cheap hotel where he lived. The little man did not smile—just laid his magazine aside.

"Jimmy," Finn said, "I've made a fool of myself!"

Mullaney reached for a cigarette. He looked past the lighted match and said, "That's right. You have." Jimmy took a deep drag. "Well, every man has his own problems to settle, Finn. What's on your mind now?"

"I want you to teach me all you know."

Jimmy stared at him. "Kid, when you were my fighter that was one thing. Now you belong to Cat. You know what he'd do to me? He might even have the boys give me a couple of slugs in the back. He's got money in you now. You think Gilman did that dive for fun? He got paid plenty, son. Because

Cat thought it would be worth it to build you up. Not that he won't see Gilman work you over when the time is ripe. Spelvin wants you for a quick killing in the bets."

"Jimmy," Finn said, "suppose you train me on the side? Then suppose I really stop those guys? Then when Spelvin's ready to have me knocked off, suppose I don't knock off so easy?"

Mullaney scowled and swore. "It's risky, kid. He might get wise, then we'd both be in the soup." He grinned. "I'd like to cross that crook, though."

"Jimmy—give it to me straight. Do you think I can be good enough to beat Gurney or Gilman?"

Mullaney rubbed out the cigarette in a saucer. "With hard work and training, you could beat Gilman, especially with him so sure now. He'll never figure you'll improve, because nobody gets better fighting setups. Gurney is a good kid. He's plenty good! He's the slickest boxer the middleweight division has seen since Kid McCoy."

Mullaney paced up and down the room, then nodded. "All right, kid. That brother of yours, he's got a big basement. We'll work with you there, on the sly." He flushed. "You'll have to furnish the dough. I'm broke."

"Sure." Finn pulled out the money from the Gilman fight. "Here's a C. Buy what we'll need, eat on it. I'll cut you in on the next fight."

When he left Mullaney, he felt good. He ran down the steps into the street—and came face-to-face with Bernie Ledsham.

Bernie halted, his eyes narrow with suspicion.

"What you doin' down here? Ain't that where Mullaney lives?"

"Sure is." Finn grinned. "I owed the guy dough. I wanted him paid off. No use lettin' him crab about it."

Ledsham shrugged. "If he gives you any trouble, you just tell me or Cat."

Downey believed Bernie's suspicions were lulled, but he didn't trust the sallow-faced man.

"Come on," he said, "I'll buy a beer!"

They walked down the street to a bar, and Finn had a Pepsi

while Bernie drank two beers and they talked. But there was a sullen air of suspicion about the gangster that Finn Downey didn't like. When he could, he got away and returned home. . . .

———

DOWNEY'S KNOCKOUT OVER Tony Gilman had made him the talk of the town. Yet Finn knew everyone was waiting to see what he would do against Webb Carter.

Carter had fought Gilman twice, losing both times, and he had lost to Gurney. He had been in the game for ten years and was accepting his orders unhappily, but was needing money.

———

THE BELL RANG in the crowded arena on the night of the fight. Finn went out fast. Coached by Mullaney, he had worked as never before, shortening his right hand, sharpening his punches, developing a left hook. Yet he showed little of it at first.

Carter met him with a fast left that Finn managed to slip, and smashed one hand, then the other, into the rock-ribbed body of the older fighter. Carter stiffened a left hook to Finn's face, and Finn threw a wicked left uppercut to the wind. Carter backed away cautiously, studying Finn with new respect, but Downey moved on in, weaving and bobbing to make Carter's left miss. Then Finn feinted and smashed a right to the ribs. In a clinch, he hammered with that right three times, and broke.

He wasted no time, but walked in close, took a chance, and deliberately missed a couple of punches. Carter was making him miss enough, anyway. More than ever, Downey realized how much he had to learn, yet he felt that even the short period he had trained for this fight had improved him.

Mullaney had warned him that he must be careful with Carter. The fighter could punch, and while it was in the bag for him to dive, Carter might slip over a couple of hard ones. A cut eye now would do Finn no good.

The second and third went by swiftly, with Finn working

with care. He missed punches, and seemed clumsy, and at times was clumsy, despite his efforts, yet his hard work had done him more good than he had realized.

In the fourth round he came out fast, and Carter moved around him, then led a left. Downey went under it and smashed that right to the ribs again, then followed it into a clinch behind two trip-hammer blows to the wind. Carter looked pale, and he glared at Finn.

"What's the matter, kid? Ain't it enough to win?"

Downey broke before the referee reached them, jabbed a left that caught Carter high on the head, then stepped in, feinting a right to the body and throwing it high and hard. It caught Webb on the cheekbone, and his face went white and his lips looked numb. He went into a clinch.

"You take it easy, kid," he growled, "or I'll lower the boom on you!"

"Anytime you're ready!" Finn snapped back.

Carter jerked free and smashed a right to Downey's head that made his knees wobble. Then he plunged in throwing them with both hands. Sensing a rally, the crowd came to its feet, and Finn, instead of yielding before the storm of blows, walked right into it, swinging with both hands.

Webb stabbed a left to Finn's mouth that made him taste blood, and Finn slid under another left and jammed a right to the heart, then a left to the wind and a right to the ear. He pushed Carter away, took a light punch going in, and smashed both hands to the body, throwing the hooks with his hip behind them.

The fifth round was a slugfest, with the fans on their chairs screaming themselves hoarse. In the sixth, as Carter came out of his corner, Finn moved in, feinted a left, and smashed a high hard right to the head. This was the round for Carter's dive, but Finn had no intention of letting him take it, and the right made Carter give ground. Finn pressed him back, weaving in under Carter's punches and winging them into the other fighter's body with all the power he had.

He broke clean and backed away, looking Carter over. There was amazed respect in Webb Carter's eyes. Finn circled, then feinted, and Carter threw a right. Downey countered with a lifting right to the solar plexus that stood Carter on his tiptoes, and before Webb realized what had happened, a whistling left hook cracked on his chin and he hit the canvas on his face, out cold!

Finn trotted back to his corner, and Bernie held up his robe, staring at Carter. Finn leaned close.

"Boy!" he whispered. "He made it look good! Better than Gilman! He stuck his chin into that punch and just let go!"

"Yeah," Bernie agreed dolefully. "Yeah, it almost fooled me!"

IT WAS AFTER the end of the fight that Finn Downey saw Pamela Gurney and her brother. They were only a few seats from his corner. Pamela's face was cold, but there was a hard, curious light in Glen's eyes.

Finn didn't show that he noticed them, but he knew that Gurney wasn't fooled. The champ knew that knockout was the McCoy. And it would puzzle him.

Well, let it! The only one Finn was worried about was Cat, but when the gambler came into his dressing room he grinned at Downey.

"Nice going, kid! That was good!"

Evidently, Spelvin knew little about fighting. He didn't know an honest knockout when he saw it.

In the month that followed, Finn spent at least four days a week in the basement gym with Mullaney. They were not training sessions. Finn just listened to Jimmy and practiced punches on the heavy bag. When he went to the regular gym for his workout, he was the same as ever. In ring sessions he worked carefully, never showing too much, but with occasional flashes of form and boxing skill. His right, always a devastating punch, was traveling less distance now, and he was hitting even harder.

In that month he had two fights, and both opponents went into the tank, but not until after a brisk, hard workout. In each fight he knew he could have stopped the man had the fight been on the level.

Now he and Jimmy had a problem, for a return match with Gilman was to be scheduled in a short time.

"They'll figure to get me this time," Finn agreed with Mullaney. "I've been scoring knockouts right and left, and Gilman has only fought once, and looked bad. The boys are saying he's through, so the betting should be at least two to one that I repeat my kayo. Cat will figure to clean up."

The writer of a sports column, a man named Van Bergen, offered the judgment of most of the sportswriters:

Tony Gilman is seeking a return match with young Finn Downey, the hard-socking battler who stopped him two months ago. If Gilman is wise he will hang them up while he has all his buttons. In his last two fights, Tony showed that he was through. Formerly a hard-hitting, tough middleweight, Gilman lacked all of the fire and dash that characterized his earlier fights. He may never be his old self again.

Downey continues to come along. After his surprise knockout over Gilman, he went on to stop tough Webb Carter, and since has followed with knockout wins over Danny Ebro and Joey Collins.

If the match is made, Downey should stop Gilman within six rounds.

Cat Spelvin called Downey in on a Tuesday morning. He was all smiles.

"Well, kid, one more fight, then I think we can get Gurney for you. The fans still like Gilman, so we'll feed him to you again. From there on, you walk right into the title."

Finn grinned back at him. "Well, I've got you to thank for it, Cat. If you hadn't helped, I'd probably still be fighting prelims."

Cat lit a cigar. "Just take it easy, kid. Gilman will be a setup for you!"

Bernie and Nick Lessack walked outside with Downey.

"Let's go get a beer," Bernie suggested. "No use killin' yourself workin' for fights that are in the bag."

"Yeah." Secretly, Finn ground his teeth. They thought he was so stupid they weren't even going to try to buy him off.

———

IN HIS GYM workouts, he fooled along. At times, when he worked hard in the ring, he told Bernie or Nick: "I've got to look good here! If the sportswriters thought I was stalling, they might smell something!"

This was reported to Cat and he chuckled. "The kid's right!" he said. "We want him to look good in the gym! The higher the odds, the better!"

In the gym in Joe's basement, Finn worked harder than ever. Then, three days before the battle, he met Pamela again. She was riding the sorrel and started to ride on by, but when he spoke, she stopped.

"Hello, Pam," he said softly.

She looked down at him, his face flushed from running, his dark hair rumpled. He looked hard and capable, yet somehow very young.

"I shouldn't think you'd train so hard," she said coolly. "Your fights don't seem to give you much trouble."

"Maybe they don't," he said, "and maybe they give me more than you think."

"You know," she said, "what you said about Glen's fights was untrue. Everything Glen won, he fought for."

"I know," he admitted. "I took too much for granted, I guess." He hesitated. "Don't you make the same mistake."

Their eyes held, and it was suddenly hard for her to believe what her brother had said—that Cat Spelvin was framing Finn Downey's fights. He looked too honest.

"If I did take a few the easy way," he said, "you couldn't blame me. My sis never had clothes like yours in her life, but she's goin' to have them, because I'm goin' to see she does— ahh, you wouldn't understand how we feel."

"Wouldn't I?" She smiled at him suddenly. "Finn, I like you. But don't start feeling sorry for yourself or making excuses. Glen never did."

"Glen!" Finn growled. "All I hear is Glen! I'd like to get in there with him sometime! Glen never felt sorry for himself or made excuses! Why should he?"

"Finn Downey," Pamela said quietly, "I hope you never get in the ring with Glen. If you do, he'll give you such a beating as you never saw! But before this goes any further, I want to show you something. Will you go for a ride with me this afternoon?"

He stared at her for a moment.

"No, I won't," he said. He looked away angrily because he was feeling such a strange emotion that something came into his eyes and into his throat when he looked at her. "I won't go for a ride with you because I think about you all the time now. I'm just a boxer from the wrong side of town. If I was to be around you too much it would tear my heart out. You'd never take a guy like me seriously, and I can't see why you should."

Pamela shook her head. "Finn, my brother is a fighter. I've nothing against fighters, it's just the kind of fighters they are. I like fighters that win their fights in the ring, not in some smoke-filled back room with a lot of fat-faced men talking about it." Her face grew grave. "You see, something's going on. I shouldn't mention it to you, but it's some sort of an investigation. It started over your fight with Gilman. One of the sportswriters, Pat Skehan, didn't like it. I don't know much, but if you should be mixed up in it, it will come out."

"So you're warning me. Why?"

"Because I like you. Maybe because I understand how you feel about your sister, about clothes and money and things."

And then, before he could say another word, she had cantered away.

———

JIMMY MULLANEY WAS in a ringside seat when Finn Downey crawled through the ropes for his return bout with Tony Gilman. Jimmy was where they had planned for him to be. His eyes were roving over the other ringsiders with a curious glint in them. Jimmy had been around for a long time and he knew pretty much what was happening tonight.

Glen Gurney had come in, and with him were his sister,

Pamela, Pat Skehan, the sportswriter, and another man. When Jimmy saw him, he began to whistle softly, for the man was Walt McKeon—and in certain quarters his name meant much.

Cat Spelvin and Nick Lessack were there, too. Every few minutes Norm Hunter would come up to Cat and whisper in his ear. Spelvin would nod thoughtfully, sometimes making a notation on a pad. Jimmy understood that, too.

Two hours before, the odds quoted on the fight had been three to one, with Finn a strong favorite, and thirty minutes before, the odds had fallen, under a series of carefully placed bets, to six to five. Norm Hunter was one of Cat's legmen, and he had been actively placing bets.

Finn felt good. He was in the best shape of his life, but he also knew he was facing the fight of his life. Regardless of the fact that he had been told Gilman was going to take a dive tonight, that had never been Spelvin's plan. Tonight he was going to cash in by betting against Finn Downey. Gilman had never liked taking that dive for him, and he was going to get even if he could by giving Finn a thorough beating. Downey understood that clearly enough. He also knew that Tony Gilman was a fighting fool, a much better fighter than any he had ever faced. Even in that previous match when Tony had been under wraps, he had made a monkey out of Finn most of the way.

Bernie Ledsham leaned on the ropes and grinned at Finn, but the grin was malicious.

"You going to take him, kid?"

Downey grinned back at him. "You can bet your last dime I am!"

The bell sounded suddenly, and Finn went out fast. The very look of Tony Gilman told him what he already knew. Gilman was out to win! Tony lanced a left to the head that jarred Finn to his heels, then crossed a whistling right that Finn slipped by a hair. Finn went in with a left and right to the body.

"All right, you pantywaist," Gilman hissed in his ear. "I'm goin' to tear you apart!"

Downey chuckled and broke free, clipping Gilman with a quick left as they moved together again. Gilman slammed a right to the body and they circled, trading lefts. Gilman rushed, throwing both hands, and the punches hurt. Finn went back to the ropes, but slid away and put a fast left to Gilman's face. He circled, watching Tony.

Gilman was anxious to get him; he was a tough scrapper who liked to fight and who was angry. He ripped into Downey, landing a hard left to the head, then a jolting right that smashed home twice before Finn could get into a clinch. His mouth felt sore and he could taste blood. Tony shook him off, feinted a left, then hooked with it. The fist clipped Finn flush on the chin, and his knees wobbled.

The crowd broke into cheers, expecting an upset, but the bell rang.

———

RETURNING TO HIS corner, Finn Downey saw the fat, satisfied smile on Spelvin's face. He dropped on the stool. For the first time he was doubtful. He had known Tony was good, but Gilman was driven by anger now and the desire for revenge, and he was even better than Finn had suspected.

The second round was a brannigan from bell to bell. Both men went out for blood and both got it. Finn took a stabbing left that sent his mouthpiece sailing. The next left cut his lips, then he took a solid right to the head that drove him to the ropes.

He came off them with a lunge and drove a smashing right to Gilman's ribs. Tony wrestled in the clinches and tried to butt, but Finn twisted free, then stepped in with a quick, short hook to the chin that shook Gilman to his heels.

In a clinch in the third round, after a wicked slugfest, Downey whispered to Gilman: "What's the matter? Can't you dish it out any better than that?"

Gilman broke away from him. His blue eyes were ugly now, and his face hard. He moved in behind a straight left that Finn couldn't seem to get away from until he had taken three on his sore mouth. Then he did get inside and drove Gilman back.

He could taste blood and there was the sting of salty sweat in the cuts on his face, and beyond the ropes there was a blur of faces. He ripped into Gilman with a savage two-fisted attack that blasted the older fighter across the ring.

"Thought I was a sap, huh? You win this one, bud, you fight for it!"

Gilman smashed him with a right cross that knocked him back on his heels. Before he could get set, Tony was on him with two wicked hooks, and the first thing he knew he had hit the canvas flat on his back!

At nine he made it to his feet, but he was shaky, and when he tried to bicycle away, Tony was on him with a stiff left, then another, then a right hook.

The terrific punch lifted him up and smashed him to the floor on his shoulder blades. He shook his head to clear it, crawled to his knees, and when he saw the referee's lips shaping nine, he came up with a lunge.

Before him he saw the red gloves of Tony Gilman, saw the punch start. He felt it hit his skull. He tried to catch his balance, knowing that a whistling right hook would follow, and follow it did. He rolled to miss the punch, but it caught him and turned him completely around!

Something caught him across the small of the back and he felt his feet lift up. Then he was lying flat on his face on the apron of the ring, staring through a blue haze at the hairy legs of Tony Gilman. He had been knocked out of the ring!

He grabbed a rope, and half pulled, half fell through the ropes, then lunged to his feet. He saw Gilman coming, ducked under the punch, then dived across the ring and brought up against the ropes.

Then Gilman was there. Tony's first punch was wild and Finn went under it and grabbed the blond fighter like a drowning man.

Then he was lying back on his stool and Mullaney was working on his eye.

"What round?" he gasped.

"The seventh, coming up!" Mullaney said quickly.

The seventh? But where—? He heard the warning buzzer and was on his feet, moving out toward Gilman.

Tony was disturbed. He had been sure of this fight; however, the clumsy, hard-hitting, but mostly ineffectual fighter he had met before had changed. Gilman was having the fight of his life. What had happened to Bernie Ledsham he didn't know, but Mullaney now was in Finn's corner.

A double cross? Was Spelvin going to cross him this time? Or was it *Spelvin* who was being crossed up?

He circled warily, looking Downey over. This called for some cool, careful boxing. He was going to have to cut Finn up, then knock him out. He would get no place slugging with him. How anything human could have survived that punch that took him out of the ring, he didn't know, to say nothing of the half dozen he had thrown before and after.

Finn, on his part, knew he was going to have to slow Tony down. Gilman was still too experienced for him, and plenty tough. He was beginning to realize how foolish he must have sounded to Glen Gurney when he told the champ how he was going to knock him out. For Gurney had beaten Gilman, and badly.

Gilman circled and stabbed a left. Finn weaved under it and tried to get in close, but Gilman faded away from him, landing two light punches.

Finn crouched lower, watching Tony. Gilman sidestepped quickly to the right and Finn missed again. He circled. Twice he threw his right at Gilman and missed. Tony was wary now, however.

Downey went under a left, then let a right curl around his neck, and suddenly he let go in a long dive at Gilman! They crashed into the ropes. Gilman stumbled back, but Finn smashed a left to the body, whipped a cracking left hook to the chin, and crossed a right to Gilman's head.

Tony broke free and backpedaled, but Finn followed him relentlessly. He landed a left, took a blow, then caught Gilman in a corner.

Tony turned loose both hands; toe-to-toe, they stood and slugged like wild men while the huge arena became one vast roar of sound.

Finn was watching his chance, watching that left of Gilman's, for he had noticed only a moment before that Gilman, after landing a left jab, sometimes moved quickly to the right.

The left came again—again, and a third time. Gilman fell away to the right—and into a crashing right hook thrown with every ounce of strength in Finn Downey's body!

Gilman came down on his shoulder, rolled over on his face.

At nine, he got up. Finn Downey couldn't imagine the effort he used to make it, but make it he did. Finn walked in, feinted a right, then whipped a left hook into Gilman's solar plexus and crossed a right on his jaw.

Tony Gilman hit the canvas flat on his face. Downey trotted to his corner. This time, Gilman didn't get up.

Mullaney threw Finn's robe around his shoulders, and he listened to the roar of sound. They were cheering him, for he had won. His eyes sought the ringside seats. Pamela was struggling through the crowd toward him.

When she reached him, she caught his arm and squeezed it hard.

"Oh, Finn, you won! You really won!"

"Nice fight, man!" Gurney said smiling. "You've shortened up that right!"

Finn grinned back. "I had to," he said, "or somebody would have killed me! Thanks for the tip."

"Yeah," Pat Skehan said, "it was a nice fight." He grinned fleetingly, then brushed by.

"Will you take that ride in the morning?" Pamela asked.

"Okay, yeah," Downey said. His head was spinning and the roaring in his ears had not yet died away.

In the dressing room, Mullaney grinned at Finn as he cut the strings on the gloves.

"Pal," he said, "you should have seen Cat! He dropped sixty G's on this fight! And that ain't all! Walt McKeon was here tonight. Walt's an investigator for the state's attorney. He was curious as to why Bernie was in your corner when Bernie works for Cat and Cat owns Gilman's contract. After some discussion, we rectified the situation!"

———

THE MORNING SUN was bright, and Finn leaned back in the convertible as it purred over the smooth paved roads.

He had no idea where he was going, and didn't care. Pamela was driving, and he was content to be with her.

The car turned onto gravel, and he rode with half-closed eyes. When the car came to a halt, he opened them and looked around.

The convertible was in a lane not far from a railroad track. Beyond the track was a row of tumbledown, long-unpainted shacks. Some housed chickens. In one was a cow.

At several of the houses, the wash hung on the line and poorly clad youngsters played in the dust.

"Where are we?" he demanded.

"In Jersey," Pamela said. "There's a manufacturing town right over there. This is where a lot of mill hands and railroad workers live, many not too long on this side of the water."

Not over fifty yards away was a small house that once had been painted green. The yard was littered with papers, sticks, and ashes.

A path led from the back door into a forest of tall ragweed.

"Let's get out," Pamela said. "I want to walk around." There was an odd look in her eyes.

It was hot and close in the jungle of ragweed. Pamela stepped carefully over the spots of mud. Finn moved carefully; he was still cut and bruised from the fight. The path led to a ditch that was crossed by a dusty plank. On the other side, the ragweed finally gave way to a bare field, littered with rusty tin cans, broken boxes, and barrels.

Pamela walked swiftly across it and into the trees that bordered the far edge. Here the path dipped to a small open space of green grass. A broken diving board hung over what had been a wide pool. Now the water was discolored by oil.

Pam sat down on a log in the shade. "Like it?" she asked curiously.

He shrugged, looking around. "How'd you know all this was here?"

Her smile vanished. "Because I used to live here. I was born in that house back there. So was Glen. Glen built that diving board. In those days, the water was still clean enough to swim in. Then the mill began dumping there and spoiled it. Even after that, I used to come here and sit, just like this. We didn't have much money, and about all we could do was dream. Glen used to tell me what he would do someday. He did it, too. He never went to school much, and all the education he got was from reading. All he could do was fight, so that's how he made it—by fighting. He paid for my education, and helped me get a job."

Finn Downey got up suddenly. "I guess I've been a good deal of a sap," he said humbly. "When I looked at you and at Glen, I figured you had to be born that way. I guess I was mighty wrong, Pam."

Pamela got up and caught his hand. "Come on! Let's go back to the car. There's a drugstore in town where we used to get cherry sodas. Let's go see if it's still open!"

They made their way back across the polluted ditch and through the overgrown lot. The convertible left a haze of dust on the road for some minutes after it departed.

Far off there was the sound of a ball bouncing, then a pause and the sound of a backboard vibrating and the *whiff* as the ball dropped through the net. A gangly youngster dribbled down an imaginary court and turned to make another shot.

The crowd went wild.

THE ROUNDS DON'T MATTER

YOU GET THAT way sometimes when you're in shape, and you know you're winning. You can't wait for the bell, you've got to get up and keep moving your feet, smacking the ends of your gloves together. All you want is to get out there and start throwing leather.

Paddy Brennan knew he was hot. He was going to win. It felt good to weigh a couple of pounds under two hundred, and be plenty quick. It felt good to be laying them in there hard and fast, packed with the old dynamite that made the tough boys like Moxie Bristow back up and look him over.

Moxie was over there in the corner now, stretched out and soaking up the minute between rounds as if it were his last chance to lie in the warm sunlight. You wouldn't think to look at him that Moxie had gone the distance three times with the champ when the champ was good. You wouldn't think that Moxie had a win over Deacon Johnson, the big black boy from Mississippi who was mowing them down.

You wouldn't think so now, because Moxie Bristow was stretched out on his stool and breathing deep. But he knew that all his breathing wasn't going to fix that bad eye or take the puff out of those lips.

Paddy was right. He was going good tonight. He was going good every night. He was young, and he liked to fight, and he was on the way up. He liked the rough going, too. He didn't mind if he caught a few, because he didn't take many. He liked to see Caproni down there in the ringside seats with Bickerstaff. They handled Tony Ketchell, who was the number-one heavyweight now. And in the articles for tonight's fight, there was a clause that said he was to fight Ketchell on the twenty-seventh of next month if he got by Bristow.

The bell clanged, and Paddy went out fast. When he jabbed that left, it didn't miss. It didn't miss the second or the third time, and then he turned Bristow with a left and hit him on the chin with a chopping right. It made Moxie's knees buckle, but Paddy Brennan didn't pay any attention to that. Their legs always went rubbery when he socked them with that inside right cross.

Moxie dropped into a crouch and bored in, weaving and bobbing. The old boy had it, Paddy thought. He could soak them up, but he was smart, too. He knew when to ride them and when to go under and when to go inside.

Paddy had a flat nose and high cheekbones, but not so flat or so high that he wasn't good-looking. Maybe it was his curly hair, maybe it was the twinkle in his eyes, maybe it was the vitality, but he had something. He had something that made him like to fight, too.

He moved in fast now, hooking with both hands. Bristow tried a left, and Paddy went inside with three hard ones and saw a thin trickle of blood start from over Moxie's good eye.

Moxie was watching him. He knew it was coming. Paddy walked in, throwing them high and hard, then hooked a left to the guts that turned Moxie's face gray. He had Moxie spotted for the right then, and it went down the groove and smacked against Bristow's chin with a sickening thud. Moxie sagged, then toppled over on his face.

———

PADDY TROTTED TO his corner, and when he looked down he could see Caproni and Bickerstaff. He was glad they were there, because he had wanted them to see it. He wished Dicer Garry were there, too. Dicer had been Paddy's best friend, and he might have guessed more of what was in the wind than anyone else.

Brennan leaned over the ropes, and Caproni looked up, his face sour.

"Now Ketchell, eh?" Paddy said. "I'm going to take your boy, Vino."

"Yeah?" Caproni said. His eyes were cold. "Sure, sure . . . we'll see."

Paddy chuckled, trotting across the ring to help Moxie to his corner. He looked down at Bristow, squeezing the other fighter's shoulder.

"Swell fight, mister. You sure take 'em."

Moxie grinned.

"Yeah? You dish 'em out, too!" Paddy squeezed Moxie's arm again and started away, but Moxie held his wrist, pulling him close. "You watch it, look out for Vino. You got it, Irish. You got what it takes. But look out."

Sammy came out of Brennan's corner. "Can it, Mox. Let's go, Paddy." He held out Paddy's robe. Sammy's face looked haggard under the lights, and his eyes shifted nervously. Sammy was afraid of Vino.

Paddy trotted across the ring and took the robe over his shoulders. He felt good. He vaulted the ropes and ducked down to the dressing rooms under the ring. Sammy helped him off with his shoes.

"Nice fight, Paddy. You get Ketchell now." But Sammy didn't look happy. "You don't want to rib Vino like that," he said. "He ain't a nice guy."

Paddy didn't say anything. He knew all about Vino Caproni, but he was remembering Dicer Garry. Dice had been good, but he hadn't got by Ketchell. Maybe Dicer could have whipped Ketchell. Maybe he couldn't. But he fought them on the up and up, and that wasn't the way Caproni or Bickerstaff liked to play.

Dicer and Paddy had worked it out between them three years ago.

"Give me first crack at it, Paddy?" Dicer suggested. "We've been pals ever since we worked on the construction crew together. You've licked me three times, and you know and I know you can do it again."

"So what?" Brennan said.

"So . . ." Garry mused. "You let me get the first crack at the champ. You let me take the big fights first. You come along after. That way maybe I can be champ before you get there. You can have a fight for the belt anytime. You'll beat me eventually if I'm still there. We've been pals too long. We know what's up."

And Garry had almost made it. He knocked out Joe Devine and Bat Turner, got a decision over Racko and a technical kayo over Morrison, all in a few months. Then they matched him with Andy Fuller, who was right up there with the best, and Dicer nearly killed him. So he was matched with Ketchell.

Caproni and Bickerstaff had worked a few years on Ketchell. He was in the big money, and he had been taken along carefully. He was good. But could he beat Dicer?

Paddy Brennan peeled the bandages and tape from his fists and remembered that last note he had from Garry.

THEY TRIED TO PROPOSITION ME. I TURNED THEM DOWN. THIS VINO AIN'T NO GOOD. HE GOT TOUGH WITH ME AND I HIT HIM. I BROKE HIS NOSE.

DICER

Sergeant Kelly O'Brien stopped in, smiling broadly. The sergeant was father to Clara O'Brien and Clara and Paddy were engaged. You could see the resemblance to Clara. O'Brien had been a handsome man in his day.

" 'Twas a grand job, son. A grand job. You've never looked better!"

"Yeah," Paddy said, looking up. "Now I get Ketchell, then the champ."

Brennan picked up his soap and stepped into the shower, put his soap in the niche in the wall and turned on the water. With the water running over him, he reached for the soap. All the time he was thinking of Garry.

If it hadn't been for that truck crashing into Dicer's car, he might be fighting his best pal for the title now, and a tough row it would have been. If it hadn't been for that truck crash, Tony Ketchell might have been out of the picture before this. Dicer Garry would have whipped Ketchell or come close to it. Vino Caproni had known that, and so had Bickerstaff.

The worst of it was, he might never have guessed about that truck if he hadn't seen the green paint on Bickerstaff's shoe sole. He'd been out to see Dicer's car, and seen the green paint that had rubbed off the truck onto the wreck. And it was almost fresh paint. Then later that day, he had talked with Bickerstaff.

The gambler was sitting with one ankle on the other knee, and there was green paint on the sole of his shoe, a little on the edge.

"That was tough about Dicer," Bickerstaff said. "Was his car smashed up pretty bad?"

"Yeah," Paddy told him, and suddenly something went over him that left him outwardly casual, but inwardly alert, and deadly. "Yeah, you seen it?"

"Me?" Bickerstaff shook his head. "Not me, I never go around wrecking yards. Crashes give me the creeps."

———

IT WAS A little thing, but Paddy Brennan went to O'Brien, who had been a friend of Garry's, too.

"Maybe it don't mean a thing," Paddy said, "or again maybe it does. But when you figure that Ketchell's had a buildup that must have cost seventy grand, you get the idea. Ketchell's good, and maybe he would have beat Dicer, but then again maybe he wouldn't. It was a chance, and guys like Vino don't take any chances."

O'Brien nodded thoughtfully.

"I've wondered about that. But it all looked so good. You know how Dicer used to drive—anything less than sixty was loafing. And he hit the truck, that was obvious enough. Of course, it would have been a simple matter to have had the truck waiting and swing it in the way. Garry drove out that road to his camp every morning.

"If you are right, Paddy, it was an almost foolproof job. The driver, Mike Cortina, he'd never had an accident before; he'd been driving for three years for that same firm. He was delivering that load of brick out that road, so he had a reason to be there. They had a witness to the crash, you know."

———

WHEN HE HAD finished his shower, he dressed slowly. The sergeant had gone on ahead with Clara, and he would meet them at a café later. Sammy loitered around, looking nervous and cracking his knuckles.

"Look, Paddy," he said suddenly, "I don't want to speak out of turn or nothing, but honest, you got me scared. Why don't you play along with Vino? You got what it takes, Paddy, an' gosh—"

Paddy stopped buttoning his shirt. "What is it? What d'you know?" he asked, staring at Sammy.

"I don't know a damn thing. Honest, I—"

"Do you know Cortina?" Paddy asked, deliberately.

Sammy sank back on the bench, his face gray.

"Shut up!" he whispered hoarsely. "Don't go stickin' your neck out, Paddy, *please!*"

Paddy stood over Sammy, he stared at the smaller man, his eyes burning.

"You been a good man, Sammy," he said thickly. "I like you. But if you know anything, you better give. Come on, *give!*"

"Farnum," Sammy sighed. "One of the witnesses—he runs a junkyard in Jersey. He used to handle hot heaps for the Brooklyn mob."

Brennan finished dressing. Then he turned to Sammy, who sat gray-faced and fearful.

"You go home and forget it, Sam. I'll handle this!"

———

SOMEHOW THE DAYS got away from him, in the gym, and on the road, getting ready for Ketchell.

"It's got to be good, Clara," he told her. "I got to win this one. It's got to be a clean win. No decision, nothing they can get their paws into."

He liked the Irish in her eyes, the way she smiled. She was a small, pretty girl with black hair and blue eyes and just a dash of freckles over her nose. Paddy held her with his hands on her shoulders, looking into her eyes.

"After this is over, we can spend all the time we want together. Until then I've got work to do."

"Be careful, Paddy," she begged him. "I'm afraid. Daddy's

been talking to someone about that man—the one with the yellow eyes."

"Vino?"

"Yes, that's the one. A friend told Daddy he used to work a liquor concession for Capone when he was young. And now he is in with some bunch of criminals who have a hot car business over in Brooklyn."

"Brooklyn?" Paddy's eyes narrowed. Car thieves in Brooklyn . . . ?

Paddy Brennan went back to the hotel and started for the elevator. The room clerk stopped him.

"Two men came in to see you, Mr. Brennan. They were here twice. They wouldn't leave their names."

"Two men?" Paddy looked out the door. "One of them short and fat, the other dark with light eyes?"

"That's right. The dark one did the talking."

If Vino was looking for him, it meant a proposition on the Ketchell fight. He picked up the phone.

"If anybody calls, I'm not in, okay?"

Let them wait. Let them wait until the last night when they couldn't wait any longer, when they would have to come out with it. Then— He dialed the phone.

———

TWO NIGHTS LATER Paddy Brennan sat on his bed in the hotel and looked across at the wiry man with the thin blond hair.

"You found him, did you?" he asked.

The man wet his lips.

"Yeah, he quit his job drivin' the truck six months after the accident. He's been carrying a lot of do-re-mi since then. I trailed him over to Jersey last night, drunk. He's sleeping it off at a junkyard right now."

Paddy got up. He took out a roll of bills and peeled off a couple.

"That's good," he said. "You stand by, okay? Then you go tell O'Brien about six o'clock, get me? Don't tell him where I am, or anything. Just tell him what I told you and don't miss. There's going to be a payoff soon. You do what I tell you, and you'll get paid a bonus."

At about nine-thirty tonight he would be going into the ring with Tony Ketchell, and the winner would get a chance at the title. In the meantime, there were things to do—the things Dicer Garry would have done if it had been Paddy Brennan whose broken, bloody body had been lifted from the wreckage of his car. They were things that had to be done now while there was still time.

———

THE JUNKYARD WAS on the edge of town. A light glowed in the office shack. Behind it was the piled-up mass of the junked cars, a long, low warehouse, and the huge bulk of the press. It was here the Brooklyn mob turned hot cars into parts, rebuilt cars, or scrap. Farnum, the convenient witness, ran the place. He had testified that Dicer Garry had hit the truck doing eighty miles an hour, that the driver hadn't had a chance to get out of the way.

Paddy Brennan's face was grim when he stopped by the dirty window and peered in. Cortina—he remembered the man from the inquest—was sitting in a chair tipped back against the wall. He had a bottle in his hand and a gun in a shoulder holster.

Farnum was there, too, a slender, gray-haired man who looked kindly and tired until you saw his eyes. There were two others there—a slender man with a weasel face and a big guy with heavy shoulders and a bulging jaw.

Paddy swung the door open, and stepped in. He carried a heavy, hard-sided case in his hand. Farnum got up suddenly, his chair tipped over.

Cortina's face tightened. "Speak of the devil! Muggs, this is Paddy Brennan, the guy who fights Ketchell tonight. He won't be the same afterward, so you'd better take a good look."

Muggs laughed, and he leaned forward aggressively. Farnum looked shocked and apprehensive. He was sitting close to Cortina, and Paddy's eyes covered them.

"What's the suitcase for? You skipping out on Ketchell?"

"Dicer Garry was a friend of mine," Paddy said quietly. He set the case down carefully on the floor.

The man with the weasel face got up suddenly.

"I'm not in this," he said. "I want out."

"You sit down," Brennan told him, pointing at the corner. "Stay out if you want but keep still."

Muggs was a big man who carried himself with a swagger, even sitting down.

"How about you?" Brennan asked. "Are you in on this, or are you going to be nice?"

Muggs got up. He was as tall as Brennan and twenty pounds heavier.

"You boxers are supposed to be good. What happens when you can't use that fancy stuff with a lot of fancy rules?"

"Something like this," Brennan said, and hit him. His right fist in a skintight glove struck with a solid crack, and Muggs was falling when the left hook hit him in the wind. It knocked him into his chair, which splintered and went to the floor with a crash.

Cortina tilted his bottle back and took another drink. He was powerful, a shorter man than Brennan, but heavier.

"Nice goin'," Cortina said. "Muggs has been askin' for that."

"You're next," Brennan said. "Garry was a pal of mine. It's going to look mighty funny when the D.A. starts wondering why the principal witness and the driver of the death car turn out to be friends and turn out to be running with a mob that backs Caproni and Bickerstaff."

"Smart pug, aren't you?" Cortina said, putting his bottle down carefully. "Well, I hate to disappoint Ketchell and the fans, but—"

His hand streaked for the gun, had it half out before Paddy kicked the legs out from under the chair. It came out, but Cortina's head smacked up against the wall, the gun sliding from his hand.

Farnum broke for the door, and Brennan caught him with one hand and hurled him back against the desk so violently that he fell to the floor. Then Brennan picked up the gun and pocketed it.

"Get up, Cortina," he said quietly. "I see you've got to learn."

The trucker made a long dive for Brennan's legs, but Paddy jerked his knee up in the Italian's face, smashing his nose. Then Brennan grabbed him by the collar, jerking him erect, and slammed him back against the wall. Before he could rebound, Paddy stepped in and hooked both hands to the body. The Italian's jaw dropped and he slumped to the floor.

Farnum was getting up. He wasn't a strong man, and the violence of that shove had nearly broken him. Brennan pushed him into a chair.

"You've got a chance to talk," he said. "I've only got a few minutes, and then I'm going to keep that date with Ketchell. You either talk, or I'm going to beat you both until you'll never feel or look the same again."

Brennan turned to Muggs, still sitting on the floor.

"You had enough, friend? Or do you take some more of that dish?"

"You busted my ribs," said Muggs.

Paddy Brennan remembered the broken body of the Dicer. He stepped up to Cortina and pulled him to his feet. He hit him a raking left hook that ripped hide from his face, then two rights to his body, then jerked the heel of his hand up along Cortina's face.

"That isn't nice," Paddy said. "I don't like to play this way, but then you aren't nice boys."

He stepped back.

"Think you can take that, Farnum?" He pulled the junk-yard operator to his feet. "What do you say? Talk or take a beating."

"Shut up, Farnum," Cortina muttered, "or I'll kill you!" Paddy hit Cortina between the eyes, and the man fell hard. Paddy walked over, and setting the case flat on the table, he popped the latches.

TEN MINUTES LATER he came out and got into his car. With him he had Farnum and Cortina. The Italian's face was raw and bloody, but Farnum was scarcely more than frightened, although one eye was growing black, and his lips were puffed. Paddy put the case in the trunk of his rented car.

———

SAMMY WAS PACING up and down the arena corridor when he came in.

"Paddy!" He rushed over, his face worried. "What happened?"

"Nothing," Brennan said quietly. He carried the heavy case to the door of the shower room and set it inside. He turned back to Sammy. "Let's get dressed."

He was bandaging his hands when Vino came in with Bickerstaff. Vino's sallow face cracked into a brief smile, and he gave Brennan a limp hand.

"Just dropped in. How about a little talk?"

"Sure," Paddy said. "Sure enough, I'll talk. Take a powder, Sammy."

Sammy hesitated. Then he turned and went out, closing the door softly behind him.

Bickerstaff sat down astride a chair, leaning on the back of it. He wore a cheap blue serge suit, and his black shoes were high-topped, but showed white socks above them. His pink, florid face looked hard now, and his small blue eyes were mean.

"Get on with it," Brennan said, drawing the bandage across his knuckles again and smacking his fist into his palm. "What's up?"

"You got plenty, kid," Vino said. "You sure made a hit beating Bristow that way. There is a big crowd out here tonight."

"You're telling me?" Brennan said. "So what?"

"We spent a lot of dough on Ketchell," Vino said carefully. "He's good, plenty good. Maybe he can beat you."

"Maybe."

"It's like this, Paddy," Vino said, striving to be genial. "We ain't in this racket for our health. Suppose you beat Ketchell. Who will you fight next? The champ? Maybe. If not there ain't a good shot in sight. Then, we lose a lot of gold. We paid off to get him where he is."

"What's on your mind?" Brennan demanded. "Get to the point." He cut a band of tape into eight narrow strips.

"Suppose you lose?" Vino suggested. "Suppose you take one in the sixth. It ain't too late to lay some bets. Then we give you a return fight, see? We all make dough. Anyway," he added, "you should tie up with us. Ketchell won't last. You will. You need a smart manager."

"Yeah?" Brennan asked. "How smart? An' where does Sammy get off?"

"Look," Bickerstaff suggested. "I got a couple of youngsters, a middle and a welter. Let Sammy take care of them. You need somebody smart, Brennan. You got color, you got a punch, you can make some real gold in there."

"What gives you the idea I think you're smart?" Paddy asked. He was putting the strips between his fingers and sticking them down. "I haven't seen any champions you boys handled. Ketchell wouldn't be in the spot he's in now if Dicer hadn't been killed."

Vino took his cigarette from his mouth very carefully. He held it in his fingers, the burning end toward him, and looked up like gangsters do in the movies.

"Maybe he would, maybe not," he said noncommittally.

"I'd like to have had another crack at Garry," Brennan said. "I wanted that guy."

Bickerstaff's face was frozen.

"I thought you two were pals," he said.

"Us?" Brennan shrugged, sliding from the rubbing table to his feet, beginning to move his arms around. "We were once. When things got serious, when he started thinking about the title . . . well, you know how those things are, the friendship didn't last."

Vino stood very still.

"Yeah?" he said.

Bickerstaff spoke up. "What about this fight? You ain't got but a few minutes."

"I'm not going to play," Brennan said. "What would I get? I can beat Ketchell. What can you guys do for me that I can't do for myself?"

"We can take care of you," Bickerstaff said. "Ketchell hasn't lost any fights since we had him."

"You got a break," Brennan said. "Just like I did when Garry got killed." He shook his head: "You know, I heard about you guys, I heard you were smart. I thought maybe when Garry got it that you guys pulled the strings. I figured you were wise, that you stood by your fighters, that you saw they won, or they lost for good money. But when I got down there, it was only an accident. So I say nuts to you."

"We can be tough," Bickerstaff said, his eyes hard.

"Don't make me laugh," Brennan told him, jabbing with his left. "What good would it do you to get tough with me after Ketchell's finished? That wouldn't be smart. I'm looking for a manager, but I want somebody smart."

Vino's eyes were cold. "Just what is this, Brennan? You're stalling."

"Sure." Paddy stopped and hitched up his tights. "Sure, I'm stalling. You said you weren't in this racket for your health. Well, I'm not either. I'm going where the dough lays. I can't see how I'm going to make out with you guys. So I'm going out there and cop a Sunday on Ketchell's chin."

The door opened, and Sammy stuck his head in.

"Better get set, Brennan. It's time to go."

When the door closed, Bickerstaff looked at Vino, then back at Brennan.

"Listen," he said. "What if we showed you how smart you would be to tie up?"

Brennan chuckled. "You look like tinhorns to me. What if some of the big mobs wanted in?"

Vino snapped his cigarette into the shower.

"I am the big mob," he said flatly.

"Yeah? You and every dago kid down on the corner."

Vino's eyes hardened, he straightened, but Bickerstaff cut in. "Get smart, kid. We take care of our boys. Look at Ketchell."

"An accident," Brennan said. "A car accident saved him."

"There's accidents, and *accidents*," Vino said, softly.

"Tryin' to kid me?" Brennan pulled his robe around his shoulders. "I saw that car and there was a witness."

"Only dumb guys make it plain," Bickerstaff said. "We know our stuff."

"Well, that would be a joke on Garry, the rat," Brennan said. "He thought he was the smart one."

"You get in there with Ketchell," Vino said. "You take one in the sixth. Make it look like an accident. Then we'll bill you with him again for a big gate, and you win. We'll see you get the title if you sign with us. And we'll take care of you."

"Listen, Vino," Brennan said. "It sounds good, but don't give me this 'accident' malarkey. You got lucky and so you're acting like a big shot. If you're real lucky maybe I'll run into a truck while I'm climbing into the ring!"

"Don't be stupid, you punk!" Vino stepped close. "I fixed Garry. He wouldn't play, see?" He paused, staring at Brennan. "I don't like boys that don't play. So I had that truck there; I had witnesses there. I even had a guy ready if the truck didn't finish it. Now you do as you're told or we'll finish you!"

Bickerstaff's face was strained. "Vino," he said, "what if he drops a dime on us?"

"Yeah?" Vino sneered. "If I even thought he'd dime us out, I'd cook him. One sign that he ain't going to play ball, and he gets it."

"I don't rat," Brennan said quietly. "I don't have to rat. All right, I'll play ball. I'll play it the way you never saw it played before."

———

THE LIGHTS WERE bright over the ring. Paddy Brennan felt good, getting away from Vino and Bickerstaff. He rubbed his feet in the resin, and the old feeling began to come over him. He trotted to his corner, where Sammy was waiting.

"What's up, kid? You goin' to tell me? Is it a flop?"

Brennan rubbed his feet on the canvas, dancing a little.

"In the sixth," he said. "They want me out in the sixth. They want to give you a welter and a middle and take me for themselves."

Sammy looked up, and Brennan realized how small he was.

"Oh?" he said. "So they want that, do they?"

"Keep your chin up, Sammy," Brennan said. "Let's get this one in the books. Then we'll talk."

When the bell clanged, Ketchell came out fast. He looked fit, and he moved right. He'd come up the easy way, but he'd had the best schooling there was. Paddy had a feeling this wasn't going to be easy. Ketchell's left licked out and touched his eye. Paddy worked around Ketchell, then feinted, but Tony backed off, smiling.

Brennan walked in steadily, feinted, feinted again, and then stabbed a quick left to the face and a right to the chin. The punches shook Ketchell and made him wary. His left jabbed again, and then again.

He circled, went in punching. He shot a left to the head, and bored in, punching for the body, then to the head, then took a driving right that bounced off his chin. It set him back on his heels for a second, and another one flashed down the groove, but he rolled his head and whipped a right to the body that made Ketchell back up.

When the round ended, they were sparring in the center of the ring, and Paddy Brennan went to his corner, feeling good. The bell came, but not soon enough. He leaped to close quarters and started slugging. He felt punches battering and pounding at him, but he kept walking in, hitting with both hands. Once Tony staggered, but he stepped away in time before Brennan could hit him again.

Then a solid right smashed Paddy on the head, and a left made the cut stream blood. Momentarily blinded, a right smashed on his chin and he felt himself falling, and then a flurry of blows came from everywhere, and he fought desperately against them. When he realized what was happening again, the referee was saying nine, and then the bell was ringing. He staggered to his corner and flopped on the stool. Sammy was working over him.

"Watch it, kid," Sammy said, gasping. "Take nine every time you're down."

"Once was enough," Paddy said. "I'm not going down again."

"Once?" Sammy's voice was very amazed. "What do you

mean—*once*?" He paused, staring at Brennan intently. "What round is this?" he demanded.

"End of the second," Brennan said. "What's the matter? You punchy?"

"*You* are," Sammy said. "This is the fifth coming up. You've been down four times."

Then the bell rang again, and Paddy went out. Ketchell was coming in fast and confident. A raking left snapped at his face, and Paddy rolled his head. Suddenly, something inside him went cold and vicious. Knock him down four times? Why, the—

His right thudded home on Ketchell's ribs with a smash like a base hit, then he hunched his shoulders together and started putting them in there with both hands. Ketchell backed up.

Suddenly Paddy Brennan felt fine again. His head was singing, his mouth was swollen, but he hooked high and low, battering Ketchell back with a rocking barrage of blows. A right snapped out of somewhere, and he barely slipped it, feeling the punch take his shoulder just below his ear.

Then, suddenly, Ketchell was on his knees with his nose broken, and blood bathing his chest and shoulders. The bell sounded wildly through the cheering, roaring crowd.

It was the sixth.

When he stood up, he could see Vino down there. Vino's eyes were on him, cold and wary. Paddy Brennan remembered Dicer.

He walked out fast, and Ketchell came in, but he could see by Ketchell's eyes what he was expecting. Paddy feinted and slid into a clinch, punching with one hand free.

"They make it easy for you, don't they?" he said. "Even murder?"

Brennan broke and saw Ketchell's face was set and cold. There was a killer in him. Well, he'd need it. Paddy walked in, hooking low and hard, smashing them to the head, slipping short left hooks and rights and all the while watching for that wide left hook of Ketchell's that would set him up for the inside right cross. Through the blur, he saw Ketchell's face, and he let his right down a little where Ketchell wanted it and saw the left hook start.

His own right snapped, and he felt his glove thud home. Then his left hooked hard but there was nothing in front of him and he moved back. He could see Tony Ketchell on the floor, and hear someone shouting in the crowd. He could see Bickerstaff on his feet, his face white, and behind him, Vino, his face twisted, lips away from the teeth. Then the referee jerked his arm up, and he knew he had won the fight.

———

CLARA CAME RUNNING to meet him in the dressing room. She had been crying, and she cried out when she saw his face.

"Oh, your poor eye!" She put up her hand to touch it, and then he grabbed her and swung her away . . . Vino was standing in the door with a gun in his hand.

"You're a real smart kid, huh? Back up, sister. Lover boy and I are walking to my car. You'll be lucky if you get him back."

Brennan lunged with his right in the groove and saw the white blast of a gun and felt the heat on his face. Then his right landed, and Vino went down.

All of a sudden, Clara had him again, and the room was full of people. Sergeant O'Brien was picking Vino up, and Vino was all bloody, and his face twisted in hate.

"Get offa me, copper!" he snarled. "You haven't got anything on me I can't get fixed—"

"You're under arrest for murder," O'Brien said to Vino. "You and Bickerstaff and Cortina. And when this hits the papers the boys in Brooklyn won't fix you up, they're going to drop you like a hot potato."

Vino's face turned a pasty white.

"You got nothing but this pug's say-so," he declared.

"Oh, yes, we have," O'Brien said. "We've got Farnum's statement, and Cortina's. But we don't need them. We were in the next room when you talked to Brennan. We had a wire recorder microphone hung on the shower partition. It was Paddy's idea."

When they had gone, Brennan sat down slowly on the table.

He pulled Clara toward him. "They're all big money fights from now on, Clara. There'll be time now . . . time for us."

"But we'll fix that eye first," she said. "I don't intend to have my man dripping blood all over everything."

She hesitated.

"I can't stand seeing you hurt, but, Paddy—I guess it's the Irish in me—oh, Paddy, it was a grand, grand fight, that's what it was!"

FIGHTERS DON'T DIVE

NIMBLY "FLASH" MORAN parried a jab and went in fast with a left to the wind. Stepping back, he let Breen get a breath. Then he flicked out a couple of lefts, put over an inside right, and as Breen bobbed into a crouch and tried to get in close, he clinched and tied him up.

They broke, and Breen came in with a flurry of punches that slid off Moran's arms and shoulders. Then Moran's hip moved and a left hook that traveled no more than four inches snapped Breen up to his toes. Breen caught himself and staggered away.

The gong sounded, and Flash Moran paused . . . then he slapped Breen on the shoulder and trotted to his corner.

Two men were standing there with Dan Kelly. He knew them both by sight. Mike McKracken, an ex-wrestler turned gambler, and "Blackie" Marollo, small-time racketeer.

"You're lookin' good, kid," Kelly said. "This next one you should win."

"You might, but you won't stop him," Marollo said, looking up. "Nobody knocks Barnaby out."

McKracken studied Moran with cold eyes. "You got paper on him?" he asked Kelly.

"I don't need any," Kelly said. "We work together."

"Well, if you had it, I'd buy a piece," McKracken said. "I need a good middle. Money in that class now with Turner, Schmidt, and Demeray comin' up."

"I wouldn't sell," Kelly said. "We're friends."

"Yeah?" Marollo shot him a glance. "I'd hate to see somebody come along an' offer him a grand to sign up. You'd see how much friendship matters."

Flash Moran looked at Marollo, then dropped to the floor beside him.

"You've a rotten way of looking at things, Blackie," he said. "We aren't all dishonest, you know!"

"You're pretty free with that lip of yours, kid. Maybe somebody will button it up one day. For keeps."

Moran turned, pulled his robe around him, and started for the dressing room.

"That kid better get wise or he won't last," Marollo said. "You tell him, Kelly."

"You told him yourself," Kelly replied. "Didn't you?"

Dan Kelly turned and walked up the aisle after Flash. Behind him, he heard Marollo mumble.

"That punk. I'll fix him!"

"You won't do nothin' of the kind," he heard McKracken growl. "We got too much ridin' on this to risk trouble."

The voices faded out with the distance, and Kelly scowled.

In the dressing room the trainer spoke up. "Keep an eye on Marollo, kid, he's all bad."

"To the devil with him," Flash said. "I know his kind. He's tough as long as he has all the odds with him. When the chips are down, he'll turn yellow."

"Maybe. But you'll never see him when he doesn't have the difference." Kelly looked at him curiously. "Where you goin' tonight?"

"Out. Just lookin' around. Say, Dan, what do you suppose is bringing Marollo and McKracken around to the gym? One or the other's been down here five days in a row."

"Probably sizing you up, figurin' the odds." Kelly knotted his tie. "Well. I've got a date with the wife."

———

SHORTY KINSELLA WAS lining up a shot when Flash Moran walked into Brescia's Pool Room. He looked up.

"Hiya, champ! How's about a game? I'm just winding up this one."

He put the last ball in the corner and walked around, holding out his hand.

Moran took it, grinning. "Sure, I'll play."

"Better watch him." The man who Kinsella had played handed Shorty five dollars. "He's good!"

Moran racked the balls. "Say, what do you know about Blackie Marollo?"

Shorty's smile went out like a light. He broke, and ran up four, then looked at Flash thoughtfully.

"Nothing. You shouldn't know anything either."

Flash Moran watched Kinsella make a three-cushion shot. "The guy's got me wondering."

"Well, don't. Not if you want to stay healthy."

Flash Moran finished his game and went out. He paused on the corner and peeled the paper from a stick of chewing gum. If even Shorty Kinsella was afraid to talk about Marollo, there must be more behind Blackie than he'd thought.

Suddenly, there was a man standing beside him. He was almost as tall as Moran, though somewhat heavier. He lit a cigarette, and as the match flared, he looked up at Flash over his cupped hands.

"Listen, sonny," he said, "I heard you askin' a lot of questions about Marollo in there. Well, cut it out . . . get me?"

"Roll your hoop." Flash turned easily. "I'll ask what I want, when I want."

The man's hand flashed, and in that instant of time, Flash saw the blackjack. He threw up his left arm and blocked the blow by catching the man's forearm on his own. Then he struck. It was a right, short and wicked, into the man's wind.

Moran had unlimbered a hard blow, and the man was in no shape to take it. With a grunt he started to fall and then Moran slashed him across the face with the edge of his hand. He felt the man's nose crunch, and as the fellow dropped, Moran stepped over him and walked around the corner.

So, Blackie Marollo didn't like to be talked about? Just who was Blackie Marollo, anyway?

Up the street there was a Chinese joint, a place he knew. He went in, found an empty booth, and sat down. He was scowling, thoughtfully. There would be trouble. He had busted up one of Marollo's boys, and he imagined Blackie wouldn't like it. If a guy had to hire muscle, he had to keep their reputation. If it was learned they could be pushed around with impunity, everybody would be trying it.

Moran was eating a bowl of chicken and fried rice when

the girl came in. She was slim, long-legged, and blond, and when she smiled her eyes twinkled merrily. She had another girl with her, a slender brunette.

She turned, glancing around the room, and their eyes met. Too late he tried to look indifferent, but his face burned and he knew his embarrassment had shown. She smiled and turned back to the other girl.

When the girls sat down, she was facing him. He cursed himself for a fool, a conceited fool to be thinking a girl of her quality would care to know anyone who earned his living in the ring.

———

SEVERAL TIMES MORAN'S and the girl's eyes caught. Then Gow came into the room and saw him. Immediately, he hurried over, his face all smiles.

"Hiya, Flash! Long time no see!"

"I've been meaning to come in."

"How are you going to do with the Soldier?"

"Think I'll beat him. How're the odds?"

"Six to five. He's the favorite. Genzel was in, the fellow who runs that bar around the corner. He said it was a cinch to go the limit."

For an instant, Flash was jolted out of his thinking of the girl.

"Genzel? Isn't he one of Marollo's boys?"

"Yes. And Marollo usually knows . . . he doesn't know about this one, does he, Flash?"

"Hell no!" He paused a moment. "Gow," he said. "Take a note to that girl over there for me, will you?"

Hurriedly, Moran scribbled a few lines.

I'D LIKE TO TALK TO YOU. IF THE ANSWER IS YES, NOD YOUR HEAD WHEN YOU LOOK AT ME. IF IT IS NO, THE EVENING WILL STILL BE LOVELY, EVEN IF NOT SO EXCITING.

REILLY MORAN

Gow shrugged, took the note, and wandered across the room. Flash Moran felt himself turning crimson and looked down. When he looked up, his eyes met those of the girl, and she nodded, briefly.

He got up, straightened his coat, and walked across the room. As he came alongside the table, she looked up.

"I'm Ruth Connor," she said, smiling. "This is Hazel Dickens. Do you always eat alone?"

She moved over and made a place for him beside her in the booth.

"No," he said. "Usually with a friend."

"Girl?" Ruth asked, smiling at him.

"No. My business partner. We're back here from San Francisco."

"Are you?" she asked. "I lived there for a while. On Nob Hill."

"Oh." He grinned suddenly. "Not me. I came from the Mission District."

Ruth looked at him curiously.

"You did? Why, that's where all those tough Irish boys come from. You don't look like them!"

He looked at her again. "Well, maybe I don't," he said quietly. "You can come a long way from the Mission District without getting out of it, though. But probably that's just what I am . . . one of those tough Irish boys."

For a moment, their eyes held. He stared at her, confused and a little angry. She seemed to enjoy getting a rise out of him but she didn't seem to really be putting him down. So many times with girls this very thing happened; it was like a test but it was one he kept failing. Her friend stayed quiet and he was unsure of what to say or how to proceed.

The door opened then and three men came in. Flash grew cold all over.

"Sit still," he told the girls softly. "No matter what happens."

The men came over. Two of them had their hands in their coat pockets. They looked like Italians.

"Get up." The man who spoke was short, very dark, and his face was pockmarked. "Get up now."

Flash got to his feet slowly. His mind was working swiftly.

If he'd been alone, in spite of it being Gow's place, he might have swung.

"Okay," Moran said, pleasantly. "I was expecting you."

The dark man looked at him. "You was expectin' us?"

"Yes," Flash said. "When I had to slug your friend, I expected there would be trouble. So I called the D.A.'s office."

"You did what?" There was consternation in the man's voice.

"He's bluffing, Rice," one of the men said. "It's a bluff."

"We'll see!" Rice's eyes gleamed with cunning. "Tell us what the D.A.'s number is."

Flash felt a sudden emptiness inside.

"It was . . ." He scowled, as if trying to remember . . . "It was seven . . . something."

"No," Ruth Connor said suddenly. "Seven was the second number. It was three-seven-four-four-seven."

Rice's eyes dropped to the girl, swept her figure with an appraising glance.

"Okay," he said, his eyes still on the girl. "Check it, Polack."

The man addressed, biggest of the three, turned to the phone book, and leafed through it quickly. He looked up.

"Hey, boss," he said triumphantly. "He's wrong, the number is different."

"It was his home phone," Ruth said, speaking up. "He called him at home. No one is in the office at this time of the night."

Rice stared at her. "You're buttin' in too much, babe," he said. "If I were you, I'd keep my trap shut."

The Polack came over, carrying the book.

"She's right, Rice. It's Gracie three-seven-four-four-seven!"

Rice stared at Moran, his eyes ugly. "We'll be waitin', see? I know your name is Reilly."

"My name is Reilly Moran," Flash said. "Just so you know where to look."

"Flash Moran?" Rice's eyes widened and his face went white. ". . . who fights Barnaby the day after tomorrow?"

"Right," Moran said, surprised at the effect of his name. Rice backed up hurriedly.

"Let's get out of here," he said.

Without another word, the three hoodlums turned and hurried out.

For a full minute, Moran stared after them. Now what was up? No man with a gun in his pocket is going to be afraid of a fighter. If they'd been afraid they wouldn't have come. They could tell by what he did to the first man that he was no pantywaist. Moran shook his head in bewilderment and sat down.

Ruth and the other girl were staring at Moran.

"Thanks," he said. "That was a bad spot. I had no idea what the district attorney's number was."

"So you're Flash Moran, the prizefighter?" Ruth Connor said slowly. There was a different expression in her eyes. "Why were those men so frightened when they heard your name?"

"They weren't," he said. "I can't understand why they acted that way." He stood up. "I guess I'd better be taking you home. It isn't safe now."

They stood up.

"Don't bother," Ruth Connor said. "I'm calling for my own car." She held out her hand. "It's been nice."

He looked into her eyes for a moment, then he felt something go out of him.

"All right," he said. "Good night."

He turned and walked swiftly outside.

———

DAN KELLY WAS sitting up in the armchair when Moran came into the apartment that they'd rented; his wife was already in bed. The old trainer looked up at him out of his shrewd blue eyes. He didn't have to look long.

"What's the matter?"

Briefly, Moran told him. At the end, Kelly whistled softly.

"Dixie Rice, was it? He's bad, son. All bad. I didn't know Rice was working for Blackie. Times have changed."

Moran looked at him. "I wonder who that girl was?" he mused. "She was beautiful! The loveliest girl I ever saw."

"She knew the D.A.'s number?" Dan scowled. "Might be a newspaper reporter."

"Well, what about tomorrow?"

"Tomorrow? You skip rope three rounds, shadowbox three rounds, and take some body exercise. That's all. Then rest all you can."

———

In THE MORNING, Flash Moran slept late. It was unusual for him, but he forced himself to stay in bed and rest. Finally, he got up and shaved. It would be his last shave before the fight. He always went into the ring with a day's growth of beard.

He was putting away his shaving kit when there was a rap on the door. Dan Kelly had gone, and Moran was alone. He hesitated only an instant, remembering Blackie Marollo, then he stepped over and opened the door. It was hardly open before a man stepped in and closed it behind him.

"Well?" Moran said. "Who the hell are you?"

"I'm Soldier Barnaby, Flash." For an instant, Flash looked at him, noting the hard, capable face, the black hair and swarthy cheeks, the broad, powerful shoulders, and the big hands. The Soldier pulled a chair over and sat astride of it. "We got to have a talk."

"If you want to work it, don't talk to me. I don't play the game. I just fight."

The Soldier grinned. "I fight, too. I don't want a setup. Not exactly."

He was studying Moran coolly. "You know," he said. "You'll make a good champ—if you play it on the level." He hesitated a moment. "You know Blackie Marollo?"

Flash Moran's eyes hardened a little. "Sure. Why?"

"Marollo's got something on my wife." The Soldier leaned forward. "She's a square kid, but she slipped up once, and Blackie knows it. If I don't do what he says, he's going to squeal. It means my wife goes to the pen . . . I got two kids."

"And what does he want?"

"Marollo says I go down before the tenth round. He says I take it on the chin. Not an easy one, as he wants it to be the McCoy."

Flash Moran sat down suddenly. This explained a lot of things. It explained why Marollo was watching him. It explained why, when they found out who he was, the gangsters had backed out of beating him up.

"Well, why see me?" Moran asked. "What can I do?"

"One thing—don't stop me before the tenth, even if you get a chance."

"Not before the tenth? But I thought you said it was in the tank?"

"I talked it over with the wife. I told her I was going sooner or later anyway, that you were a good kid and would make a good champ, and that I'd sooner you had it than the others. I knew you were on the level, knew Dan was, too.

"But she said, nothing doing. She said that she'd take the rap rather than see this happen. That if I lose this fight for Blackie, he'll force me to do other things. Eventually, I'll have to kill him or become a crook.

"She told me to come and see you. She said that not only must I not take a dive, but there mustn't be any chance that he'd think I took it.

"Then she asked me if I could beat you." Barnaby looked at Flash Moran and grinned. "Well, you know how fighters are. I told her I could! Then she asked me if it was a cinch and I told her no, that the betting was wrong. It should be even money, or you a slight favorite. You're six years younger than me, and you are coming up. I'm not. That makes a lot of difference."

Flash Moran looked at the floor. He could see it all. This quiet, simple man, talking quietly with his wife over the breakfast table, and deciding to do the honest thing.

"Then you want me to ease up on you in case I have you on the spot?" he said slowly. "That's a lot to ask, Soldier. You aren't going to be easy, you know. You're tough. Lots of times it's easier to knock a man out in the first round than any other time in the fight. Get him before he's warmed up."

"That's right. But you ain't going to get me in the first, kid. You might tag me about eight or nine, though. That's what I want to prevent.

"You see, the thing that makes guys like Marollo dangerous is money. They got money to buy killers. Well, I happen to know that Marollo has his shirt on this fight. He figures it's a cinch. He knows I'm crazy about my wife. He doesn't know that she'd do anything rather than let me do something dishonest. One bad mark against the family is enough, she says. But if we can make Marollo lose, we got a chance."

Flash Moran nodded. "I see. Yes, you've got something, all right."

"I think I can beat you, Moran. I'm honest about that. If I can, I will. I came because I'm not so dumb as to believe I can't lose."

"Okay." Moran stood up. "Okay, it's a deal. They want you down before the tenth. I won't try to knock you out until the eleventh round. No matter how hard it is, I'll hold you up!"

The Soldier grinned. "Right, then it's every man for himself." He thrust out his hand. "Anyway, Flash, no matter who wins, Blackie Marollo loses. Okay?"

"Okay!"

WHEN BARNABY WAS gone, Flash Moran sat down and pulled on his shoes. It might be a gag. It might be a stall to get him to lay off. It would be good, all right. They all knew he was a fast starter. They all knew his best chance would be quick.

Yet Barnaby's story fit the situation too well. It was the only explanation for a lot of things. And, he remembered, both Marollo and McKracken had been talking the impossibility of a knockout. That would be right in line. They would do all they could to inspire confidence in the fight going the distance, and then bet that it wouldn't go ten rounds.

He took his final workout, and then left the gym. It was late afternoon, and he walked slowly down the street. He'd never worked a fight. It wasn't going to be easy, for all his life he had thrown his punches with purpose. Well, he thought ruefully, it would probably take him all of ten rounds to take the Soldier, anyway.

Suddenly, he remembered . . . the Soldier had made no such promise in return.

He turned a corner, and found himself face-to-face with Ruth Connor, walking alone.

Her eyes widened as she saw him, and she made as if to pass, but he stopped her.

"Hello," he said. "Weren't you going to speak?"

"Yes," she said. "I was going to speak, but I wasn't going to stop."

"You don't approve of fighters?" he asked, quizzically.

"I approve of honest ones!" she said and turned as if to go by. He put his hand on her sleeve.

"What do you mean? I'm an honest fighter, and always have been."

She looked at him.

"I'd like to believe that," she said sincerely, "I really would. But I've heard your fight tonight was fixed."

"Fixed? How was it supposed to go? What was to happen?"

"I don't know. I heard my uncle talking to some men in his office, and they were discussing this fight, and one of them said it was all framed up."

"You didn't hear anything else?" he asked.

"Yes, when I come to think of it, I did! They said you were to win by a knockout in the twelfth round."

"In the twelfth?" he asked, incredulous. "Why, that doesn't make sense."

She glanced at her watch.

"I must go," she said quickly. "It's very late. . . ."

"Ruth!"

"Yes?"

"Will you reserve your opinion for a few hours? A little while?"

Their eyes met, then she looked away.

"All right. I'll wait and see." She looked back at him again, then held out her hand. "In the meantime—good luck!"

Reilly Moran walked all the way back to the hotel and told Dan Kelly the whole story.

Kelly was puzzled.

"Gosh, kid! I can't figure it. The setup looks to me like a double double-cross any way you look at it. Maybe the story about Barnaby's wife is all hokum. Maybe it ain't true. It sounds like Blackie Marollo all right. I don't know what to advise you. I'd go out and stop him quick, only we know you've got blamed small chance of that."

"Supposing the fight went the distance . . . all fifteen rounds?" Flash said thoughtfully. "Suppose I didn't stop him?"

"Then neither way would pay off and the average bettor would come out on top. That's not a bad idea, but hard, Flash, damned hard to pull off."

———

THE PRELIMINARIES WERE over before Flash Moran walked into the coliseum. He went to his dressing room and began bandaging his hands. It was a job he always did for himself, and a job he liked doing. He could hear the dull roar of the crowd, smell the strong smell of wintergreen and the less strong, but just as prevalent, odor of sweat-soaked leather.

Dan Kelly worked over him quietly, tying on his gloves, and Sam Goss gathered up the bucket and the bottles.

Flash Moran never had felt like this about a fight before. When he climbed through the ropes, hearing the deep-throated roar of the crowd, he knew that something was wrong. It was, he was sure, stemming from his own uncertainty. All he'd ever had to do was to get in there and fight. There had been no other thought but to win. Tonight his mind was in turmoil. Was Soldier Barnaby on the level? Or was he double-crossing him as well as Marollo?

What if he threw over his bargain and stopped the Soldier quick? That would hit the customers who were betting against a quick knockout hard. It would make money for Blackie Marollo. On the other hand, he would be betraying his promise to Barnaby.

When they came together in the center of the ring, he stared at the floor. He could see Barnaby's feet, and the strong, brown muscular ankles and calves. Idly, he remembered what Dan Kelly had told him one day.

"Remember, kid, anytime you see two fighters meet in the center of the ring, and one of them looks at the other one, or tries to look him in the eye, bet on the other guy. The fellow who looks at his opponent is uncertain."

They wheeled and trotted back to their corners, and then the bell rang.

HE WENT OUT fast and led with a left. It landed, lightly, and he stepped in and hooked. That landed solidly and he took a left himself before he tied the Soldier up. This preliminary sparring never meant anything. It was just one of those things you had to go through.

Barnaby was hard as nails, he could see that, and fast on his feet. . . . A blow exploded on Moran's chin and he felt himself reel, falling back against the ropes.

The Soldier was coming in briskly, and Moran rolled away, straightened up, and then stopped Barnaby's charge with a pistonlike left. He stepped in, took a hard punch, but slipped another and smashed a wicked right to the heart.

He was inside then and he rolled with the punch and hooked his left to the ribs, and then with his head outside the Soldier's right he whipped his own right to Barnaby's head.

It was fast, that first round, and both men were punching. No matter what happened later, Moran decided, he was still going to soften Barnaby up plenty.

When the bell rang for the second, Flash Moran ran out and missed a left then fell into a clinch. As they broke, he hooked twice to the Soldier's head, but the Soldier got inside with a right. Moran smashed both hands to the body and worked around. The Soldier fought oddly, carried himself in a peculiar manner.

It was midway through the third when Flash figured it out. The Soldier was a natural southpaw who had been taught to fight right-handed. His stance was still not quite what a natural right-hander's would be, but the training had left him a wicked two-handed puncher.

Soldier Barnaby was crowding the fight now and they met in mid-ring and started to swap it out.

Outside the ropes all was a confused roar. With the pounding of that noise in Moran's ears and the taste of blood in his mouth, he felt a wild, unholy exhilaration as they slugged for all they were worth.

The first seven rounds went by like a dream. It was, he knew, a great fight. Those first seven rounds had never given the crowd a chance to sit down, never a chance to stop cheering. It was almost time for the bell, time for the eighth.

He got up eager to be going, and suddenly, out of the ringside seats, beyond the press benches, he saw Blackie Marollo. The gambler was sitting back in his seat, his eyes cold and bitter. Beside him was McKracken, his big face ugly in the dim light.

Before the tenth.

He remembered the Soldier's words. Would Barnaby weaken and take a dive? And if he got a chance, should Moran knock him out?

———

THE BELL SOUNDED for the eighth and they both came out slower. Both men were ready, and they knew that this was a critical time in the fight. As Barnaby stepped forward, Flash looked him over coolly. The older fighter had a lump on his cheekbone. Otherwise, he was unmarked. That brown face seemed impervious, seemed granite-hard. How like the old Dempsey Barnaby looked! The shock of dark curly hair, the swarthy, unshaven face, the cold eyes.

Moran circled warily. He didn't like the look of things. What if the Soldier stopped him before the tenth? How was Marollo's money bet, anyway? Was it bet on a knockout before the tenth? Or on Moran to stop Barnaby?

Barnaby came in fast, landed a hard left to the head, then a right. Moran started to sidestep, his foot caught and for an instant he was off balance. He saw the Soldier's left start and tried to duck but caught the blow on the corner of the jaw. It spun him halfway around. Then, as Barnaby, his eyes blasting with eagerness, closed in, he caught a left to the body and a right to the chin. He felt himself hit the ropes and slide along them. Something exploded in his face and he went down on his knees in his own corner.

Through a haze of roaring sound, he stared at the canvas, his head spinning. He got one foot on the floor, shook his head, and the mists cleared a little. At the same instant, his gaze fell upon Marollo. The racketeer's face was white. He was half out of his chair, screaming.

At the count of nine, something happened to his legs and they straightened him up. As the Soldier charged, Moran ducked a driving right and clinched desperately. The referee fought to get them free. When they broke, Moran stabbed the Soldier with a stiff left to the mouth that started a trickle of blood down his face, then crossed hard right to the chin and the startled Soldier took a step back.

But he slipped the next left and came in, slamming both hands to Moran's body. Smiling grimly, Moran stabbed three times to Barnaby's split lip, stepped in, and hooked high and low with the left.

Barnaby's eyes were wild now. He charged with a volley of hooks, swings, and uppercuts that drove Flash Moran back and back. Moran got on his bicycle, fled along the ropes, and circled into the center of the ring, where he feinted with a right. As Barnaby came in, Flash Moran crossed his right to the chin.

The blow caught the Soldier coming forward and knocked him back on his heels. Moran followed it up fast and staggered Barnaby with a left, then stabbed another left to the mouth and crossed a hard right which caught the Soldier high on the head. Barnaby staggered and almost went down. Clinching, the Soldier hung on. At last he broke and tried a wild swing to the head. It missed, but the next caught Moran on the chin.

He went down—hard!

————

THE BELL SOUNDED as Moran was getting up. Flash turned and walked back to his corner. He was dead tired,

tired and mad clear through. Two knockdowns! It was the first time he had ever been off his feet!

"How's it, kid? Hurt?"

"No. Just mad."

Kelly grinned. "Don't worry. This round coming up will be yours. Lots of left hands now, and watch that left of his."

The gong sounded. They both came out fast and the Soldier bored in. Flash Moran needled Barnaby's mouth with a left jab, then put a left to the body and one to the head. He side-stepped quickly to the right and missed with a right hand.

Now Flash Moran got up on his toes and began to box. He boxed neatly and fast. He piled up points. He kept the Soldier off balance and rocked him with a couple of stiff right hands.

For two and a half minutes of the ninth round, he outboxed the Soldier and piled up points. Barnaby had taken the eighth by a clear margin. The two knockdowns had seen to that.

As for himself, Moran knew he had won the first round and the seventh, while the Soldier had taken the second, third, and fourth. The fifth and sixth were even. It left the Soldier with a margin toward the decision; those knockdowns would stick in the judges' minds.

Moran stabbed in with a left, crossed a right, and then suddenly spotted a beautiful shot for the chin.

He let it go—right down the groove!

And then something smashed against his jaw like the concussion of a six-inch shell. Again he went down, hard.

The first thing he heard was five. Someone was saying "five." No, it was six . . . seven . . . eight . . .

Moran did a push-up with his hands and lunged forward like the starter in a hundred-yard dash.

The Soldier was ready. He set himself, and Flash could see the fist coming. It had to miss, had to miss, had to—miss!

He brought up hard against the Soldier's body, tied him up, and smashed two solid rights to Barnaby's midsection as the round ended.

He wheeled, ran to his corner, and sat down. As he sat he saw a small, wiry man sitting next to McKracken get up and slip out along the aisle.

A moment later the little man was in the Soldier's corner.

Flash Moran sat up. He shook his head, felt the blast of the smelling salts under his nose and the coolness of the water on the back of his neck. Dan Kelly wasn't talking. He was looking at Moran. Then he spoke.

"All right, kid? Got enough?"

Moran grinned suddenly.

"I'm just getting started! I'm going to stop this lug!"

He went out fast at the bell, feinted a left and crossed a solid right to the head. He hooked a left, and the Soldier clinched.

"To the devil with it, kid!" Barnaby said in his ear. "I'm going into the tank. Marollo will kill me if I don't!"

Flash Moran fought bitterly, swapping punches in the clinch with the Soldier, then the referee broke them apart. Suddenly, Flash Moran knew what Barnaby had said couldn't be true. The Soldier was too good a man. What if Barnaby had tried to double-cross him? What if—he stabbed a left to the Soldier's mouth, smashed both hands to the body, and then went inside and clinched.

"You dive and I squeal the whole thing!" he muttered. "I won't let you dive! I'll talk right here, from the ring. If you go out during the round, I'll spill it right here."

"Marollo would kill you, too!" Barnaby snarled. They broke, sparred at long range, and Flash Moran let go with a right. Even as the punch started, he knew the Soldier was going to take it. The punch was partially blocked, and Barnaby began to wilt.

Like a streak Moran closed in and clinched, heaving him back against the ropes.

"I told you!" Moran muttered. "Fight, you yellow skunk! Real fighters don't dive!"

Barnaby broke loose, his eyes cold. He stabbed a left to the mouth, crossed a right, and Flash went inside with both hands to the body. He staggered Barnaby with a left, and knocked him into the ropes. As they rolled along the ropes, the Soldier tried to fall again, but Flash brought him up with a left just as the bell sounded. At this moment, Moran looked over the Soldier's shoulder right into Marollo's eyes.

BLACKIE MAROLLO WAS looking like a very sick man. McKracken, his big, swarthy face yellow, was also sagging. Instantly, Moran knew what had happened. They had overbet and they wouldn't be able to pay up!

The bell clanged again, and the referee broke the two fighters and they went to their corners.

The eleventh was quieter. Flash knew nothing would happen in the eleventh. Marollo had frightened the Soldier into trying to dive in the tenth, but the Soldier's money was bet on a dive in the twelfth round.

Flash Moran walked in and feinted to the head, then uppercut hard with a left to the liver. He stepped in a bit more and brought up his right under the Soldier's heart. He landed two more punches to the body in a clinch and they broke. Moran was body punching now. He slipped a left and rapped a right over Barnaby's heart, then hooked a left. He landed twice more to the body as the bell rang.

The twelfth opened fast. Both men walked to the center of the ring and Moran got in the first punch, a left that started the blood from the Soldier's mouth. As he slipped a left, they began to slug, fighting hard. They battered each other from corner to corner of the ring for two solid minutes. There was no letup. This was hard, bitter, slam-bang fighting. Suddenly, Barnaby caught a high right and started to fall.

Moran rushed him into the ropes before he could hit the canvas and smashed a right to the head. Angry, Barnaby jerked his head away from a second punch, and slugged Flash Moran in the wind. Moran's mouth fell open as he gasped for breath. As he staggered back, all the fighter in Barnaby came back with a rush. This was victory! He could win!

Seeing a big title fight just ahead of him, Barnaby came in slugging!

Half covered, Moran reeled under the storm of blows and went down. He staggered up at ten, and went down again. Just before the bell rang, he straightened up. They clinched.

"You played possum, blast you!" Barnaby snarled.

"Sure! I always liked a fight!" Moran said and let go with

a left that narrowly missed the Soldier and slid by him, almost landing on the face of the referee. The referee jerked back like he'd been shot at, and glared at Moran.

"Naughty, naughty!" Barnaby said with a grin.

The bell rang.

When they came out for the thirteenth, they came out fast.

"All right!" Barnaby snapped. "You wanted a fight. Well you're gonna get one!"

He ducked a left and slammed a wicked right to Moran's middle. Moran gasped with pain and Barnaby crowded on in, driving Moran back into the ropes with a flurry of wicked punches. A steaming right caught Flash on the chin, but he set himself and smashed a right to the body, a left to the head, and a right to the body.

Slugging like a couple of madmen, they circled the ring. Flash hung the Soldier on the ropes and smashed a left to the chin. The Soldier came off the ropes, ran into a stiff left, and went to his knees. He came up slugging and, toe-to-toe, the two men slugged it out for a full thirty seconds. Then Moran threw a left to the Soldier's mouth and the blood started again.

Barnaby broke away from a clinch, hooked a high right to the head, and followed it up with a stiff left to the wind. They battered each other across the ring and Barnaby split Moran's lip with a left. The Soldier moved in and knocked Moran reeling with another left. Following it up, he dropped Moran to his knees.

There was a taste of blood in Moran's mouth and a wild buzzing in his head as he waited out the count. He could smell the rosin and the crowd and the familiar smell of sweat and the thick, sweetish taste of blood. Then he was up.

But now he had that smoky taste again and he knew he was going to win. The bell rang. Wheeling, they both trotted back to their corners and the whole arena was a bedlam of roaring sound.

———

THE FOURTEENTH ROUND was three minutes of insanity, sheer madness on the part of two born fighters, wild with the lust of battle. Bloody and savage, they were each berserk with the desire to win.

Every one of the spectators was on his feet, screeching with excitement. Even the pale and staring Marollo sat as though entranced as he watched the two pugilists amid the standing figures around him.

The Soldier dropped, got up, and Moran went down. It was bloody, brutal, sickening yet splendid. All thought of money was gone. For Moran and Barnaby there was no crowd, no bets, no arena. They were just two men, fighting it out for the glory of the contest and of winning.

The fifteenth opened with the sound unabated. There was a continual roar now, as of breakers on a great reef. The two men came together and touched gloves and then, impelled by driving fury, Flash Moran waded in, slugging with both hands.

Barnaby lunged and Moran hit him with a right that shook him to his heels. The Soldier started a left and again Flash brushed it aside and brought up his own left into Barnaby's wind.

Then the Soldier backed off and jabbed twice. After the first jab, he dropped his left before jabbing again. Louis had done that in his first fight with Schmeling. He was tiring now and falling back on habits that were unconscious yet predictable.

Flash Moran backed off and waited. Then that left flickered out. Moran took the jab and it shook him to his heels. But he saw the left drop before the second jab. In that brief instant, he threw his right and he put the works on it.

He felt the wet and sodden glove smash into Barnaby's jaw and saw the Soldier's knees buckling. He went in with a left and a right to the head. The Soldier hit the canvas and rolled over on his face and was counted out.

It was over! Flash Moran turned and walked to his corner. In a blur of exhaustion, he felt the referee lift his right hand, and then he slumped on the stool. They put his robe around him and he was half lifted from the stool and as he stepped down to the floor, he saw Ruth and with her was a tall, gray-haired man who was smiling.

"Great fight, son—a great fight. We'd heard Barnaby was to quit in the twelfth. Glad the rumor was wrong, it would have ruined fighting in this state."

Flash Moran smiled.

"He wouldn't quit, sir. Soldier Barnaby's a great fighter."

Moran turned his head then and saw the Soldier looking at him, a flicker of wry humor in his swollen eyes.

The older man was speaking again.

"My name is Rutgers, Moran," he said. "I'm the district attorney, you know. This is my niece, Ruth Connor. But then I believe you've met."

"That's right," Flash said. "And we'll meet again, tomorrow night? Can we do that, Ruth?"

"Of course," she said with a smile. "I'll be at Gow's place—waiting."

GLOVES FOR A TIGER

THE RADIO ANNOUNCER'S voice sounded clearly in the silent room, and "Deke" Hayes scowled as he listened.

"Boyoboy, what a crowd! Almost fifty thousand, folks! Think of that! It's the biggest crowd on record, and it should be a great battle.

"This is the acid test for the 'Tiger Man,' the jungle killer who blasted his way up from nowhere to become the leading contender for the world's heavyweight boxing championship in only six months!

"Tonight he faces Battling Bronski, the Scranton Coal Miner. You all know Bronski. He went nine rounds with the champ in a terrific battle, and he is the only white fighter among the top contenders who has dared to meet the great Tom Noble.

"It'll be a grand battle either way it goes, and Bronski will be in there fighting until the last bell. But the Tiger has twenty-six straight knockouts, he's dynamite in both hands, with a chin like a chunk of granite! Here he comes now, folks! The Tiger Man!"

Deke Hayes, champion of the world, leaned back in the chair in his hotel room and glanced over at his manager. "Toronto Tom" McKeown was one of the shrewdest fight managers in the country. Now he sat frowning at the radio and his eyes were hard.

"Don't take it so hard, Tom," Deke laughed. "Think of the gate he'll draw. It's all ballyhoo, and one of the best jobs ever done. I didn't think old Ryan had it in him. I believe you're actually worried yourself!"

"You ain't never seen this mug go," McKeown insisted.

"Well, I have! I'm telling you, Deke, he's the damnedest fighter you ever saw. Talk about killer instinct!

"There ain't a man who ever saw him fight who would be surprised if he jumped onto some guy and started tearing with his teeth. This Tiger Man stuff may sound like ballyhoo but he's good, I tell you!"

"As good as me?" Deke Hayes put in slyly.

"No, I guess not," his manager admitted judiciously. "They rate you one of the best heavyweights the game ever saw, Deke. But we know, a damned sight better than the sportswriters, that you've really never had a battle yet, not with a fighter who was your equal.

"That Bronski thing looked good because you let it. But don't kid yourself, this guy isn't any sap. He's different. Sometimes I doubt if this guy's even human."

Toronto Tom McKeown tried to speak casually. "I talked to Joe Howard, Deke, Joe was his sparrin' partner for this brawl. That Tiger guy never says anything to anybody! He just eats and sleeps, and he walks around at night a lot, just . . . well, just like a cat! When he ain't workin' out, he stays by himself, and nobody ever gets near him."

"Say, what the devil's the matter with you? Got the willies? You're not buyin' this hype?" Deke Hayes demanded.

But the voice from the radio interrupted just then, and they fell silent, listening.

"They're in the center of the ring now, folks, getting their instructions," the excited announcer said. "The Tiger Man in his tiger-skin robe, and Bronski in the old red sweater he always wears. The Tiger is younger, but Bronski has the experience, and—man, this is going to be a battle!" the announcer exclaimed.

The bell clanged. "There they go, folks! Bronski jabs a left and the Tiger slips it! Bronski jabs again, and again, and again! The Tiger isn't doing anything now, just circling around. Bronski jabs again, crosses a right to the jaw.

"He's getting confident now, folks, and—there, he's stepping in with a volley of punches! Left, right, left, right—but the Tiger is standing his ground, just slipping them!"

"Wow!" the radio voice hit the ceiling.

"Bronski's down! The Battler led a left, and quick as a flash the Tiger dropped into a crouch, snapped a terrific, jolting right to the heart, and hooked a bone-crushing left to the jaw! Bronski went down like he was shot, and hasn't even wiggled!

"There's the count, folks!—eight—nine—ten! He's out, and the Tiger wins again! Boyoboy, a first-round knockout!

"Wait a minute, folks, maybe I can get the Tiger to say something for you! He never talks, but we might be lucky this time. Here, say something to the radio fans, Tiger!" the announcer begged.

"He won't do it," McKeown said confidently. "He never talks to nobody!"

Suddenly, a cold, harsh voice spoke from the radio, a voice bitter and incisive, but then dropping almost to a growl at the end.

"I'm ready now. I want to fight the champion. Come on, Deke Hayes! I'll kill you!"

In a cold sweat Hayes snapped erect, face deathly pale. His mouth hung slack; his eyes were ghastly, staring.

"My God . . . that voice!" he mumbled, really scared for the first time in his life.

McKeown stared strangely at Hayes, his own face white. "Who's punchy now? You look like you've seen a ghost!"

Hayes sagged back in his chair, his eyes narrowed. "No. I ain't seen one. I heard one!" he declared enigmatically.

RUBY RYAN, VETERAN trainer and handler of fighters, looked across the hotel room. The Tiger was sitting silent, as always, staring out the window.

For six months Ryan had been with the Tiger, day in and day out, and yet he knew almost nothing about him. Sometimes he wondered, as others did, if the Tiger was quite human. Definitely he was an odd duck, and Ruby Ryan, so-called because of his flaming hair, had known them all.

Jeffries, Fitzsimmons, Ketchell, Dempsey. But he had seen nothing to compare with the animal-like ferocity of the Tiger. Through all the months that had passed since Ryan received that strange wire from Calcutta, India, he had wondered about this man. . . .

Who sent the cablegram Ruby Ryan didn't know. Who was the Tiger? Where had he come from? Where had he learned his skill? He didn't know that, either. He only knew that one night some six months before, he had been loafing in Doc Hanley's place with some of the boys, when a messenger had hurried to him with a cablegram. It had been short, to the point—and unsigned.

WOULD YOU LIKE TO HANDLE NEXT HEAVYWEIGHT CHAMPION STOP READ CALCUTTA AND BOMBAY NEWS REPORTS FOR VERIFICATION STOP EXPENSES GUARANTEED STOP COME AT ONCE.

Ryan had hurried out and bought the papers. The notes were strange, yet they fascinated the fight manager with their possibilities. Ever alert for promising material, this had been almost too good to be true.

The news reports told of a strange heavyweight—a white man with skin burnt to a deep bronze. A slim, broad-shouldered giant, with a robe of tiger-skins and the scars of many claws upon his body, who fought with the cold fury of a jungle beast.

The *China Clipper* carried Ruby Ryan to the Far East. He found his man in Bombay, India. In Calcutta, the Tiger Man had knocked out Kid Balotti in the first round, and in Bombay, Guardsman Dirk had lasted until the third by getting on his bicycle.

Balotti was a former top-notcher, now on the downgrade, but still a capable workman with his fists. He had been unconscious four hours after the knockout administered by the Tiger.

In Bombay, the Tiger, a Hercules done in bronze, had floored Guardsman Dirk in the first round, and it had required all the latter's skill to last through the second heat and one minute of the third. Then, he, too, had gone down to crushing defeat.

Ruby Ryan found the Tiger sitting in a darkened hotel

room, waiting. The big man wore faded khakis and around his neck was the necklace of tiger claws Ryan had heard of.

The Tiger stood up. He was well over six feet tall and well muscled but he had a startling leanness and coiled intensity to his body. Looking at him, Ryan thought of Tarzan come to life. There *was* something catlike about the man, something jungle-bred. One felt the terrific strength that was in him, and knew instantly why he was billed as "The Tiger."

"We go to Capetown, South Africa. We fight Danny Kilgart there," the man said bluntly. "In Johannesburg, we fight somebody—anybody. If you want to come on you get forty percent of the take. I want the championship within a year. You do the talking, you sign the papers; I'll fight."

That was all. The man knew what he wanted and had a good idea of how to get it.

Danny Kilgart, a good, tough heavyweight with a wallop, went down in the second under the most blistering, two-fisted attack Ruby Ryan had ever seen. The next victim, the Boer Bomber, weighing two hundred and fifty pounds, lasted just forty-three seconds . . . that had been in Johannesburg.

―――

THE TIGER DIDN'T speak three words to Ruby Ryan in three weeks. But Ryan knew what he was looking at—that potentially, the Tiger was a coming champion. Of course it was unlikely that he was good enough to beat Deke Hayes. Hayes was the greatest heavyweight of all time, a master boxer with a brain-jolting wallop. And Hayes trained scientifically and thoroughly for every fight; Ryan's Tiger Man was, to push the allusion too far, an animal. Brutally strong, unbelievably aggressive, but he hadn't been in the ring daily with the best fighters in the world. . . . The Tiger wasn't just a slugger, he was better than that, but it was unlikely that he had the skill of the champ.

―――

IN PORT SAID, Egypt, accompanied by an internationally famous newspaper correspondent, Ryan and the Tiger had been set upon by bandits. The Tiger killed two of them with his bare hands and maimed another before they fled.

The news stories that followed set the world agog with amazement, and brought an offer from Berlin, Germany, to go fifteen rounds with Karl Schaumberg, the Blond Giant of Bavaria.

Schaumberg, considered by many a fit opponent for the champion himself, lasted three and a half rounds. Fearfully battered, he was carried from the arena, while the Tiger Man, mad with killing fury, paced the ring like a wild beast.

Paris, France, had seen François Chandel go down in two minutes and fifteen seconds, and in London the Tiger had duplicated Jeffries's feat of whipping the three best heavyweights in England in one night.

Offered a fight in Madison Square Garden, the Tiger Man had refused the battle unless given three successive opponents, as in England. They agreed—and he whipped them all! One of them was unfortunate—he had lasted into the second round, and took a terrific pounding.

Then had followed a tour across the country. The best heavyweights that could be brought against the mystery fighter were carried from the ring, one after the other.

Delighted and intoxicated by the Tiger Man's color and copy value, sportswriters filled their papers with glowing stories of his prowess, of his ferocity, and of the tiger-skin robe he wore. The story was that the skins were reputed to have been taken with his bare hands.

Ruby Ryan, after the Bronski fight, was as puzzled as ever. He had his hands on the gimmick fighter of the century, a boxer who made his own press, packed stadiums, and had launched himself into the imagination of the public like a character from the movies. The Tiger Man had created a public relations machine beyond anything Ryan had ever seen but what bothered the old trainer to no end was that he wasn't in on the joke. His fighter played the part every hour of the day. He was good at it, so good that you'd swear the vague stories were real. Ryan, however, knew no more about his man than the average kid on the street—and sometimes thought he knew less.

Ryan drank the last of his coffee and turned to the man seated in the window.

"Well, Tiger, we've come a long way. If we get the breaks, the next fight will be for the title. It's a big if, though; Hayes is good, and he knows it. But McKeown won't let him fight you yet, if he can help it. I think we've got McKeown scared. I know that guy!"

"He'll fight. When he does I'll beat him so badly he'll never come back to the game . . . maybe I'll kill him."

The Tiger got up then, squeezed Ryan's shoulder with a powerful hand, and walked into the bedroom.

Ruby Ryan stared after him. His red face was puzzled and his eyes narrowed as he shook his head in wonderment. Finally, he got up and called Beck, his valet-handyman, to clear the table.

"I got an idea," Ryan told himself, "that that Tiger is a damned good egg underneath. I wonder what he's got it in for the champ for?"

Ruby Ryan shook himself with the thought. "Holy mackerel! I'd hate to be the champ when my Tiger comes out of his corner!"

Beck came in and handed the manager a telegram. Ryan ripped it open, glanced at it briefly, and swore. He stepped into the Tiger's room and handed him the message.

COMMISSION RULES TIGER MUST FIGHT TOM NOBLE STOP WINNER TO MEET CHAMPION.

"Now *that's* some of Tom McKeown's work!" Ruby exclaimed, eyes narrow. "They've ducked that guy for five years and now they shove him off on us!"

"Okay," the Tiger said harshly. "We'll fight him. If Hayes is afraid of him, I want him! I want him right away!"

Ruby Ryan started to speak, then shrugged. Tiger walked out, and in a few minutes the pounding of the fast bag could be heard from the hotel gym.

THE CANVAS GLARED under the white light overhead. In his corner, Tom Noble rubbed his feet in the resin. Under the lights, his black body glistened like polished ebony. This was his night, he was certain.

For years the best heavyweights had dodged him. They had drawn the "color line" to keep from fighting big, courageous Tom Noble. His record was an unbroken string of victories and yet even the fearless Deke Hayes had never met him.

A fast, clever boxer, Noble was a pile-driving puncher with either hand, and most dangerous when hurt. He weighed two hundred and forty pounds; forty pounds heavier than the slim, hard-bodied Tiger.

The Tiger Man crawled through the ropes, throwing his black and orange robe over the top rope, and crouched in his corner like an animal, shifting uneasily, as if restless for the kill.

If he won tonight, he would meet the champion. Meet Deke Hayes! Even the thought made his muscles tense with eagerness. It had been a long time. A lifetime . . . in some ways it had almost been a lifetime.

THE TIGER STIRRED restlessly, staring at the canvas. He remembered every detail of that last day of his old life. How Deke and himself, on an around-the-world athletic tour nine years before, had decided to visit Tiger Island.

Rumor had it there were more tigers on the island than in all Sumatra, perhaps in all the Dutch East Indies. The hunting was the best in the world but they had been warned; the big cats were fierce, and they were hungry. The greatest of care had to be taken on Tiger Island . . . more than one hunter had died.

Deke Hayes, however, had insisted. And Bart Malone—who was later to become the feared Tiger Man—had gone willingly enough.

For years the two had been friends. They had often trained together, and had boxed on the same card. The two were evenly, perfectly matched in both skill and stamina. Toward the end, as they had risen in the rankings, Bart Malone had seemed to get a little better. Then two things happened: both men were booked on an exhibition tour that was to take them around the world, and Margot had come into the picture. From the beginning she had seemed to favor Bart.

They had been in a tree stand, waiting fifty yards from the body of a pig they had killed to bait the tigers. Suddenly, Hayes discovered the ammunition he was to have brought had been forgotten.

Despite Bart Malone's protests, he had gone back to the boat after it. A tiger had come along, and Malone had killed it. But as the sound of the shot died away, he heard the distant roar of a motor.

At first Malone wouldn't believe it. In the morning, when he could leave the tree with safety, he had gone down to the beach. The motorboat that had brought them over from Batavia was gone. On the beach was a little food, a hunting knife, and an axe.

Deke Hayes had never expected him to live, but he had reckoned without the strength, the adaptability, the sheer energy of Bart Malone. With but six cartridges remaining, Malone had made a spear, built a shelter, and declared war on the tigers.

It had been a war of extermination, a case of survival of the fittest. And Bart Malone had survived. He had used deadfalls and pits, spring traps, and traps that shot arrows.

He had learned to kill tigers as hunters in Brazil kill jaguars—with a lance. For nearly eight years he had lived on the remote island, then he had been rescued—and returned to the world as the "Tiger Man."

———

THE TIGER MAN shook himself from his reverie, and rubbed his feet in the resin.

And in the champion's apartment, Tom McKeown toyed with the dials, seeking the right spot on the radio.

"You should see him fight, champ. Might get a line on him. This will be his big test. And if Noble beats him, as he probably will, we'll have to fight a Negro."

Hayes snorted. "I don't care. Noble is a sucker for a left uppercut. I can take him. I'd have fought him two years ago if you'd let me!"

"There's plenty of time, if you have to. He ain't getting any younger. You got seven years on him, champ," McKeown said smoothly. Deke Hayes grinned.

"That was neat work, McKeown, steering the Tiger into Noble. No matter who wins, we got a drawing card. And no matter who wins, if we move fast, he'll be softened by this fight. So the goose hangs high!"

———

THE BELL CLANGED. Tom Noble was easy, confident. He came out fast, jabbed a light left to the head, feinted, and hooked a solid right to the body. The Tiger circled warily, intent.

Noble put both hands to the head, and then tried a left. The Tiger slipped inside, but made no attempt to hit. As they broke the crowd booed, and the Negro looked puzzled.

The Tiger circled again, still wary. Noble landed a left, tried to feint the Tiger in, but it didn't work. The Tiger circled, feinted, and suddenly sprang to close quarters, striking with lightning-like speed.

A swift left, followed by a hard right cross that caught the Negro high on the side of the head. Tom Noble was stepping back, and that took the snap out of the punch; but it shook him, nevertheless.

Noble stepped in, jabbed a left three times to the head, and crossed with a right. The Tiger slipped inside Noble's extended left and threw two jarring hooks to the body.

The fans were silent as the round ended. The usual killing rush of the Tiger hadn't been there. Noble looked puzzled. The Tiger glanced up at Ruby Ryan, then bared his teeth in sort of a smile.

Noble boxed carefully through the second and third rounds, winning both by an easy margin. The Tiger seemed content to circle, to feint, and to spar at long range. The killing rush failed to come, and the Negro, who carefully studied each man he fought, was puzzled. The longer the Tiger waited, the more bothered Noble became.

The giant Negro could sense the repressed power in the steel of the Tiger's muscles. When they clinched, Noble could feel his great strength; but still the Tiger waited. He stalled, and Noble began to feel like a mouse before the cat.

In the fourth round, Tom Noble opened hostilities with a hard left to the head, and then crossed a terrific right to the jaw that snapped the Tiger's head back and split his lip.

Noble, eager, whipped over another right, but the Tiger slid under it and drove a powerful left hook to the body that jarred the Negro to his heels.

Before Noble could recover from his surprise, a hard right uppercut snapped his head back, and a steaming left hook slammed him to the floor in a cloud of resin dust!

Wild with pain and rage, the Negro scrambled to his feet and rushed. Toe-to-toe, they stood in the center of the ring and swapped punches until every man in the house was wild with excitement.

Bronze against black, Negro from the Baltimore rail yards against the mysterious Tiger Man, they fought bitterly, desperately, their faces streaked with blood and sweat, their breath coming in great gasps.

The crowd, shouting and eager, saw the great Negro boxer, the man whom all white fighters were purported to fear, slugging it out with this jungle killer—the strange white man, bronzed by sun and wind, who had come out of the tropics to batter all his competition into fistic oblivion!

———

WHEN THE BELL rang for the fifth round, the Tiger came out like a streak. His wild left hook missed. Overanxious, he stumbled into a torrid right uppercut that slammed into his jaw with crashing force. The Bronze Behemoth slid forward on his face, to all intents and purposes out cold!

For a moment the crowd was aghast. The Tiger Man was down! For the first time in his career, the Tiger Man was down! Roaring with excitement, the crowd jumped up on their chairs, shrieking their heads off.

Then suddenly, the Tiger Man was up! All the stillness, the watching, the waiting was gone from him now. Like a beast from the jungle, he leaped to the fray and with a torrent of smashing, bone-crushing blows, he battered the giant black man across the ring!

Twice the Negro slipped to one knee, and both times came up without a count. Like a fiend out of hell he battled, cornered, fierce as a wounded lion.

But with all his ferocity, all his great strength, it was useless for Tom Noble to stand up against that whirlwind of blows that drove him back, back, and back!

The Tiger was upon him now, fighting like a madman! Suddenly, a steaming right cross snapped the Negro's head back, and he came down with a crash! Like an animal, the Tiger whirled and leaped to his corner.

Tom Noble was up at nine. A great gash streaked his black face. One eye was closed tight, and his lips had been reduced to bloody shreds of flesh. His mouthpiece, lost in the titanic struggle, had failed him when most needed.

Noble was up, and bravely he staggered forward. But the Tiger dropped into a crouch. Grimly, surely, he stalked his opponent.

Seeing him coming, Tom Noble backed off, suddenly seeming to realize that no human effort could stem that tide of blows he knew would be coming.

He backed away, and the Tiger followed him, slowly herding him toward the corner, set for the kill. Not a whisper stirred the crowd. They were breathless with suspense, realizing they were seeing the perfect replica of a jungle kill. A live tiger from Sumatra couldn't have been more fierce, or more deadly!

Then, suddenly, Noble was cornered. Vainly, desperately, he tried to sidestep. But the Tiger was before him and a short, jolting left set Noble's chin for the right cross that flickered over with the speed of a serpent's tongue. The great legs tottered, and Tom Noble, once invincible, crashed to the canvas, a vanquished gladiator.

IN HAYES'S APARTMENT, there was silence. McKeown wiped the sweat from his forehead, although he suddenly felt cold. He looked at the champion, but Hayes's face was a mask that told nothing.

"Well," Tom McKeown said at last. "I guess we overrated Noble. It looks now like he was a setup!" But in his heart there was a chill as he thought of those crashing fists.

"Setup, hell! That guy could fight!"

Hayes whirled.

"Listen, McKeown: you find out who this Tiger is; where he came from—and why! He started in Calcutta. Okay! I want to know where he was before then! I think I know that guy, and if I do—"

Toronto Tom McKeown walked out into the street. He stood still, looking at nothing. The Tiger had the champ's goat. What was behind it all? One thing he knew: if there was any way to prevent it, the Tiger would never meet Deke Hayes.

———

RUBY RYAN WALKED into the hotel room and threw his hat on the table. His eyes were bright with satisfaction.

"Well, that settles that! I guess McKeown has tossed every monkey wrench into the machinery that he can think of—but nevertheless, the fight goes on, and no postponements. The commission accepted my arguments, and agreed that Hayes has got to meet the Tiger—and no more dodging."

Beck looked up from the sport sheet he was reading. He seemed worried.

"Maybe it's okay, but you and me know Tom McKeown, and he's nobody's fool. There'll be trouble yet!" Beck opined.

"It'll have to be soon, then. Tomorrow night's the night," the manager said grimly.

Suddenly the door burst open and the Tiger staggered in. He was carrying "Pug" Doman, one of his sparring partners. Over the Tiger's eye was a deep cut from which a trickle of blood was still flowing.

"What th'—" Ryan's face was white, strained. "For cryin' out loud, man, what's happened?"

"Five men jumped us. I heard them slipping up from behind. We fought. Four of them are out there"—he jerked a thumb toward the door—"in the road, Doman got in the way of a knife."

"Well, that's more of McKeown's work!" Ryan said angrily. "I'll get that dirty so-and-so if it's the last thing I ever do! Look at that cut over your eye. And I just put up the same amount McKeown did—to guarantee appearance, and no postponements!"

———

THE TIGER MAN crawled through the ropes, stood rubbing his feet in the resin. Ruby Ryan, his face hard, was staring up the aisle for Hayes to appear. Beck arranged the water bottle and stood silent, waiting. Behind them the excited crowd continued to swell. The arena was fairly alive with tension.

Now Deke Hayes was in the ring. The two men stepped to the center for instructions. Hayes's eyes were fastened on the Tiger with a queer intensity. The Tiger looked up, and there was such a light in his eyes as made even the referee wince.

"It's been a long time, Deke Hayes!" the Tiger growled. "A long time! But tonight, you can't run off and leave me.

"You gypped me out of my girl. You tried to gyp me out of the title, too. Now I'm going to thrash you until you can't move! After tonight, Hayes, you're through!"

"I don't know what you're talkin' about!" Hayes sneered. Then they were back in their corners, and the bell clanged.

Hayes was fast. The Tiger, circling to the center, realized that. He was even faster than Tom Noble. Probably as good a boxer, too. Hayes feinted a left, then hurled a vicious right that spun the Tiger halfway around and made him give way. Deke Hayes bored in promptly, punching fast, accurately.

But the Tiger danced away, boxing carefully for the first time. Hayes's left flicked at the wounded eye, but was just short, and the Tiger slipped under it, and whipped both hands to the body as the round ended.

Deke Hayes came out fast for the second heat, and a right opened the cut over Tiger's eye. Hayes sprang in and, punching like a demon, drove the Tiger across the ring, where he hung him on the ropes with a wicked right uppercut that jerked his head back and slammed him off balance into the hemp.

The Tiger staggered, and almost went down. He straightened and by a great effort of will, tried to clinch, but Deke Hayes shook him loose, floored him with a wicked left hook.

The crowd was on its feet now, in a yelling frenzy. Ryan sat in the corner, twisting the towel in his hands, chewing on the stump of a dead cigar. But even as the referee counted nine, the Tiger was up!

He tried to clinch, but Hayes shook him off. Confident now, he jabbed three fast lefts to the bad eye, then drove the Tiger to a corner with a volley of hooks, swings, and uppercuts. A short right hook put the Tiger down a second time—and then the bell rang!

The arena was a madhouse as the Tiger came out for the third round, his brain still buzzing. He couldn't seem to get started. Hayes's left flicked out again, resuming the torture. Hayes stepped in and the Tiger evaded a left, then clinched. He caught Hayes's hands, hung on until the referee broke them, warning him for holding.

———

THROUGH THE FOURTH, fifth, and sixth rounds, Hayes boxed like the marvel he was, but the Tiger kept on. In the clinches he hung on until the referee broke them; he slipped, ducked, and rode punches. He tried every trick he knew.

Only the terrific stamina of those long jungle years carried the Tiger through now; only the running, the diving, the swimming he had done, the fighting in the jungle, the bitter struggle to live, sustained him, kept him on his feet.

Strangely, as the seventh round opened, the Tiger felt better. His natural strength was asserting itself. Hayes came out, cocky, confident. The Tiger stepped in, but his feet were lighter. Some of the confusion seemed to have gone from his mind. Between rounds the blood from his cut eye had been stopped. He was getting his second wind.

Deke Hayes rushed into the fray, throwing both hands to the head, but the Tiger was ready this time. Dropping into a crouch, he whipped out a snapping left hook and dug a right into the solar plexus.

But the champion fired a left to the head that shook the Tiger to his heels, then threw a right that cracked against his jaw with the force of a thunderbolt. The Tiger went to one knee; but came up, fighting like a demon!

He ripped into the champion with the fury of an unleashed cyclone, battering him halfway across the ring. But when the champion caught himself, he drove the Tiger back onto his heels with a straight left, crossed a right, and then threw both hands to the body.

The Tiger took it. He stepped in, swapping blow for blow, taking the champion's hardest punches with scarcely a wince. Deke Hayes backed off, jabbed a left, but was short, and then the Tiger was inside, tearing away at the other's body with the fury of a Gatling gun. He ripped a mad tattoo of punches against Deke Hayes's ribs; then, stepping back suddenly, he blocked Hayes's left and hooked his own solid left to the head.

The champion staggered, and as the crowd roared like a typhoon in the China Sea, the Tiger tore in, punching furiously. There was no stopping now. Science was cast to the winds, it was the berserk brawling of two killers gone mad!

———

ROUND AFTER ROUND passed, and they slugged it out, two fighting fools filled with a deadly hatred of each other, fighting not to win but to kill!

Hayes, panic-stricken, was fighting the fight of his life, backed into a corner by Fate and the enemy he thought he had left behind for good—the man he had cheated and left to die.

Now that man was here, fighting him for the world's title, and Hayes battled like a demon. Staggering, almost ready to go down, the champion whipped up a desperate right uppercut that blasted the Tiger's mind into a flame of white-hot pain! But the Tiger set his teeth, and bored in.

Shifting quickly, he brought down a short overhand punch, and then deliberately stepped back. As the champion lunged forward instinctively, the Tiger Man knocked him flat with a straight right.

Then the champion was up again at the count of seven. Suddenly, with every ounce of strength at his command, he whipped up a mighty left to the Tiger's groin—a deliberately foul blow! The crowd leaped to its feet, roaring with anger; cries of rage came from officials at the ringside.

The Tiger, tottering, collapsed to his face in the center of the ring—just as the bell rang. The referee angrily motioned the champion to his corner amid a thunder of boos, and the Tiger was helped up.

Even Tom McKeown looked in disgust at his fighter as he worked over him. The angry referee strode to the Tiger's corner, and asked whether he could continue. The official, thoroughly enraged at the foul blow, was all for declaring the Tiger the winner, then and there.

But the Tiger, through his daze of pain, shook his head. "Not that way!" he gritted. "We fight . . . to the finish!" and the referee, cursing the champion, let the challenger have his way.

THEN THE BELL rang. But now it was different; and even the maddened crowd sensed that. Deke Hayes looked over at the slowly rising Tiger with real fear in his eyes. Why, the man wasn't human! No one could take a blow like that and keep coming!

Eyes red with hatred, the Tiger came out in a steel-coiled crouch. Hayes, wary now, had come to the end, and he knew it. He advanced slowly to the center of the ring, and the Tiger met him—met him with a sudden, berserk rush that drove the now frightened champion to the ropes.

There he hung, while the Tiger ripped punch after vicious punch to his body, pounded his ears until they were swollen and torn, cut his eyebrows with lightning-like twists of hard, smashing gloves.

A bloody, beaten mess, marked for life, the champion slipped frantically away along the ropes. Trembling with fright, he set himself desperately, shot a steaming right for the Tiger's chin.

But the Tiger beat him to the punch with an inside right cross that jerked Hayes back on his heels! Before the blood-covered champion could weave away, the Tiger—Bart Malone—whipped up a lethal left hook that started at his heels. Spinning completely around, the champion toppled to the canvas, out like a log, his jaw broken in three places!

The referee dismissed the formality of a count as the crowd went wild. Without a word, the referee raised the Tiger's hand in victory, as the rafters shook with the roaring of thousands of frenzied voices.

Ruby Ryan was beside himself with joy. "You made it, kid!" he yelled. "You made it! I never saw such nerve in my life! The greatest fight I ever seen! Damn, how did you do it?"

The Tiger looked down at him, grinned, though his body was a throbbing pain from the punishment he had absorbed.

"Somethin' I learned in the jungle," he growled.

THE GHOST FIGHTER

THE BELL CLANGED. The narrow-faced man tipped his chair away from the gym wall and sat suddenly forward. Had he not known it to be impossible, he would have sworn the husky young heavyweight in the black trunks was none other than "Bat" McGowan, the champion of the world!

Tall, bronzed, the fighter glided swiftly across the ring, stabbing a sharp left to his opponent's head; then, slipping over a left hook, he whipped a steaming right to the heart.

"Salty" Burke staggered, and his hands dropped slightly. Quickly Barney Malone jabbed another left at his face, and then a terrific right cross to the jaw. The blow seemed to travel no more than six inches, yet it exploded upon the angle of Burke's chin like a six-inch shell, and the big heavyweight crashed to the canvas, out cold!

———

RUBY RYAN, TRAINER of Bat McGowan, turned as "Rack" Hendryx relaxed and leaned back in his seat. His keen blue eyes were bright with excitement.

"See? What did I tell you? The kid's got it. He can box an' he can hit. He's just what you want, Rack!"

"Yeah, that's right. But he can't take it. . . ." Hendryx mused. "Well, he's a ringer for the champ, that's for sure. Hell, if I didn't know better, I'd swear that was him in there! Why, they could as well be twins!"

"Sure," Ryan nodded wisely. "Stick the kid in an' let him box these exhibitions as the champion, an' nobody the wiser. You've heard of these 'ghost writers,' haven't you? Well, Malone can be your 'ghost fighter'! No reason why you should miss collecting just because that big lug wants to booze and raise hell. It's a cinch."

"Yeah," Hendryx agreed. "As long as nobody taps that glass jaw of his . . . Okay, we'll try it. This kid is good, an' if he's just a gym fighter, so much the better. We don't want him gettin' any ideas."

———

THE NEXT NIGHT three men loafed in the expensive suite at the Astor where Hendryx maintained an unofficial headquarters. Rack Hendryx did not confine himself merely to managing the heavyweight champion of the world. From behind a score of "fronts" he pulled the wires that directed a huge ring of vice and racketeering. Even Bat McGowan knew little of this, although he surmised a good deal. The three had become widely known figures: Bat McGowan, the champion; Rack Hendryx, his manager; and Tony Mada, Hendryx's quiet, thin-lipped bodyguard.

"Say, when's this punk going to show up?" McGowan growled irritably. "He hasn't taken a powder on you, has he?"

"Not a chance. Ruby's bringin' him up the back way. We can't have nobody gettin' wise to this. Why, the damned papers would howl bloody murder about the fans payin' to see the champ an' only seein' some punk gym fighter who can't take it on the chin!" Hendryx laughed harshly.

"What about the guys that already seen him?" McGowan demanded.

"He's from South Africa. An Irishman from Johannesburg. He only fought here once, and that was some little club in the sticks. Ruby Ryan also saw him in the gym."

There was a sharp rap at the door, and when Mada swung it open, Ryan stepped in with Barney Malone at his heels. For a moment, there was silence while Malone and Bat McGowan stared at each other.

"Well, I'll be—" McGowan exclaimed. "The punk sure does look like me, don't he?" Then he walked over and looked Barney Malone up and down. "Don't you wish you could fight like me, too?"

"Maybe I can," Malone snapped, his eyes narrowing coldly.

McGowan sneered. "Yeah?" Quick as a flash he snapped a left hook to Malone's head, a punch that caught the new-comer flush on the point of the chin. Without a sound the young fighter crumpled to the floor!

"Are you crazy?" Rack Hendryx grabbed McGowan by the arm and jerked him back, face livid. "What the hell d'you think you're tryin' to do, anyway? Crab the act?"

"Aw, what the hell—the punk was gettin' wise with me. I might as well put him in his place now as later."

Helped by Ruby Ryan, Malone was slowly getting to his feet, shaking his head to clear it. The old trainer's Irish face was hard, and the light in his eyes when he looked at McGowan was not good to see.

"Now lay off, you big chump!" Hendryx snapped angrily. "What d'you think this is, an alley?"

Malone looked at McGowan, his eyes strange and bleak. "So you're a champion?" he said coldly. McGowan stepped forward, his fist raised, but Hendryx and Mada intervened.

"You should know, lollypop." Bat turned and picked up his hat, then looked back at Malone and laughed.

"Just another cream puff! Well, you can double for me, but don't get any ideas, see, or I'll beat you to jelly." He turned and walked out.

"Forget that guy, Malone," Hendryx broke in, noticing the gleam in the youngster's eye. "Just let it slide. We got to talk business!"

"Nothing doing." Barney Malone looked at Hendryx and shook his head. "Not for a guy like that!"

"Come on . . . Bat won't be around much. He'll be busy with the girls. An' where can you lay your mitts on five hun-dred a week? Forget that guy; this is business."

"All right," Malone said. "But not for five hundred. I want five hundred, and ten percent of the take from all exhibitions I work as champion!"

"Not a chance!" Hendryx snapped angrily. "What you tryin' to do, pull a Jesse James on me?"

"Then let me out of this joint," Malone said grimly. "I'm through."

For a half hour they argued, and finally Hendryx shrugged his shoulders. "Okay, Malone, you win. I'll give it to you. But remember—one move that looks like a double cross and I give Tony the nod, see?"

Malone glanced at Tony Mada, and the little torpedo parted his lips in a nasty grin. Whatever else there was about the combination, there wasn't any foolishness about Tony Mada. He was something cold and deadly.

———

A MONTH AND nine exhibitions later, in the dressing room of the Adelphian Athletic Club, Barney Malone sat on the table, taping his hands. The champion's silk robe over his broad shoulders set them off nicely. He looked fit and ready.

"This Porky Dobro is tough, see?" Ryan advised. "He's tougher than we wanted right now, but we couldn't dodge him. He knows McGowan, an' has a grudge against him. You gotta be nasty with this guy, Barney. Get tough, heel your gloves, use your elbows and shoulders, butt him, hold and hit—everything! That's the way the champ works; he was always dirty. This guy will expect it, so give him the works. But, no matter what, don't let him near that jaw of yours . . . you can outbox him, so don't try anything else."

"That's right, kid," Hendryx agreed. "You been doin' fine. But this Dobro isn't like the others, he's bad medicine—an' he ain't going to be scared!"

———

HENDRYX WALKED OUT, with Mada at his heels. Malone watched them go, and then looked back at Ruby Ryan. The old Irishman was tightening a shoelace.

"How'd you happen to get mixed up with an outfit like that, Ruby?"

Ryan shrugged. "Same way you did, kid. A guy's got to live. Rack knew I was a good trainer, an' he hired me. I made McGowan champ. Now they both treat me like the dirt under their feet."

They hurried down the aisle to the ring, where Porky Dobro was already waiting for them. He was a heavy-shouldered fighter with a square jaw and heavy brows. A typical slugger, and a tough one.

"All right, champ, box him now!" Ryan murmured as the bell sounded.

Dobro broke from his corner with a rush. He was a huge favorite locally, and it was the real thing for the hometown fans to see a local heavyweight in a grudge battle with the world's champion.

Dobro rushed to close quarters but was stopped abruptly by a stiff left jab that set him back on his heels. Before he could regain his balance, Malone crossed a solid right to the head, and hooked two lefts to the body, in close. Dobro bored in, taking more blows. Bobbing and weaving, he tried to go under Malone's left, but it followed him, cutting, stabbing, holding him off.

Then Barney's left swung out a little, and Dobro managed to drive in close, where he clinched desperately, cursing. Malone tied him up calmly and pounded his body with a free hand. Ryan was signaling from his corner and, remembering, Malone jerked his shoulder up hard under Dobro's chin. As the crowd booed, he calmly pushed Dobro away and peeled the hide from a cheekbone with the vicious heel of his glove.

The crowd booed again, and Dobro rushed, but brought up sharply on the end of a left that split his lips and started a stream of blood. Before he could set himself, Malone fired a volley of blows to his body. The bell sounded, and the crowd mingled cheers with the booing.

"Nice goin', kid," Ryan assured him. "You should be in the movies. You look so much like McGowan, I hate you myself! But keep up the rough stuff, that's what we want."

The clang of the bell had scarcely died when Dobro was across the ring, but again he met that snapping left. He plunged in again, and again the left swung a little wide, letting him in. Then Malone promptly tied him up.

As they broke, Dobro took a terrific swing at Malone's jaw, slipped on some spilled water, and plunged forward, arms flailing. Stumbling, he tried to regain his balance, then plunged headfirst into a steel corner-post! He slumped, a dead weight upon the canvas, suddenly still.

Quickly, Malone bent over him, helping him to his feet, face white and worried. The referee and the man's seconds crowded around, working madly over the fighter, who had struck with force enough to kill. Malone was suddenly conscious of a tugging at his arm, and looked up to find Ruby Ryan motioning him to the corner.

"He's all right, kid," Ryan assured him. "But if he came to and found you bent over him, worried like that, the shock would probably kill him! Remember, you're supposed to hate him and everything about him."

Finally, Dobro came around, but insisted on going on with the fight after a brief rest.

When the bell sounded again, Dobro came out fast, seemingly none the worse for his bump, but Malone stepped away, sparring carefully. Dobro plunged in close and slammed a couple of stiff punches to the body, then hooked a hard left to the head without a return. Malone stepped away, boxing carefully. He could still see Dobro's white face and queer eyes as he lay on the canvas, and was afraid that a stiff punch might—

A jolting right suddenly caught him on the ear, knocking him across the ring into the ropes. He caught himself just in time to see Dobro plunging in, his eyes wild with killer's fire. Malone ducked and clinched. As Dobro's ear came close, he whispered:

"Take it easy, you clown, an' I'll let you ride awhile!"

Then the referee broke them, and Malone saw Dobro's brow wrinkle with puzzlement. He realized instantly that he had overplayed his hand. Hesitant to batter Dobro after his fall, he had acted as Bat McGowan would never have acted. Dobro bored in, and Malone put a light left to his mouth, but passed up a good shot for his right. Suddenly, in close, his eye caught Dobro's; Dobro went under a left and clinched.

"Say, what is this?" he growled. "You're—"

Panic-stricken, Malone shoved him off with a left and

hooked a terrific right to the chin that slammed Dobro to the canvas. But he was up at nine, boring in, still puzzled, conscious that something was wrong. Malone put two rapid lefts to the face, and then stepped back, feinting a left and then letting it swing wide again. But this time, as Dobro lunged to get in close, Malone caught him coming in with a short, vicious right cross to the chin that stopped him dead in his tracks. Dobro weaved and started to drop, already out cold, but before he could fall, Malone whipped in a steaming left hook that stretched him on the canvas, dead to the world.

———

THE NEXT MORNING, Ruby Ryan walked into the room where Barney Malone was playing solitaire and handed him a paper.

"Take a gander at that, son. Looks like they're eating it up; but just the same, I'm worried. Porky is dumb enough, but even a dumb guy can stumble into a smart play."

On one side of the sport sheet, black headlines broadcast the fight of the previous evening:

MCGOWAN STOPS DOBRO IN SECOND
*Champ Looks Great in Grudge Battle
with Slugging Foe*

But across the page, and in a column of comment, Malone read further:

How does he do it? In the past thirty days, Bat McGowan has flattened ten opponents in as clean-cut fashion as ever a champion did. But in the same space of time, he has been seen drunk and carousing no less than seven times. Even Harry Greb in his palmy days never displayed such form as the champion has of late, while at the same time burning the candle at both ends.

We have never cared for McGowan; the champion has been as consistently dirty, and as unnecessarily foul as any fighter we have ever seen. But last night with Porky Dobro, he intentionally coasted after the man had been injured by a fall. It was the act of a champion—but somehow, it wasn't like McGowan as we have known him.

"Well, what do you think, kid?" Ryan looked at him curiously. "You're making the champion a reputation as a good guy."

"It's all the same to me, Ruby. Champion or no champion, I've been giving the fans a run for their money. I'm going to keep it up, even if McGowan does get the credit."

"You know, son, you've changed some lately, do you realize that?"

"How d'you mean?"

"You stopped Porky Dobro in the second round last night. The last time they fought, McGowan needed seven rounds to get him, and had quite a brawl. And Dobro stayed the distance with him twice before, once in Reno, and again in Pittsburgh. You've improved a lot."

———

THERE WAS A sharp rap at the door, and Ryan looked up, surprised. When he opened the door it was to admit Bat McGowan, Tony Mada, and a very excited Rack Hendryx.

"All right, Ryan, you were smart enough to tip me off to this ghost fighter business. Now give me an out!"

"What's up?"

"Almost everything. Major Kenworthy called me this morning and told me to come to the Commission offices, and right away. I went, and they want to know why McGowan is gallivanting around the country, knocking off setups and not defending his title. They say the six months are up, and they want him to defend his title at once. They had Dickerson, the promoter, up there, and had papers all ready to sign, and wanted to know if I had any objections to letting the champ defend his title against Hamp Morgan—and in just six weeks! McGowan here can't get in shape to fight in that time!"

"Hamp Morgan, eh?" Ryan frowned. "He's a tough egg, and been comin' up fast the past few months. Can't you stall a little?"

"Stall? What d'you think I've been tryin' to do? They say the champ's in great shape, they saw him beat Dobro and a couple of other guys. There's a lot of talk now, and they say it will draw like a million bucks. And when we got the fight for the title, we posted ten thousand bucks in agreeing to defend the title in six months!"

"Why not let Barney fight?" Ryan asked softly.

"Malone? Say, what are we talkin' about? Hamp Morgan is no setup!" McGowan snarled angrily. "Think I want that punk to lose my title for me? You're nuts!"

"Yeah? What about Porky Dobro? How long did it take you to stop him last time? And did he or did he not bust you around plenty?" Ryan demanded. "Maybe Barney can't take it—but how many of these bums been touchin' him? Well, I'll tell you—none of them have! He was hurt on the ship workin' his way over from South Africa and hasn't been able to take 'em around the head since. But he can box, an' he can hit."

"Maybe we don't have a choice, Ruby," Hendryx said thoughtfully. "Bat is hog-fat. He'd be twenty pounds over Malone's weight easy."

"Hey!" the champ scowled at Hendryx.

"You are! You'd be in a hell of a spot if the Commission put you on a scale. I ain't made much money with this title, an' I can't afford to gamble. It looks to me like Barney has to fight Morgan."

Bat turned suddenly, facing Malone. "Well, what d'you say about it? Are you game? Or are you yella?"

Barney Malone got up slowly. For a minute he stared coldly at Bat McGowan. Then he turned to face Hendryx. "You're the one that has it to lose. Sure, I'll fight Morgan. I've been playin' champ a month now, an' I like it!"

"Kind of cocky, ain't you?" McGowan said suddenly, his eyes hard. "It seems to me you're gettin' pretty smart for a guy with a glass chin! Why, I just brushed you with a left and flattened you the first time I ever laid eyes on you!"

"Fight him yourself!" Barney snapped back.

"Forget it," Hendryx barked. "Sit down, Bat, an' shut up.

What're you always gettin' hard around Barney for? He's been doin' your dirty work, and makin' money for all of us."

"Why? Because he's yella, because he's too pretty to suit me! Because he thinks he's a nice boy! Why, I'd—"

"You'd nothing!" hissed Hendryx. "If you were just another pug I'd have your knees broken—I'd have you whacked! You're the pretty face around here, and you're lettin' someone else do all the work. Now everybody listen close; Malone, you win this fight or I'll make you sorry . . . and Bat, you stop drinkin' and get yourself in shape! If you don't make me some money I'm gonna let you swing, understand?"

———

FOR A LONG time after they'd left, Malone stared out the window into the gathering darkness. Ryan walked up finally and stood by his chair.

After a moment—"Well, kid," he began, "we've come a long way together. When I first spotted you in that gym, I knew you had it. If you don't get careless, none of these punks are goin' to hit you. But just remember, Barney—the champ knows, see? An' if you ever let McGowan start a fight with you, he'll try to kill you!"

"I know. Hell, Ruby, everything looked good when I left Capetown. I'd had seventeen fights, and won them all by knockouts. Then I had that fall, and the doc told me I could never fight again. But I have to fight. It's all I know. I was stopped twice in the gym, and then practically knocked out that day by McGowan."

"Ain't there anything a doctor can do?" Ryan asked.

"Doesn't seem so. But this doc told me I might get over it, in time. An' Ruby, do you remember the Dobro battle? He hit me twice on the head, an' though one of them hurt, I didn't go down."

———

SIXTY THOUSAND PEOPLE crowded the vast open-air arena to see Bat McGowan defend his heavyweight title against Hamp Morgan, the Butte, Montana, miner. For only six weeks the publicity barrage had been turned on the title fight, but it had been enough. Morgan's steady string of victories and the champion's ten quick knockouts in as many exhibitions had furnished the heat for the sportswriters. They all agreed that it should be a great battle. Morgan had lost but two decisions, and these almost three years before. The champion looked great in training, and everyone marveled at his recent record even during a long period of dissipation. The betting was three-to-one on the champ.

In Hamp Morgan's dressing room "Dandy Jim" Kirby was giving his fighter a few last-minute tips. Salty Burke, Morgan's sparring partner and second, whom Barney Malone had knocked out on the day Ryan spotted him, stood nearby. Porky Dobro had dropped in to wish Morgan the best of luck and a better "break" than he himself had got. Though they had all been competitors at one time or another, there was one thing they could all agree on: No one liked the champ.

"You know, Hamp," Dobro mused, "it's funny, but Bat eased up on me in the last scrap we had. He was boxing like a million, had me right on the spot after I got hurt, and then offered to let me ride. If I hadn't known him so well, I'd have sworn there was something crooked about the deal. McGowan has a trick of cussing a guy in the clinches, an' a funny way of biting his lip, an' that night he didn't do either!"

Burke looked up and grinned. "Maybe Hendryx stumbled on that punk I fought a few months ago."

Kirby looked queerly at Burke, his eyes narrowing slightly. "What d'you mean, the guy you fought?"

"Why, several months ago I boxed a guy who looked enough like McGowan to be his twin. A fella named Barney Malone, from Johannesburg, South Africa. He stopped me quick. Hit like a mule, he did, but I'd seen him get stopped in the gym a couple of times by small boys, and figured I could take him."

"And you say he looked like the champ?" Kirby said thoughtfully.

"Yeah," Burke agreed. "An' say, I hadn't remembered it before, but I seen him talkin' to Ryan one time. . . ."

"Did he sound like he was from South Africa, you know, did he have an accent?" Kirby asked Dobro.

"Had the mouthpiece in—he sounded like a guy talkin' past the world's biggest chaw."

"You say he was stopped by somebody?"

"Yeah, hit on the head, both times. Back around the ear. I thought I could cop him myself, but he was in better shape, an' he never give me no chance."

———

NEARLY RING TIME. "Dandy Jim" Kirby walked slowly down the aisle toward his ringside seat, a very thoughtful man. Kirby was nobody's fool. He had been around the fight racket as a kid, and he'd heard the smart fight managers talk, guys who'd been in the business since the days of Gans and Wolgast. He knew Rack Hendryx well enough to know he was no more honest than he had to be. Somehow—He paused momentarily, running his long fingers through his slightly graying hair.

Now, let's see: McGowan, nasty as they make 'em, wins the title by a kayo. He is a slugger with a chunk of dynamite in each mitt, and plenty tough. He starts drinking and chasing women. Then, about two months later, he suddenly starts a campaign of exhibition fights.

McGowan carouses, and yet is always in perfect shape. Tonight his face is puffy and eyes hollow—tomorrow he is lean, hard, and clear-eyed. There is another heavyweight who looks like McGowan, and Ruby Ryan knows them both. . . .

Kirby dropped his cigarette and rubbed it out with his toe. Then he turned and walked back toward the dressing room. His eyes were bright. He met Hamp Morgan coming toward the ring.

"Listen, Hamp," he said quickly. "When you go out there tonight, I want you to hit this guy on the ear, see? Hit him, an' hit him hard, get me?"

———

FOR YEARS, FANS were to remember that fight. It was one for the books. For four rounds, it was one of the most terrific slugging matches ever seen, with both boys moving fast and slamming away with a will. It was a bitter, desperate fight, and when the bell rang for the fifth, the crowd was on the edge of their seats, every man hoarse from yelling.

The "champion" stopped Morgan's first rush with a lancing left jab. A hard right to the body followed, and Morgan backed up, taking two lefts as he was going away. Then he lunged in, whipped both hands for the body, and then missed a long overhand right to the head. The "champion" backed away and Morgan followed. Suddenly Barney Malone stopped, feinted a left, and shook Morgan to his heels with a driving right to the jaw. Hamp Morgan dropped swiftly to a crouch, and suddenly, so quickly that the eye could not follow, he whipped over a terrific right to the head that crashed against Malone's ear! With a sound, the "champion" pitched forward on his face and lay still.

Amid the roar of the crowd, the referee's hand began to rise and fall, slowing tolling off the seconds. In the ringside seat, Rack Hendryx sat tensely, swearing under his breath in a low, vicious monotone. Ryan leaned over the edge of the ring, fists clenched, almost breathless.

Kirby, the championship almost in his hands, was watching Hendryx, and then his eyes slid over to Tony Mada.

The crowd was in a frenzy, but Mada was cold and silent. He was not looking at the ring; his gaze was fastened upon "Dandy Jim" Kirby. Kirby felt his mouth go dry with fear. Then, amid the roaring of the crowd, the bell sounded. Probably not more than a dozen people heard it, but it sounded at the count of nine.

The first thing Barney Malone understood was the dull roar in his ears and the bright lights over the ring. He felt someone anxiously shaking his head, and a whiff of smelling salts nearly tore his skull off.

———

THEN—"COME ON, son, you got to snap out of it!" Ryan was pleading. "Come on!" As Malone's eyes opened, Ryan leaned forward, whispering, "Now's your chance! Go out there like you were gone, see? Stagger out, act like you don't know where you are. Then let him have it, just as hard as you can throw it, get me?"

The sound of the bell was lost in the howl of the crowd, and Hamp Morgan was crossing the ring, tearing in, punching like a madman, throwing a volley of hooks, swings, and uppercuts that had Barney Malone reeling like a drunken man; reeling, but just enough to keep most of Morgan's blows pounding the air. And then, like a shot from the blue, his right streaked out and crashed against Morgan's chin with the force of a thunderbolt. Hamp Morgan spun halfway around and dropped at full length on the canvas!

———

MALONE CRAWLED STIFFLY out of bed and sat staring across the room. One eye was swollen, and he felt gingerly of his ear. Thoughtfully, but cautiously, he worked his jaw around to find the sore spots. There were plenty.

He was shaving when suddenly the sound of the key in the lock made him look up. It was Ruby Ryan.

"Look, kid," he said excitedly, "we got to scram. Somebody is stirrin' up a lot of heat! Look at this!"

He pointed at the same daily column of sports comment that had been giving so much space to the activities of the champion, both in and out of the ring.

Where is Barney Malone? That question may or may not mean anything, but this A.M., as we recovered from last night's fistic brawl in which Bat McGowan (or somebody) hung a kayo on Hamp Morgan's chin, we received an anonymous note asking this very question: Where is Barney Malone?

Now, it is true that we are not too well aware of who this Malone party is, but an enclosed clipping from a Capetown, South Africa, paper shows us a picture entitled BARNEY MALONE, a picture of a fighter whose resemblance to Bat McGowan is striking, to say the least. The accompanying story assures the interested reader that Mr. Malone is headed for pugilistic fame in the more or less Land of the Free.

Can it be possible that this accounts for the startling alterations in the appearance and actions of Bat McGowan? And if so, who knocked out Hamp Morgan? Was it indeed our beloved champion, or was it some guy named Jones, from Peoria, or perhaps Malone, from Capetown?

I wonder, Major Kenworthy, if Bat McGowan has a large ear this morning?

There was a light step behind them as Malone finished reading, and they whirled about to confront Tony Mada. He smiled.

"Hello, kid, the boss wants to see you."

"Hendryx? Why don't he come over here like he always does?" Ryan demanded. "He knows it's dangerous to have Barney on the streets."

"We got a car, Barney, a closed car. Come on, he's waiting for you."

Ryan was standing by the window, and he turned his head slightly, glancing at the car across the street. Suddenly his face went deathly white. Behind the wheel was "Shiv" McCloskey, another of Hendryx's muscle men. He had the feeling that Barney Malone was about to disappear, forever.

Malone picked up his hat, straightened his tie. In the mirror he caught a glimpse of Ryan's face, white and strained. A jerk of the head indicated the car, with McCloskey at the wheel. Mada was lighting a cigarette.

WITHOUT A WORD, Barney Malone spun on his heel, and as Mada looked up, his fist caught the torpedo on the angle of the jaw. Something crunched, and the gunman toppled to the floor. Quickly, Ryan grabbed the automatic from Mada's shoulder holster.

"Come on, kid, we got to scram—"

Suddenly in the door of the room stood Major Kenworthy, Rack Hendryx, Bat McGowan, and two reporters. Kenworthy stepped over to Mada, and then glanced out the window. He turned slowly to Hendryx.

"I don't know quite what this is all about yet, Hendryx," he said dryly, "but I'd advise you to call off your dog out there. He might become conspicuous. It seems"—he smiled at Ryan and Malone—"that your other shadow has met with an accident."

"Are you Malone?" asked one of the reporters.

"Of course he's Malone," Kenworthy interrupted. "Just what else he is, we'll soon find out. But before asking any questions or listening to any alibis, I'm going to speak my piece. Apparently, Malone"—he eyed Barney's bruised ear—"fighting as the champion, defeated Hamp Morgan. This means"—he looked at Hendryx—"that your ten thousand dollars is forfeit. Apparently, Malone, you scored ten knockouts while posing as champion. This is all going to be public knowledge, but you and McGowan are going to get a chance to make it right with the fans. A chance I'd not be giving either of you but for the good of the game. You can fight each other for the world's title, the proceeds, above training expenses, to go to charity . . . that, or you can both be barred for life. And if you can also be prosecuted, I'll see that it's done. What do you men say?"

"I'll fight," Barney Malone said. "I'll fight him, and only too willing to do it."

Hendryx agreed, sullenly, for the scowling McGowan.

———

"DON'T MISS ANY guesses, Barney," Ruby Ryan whispered. "Watch him all the time. Remember, he won the title, and he can hit. He's dangerous, experienced, and a killer. He's out for blood and to keep his title. Both of you got everything to fight for. Now, go get him!"

The bell clanged, and Malone stepped from his corner, stabbing a lightninglike jab to McGowan's face. McGowan slid under another left and slammed both hands into Malone's ribs with jolting force, then whipped up a torrid right uppercut that missed by a hairsbreadth. Malone spun away, jabbing another left to the chin, and hooking a hard right to the temple that shook McGowan to his heels.

But Bat McGowan looked fit. For two months, he had trained like a demon. Ryan had not been joking when he said that McGowan was out for blood. He crowded in close, Malone clinched, and McGowan tried to butt him, but took a solid punch to the midsection before the break.

McGowan crowded in again, slugging viciously, but Malone was too fast, slipping over a left hook and slamming him on the chin with a short right cross. Bat McGowan slipped under another left, crowded in close to bury his right in Malone's solar plexus.

Malone staggered, tried to cover up, but McGowan was on him, pulling his arms down, driving a terrific right to the side of his head that slammed him back into the ropes. Before he could recover, McGowan was throwing a volley of hooks, swings, and uppercuts, and Malone was battered into a corner, where he caught a stiff left and crashed to the canvas!

He was up at nine, but McGowan came in fast, measured Malone with a left, and dropped him again. Slowly, his head buzzing, the onetime ghost fighter struggled to his knees, and caught a strand of rope to pull himself erect. McGowan rushed in, but was a little too anxious, and Malone fell into a clinch and hung on for dear life.

At the break, McGowan missed a hard right, and the crowd booed. Malone circled warily, boxing. Bat McGowan crowded in close, but Malone met him with a fast left that cut his eyebrow. Then just before the bell, another hard right to the head put Malone on the canvas again. The gong rang at seven.

"Say, you sap," Ruby Ryan growled in his ear, "who said you couldn't take it? Whatever has been wrong with you is all right. You've taken all he can dish out now. Keep that left busy, and keep this guy at long range and off balance, got me?"

The second round opened fast. Malone was boxing now, using all the cleverness he had. McGowan bored in, then hooked both hands to the head. But Malone took them going away. A short right dropped Bat McGowan to his knees for no count, and then the champion was in close battering away at Malone's ribs with both hands. Just before the bell, Malone staggered the champion with a hard left hook, and then took a jarring right to the body that drove him into the ropes.

Through the third, fourth, fifth, and sixth rounds the two fought like madmen. Toe-to-toe, they battered away, first one having a narrow lead, then the other. It was nobody's fight. Bloody, battered, and weary, the two came up for the seventh berserk and fighting for blood. McGowan's left eye was a bloody mess, his lips were in shreds; Malone's body was red from the terrific pounding he had taken, his lip was split, and one eye was almost closed. It had been a fierce, grueling struggle with no likelihood of quarter.

McGowan came out slowly and missed a hard right hook, which gave Malone a chance to step in with a sizzling uppercut that nearly tore the champion's head off! Quickly Malone feinted a left, tried another uppercut, but it fell short as McGowan rolled away, then stepped in, slamming both hands to the body, and then landed a jarring left hook to the head. Slipping away, Malone jabbed a left four times to the face without a return, danced away. McGowan put a fist to Barney's sore mouth, but took a fearful right and left to the stomach in return that made him back up hurriedly, plainly in distress. McGowan swung wildly with a left and right, Malone ducked with ease, and fired a torrid right uppercut that stretched the champion flat on his shoulder blades!

McGowan came up at seven and, desperate, swung a wicked left that sank into Malone's body, inches below the belt!

There was an angry bellow from the crowd and a rush for the ring amidst a shrilling of police whistles! But Malone caught himself on the top rope, and as McGowan rushed to finish him, the younger fighter smashed over a driving right to the chin that knocked the champion clear across the ring. Staying on his feet with sheer nerve, Barney Malone lunged across the canvas and met McGowan with a stiff left as he bounded off the ropes, then a terrific right to the jaw and McGowan went down and out, stretched on the canvas like a study in still life!

———

RUBY RYAN THREW Malone's robe across his shoulders, grinning happily. "Well, son, you made it! What are you going to do now?"

Barney Malone carefully raised his head. "A couple more fights. Then I'm goin' back home . . . buy a farm up north near Windhoek . . . find a wife. I need to be in a place where a man can just be himself without having to be someone else first!"

———

IN THE PRESS benches, a radio columnist was speaking into the mike: "Well, folks, it's all over! Barney Malone is heavyweight champion of the world, after the first major ring battle in recent years in which neither fighter was paid a dime! And"—he glanced over at McGowan's corner, where Hendryx was slowly reviving his fighter—"if Major Kenworthy is asked tomorrow morning whether Bat McGowan has a large ear, he will have to say 'Yes,' and very emphatically!"

About Louis L'Amour

"I think of myself in the oral tradition—as a troubadour, a village taleteller, the man in the shadows of the campfire. That's the way I'd like to be remembered—as a storyteller. A good storyteller."

I T IS DOUBTFUL that any author could be as at home in the world recreated in his novels as Louis Dearborn L'Amour. Not only could he physically fill the boots of the rugged characters he wrote about, but he literally "walked the land my characters walk." His personal experiences as well as his lifelong devotion to historical research combined to give Mr. L'Amour the unique knowledge and understanding of people, events, and the challenge of the American frontier that became the hallmarks of his popularity.

Of French-Irish descent, Mr. L'Amour could trace his own family in North America back to the early 1600s and follow their steady progression westward, "always on the frontier." As a boy growing up in Jamestown, North Dakota, he absorbed all he could about his family's frontier heritage, including the story of his great-grandfather who was scalped by Sioux warriors.

Spurred by an eager curiosity and desire to broaden his horizons, Mr. L'Amour left home at the age of fifteen and enjoyed a wide variety of jobs, including seaman, lumberjack, elephant handler, skinner of dead cattle, miner, and an officer in the transportation corps during World War II. During his "yondering" days he also circled the world on a freighter, sailed a dhow on the Red

Sea, was shipwrecked in the West Indies, and stranded in the Mojave Desert. He won fifty-one of fifty-nine fights as a professional boxer and worked as a journalist and lecturer. He was a voracious reader and collector of rare books. His personal library contained 17,000 volumes.

Mr. L'Amour "wanted to write almost from the time I could talk." After developing a widespread following for his many frontier and adventure stories written for fiction magazines, Mr. L'Amour published his first full-length novel, *Hondo,* in the United States in 1953. Every one of his more than 120 books is in print; there are more than 300 million copies of his books in print worldwide, making him one of the bestselling authors in modern literary history. His books have been translated into twenty languages, and more than forty-five of his novels and stories have been made into feature films and television movies.

His hardcover bestsellers include *The Lonesome Gods, The Walking Drum* (his twelfth-century historical novel), *Jubal Sackett, Last of the Breed,* and *The Haunted Mesa.* His memoir, *Education of a Wandering Man,* was a leading bestseller in 1989. Audio dramatizations and adaptations of many L'Amour stories are available from Random House Audio publishing.

The recipient of many great honors and awards, in 1983 Mr. L'Amour became the first novelist ever to be awarded the Congressional Gold Medal by the United States Congress in honor of his life's work. In 1984 he was also awarded the Medal of Freedom by President Reagan.

Louis L'Amour died on June 10, 1988. His wife, Kathy, and their two children, Beau and Angelique, carry the L'Amour publishing tradition forward with new books written by the author during his lifetime to be published by Bantam.

The Worst
Drought In
Memory . . .

In Louis L'Amour's classic tale of loyalty and betrayal . . .

Praise for
Law of the Desert Born

"This actually may be the story's ideal form....
The result is stunning and richly textured."
—*Publishers Weekly*

"Yeates' artwork is incredible."
—GraphicNovelReporter.com

"*Law of the Desert Born* is a fantastic
example of how relevant the Western can be."
—Suvudu.com

"The richer plot and characters from
L'Amour's son Beau and collaborator Kathy
Nolan add appeal and value in addition to
the finely crafted visuals."
—*Library Journal*

"The novel's illustrations add a new
dimension to an already gripping tale."
—*American Cowboy*

"An amazing level of detail and ambience
that breathes new life into Louis L'Amour's
already stunning story."
—*Cowboys & Indians*